Jack McDevitt is a former naval officer, taxi driver, English teacher, and motivational trainer, and is now a full-time writer. Eleven of his novels have been Nebula finalists. *Seeker* won the award in 2007. McDevitt lives in Georgia with his wife Maureen.

Praise for Jack McDevitt:

'You're going to love it even if you think you don't like science fiction. You might even want to drop me a thank-you note for the tip before racing out to your local bookstore to pick up the Jack McDevitt backlist'
Stephen King

'A real writer has entered our ranks, and his name is Jack McDevitt'
Michael Bishop, Nebula Award winner

'Why read Jack McDevitt? The question should be: Who among us is such a slow pony that s/he isn't reading McDevitt?'
Harlan Ellison, Hugo and Nebula Award winner

'You should definitely read Jack McDevitt'
Gregory Benford, Nebula and Campbell Award winner

'No one does it better than Jack McDevitt'
Robert J. Sawyer, Hugo, Nebula and Campbell Award winner

Jack McDevitt titles published by Headline:

The Alex Benedict Novels
A Talent For War
Polaris
Seeker
The Devil's Eye
Echo
Firebird

The Academy (Priscilla Hutchins) Novels
The Engines Of God
Deepsix
Chindi
Omega
Odyssey
Cauldron

Jack McDevitt

POLARIS

headline

First published in Great Britain in 2013 by
HEADLINE PUBLISHING GROUP

First published in 2004 by Ace Books
A division of Penguin Group (USA) Inc.

1

Cataloguing in Publication Data is available from the British Library

ISBN 978 1 4722 0309 0

Typeset in Sabon LT Std by Palimpsest Book Production Limited,
Falkirk, Stirlingshire

Printed and bound in Great Britain by
Clays Ltd, St Ives plc

Headline's policy is to use papers that are natural, renewable and
recyclable products and made from wood grown in sustainable
forests. The logging and manufacturing processes are expected
to conform to the environmental regulations of the country of origin.

HEADLINE PUBLISHING GROUP
An Hachette UK Company
338 Euston Road
London NW1 3BH

www.headline.co.uk
www.hachette.co.uk

For Bob Carson,
the world's finest history teacher

Acknowledgments

I'm indebted to David DeGraff of Alfred University, and to Walter Cuirle, for technical assistance; to Christopher Schelling for his patience, and Ralph Vicinanza for many years of encouragement. To Athena Andreadis, whose compelling book *To Seek Out New Life* (Three Rivers Press, 1998) was helpful; and to Michael Shara, whose excellent article 'When Stars Collide' (*Scientific American*, November 2002) inspired the setup. To Ginjer Buchanan, for editorial guidance. To Julie E. Czerneda and Maureen McDevitt, who helped with early versions of the manuscript. And to Sara and Bob Schwager for their insight.

Prolog

I.

It no longer looked like a sun. When they'd arrived, only a few days ago, Delta Karpis had been a standard class G star, serene, placid, drifting quietly through the great deeps with its family of worlds, as it had done for six billion years. Now it was a misshapen bag, dragged through the night by an invisible hand. Its mass seemed to have shriveled beneath the tidal pressures; and a stream of radiant gas, millions of kilometers long, jetted from the neck of the bag, connecting the stricken star with a glowing point.

A *point*. Chek Boland looked at it a long time, marveling that something so small as to be virtually invisible could be so disruptive, could literally distort a *sun*.

You haven't seen anything yet, the astronomers from the other ships were saying. It hasn't even begun.

He turned his attention to Klassner. 'Nine hours left, Marty,' he said. 'Showtime.'

Klassner was sitting in his favorite chair, the gray-green one with the side table, his unfocused eyes fixed on the bulkhead. Gradually he blinked and turned toward Boland. 'Yes,' he said. And then: 'Showtime for what?'

'The collision.'

He was wearing the puzzled expression that they saw all too often now. 'Are we going to hit something?'

'No. The dwarf is about to hit Delta Kay.'

'Yes,' he said. 'It *is* remarkable. I'm glad we came.'

The telescopes revealed the point to be a dull red disk surrounded by a ring of shining gas. It was a white dwarf, the naked core of a collapsed star. Its electrons had been torn from their nuclei and jammed together, producing an object one step short of a black hole. A year ago, it had penetrated the planetary system, scattering worlds and moons, and now it had become a dagger aimed directly at the heart of Delta Karpis itself.

Klassner had been lucid last evening, and they'd been talking about the human tendency to project personality onto inanimate objects. To develop loyalty to a ship. To think that a childhood home welcomes one back. Now they could not escape a sense of sadness, watching the death struggle of the star, as if it were a living thing, somehow conscious of what was happening to it.

Nancy White had been part of the conversation. Nancy was a popularizer of science and had produced shows watched by millions. She'd commented that it was nonsense, that she couldn't bring herself to indulge in that particular fantasy when a genuine catastrophe was taking place on the third world, which was home to large animals, living oceans, and vast forests. They called the place Kissoff in sullen reaction. Kissoff had, so far, survived the general turmoil in the system caused by the presence of the interloper. Its orbit had become eccentric, but that was of no moment compared with what was about to happen to it and its biosphere. Within the next few hours, its oceans would boil off, and the atmosphere would be ripped away.

On a different scale, watching the approaching destruction of Martin Klassner was also painful. Klassner had demonstrated, after thousands of years of speculation, that alternate universes did exist. It was the breakthrough everyone had thought impossible. They're out there, and Klassner had predicted that one day

2

transportation to them would become possible. Now they were called Klassner universes.

Last year he'd come down with Bentwood's Syndrome, which induced occasional delusions and bouts of memory loss. His long, thin hands trembled constantly. The disease was terminal, and there was doubt whether he'd survive the year. The medical community was working on it, and a cure was coming. But Warren Mendoza, one of two medical researchers on board, insisted it would be too late. Unless Dunninger's research held the answer.

'Kage.' Klassner was addressing the AI. 'What is its velocity now?' He meant the white dwarf.

'*It has increased slightly to six hundred twenty kilometers, Martin. It will accelerate another four percent during its final approach.*'

They'd just finished dinner. Impact would take place at 0414 hours ship time.

'I never expected,' said Klassner, turning his gray, watery eyes on Boland, 'to see anything like this.' He was back. It was amazing the way he came and went.

'None of us did, Marty.' The frequency of such an event anywhere within the transport lanes had been estimated at one every half billion years. And here it was. Incredible. 'God has been very kind to us.'

Klassner's breathing was audible. It sounded whispery, harsh, labored. 'I would have wished, though, if we were going to have a collision,' he said, 'it could have taken place between two *real* stars.'

'A white dwarf is a real star.'

'No. Not really. It's a burned-out corpse.' Part of the problem with Bentwood's was that, along with its other effects, it seemed to reduce intelligence. Klassner's enormous intellect had at one time glowed in those eyes. You could look at him and literally see his brilliance. There were times now when it seemed he was on automatic, that no one was behind the wheel. It would not have been correct to say that his gaze had turned vacuous, but the genius was gone, save for an occasional glimmer. And he knew it, knew what he had once been. *It's a burned-out corpse.*

'I wish we could get closer,' Boland said. The link to the bridge was on, and he intended the comment for Madeleine English, their pilot.

'As far as I'm concerned,' she responded, *'we're already too close.'* Her voice was cool and crisp. She wasn't impressed by the six celebrities who constituted the entire passenger list for the *Polaris*.

The *Sentinel* was somewhere above Delta Kay's north pole; the *Rensilaer* lay on the far side of the dwarf. Both were filled with working researchers, measuring, counting, recording, gathering data that specialists would still be analyzing years hence. One of the major objectives of the mission was to measure, finally, the natural curve of space-time.

The conversations among the ships had grown increasingly enthusiastic during the buildup. *You ever see anything like this? I feel as if everything I've done has been leading up to this moment. Look at that son of a bitch. Cal, what are you getting on acceleration?* But it had all died away during the last few hours. The comm links were silent, and even Boland's fellow passengers had little to say.

They'd all gone back to their cabins after dinner, to work, or read, or while away the final hours however they could. But the herd instinct had taken over, and one by one they'd filtered back. Mendoza in white slacks and pullover, always a brooding figure, absorbed to the exclusion of everything else by the drama playing out in the sky. Nancy White, scribbling notes to herself between exchanges with Tom Dunninger, Mendoza's occasional colleague. They were microbiologists. Dunninger had earned an extraordinary reputation in his chosen field. He'd dedicated the latter years of his career to pursuing a way to stave off the ageing process. And Garth Urquhart, who had for two terms been one of the seven councillors of the Associated States.

On the screens, the torture of Delta Karpis grew more intense.

The solar bag was becoming more and more stretched. 'Who would have believed,' said Mendoza, 'that one of these things could become that distorted without blowing up.'

'It's coming,' said White.

The hours counted down, and the conversation never wandered from the spectacle. *What's the mass of that thing anyhow? Is it my imagination, or is the sun changing color? The ring around the dwarf is getting brighter.*

Shortly before midnight they set up a buffet. They wandered around the table, sampling fruit and cheese. Dunninger opened a bottle of wine and Mendoza offered a toast to the dying giant outside. 'Unmarked for six billion years,' he said. 'All that time just waiting for us.'

Unlike the researchers in the *Sentinel* and the *Rensilaer,* they were no more than casual observers. No work was being done, no measurements taken, no records kept, by any of them. They were there simply to enjoy the show, which consisted of slices of feeds from all three ships and from dozens of probes and satellites. They would sit quietly, or noisily if they preferred, and watch. Survey and the scientific community were saying thanks for their assorted contributions.

The *Polaris* wasn't designed as a research vessel. It was a supplemental carrier, a luxury vehicle (by Survey's spartan standards) that transported VIPs whom the director wanted to impress. Usually, these were political figures. This, however, was a different sort of occasion.

The images of Delta Karpis and the white dwarf on the wall screen were better than anything they could see with the naked eye. Still, Boland, who was a psychiatrist, noticed they all had a tendency to station themselves near the viewports, as if that were the only way to be really present at the event.

Huge explosions erupted periodically from the surface of the sun and vast waves of glowing gas were flung into the darkness of space.

5

A streak of white light ripped outward from the dwarf. 'Looks like a piece broke off,' said Urquhart.

'Not possible,' said Klassner. 'Nothing's going to break off a neutron star and float away. It was gas.'

Boland was the youngest of the passengers. He was probably forty, with black hair, trim good looks and a self-confident demeanor that never failed to turn women's heads. He had started out doing mind wipes and personality reconstruction for violent criminals, converting them into contented – or at least, law-abiding – citizens. But he was best known for his work in the neurological sciences, and for the Boland Model, which purported to be the most comprehensive explanation ever devised of how the brain worked.

Delta Kay's remaining worlds moved serenely in their orbits, as if nothing unusual were occurring. Except for the innermost, which had been a gas giant so close to the sun that it literally sailed through its outer atmosphere. That was Delta Karpis I. It had no other name, and now it was gone, swallowed by a flare. They'd seen it happen. It had plunged in, but only a couple of its moons had emerged on the other side.

When the dwarf arrived, a year ago, Delta Kay had possessed a planetary system containing five gas giants, six terrestrial worlds, and a couple of hundred moons. The outermost was still there, a world of blue crystal and brilliant silver rings, with only three satellites. Boland thought it the loveliest celestial object he'd ever seen.

Kissoff was also still relatively untouched by the disaster. Its oceans remained placid, and its skies were quiet except for a hurricane in one of the southern seas. It was just getting started, but it would not have an opportunity to develop. Most of the other worlds had been dragged from their orbits and were now outbound. Delta Karpis IV had been a double planet, two terrestrial worlds, each with a frozen atmosphere. They'd been ripped apart and were now headed in almost diametrically opposite directions.

The dwarf was smaller than Rimway, smaller even than Earth. But it packed more mass than Delta Kay, and Boland knew that if somehow he could reach the surface of the object, he would weigh billions of tons.

At 2:54 A.M., the dwarf and its shining ring slipped into the chaos and disappeared. Urquhart said he didn't care what anybody said, something that small couldn't possibly avoid getting swallowed by the conflagration. Tom Dunninger commented how it could just as easily have been a sun warming one of the Confederate worlds. 'It's a sobering moment,' he said. 'Makes you realize nobody's safe.'

The comment seemed pointed, and Boland wondered if he was sending a message.

Huge explosions ripped through the stricken sun, and the AI reported that temperatures on its surface were soaring. Its basic yellow-orange hue was fading to white. Wild forest fires had broken out on Kissoff. And enormous clouds of mist were rising out of the oceans. Abruptly, the picture went blank.

'Lost at the source,' said the AI.

Delta Kay V was adrift, sucked in toward the collision. It was normally ice-covered, with only a wisp of atmosphere. But the ice had melted, and its sky was full of thick gray clouds. Two of the satellites orbiting the gas giant Delta Kay VII collided. Its rings, brown and gold like a sunset, began to shimmer and break apart.

Maddy's voice sounded over the link: *'The* Rensilaer *is saying the sun'll put out as much energy during the next hour as it has over the last hundred million years.'*

The *Sentinel* reported that it was taking more radiation than it had been prepared for and was withdrawing. Its captain told Madeleine, in a transmission mistakenly relayed to the passengers, to be careful. *'That's bad weather out there.'*

Madeleine English stayed on the bridge. Usually she did not hesitate to join her passengers in the common room when circumstances allowed, but at the moment conditions demanded she remain in the pilot's seat. She was a beautiful woman, with blue eyes, lush blonde hair, perfect features. But there was no softness in her, no sense that she was in any way vulnerable.

Mendoza asked whether they were too close.

'*We're at a safe distance,*' Maddy said. '*Don't worry. At the first sign of overload, we'll skedaddle.*'

One hour, eight minutes after it had vanished into the inferno, the dwarf reappeared. It had plowed directly through the sun, *sailed* through, according to the experts on the other ships, like a rock going through fog. The solar stream that had reached out toward it during its approach had collapsed back into the turbulence, and a new one was forming on the opposite side, dragged out of the dying star by the enormous gravity. Then a titanic explosion obscured the view.

'*I'm closing the viewports,*' said Maddy. '*You'll have to settle for watching the feeds now. If it goes prematurely, we don't want anyone blinded.*'

Dunninger napped. And even Mendoza. Nancy White looked tired. She'd tried to get some rest during the day, but it didn't matter. Circadian rhythms were what they were, and it happened that ship time coincided with Andiquar time, so it really was close to 4:00 A.M. She had taken something to stay awake. Boland didn't know what it was, but he knew the symptoms.

Boland was startled by the tug of the ship's engines. Madeleine appeared briefly at the door to report that it was getting 'a little bit hot outside,' and she was going to withdraw to a safer distance. 'Everybody belt down.'

They secured Mendoza and Dunninger without waking them. And then Boland settled into his own harness.

Incredibly, it didn't seem as if the dwarf had even slowed down. It was still dragging the entrails of the sun behind it. The scene reminded Boland of a cosmic taffy pull.

The senior expert on stellar collisions was on the *Sentinel*. He'd predicted that the sun would collapse during the course of the event. Final demolition would occur, he said, when the various forces generated by the passage of the dwarf had time to penetrate the outer layers. Delta Karpis was more massive than their home sun by about a quarter, more massive than Sol by a third.

Maddy piped in the voice of one of the experts from the *Rensilaer*: '*Any minute now.*'

They woke Mendoza and Dunninger.

'It's starting to go,' said Klassner. 'What you'll see first is a general collapse.' Moments later, that character-switch came over him, and he was someone else. He looked first puzzled, then sleepy. Boland watched his eyelids sag. Within minutes, Klassner was asleep.

What they saw first was a bright white light that blew all the pictures off the monitors. Somebody inhaled, but no one spoke. Mendoza, seated beside Klassner, looked toward Boland, and their eyes locked. Boland knew Mendoza well. They'd been friends a long time, but something deeper passed between them in that moment, as if they were comrades standing on a dark shore.

They jumped out past the orbit of the fifth planet, to a prearranged location, where they rejoined the other ships. Klassner woke during the jump and looked devastated when they told him it was over. 'You slept through it, Marty,' said Mendoza. 'We tried to wake you, but you were seriously out.'

'It's okay,' White told him. 'You'll get another chance.' From this range, the explosion hadn't occurred yet, was still forty minutes away, and the researchers were able to set up and wait for the event to happen again. Klassner swallowed his disappointment, and commented that his daughter wouldn't be a bit surprised when he told her what had happened. Boland understood that Klassner had no children.

From their present range, Delta Karpis would normally have been a relatively small disk. But the disk was gone, replaced by a yellow smear twisted into the shape of a pear.

Nancy White was sitting with a notebook, recording her impressions, as if she would one day publish them. Her reputation had come from creating and moderating a series of shows, *Nancy White's Fireside Chats*, in which she talked science and philosophy with her audience; and *Time-Out*, a panel discussion that allowed her to sit each week with simulated historical figures ranging from Hammurabi to Adrian Cutter to Myra Kildare to discuss the issues of the day. The show had never been enormously popular, but – as the producers liked to say – the people who counted loved it.

Urquhart talked quietly with Mendoza. Dunninger had opened a book but wasn't really paying any attention to it.

They counted down, and it all happened again. Except at this range it was less painful to watch. The pear buckled, and the light coming through the viewports alternately brightened and darkened. And finally subsided into a hostile red glow.

It was odd, living through an event twice. But that was what FTL did for you. When you could outrun light, you could travel in time.

Within two hours, Delta Karpis was gone, and the light in the solar system had gone out. Only a blaze of luminous gas, and the bright golden ring around the dwarf, remained. They watched while the neutron star proceeded quietly on its way.

II.

Rondel (Rondo) Karpik was chief of the communications watch at Indigo Station, near the outer limits of Confederate space. His title, *chief*, was largely nominal since, except during major operations, he was the only person on the watch. The Delta Kay mission had ceased to be a major operation. Sensor packages had been laid at strategic points, data from the three ships had been relayed and stored, the on-station experts had expressed their admiration for the efficiency with which the researchers had carried out their assigned tasks, but they were predicting it would be months before we knew what we'd learned. There had been a journalist with the *Sentinel*, reporting to a pool. The pool had filed stories that went on about the majesty of it all until Rondo thought he was going to throw up. Then the fleet had announced its homebound schedule, and the experts and journalists had retired down to Cappy's gumpo shop, and he hadn't seen them since.

There was still some tracking data coming in, and a few other odds and ends, but the excitement was clearly over. Well, he had to admit he'd never seen a star blow up before, at least not from close by.

'*Indigo, we're ready to make our jump.*' Bill Trask's image gazed at him from the center of the room. Bill was captain of the *Rensilaer* and, in Rondo's view, the biggest horse's ass among the assorted skippers who passed through Indigo. He had no time for peasants, and he let you know exactly how you rated. He was big, ponderous, with white hair and a deep, gravelly voice, and everybody was afraid of him. At least all the communications people. '*We estimate timely arrival, Indigo. Keep the stewpots warm.*'

The message had been sent fifteen hours earlier. Trask signed off, and his image vanished.

Rondo opened a channel but kept it audio only. 'Acknowledge, *Rensilaer*,' he said. 'We'll be looking for you.'

All three ships would, of course, stop there before proceeding to Rimway. Indigo was a cylinder world, orbiting Planter's Delight, which had been settled less than thirty years before and already boasted 17 million inhabitants. Indigo had almost half a million more.

The past few days had been historic, but it was hard to get excited. He was up for a department manager's job, and that was all he cared about at the moment. Events like this were a hazard. They were no-win situations. Handle them right, and nobody would notice. Screw up somewhere, say the wrong thing to one of the journalists, and it would be bye-bye baby. So he concentrated on maintaining a professional attitude. Keep the experts happy.

And make sure the assorted hyper-light transmissions were received in good order, made available, and relayed to Rimway. It was simple enough. All he really had to do was to let the AI handle the details, be on his best social behavior, say good things about everybody, and keep close in case of a problem.

He watched the *Rensilaer*'s status lights, and when they went blue, he informed operations that the ship had made its jump, and he gave them its ETA.

Ten minutes later, the *Sentinel*'s captain appeared, Eddie Korby, young, quiet, studious. Look at him and you thought he was timid. The last person in the world you'd think would be piloting a starship. But he always had an attractive woman on his arm. Sometimes two or three.

'Indigo,' he said, '*we'll be departing in four minutes. I hope you got to watch the show. Delta Kay literally imploded. The passengers seem pretty happy with the mission. See you in a couple of weeks. Sentinel out.*'

Next up was Maddy. '*Coming home, Rondo,*' she said. '*Departure imminent.*' Behind her, on his operational screen, the dying star gave her an aura. She looked positively supernatural, standing there, silhouetted against the conflagration. A first-class babe, she was. But there was something about her that warned him *don't touch*. 'Polaris *out*.'

He took another sip of his gumpo, which was an extract from a plant grown on the world below, and to which he'd long since become accustomed. Lemon with a sting, but when it settled, it provided a general sense of warmth and well-being.

Sentinel's status lamps went blue. On her way.

He passed it on, not that anyone in Ops really cared, but it was procedure. He checked the logbook, made the entry for the *Sentinel,* and waited for *Polaris*'s lights to change.

The lamps showed white when the ship was in linear space, and they would go to blue when she'd made her jump. Twenty minutes after Maddy said they were ready to leave, they were still white.

That shouldn't be. 'Jack,' he told the AI, 'run a diagnostic on the board. Let's make sure the problem's not at this end.'

The systems whispered to one another, status lamps winked on and off, turned yellow, turned green, went back to white. *'I do not detect any problem with the system, Rondo,'* said Jack.

Damn. He disliked complications. He waited another few minutes, but the lamp remained steadily, defiantly unchanged.

White.

He hated problems. Absolutely hated them. There was always a big hassle, and it usually turned out that somebody had fallen asleep. Or hadn't thrown a switch. Reluctantly, he informed operations.

'*Polaris* twenty-five minutes after scheduled jump. Unaccounted for.'

Rondo's supervisor, Charlie Wetherall, showed up a few minutes later. Then one of the techs, who'd heard what was happening. The tech ran tests, and said the problem was at the other end. At forty-five minutes, the first journalists arrived. Heard something was happening. What's wrong?

Rondo kept quiet and let Charlie do the talking. 'These things happen,' Charlie said. 'Communications breakdowns.' Sure they do.

What Rondo couldn't figure was why they hadn't heard from Maddy if she'd been unable to jump.

'Busted link,' said Charlie, helpfully, using his expression to suggest that Rondo not say anything alarming to the journalists. Or to anyone at all.

'Then you don't think they're in trouble?' one of them asked. Her name was Shalia Something-or-other. She was a dark-skinned woman who'd sulked for weeks because they hadn't made room for her on the mission.

'Hell, Shalia,' said Charlie, 'for the moment we just have to wait until we have more information. But no, there's nothing to be worried about.'

He ushered the journalists into a conference room and found someone to stay with them, talk to them, keep them happy. He promised to let them know as soon as the station heard from the *Polaris*.

Charlie was small and round. He had a short temper when people made mistakes that impacted on him, and he was obviously thinking that Maddy had screwed up somehow, and he was getting irritated with her. Better with her, Rondo thought, than with *me*. Back in the comm center, they replayed the *Polaris* transmission. It was audio only. '*Coming home, Rondo. Departure imminent. Polaris out.*'

'Doesn't tell us much,' said Charlie. 'What's *imminent* mean?'

'Not an hour.'

'Okay. I'm going to check with upstairs. Stand by.'

Ten minutes later he was back with the station's director of operations. By then there was a crowd, and the journalists, who had broken out of their holding cell, were back. The director promised to make a statement as soon as he had something, and assured everyone it was just a technical glitch.

They played Maddy's transmission over and over. The director confessed he had no idea what the situation might be and asked Charlie whether anything like this had happened before. It had not.

'Give it another hour,' the director said. 'If nothing changes by' – he consulted the time – 'by five, we'll send somebody in. Can we turn one of the other two ships around?'

Charlie consulted his display. 'Negative,' he said. 'Neither has enough fuel to make a U-turn.'

'Who else is out there?'

'Nobody who's close.'

'Okay. Who's not close?'

Rondo tapped the screen to show his boss. 'Looks like Miguel,' said Charlie.

Miguel Alvarez was the captain of the *Rikard Peronovski*. Carrying supplies to Makumba and running some sort of AI tests.

14

'How long'll it take him to get there?'

While Charlie watched, Rondo ran the numbers. 'Four days after he reorients and is able to jump. Add time for the request to reach him, and for maneuvering at Delta Kay, figure a week. No less than that.'

'Okay. If we don't hear by five, tell him to go find the *Polaris*. Tell him to expedite.' The director shook his head. 'It's a bitch. Whatever we do here, we're going to have some very unhappy people. What's the captain's name again, Charlie?'

'Miguel.'

'No. On the *Polaris*.'

'It's Maddy. Madeleine English.'

'We ever have trouble with her before?'

'Not that I know of.' He looked at Rondo, who shook his head. No. Never any trouble.

'Well, I'll tell you, when this is over she better have a good story, or we're going to have her license.'

Rondo turned the comm center over to his relief and retired to his quarters. He showered and changed and went down to the Golden Bat, where he had dinner, as he customarily did, with friends. He started to describe what had happened, but word had already gotten around.

He was midway through a roast chicken when Talia Corbett, an AI specialist, showed up and told them that nothing had changed, they had not yet heard anything from the *Polaris*. The call had gone out to the *Peronovski*. Miguel was riding to the rescue.

There was a lot of talk that there must have been a major comm malfunction because nothing else could explain what was happening. Other than a catastrophic event. When you say *catastrophic event* in a situation like that, you tend to get a lot of attention.

He'd been trying to coax Talia into his bed for the better part of a year. That night he broke through. Afterward, he concluded that the business with the *Polaris* had, in some way, been responsible. It's an ill wind . . . he thought. Meantime, the *Polaris* lamps remained white.

III.

Delta Kay's surviving worlds and moons were scattering. A great ring of light marked the progress of the dwarf star. Near the position from which the *Polaris* had sent its last transmission, a set of lights blinked on, and the iron gray bulk of the *Rikard Peronovski* appeared apparently from nowhere.

Miguel Alvarez, who usually rode alone in the big freighter, was glad to have a passenger along this time. If the *Polaris* was really in trouble, another hand would be helpful.

He knew Madeleine. Not well, but well enough to know she was no dummy. It had been almost six days since Maddy's last transmission, and there'd been no word from the ship since. A communication problem, no doubt. Had to be. He did not expect to find anything in the area, because Maddy was undoubtedly in Armstrong space, her comm systems down, but headed home. If that was the case, she would arrive back at Indigo in another ten days or so.

The *Peronovski* was transporting general supplies, food, spare parts, environmental gear, and assorted odds and ends to the newly established colony at Makumba. Survey had elected to use the opportunity to test Mariner, which was, as his passenger insisted on calling it, a deep-space intelligence and docking system. The passenger was Shawn Walker, an AI specialist.

Miguel had expected to be overtaken en route by a second message, *It's okay, we've heard from them, continue your scheduled flight.* But Indigo's hourly updates, *Nothing yet; Still no word,* simply confirmed his suspicion that the ship was homeward bound, hidden in the folds of Armstrong space. He imagined Maddy's frustration, aware that they'd be scrambling to find her but unable to communicate with anyone.

Walker was on the bridge with him when they arrived. Miguel

wasn't sure what he expected to see. His instruments told him that vast clouds of gas were out there, but nothing was visible other than the ring of light around the neutron star.

Shawn Walker was about forty, average height, a bit overweight. He didn't look particularly smart, and maybe he wasn't. He was one of these guys who knew his way around AIs, and didn't seem to care much about anything else in the world. When they sat and talked at meals, it was all shop. Walker was married, and Miguel wondered if he was like that at home.

He turned toward the last-known position of the *Polaris*, accelerated, and began scanning for the ship he didn't expect to find. Miguel sent off a message to Indigo, bringing them up to date. Then he asked Sebastian, Shawn's experimental AI, when they could expect to locate the lost vessel.

'*If it is in the area,*' Sebastian said, '*and if it maintained course and speed, as one would expect, we should see it within a few hours.*'

'What happens,' Shawn asked Miguel, 'if they're not there?'

'We'll look elsewhere.'

'No. I mean, what happens if they're on their way back to Indigo?'

'I guess,' Miguel said, 'we'll be stuck here until Indigo tells us they've shown up.' Walker looked distressed. 'You okay, Shawn?'

'I know Warren Mendoza. He was on board. He's an old friend.'

'I'm sure they'll be all right.'

'And Tom Dunninger, too. Not well, but I met him.'

They had dinner, played cards, watched a video, went back to the bridge, and looked out at the relentless sky.

Miguel didn't sleep well. He wasn't sure why. He'd done a rescue mission once before, bailing out a ship whose engines had exploded. That had been the *Borealis*. Ten years ago. They'd been lucky: The captain had eleven people on board, and ten had survived. They'd given him a citation for that, and the rescued passengers had thrown a party for him. It had been one of the great moments of his life.

But there was something different about this. He wasn't sure what was bothering him, but his instincts kept him from closing his eyes. Kept him from relaxing at all.

In the morning there was still no sign. He had an early breakfast, then an hour later sat drinking coffee while Shawn ate. Sebastian was still reporting empty skies.

He prowled through the ship. He wandered from the common room to the bridge, took the zero-gee tube down to the cargo hold, glanced toward the two additional cabins they maintained just off the main storage bins, and inspected the Makumba shipment, which they were supposed to deliver in a couple of days. Eventually he climbed into the shuttle and took a seat. Shawn came down and asked if he was okay.

'Sure,' he said. 'I'm just not anxious to spend the next two weeks here.'

'*Miguel.*' It was Sebastian. '*We have searched the entire area in which they should be. The* Polaris *is not there.*'

'So they jumped?'

'*Or changed course. Or accelerated.*'

Miguel had no doubt the *Polaris* was on its way home. 'Okay,' he said, 'if we have to hang around, let's do it right. Sebastian, expand the search. Let's assume they got blown off course by the event. We'll look deeper. Away from wherever the central luminary used to be.

'Waste of time and money,' he grumbled. 'But we'll do it by the book.'

Miguel was becoming annoyed with Maddy. It would have been thoughtful of her to leave a satellite at the place where the ship should have been, informing any potential rescuer that she was okay and on her way to Indigo. It would have saved all this hassle.

They played some more cards. He started the latest Chug

18

Randall thriller, in which Chug has to outwit a gang of interstellar pirates who are after a shipment of priceless works of art. He watched some talk shows. (Miguel loved watching people argue. He didn't much care what they argued about, as long as it got loud and passionate. And nothing got louder than panels on politics and religion.)

He was eating more than he would have on a normal flight. And skimping on his daily workout. He promised himself that he'd get back to his routine the next day.

Then they were at the end of another evening, and he said good night to Shawn, who seemed able to entertain himself going through Sebastian's specs. Miguel had not slept well the first night because he was worried that they would find the *Polaris*. Now he didn't sleep well because he was bored and annoyed. He'd mention it to Maddy next time he saw her.

He finally dropped off at about 0200 hours. And Sebastian woke him ten minutes later. '*Miguel, I can see the* Polaris.'

It was substantially off course, moving at about forty degrees off its original heading. And angled down, out of the plane of what used to be the planetary system. It was running at a lower velocity than he'd been led to expect. He sent off a transmission to Indigo, then woke Shawn.

The specialist looked relieved. 'At least we know where they are,' he said.

But why are they here? There was no simple explanation that didn't involve either catastrophe or an unlikely breakdown of both comms and propulsion. There was a possibility he'd pushed to the back of his mind: They might have been punctured by debris, by rocks blown away from the dying sun. Or maybe a burst of radiation had penetrated the shielding.

'Range, Sebastian?'

'*Six point six million kilometers.*'

'Open a channel.'

'*Channel open.*'

'*Polaris,* this is *Peronovski.* Madeleine, is everything okay?' Miguel took a deep breath and settled down to wait. Round-trip for the signal would be almost a minute, plus whatever time Maddy needed to respond.

'*Power signature is normal,*' said Sebastian. An image of the *Polaris* appeared on the shuttle screen. It was running without lights.

He counted off a minute. Then two.

'Maddy, please answer up.'

Shawn wiped the back of his hand against his mouth. 'What do you think?' he asked.

'Don't know. Madeleine, are you there?'

Silence filled the bridge.

'Sebastian,' he said, 'can you contact the AI?'

'*Negative, Miguel. There is no response.*'

'Okay,' he said. 'Shawn, let's go have a look.'

The *Polaris* was small and showy. It was silver and black, with a flared rear end and teardrop pods along its flanks and a swept-back fuselage and a wraparound bridge over the prow. None of these features was necessary, of course. The only things a starship needs are symmetry and engines. Beyond those, appearance doesn't matter much. But the *Polaris* had been intended to impress VIPs, so Survey had spent money.

They went over in the shuttle, and he inspected the hull. There was no sign of damage. And no indication of movement on the bridge. 'Depressurize the cabin, Sebastian. And take us directly alongside the main airlock.'

The AI complied. Miguel and Walker checked each other's pressure suits, and, when the lamps turned green, left the shuttle and jumped to the *Polaris.*

The outer hatch responded to the control panel and swung open. They entered the airlock, the hatch closed behind them, and the air pressure started to rise. When it reached normal, the inner door opened.

The artificial gravity was on, but the interior was dark. Temperature was within normal range. They switched on wrist lights and removed their helmets. 'Kage,' he said addressing the AI, 'hello. Answer up, please. What's going on?'

Shawn flashed his lamp around at a table and chairs. They were in the common room. And other than the fact the lights were off, and nobody was there, everything looked normal.

'Kage?'

He would not have been able to give instructions to the AI, but she should respond to him.

Shawn tried his luck and shook his head. 'She's not functioning,' he said.

Miguel looked on the bridge. Nobody there. And no visible damage.

'Are they dead?' asked Shawn.

'Don't know.'

'Any way that could happen?'

'Not without leaving a hole in the hull.'

'How about a madman? Maybe somebody went berserk.'

'Somebody running amok with an ax?' Ridiculous. Especially among this crowd. Every one of them had led an exemplary existence. He'd checked their backgrounds while they were en route. Pillars of the community. All of them. But the prospect chilled him nonetheless. Had there been a maniac, he'd still be on board.

'We need light,' Miguel said. He crossed the bridge and sat down in the pilot's chair. The control board looked standard. He threw a couple of switches. Lights came on. 'Kage, do you hear me?'

The silence rolled back. Shawn knelt and opened a black box at the base of the pilot's chair. 'The circuits seem to be intact.' He touched a switch, pushed it forward. 'Try it now.'

'Kage, are you there?'

'Hello.' A female voice. 'To whom am I speaking?'

'Captain Miguel Alvarez. Of the *Peronovski*. Kage, what happened here?'

'*Captain, I am sorry, but I do not understand the question.*'

'You were supposed to start back to Indigo six days ago. Instead, you're adrift near Delta Kay. Where Delta Kay *was*. What happened?'

'*I don't know, Captain.*'

'Did somebody turn you off, Kage?'

'*Not that I'm aware of.*'

He peered into the black box. Someone could have disconnected one of the core circuits without her being aware it was happening. That would have shut her down. But if that's what happened, they went to the trouble to reconnect, but did not throw the switch to reactivate the AI. Why would anyone do that?

'Kage, what are your last recollections?'

'*We were getting ready to make the jump into Armstrong space. At the end of the mission.*'

'And then what happened?'

'*That's what I remember. Next I was talking to you. I am not aware of the passage of time between those events.*'

'Kage,' he said, 'where's Madeleine?'

'*I don't know. I don't see her.*'

'How about the others?'

'*I don't see anyone.*'

'Miguel,' said Shawn, 'she has a restricted view of the ship. AIs always do. We're going to have to find them ourselves.'

They put the lights on and started aft. Through the common room. Down the main passageway, which was lined with doors, four on each side. Miguel had never before been aboard the *Polaris,* but he knew that these were the quarters for the captain and her passengers.

'Madeleine?' he called. 'Hello? Anybody home?' His voice echoed through the ship.

'Spooky,' said Shawn.

'Yes, it is. Stay close until we figure out what's going on here.' He touched the pressure plate on the first door, the captain's

22

quarters, and it opened. It was empty, but Maddy's clothes were hung up.

The cabin across the passageway was also empty. As were the others, and each of the washrooms.

'What's below?' Shawn asked, his voice barely a whisper.

'Cargo, engine room, and lander.'

They went down and looked. There was nobody in cargo.

'This is crazy,' said Shawn.

Miguel led the way into the power room. Nobody lurking in the spaces between the engines. Nobody in storage. Nobody in the launch area.

They approached the lander, which was the only place on the ship where they hadn't looked. Alvarez opened the hatch and peered in.

Nobody in the front seat. Nobody in the back.

The place felt haunted. 'What the hell,' he said, 'is going on?'

There was a spare washroom on the lower deck, but it was empty. Cabinets lined one bulkhead. Several of them were big enough to hide in, so he opened them one by one. They were also empty.

They found two pressure suits. 'Kage,' he said, 'how many pressure suits are on board?'

'Four, Captain.'

'We're looking at two of them.'

'There are two more on the bridge.'

'They're there now?'

'Yes, sir.'

'So all four suits are accounted for.'

'Yes, sir.'

And the lander lay snugly within its restraints. 'They have to be here somewhere.'

There were clothes in seven of the eight compartments. That figured, since there had been a captain and six passengers. Shoes were laid out in two of the rooms, personal gear in drawers everywhere. Readers, toothbrushes, combs, bracelets. In one, a copy of *Lost Souls* had fallen onto the deck.

'What could have happened?' asked Shawn.

'Kage, is there any place in the entire system currently habitable?'

'Negative, Captain. Not now.'

He'd forgotten. The sun had gone out. That seemed a trivial point at the moment. 'There was a living world here, wasn't there?'

'Yes. Delta Karpis III.'

'Would it have supported humans?'

'Yes. If they were careful.'

'No point to this,' said Shawn. 'They had no way to get off the ship.'

They turned out the lights and set the *Polaris* for power-save mode. Then they went back out through the airlock, left the outer hatch open, and boarded the shuttle.

He was glad to get back to the *Peronovski*. He hadn't realized how chilled he'd been until the warm air hit him. Then he activated the hypercomm.

'What are you going to tell them?' asked Shawn.

'I'm still thinking about it,' he said. He sat down and opened the channel, but before he said anything for the record, he directed the AI to move well away from the *Polaris*. 'Give us some space,' he said.

1

Say what you will, murder is at least a straightforward crime, honest and direct. There are other acts far worse, more cowardly, more cruel.

—Edward Trout,
during the penalty phase of the trial of Thomas Witcover

SIXTY YEARS LATER.
1428TH YEAR SINCE THE WORLD FOUNDATION OF
ASSOCIATED STATES (RIMWAY).

I would probably never have gotten involved with the *Polaris* business had my boss, Alex Benedict, not figured out where the Shenji outstation was.

Alex was a dealer in antiquities, although he could be infuriating because his passion for artifacts inevitably took second place to his interest in profits. He was in it for the money. His job consisted largely of schmoozing with clients and suppliers, and he liked that, too. Furthermore, his career choice brought him more prestige than he could ever have earned as an investment banker or some such thing.

The truth is that I did most of the work at Rainbow. That was his corporation. He was the CEO, and I was the workforce. But I shouldn't complain. The job was intriguing, and he paid me well.

My name's Chase Kolpath, and I was with him during the *Corsarius* affair, two years earlier. Which, as you might know, led to some rewriting of history. And a small fortune for Alex. But that's another story.

In his chosen profession, he was a genius. He knew what collectors liked, and he knew where to find it. Rainbow was primarily a wheel-and-deal operation. We located, say, the pen with which Amoroso the Magnificent had signed the Charter, talked its owner into selling it to our client, and took a generous commission. Occasionally, when the prices looked especially appealing, we bought the objects and turned them over at prices more commensurate with their value. During all the years I worked with him, Alex seemed invariably to be correct in his judgments. We almost never lost money.

How he managed that without giving a damn about the objects themselves, I've never understood. He kept a few around the country house that served as his private residence and corporate headquarters. There was a drinking cup from the Imperial Palace at Millennium, and a tie clasp that had once belonged to Mirandi Cavello. That one goes back two thousand years. But he didn't really connect with them, if you know what I mean. They were there for show.

Anyhow, Alex had located a previously unknown Shenji outstation. In case you don't stay up with these things and have no idea what an outstation is, corporations used them as bases when travel around the Confederacy took *weeks,* and sometimes *months.* I know I'm dating myself when I admit that I was a pilot in the days before the quantum drive, and I remember what it was like. You left Rimway and headed out and it took a full *day* to go twenty light-years. If you were doing some serious traveling, you got plenty of time to improve your chess game.

Outstations were placed in orbit at various strategic points so that travelers could stop and get refreshed, pick up spare parts, refuel, replenish stores, or just get out of the ship for a while. Some were run by governments, most were corporate. Unless you've been on an old-style flight, you have no idea what sitting inside one of those burners for weeks at a crack can be like. It's all strictly eyeblink now. Turn it on, and you can be halfway across the Arm before you finish your coffee. No limit other than the one imposed by fuel. Alex gets credit for that, too. I mean, he was the one who found the original quantum drive. And I won't be giving away any secrets if I tell you that it hasn't made him happy that he was never able to cash in. It seems you can't patent historical inventions that somebody else, uh, *invented*. Even if no living person knew about it anymore. The government gave him a medal and a modest cash prize and thanked him very much.

If you've read Alex's memoir, *A Talent for War*, you know the story.

The outstation was orbiting a blue giant whose catalog number I've forgotten. Doesn't matter anyhow. It was close to six thousand light-years from Rimway, on the edge of Confederacy space. If the sources were accurate, it was eighteen hundred years old.

Outstations are almost always reconfigured asteroids. The Shenji models tended to be *big*. This one had a diameter of 2.6 kilometers, and I'm talking about the station, not the asteroid. It was in a seventeen-year orbit around its sun. Like most of these places that have been abandoned awhile, it had developed a distinct tumble, which, of course, tends to shake up whatever might be stored inside.

It was the first time in its history Rainbow Enterprises had discovered one of these things. 'Are we going to register it?' I asked. We would do that to claim ownership.

'No,' he said.

'Why not?' It would have been just a matter of informing the Registry of Archeological Sites. You gave them a brief description of the find, and its location, and it was legally yours.

He was looking out at the station. It was dark and battered, and you could easily have missed seeing what it was. In its glory days it would have said hello and invited you over for some meals and a short vacation. 'Off-world law enforcement doesn't exist,' he said. 'All we'd be doing is giving away the location of the site.'

'Maybe that's what we should do, Alex.'

'What is?'

'Give it away. Contribute it to Survey. Let them worry about it.'

He stuck his tongue into the side of his jaw. 'That might not be a bad idea, Chase,' he said. We both knew we could carry off pretty much everything of value, short of the site itself. Giving it to Survey would generate goodwill with an organization that had always supplied well-heeled clients. And Rainbow Enterprises would get plenty of free publicity. 'Exactly what I was thinking, my little urchin.'

Most of its space had been given over to docking and maintenance. But there had also been a couple of dining areas, living accommodations, and recreational facilities. We found the remains of open spaces that had once been parks. There'd been a lake. And even a beachfront.

It was all gray and cold now. Eighteen centuries is a long time, even in near vacuum.

There was no power, of course, hence no gravity. And no light. But that was okay. We had made a serious strike, and Alex, usually staid, complacent, one might even say *dull,* became a child in a toy store as we toured the place, dragging spare air tanks with us.

But the toys turned out to be pretty well smashed. Personal items left behind by the inhabitants were afloat everywhere, going round and round with the station. Chairs and tables, stiffened fabrics, knives and forks, notebooks and shoes, lamps and cushions. And a lot of stuff that was beyond recognition, bits and pieces of everything, whatever might have broken off over the years. The place was turning on its axis every seven and a half minutes, an action that sent clouds of loose objects bumping around the bulkheads. 'The thing's a giant blender,' said Alex, trying to swallow his disappointment.

Shenji culture is best remembered today for its flared towers (which look like rockets waiting to roar into the sky), their asymmetric architectural designs, their affinity for showy tombs, the dramas of Andru Barkat (which are still periodically revived on some of the snobbier stages around town), and their descent into the series of religious wars that eventually destroyed them. And maybe their drive to find nonhuman civilizations, which went on almost without pause, and without noticeable result, for two millennia. The Shenji were not people who gave up easily. But during their golden age, before the prophet Jayla-Sun showed up, they were convinced there were others out there and that the human race wouldn't fulfill its destiny until it could sit down with them and talk philosophy. Even that effort was largely a religious thing, but if it cost a lot of resources, it caused no damage. The common wisdom now is that there is nobody else anywhere in the Milky Way, except us, and the Ashiyyur. The Mutes. (All this with the Shenji, of course, happened before Gonzalez discovered the Mutes. Or, if you want to be factual, before they discovered *him*.) And I don't mind telling you that it wouldn't be a bad thing if *they* would pack up and move on. Andromeda would be a good place for them.

There are still a few people walking around who claim to be pure-blooded Shenji. I don't know why they would. Their history is a mixed bag at best. When they weren't exploring, they were running pogroms and inquisitions; but they've been dead and gone a long time, and that fact alone seems to make them intriguing to some folks. Alex has commented that being dead for a sufficiently long time guarantees your reputation. It won't matter that you never did anything while you were alive; but if you can arrange things so your name shows up, say, on a broken wall in a desert, or on a slab recounting delivery of a shipment of camels, you are guaranteed instant celebrity. Scholars will talk about you in hushed tones. You will become a byword, and an entire age might even be named for you. History used to be simpler back when there wasn't so much of it.

Historians are forever announcing how they'd like to sit down with someone who'd actually hung out at the Parthenon during the years of Athenian hegemony, or had attended a Shenji parade. A survivor, if one could be found, would be hustled around town in the most luxurious skimmers, treated to the best meals, and taken to see the Council. He would show up as a guest on *The Daylight Show.*

Go to Morningside today, the Shenji home world, and you'll find a modern, skeptical, democratic society populated by waves of outsiders, people from all over the Confederacy. The tribes of true believers are gone, everybody's a skeptic, watch your purse, and if you really think there are more aliens out there, I have a bridge I'd like you to look at.

Alex had the kind of looks that could get lost easily in a crowd. His face was sort of bureaucratic, and you knew immediately that he liked working in an office, that he preferred a regular schedule, no surprises, and took his coffee with a sweetener. That was all true, actually. Although I have to confess we had a brief romantic fling years ago. But he was never going to commit to marriage, and I wanted him as a friend rather than a lover anyhow. So there you are.

He was about average height, brown hair, dark brown eyes, and he looked out of place in a pressure suit. Or in an ancient outstation, drifting down dark corridors, with a lamp in one hand and a laser cutter in the other.

He was reasonable, quiet, and he thought well of himself. He had never liked starships. In the early years, when we were using the old jump engines, he used to get sick every time we made the transition into or out of Armstrong space. He was interested primarily in number one. Liked making money, liked wielding influence, enjoyed being invited to the right parties. But at heart he was a good guy. He'd take care of a stray cat, always kept his word, and watched out for his friends. I should add that he was a reasonable boss. If occasionally erratic.

We needed the cutters because the hatches, both inside and out, were nonfunctional, so we had to slice our way through a lot of them. My job was to do the slicing and pack any salable objects. His was to point out the stuff we'd take back.

But after three days wandering around the station we had virtually nothing to show for it.

He'd figured out the location of the place from clues left in Shenji archives. Just finding this outpost of Shenji culture would have considerable public relations value, but it wasn't going to bring a cascade of wealth, which was what he'd expected.

His good humor began to drain. As we fished pieces and bits, knobs and filters and chunks of dishware and broken glass and shoes and timers out of the debris, he took to sighing, and I'm sure inside the helmet he was shaking his head.

I'd seen him like that before. What happens is that he begins to talk about the historical value of the artifacts and what a loss it is to the human race to find them in such terrible condition. He becomes a great humanitarian when things go wrong.

The original plan had been to set up a base inside the station, but Alex wondered whether it was worth the effort. So every evening when we got tired, or bored, wandering around the place, we returned to the *Belle-Marie* for dinner. And then we looked at whatever we'd salvaged. It was a depressing time, and when I told him that maybe we should just close up shop and head home, he replied that I was giving up too easily.

On the sixth day, when we were getting ready to pack it in, we found a chamber with odd damage. It appeared to be a conference room. It contained a table that could have seated about ten, and gray mottled bulkheads, one of which might once have been a display screen. The screen was smashed. Not smashed because objects were getting rolled around the room, because nothing was moving in there with much force. But smashed the way it would be if someone had taken a hammer to it.

The table and chairs and some gunk that might once have been fabric were working their way across the overhead. The only thing that held us upright was our grip shoes, and I should tell you that standing there watching everything move around the room tended to make your head spin.

'Vandals,' Alex decided, standing in front of the wall screen. He hated vandals. 'Damn their hides.'

'It happened a long time ago,' I said.

'Doesn't matter.'

The next room might have been a VR chamber. We checked the equipment, which was locked in place, and in fact everything in that room was secured, and the door had been closed, so it was in decent condition. Not that the equipment would work, of course. But it looked good. And I could see Alex brighten, mentally tagging some of the gear for shipment home.

Then we found more signs of vandals, more damage to stationary objects. 'They probably came in on a looting expedition,' he said. 'Got exasperated at the conditions, and started breaking things up.'

Yeah. Those looters are just terrible.

But maybe they'd gotten discouraged too soon. We eventually wandered into what appeared to be the control room. And that was where we found the jade bracelet. And the corpse.

The bracelet was on the left wrist. It was black, and engraved with an ivy branch.

The corpse was in pieces, and the pieces were adrift. The torso was moving across the deck when we moved in. At first I didn't know what it was. It was mummified, and it looked as if it had been either a woman or a child. While we were trying to decide about that, I discovered the bracelet. The arm was the only limb still attached.

It wasn't readily visible unless you handled the remains. Don't ask me why I did. It was just that the corpse shouldn't have been there, and I wondered what had happened.

And there was the bracelet. 'I think she got left behind,' I told Alex. There was no sign of a pressure suit, so she hadn't been with the vandals.

We had nothing to wrap her in, no way to secure the body. Alex stood staring at her a long time. Then he looked around the room. There were three control positions. They opened the outer doors remotely, maintained station stability, managed communications, kept an eye on life support, probably controlled the bots that serviced the living quarters.

'I think you're right,' he said at last.

'Probably didn't check when they left to be sure they had everybody.'

He looked at me. 'Maybe.'

She was shriveled, dry, the face smoothed out, the features missing altogether. I thought how it must have been when she realized she'd been left behind. 'If it really happened,' Alex said, 'it had to have been deliberate.'

'You mean, because she could have called them? Let them know she was here?'

'That's one reason.'

'If they were shutting down the station,' I said, 'they'd have killed the power before they left. She might not have known how to turn it back on.' He rolled his eyes. 'So what other reason is there?'

'They'd have used a team for a project like shutting down the station. There's no way someone could have been here and not noticed what was going on. No. This was deliberate.'

Three walls had been converted into display screens. There was lots of electronic gear. The rear wall, the one the corpse was climbing, was given over to an engraving of the mountain eagle that for centuries was the world symbol of the Shenji Imperium. Two phrases were inscribed below the eagle.

'What's it say?' I asked.

Alex had a translator. He poked the characters into it and made a face. '*The Compact*. It's the way the Shenji of that era referred to their nation, which was a polity of individual states. *The Compact*.' He hesitated. 'The second term is harder to translate. It means something like *Night Angel*.'

'*Night Angel*?'

'Well, maybe *Night Guardian*. Or *Angel of the Dark*. I think it's the name of the station.'

An outstation always had a dozen or so rooms set aside as accommodations for travelers. You want to stay overnight, and maybe even sneak someone into your apartment without the rest of the world finding out, this was the place to do it. The room usually consisted of a real bed, as opposed to the fold-outs on the ships. Maybe a chair or two. A computer link. Possibly a small table and a reader.

The compartments at the Night Angel were located two decks above the control room and about a kilometer away. We were looking to see if any appeared to have been lived in, but the passage of time was too great, and the contents of the rooms too thoroughly scrambled, so it was impossible to determine whether any of them might have been used by the victim.

Eventually, we opened an airlock and, after retrieving the bracelet, gave the body to the void. I wasn't sure it was the proper thing to do. After all, she'd been dead a long time and had herself become an object of archeological interest. I had no doubt Survey would have liked to have the corpse. But Alex wouldn't hear of it. 'I don't like mummies,' he said. 'Nobody should be put on display after they're dead. I don't care how long ago they died.'

Sometimes he got sentimental.

So we watched her drift away, then we went back inside. The best finds came out of one of the dining rooms. Fortunately, everything there had been locked down, and it was in good condition. We spent two hours gathering glasses and plates and chairs, and especially stuff that had the station's name on it, Night Angel.

That's where the money is. Anything with a seal. We also collected circuit boxes, switches, keyboard panels whose Shenji inscriptions, after a careful cleaning, were still visible. We removed vents and blowers and the AI (a pair of gray cylinders) and a water nozzle and a temperature gauge and a hundred other items. It was by far our best day at the outstation.

We found a group of seventeen wineglasses, carefully stored, each glass engraved with the image of the mountain eagle. That alone would be worth a small fortune to a collector. We needed two more days to haul everything back to the *Belle-Marie*.

Alex, celebrating our success, gave me a raise and invited me to take a couple of souvenirs. I picked out some settings, dinner dishes, saucers, cups, and silver. Everything except the silver was made of cheap plastic, but, of course, that didn't matter.

When we'd filled *Belle*'s storage area, there were still some decent items left over. Not great stuff, but okay. We could have come back to get them, made another flight, but Alex said no. 'It'll be part of the bequest to Survey.'

By God he was a generous man.

'We've got the pick of the merchandise,' he continued. 'Survey will send the rest of it around to every major museum in the Confederacy. And they'll be representing us. Everywhere they go on display, Rainbow will be mentioned.'

As we slipped away from the platform, Alex asked what I made of the corpse.

'Left by a boyfriend,' I suggested. 'Or a husband.'

Alex looked at me oddly, as if I'd said something unreasonable.

2

History is a collection of a few facts and a substantial assortment of rumors, lies, exaggerations, and self-defense. As time passes, it becomes increasingly difficult to separate the various categories.

—Anna Greenstein,
The Urge to Empire

We left the Shenji outstation just after breakfast on the tenth day. We used nine hours to charge the quantum drive, so we were back in the home system in time for a late dinner. Of course, we needed another two days to travel from the arrival point to Skydeck, the Rimway orbital station.

I was in favor of calling a press conference to announce our find, but Alex asked me coolly who I thought would come.

'Everybody,' I said, honestly surprised that he didn't see the advantage in culling maximum publicity out of the discovery.

'Chase, nobody cares about a two-thousand-year-old space station. *You* do, for obvious reasons. And a handful of collectors. And maybe some researchers. But to the general public, it's not sexy. It's just a piece of leftover junk.'

So okay. I gave in, grumbling a bit over a lost opportunity to talk to the media people. I confess I enjoy the spotlight, and I love being interviewed. So while we cruised into the inner system, I contented myself by putting together an inventory and writing a cover letter detailing what we'd found. Alex changed the emphasis here and there, and we transmitted it to our assorted clients and other possibly interested parties, and also to most of the major museums on Rimway. It described a dozen or so of the objects we'd brought back, advising prospective buyers to get in touch if they wanted to see the complete inventory. So when we docked at Skydeck, nobody was there, and no bands played. But we already had a few bids.

And that evening, back in Andiquar, we had a celebratory dinner at Culp's on the Tower.

By morning we'd had more than a hundred responses. Everybody wanted details, most inquired about starting negotiations, and others wanted to know when they could see specified objects. I referred the money issues to Alex, while I arranged to have the merchandise shipped down from orbit.

Rainbow had always been a profitable venture for him, and it had provided a good situation for me. It paid better than running around in an interstellar bus, it was less disruptive to my personal life, and in fact I loved the work.

It's an odd thing about collectors. The value of an artifact tends to be in direct proportion to the proximity the object would have had to the original owner, or at least the degree to which it could have been seen or handled by him. That's why dinner plates and glasses are so popular, why a collector will pay good money for a panel board, while turning thumbs down on the recycler or generator that it controlled.

If Alex had been one of those people given to framing an epigraph and hanging it on the wall, it would have read, THE PAYOFF'S IN FLATWARE. People love dishes and cups and forks and, if the historical background is right, they'll pay almost anything to own them. Especially if a ship's seal is present. The truth about our customers was that none of them was going to show up at the bargain store. In fact, it had become obvious to me that, unlike standardized goods, antiquities tend to become more sought after as the price goes up.

The routine work took several days. By the end of the week money had begun to come in, and we were shipping off the first Night Angel objects. Although we hadn't communicated directly with Survey, they'd learned of the find, as we knew they would, and the director got in touch with Alex. Where was the outstation? Was there any chance they could see it? Alex said he would try to arrange something. It was, of course, the signal for us to demonstrate our munificence. 'How did you want to handle it?' I asked.

'*You* take care of it, Chase. Go see Windy.'

'*Me?* Don't you think you should do this personally? Give it to Ponzio himself? You're making a pretty big donation.'

'No. I'd have a hard time containing myself. If we're going to get maximum value out of this, humility is the way to go.'

'You're not good at that.'

'My thought exactly.'

Winetta Yashevik was the archeological liaison at Survey, and an old friend. We'd gone to school together. She didn't approve of Alex because of his profession. Turning antiquities into commodities and selling them to private buyers struck her as grossly incorrect. When I'd gone to work for Rainbow twelve years earlier she told me it was a sellout.

But she listened carefully while I described what we'd seen. She gazed at the ceiling with a help-me-stay-calm-Lord expression when I told her we'd taken 'some' of the artifacts, and finally nodded solemnly when I announced the gift.

'Everything you couldn't carry off, I presume?' We were sitting on a love seat in Windy's office. Old pals. It was a big office, on the second floor of the Kolman building. Lots of pictures from the missions on the paneled walls, a few awards. Winetta Yashevik, employee of the year; Harbison Award for Outstanding Service;

Appreciation from the United Defenders for contributions to their Toys for Kids program. And there were pictures of dig sites. I recognized the collapsed towers at Ilybrium, but the others were just people standing around excavations.

'We could have gone back,' I said. 'We could have stripped the place clean.'

She stared at me intensely for a moment, then relented. Windy was tall, dark, send-in-the-cavalry. She'd trained originally to be an archeologist, and had some field experience. She had a lot of good qualities, but she wasn't someone *I'd* have put in a position that required diplomacy and tact. 'How'd you find it?' she asked.

'The archives.'

A water clock in a corner of the room made a gurgling sound. 'Incredible,' she said.

'There's something else,' I said. 'We found a corpse. A woman.'

'Really? You mean an *old* corpse?'

'Yes. It looked as if she was left behind when they cleared out.'

'No idea why? Or who she was?'

'None.'

'We'll look into it when we get there. Maybe we can turn up something. I don't suppose you brought it back with you?'

I hesitated. 'We put it out the airlock.'

Her eyes closed, and she stiffened. 'You put *what* out the airlock?'

'The corpse.' I wanted to say, hey, it wasn't my idea, it was Alex, you know how he is. But I didn't want her going after my employer and saying how I'd pointed the finger at him.

'Chase,' she said, 'you *didn't*.'

'Sorry.'

'Hell of a time for you two to get a conscience.'

The windows began to darken. Storm coming. It seemed like a good time to change the subject. 'Alex thinks there are a dozen more of them out there.'

'Corpses?'

'Outstations.'

40

'As far as we can tell, the Shenji built a lot of them.' People had started establishing outstations almost as soon as they'd left the home world. 'Listen, Chase: If he finds another one, how about letting us take a look first? Before you guys charge in.'

'This one took him the better part of two years.'

She sighed at the injustice of it all. 'We've had people devote whole lifetimes and come away empty.'

'Alex is pretty good at what he does, Windy.'

She got up, walked over to the window, turned her back to it, and half sat against the sill. 'You want nothing in return?' she asked.

'No. It's free and clear.' I handed her a chip. 'This is the location. And the transfer of all rights.'

'Thank you. We'll see that you get full credit.'

'You're welcome. I hope you find it useful.'

She opened a drawer in her desk and put the chip inside. 'I'll have the director get back to Alex. Express his appreciation.'

'That would be nice,' I said. 'And by the way I have something for *you*.' I'd brought a couple of samples with me, pieces from the life-support system, a section of tubing, a filter, and a tiny motor. I took them out of my carrying case and held them out to her. Now this is not going to seem like much to the casual reader, but I knew Windy, and I watched the tension drain away and saw her eyes light up. She reached out tentatively for them, and I put them in her hands.

She held them, letting the centuries flow through her, then she put them on the desk and hugged me. 'I appreciate it, Chase,' she said. 'You're okay.'

'You're welcome,' I said.

'But I still think you two are grave robbers.'

Ten minutes later she was walking me into the office of the director. His name was Louis Ponzio. A man of boundless importance. Ramrod straight. Used to giving directions. Took himself very seriously.

He was a little guy, narrow eyes, narrow nose, lots of energy. Always ready to shake your hand and take you into his confidence. You and I know how things are, he seemed to say. We can trust each other. You always knew when he was in the room. And you knew he was accustomed to getting his way. He was *Dr Ponzio*. Nobody would ever have called him *Louie*.

Windy explained about the Shenji platform, and Ponzio smiled and tried to look overwhelmed by it all. I didn't know him that well, but he was a mathematician and a political appointment. That was a double whammy. Political appointments were inevitably people who were getting paid off. And I'd had several bad experiences with mathematicians over the years. Never knew one who could get passionate about anything other than sex and numbers. And not necessarily in that order.

We shook hands all around. Filled the glasses for everyone. He'd always admired Rainbow's efforts. If there was anything he could do, please don't hesitate.

I always say that when you do the right thing, you get rewarded. Windy did some research and was able to date the outstation a little more precisely than we had, to the end of the Imperium years.

A couple of days later she called me at home in a state of suppressed excitement. *'I think I know who the victim was.'*

I'd slept late, and was just getting out of the shower. Since I wasn't appropriately dressed, we stayed on audio. 'Who?'

'Lyra Kimonity.'

'Is she someone I should know?'

'Probably not. She was the first wife of Khalifa Torn.'

Ah. Torn I knew. Attila. Bogandiehl. Torn. Three of a kind. He had finished off the Imperium, seized power for himself, and ruled four years, murdering millions, before his own guards took him out. He had seen no need for the outstations, which were simply a drain on the treasury, so he shut them down.

'Torn liked to sleep with the wives of his staff and officers. Lyra made a fuss.'

'Ah.'

'She disappeared.'

'What makes you think it was her at the outstation?'

'Most historians think he exiled her. His stooges might have misunderstood his intention, because later he changed his mind. Tried to get her back. Or maybe he just forgot his original instructions. Anyhow, the person he'd given her to couldn't produce her. When he found out the details of what had happened – the archives don't specify what that was *– he executed the people responsible. One of them was'* – she paused to look at her notes – *'Abgadi Diroush. And there was a second one whom he personally drowned. Berendi Lakato. Lakato was responsible for shutting down the outstations. And Diroush headed up the team that actually did the work. In any case, Lyra was never seen again.'*

'Well,' I said, 'that's good news.'

That startled her. *'How do you mean?'*

'Makes the artifacts more valuable. Everybody loves a monster. You don't think he ever visited the station personally, do you?'

She let me see that she was shocked. *'No,'* she said, *'I don't think so. He didn't like to travel. Afraid somebody might seize power while he was gone.'*

'That's a pity.'

'I sent you a picture of her.'

I put it on-screen. Lyra had been a red-haired beauty. Big almond eyes. A fetching smile. I wondered how she'd gotten involved with Khalifa. And it occurred to me it's not always an advantage to look good.

'Look at the wrist,' she said.

I knew what I was going to find: the jade bracelet. And there it was. I could even make out the sprig of ivy.

'Is it the same as the one you found?'

'Yes.'

'That confirms it, then.'

'Yeah.' Lyra was maybe twenty-two when the picture was taken. 'How old would she have been?'

'We can't get it exactly, but she was still young. Twenty-seven, maybe.'

I thought about her, marooned on the station. I wondered whether they'd at least left the lights on for her.

'Something else,' Windy said. 'You brought back a boatload of artifacts, right? From the Night Angel.'

'We salvaged a few items, yes.'

'I was thinking that we might provide you with some publicity. Help you sell the merchandise.'

'What did you have in mind, Windy?'

'Why not put the artifacts temporarily in our hands? We could create an exhibition at the museum. Put everything on display for, say, a month. I suspect that sort of event would enhance their value considerably.'

'We might consider making some of them available,' I told her. 'What do we get in return?'

'I beg your pardon?'

'You get a Shenji exhibition. What do we get?'

'Chase, you're going to get a ton of museum exposure.'

'I think Survey comes out way ahead on that arrangement.'

'Okay. I'll tell you what. Let us have the artifacts, and I'll let your boss in on something.'

'Nothing up this sleeve,' I said.

'Hear me out.'

'What's the something?'

'We're approaching the sixtieth anniversary of the loss of the Polaris.'

I tossed the towel into a hamper and pulled on a robe. 'You alone, Windy?'

'Yes.'

I went out to the living room and switched over to visual. She was sitting behind her desk.

'Must be nice to be able to keep those kinds of hours,' she said.

'I'm paid for what I know.'

'Of course. I've always thought that.'

'What's the something you're prepared to offer?'

'Next week, to mark the anniversary, several books are being released. A major studio production has been put together, and one of the networks even has a psychic who's going around explaining what happened.'

'Aboard the *Polaris*?'

'Yes.'

'What's he say? The psychic?'

'Ghosts got 'em.'

'Why am I not surprised to hear that?'

'I'm not kidding. Ghosts. More or less. Some sort of supernatural fog. Goes right through the hull.'

'Okay.'

'The guy's good. He's got a track record.'

'I'm sure.'

'The point is that there'll be a lot going on about the Polaris *over the next couple of weeks. We're doing a banquet, inviting some VIPs, and we've been holding off on the dedication so we could do everything at once.'*

'The dedication?'

'*A new wing. For the* Polaris.'

'You're just getting around to it now?'

She laughed. *'You'll have to ask somebody else about that, Chase. I've only been here a few years. But, off the record, I suspect it was always a bit too spooky for Survey. Seven people vanish off a ship? It was a downbeat story for a long time. I don't think they wanted to remind anybody. Now it's mostly legend. You know what I mean? Anyhow, we're going to make it into a two-week-long extravaganza. Now what I think you'll be interested in is that we're going to sell off some Polaris artifacts. At auction.'*

'Artifacts?' That was a surprise. 'I didn't know you had any.'

'They were stored at the time of the event. They're personal items mostly, slates, pressure suits, pens, mugs, you name it. And some gear, but not much.'

'Why? I mean, why'd they go into storage?'

'There were a lot of investigations. When the big one was done, the Trendel Commission, they sold the ship and probably forgot about the stuff. Or maybe somebody thought it'd be worth hanging on to.'

Artifacts from the *Polaris*. They'd be worth a fortune.

'Anyway, we'll be issuing invitations to the banquet for you and Alex.'

I couldn't help a wide smile. 'You get access to the Night Angel artifacts, and we get an invitation to dinner.'

She actually managed to look hurt. *'It's not just a dinner. Some of our most important supporters will be there. It'll be very exclusive. It's going to get coverage.'*

'Windy,' I said, 'I tell you what I'll do. We'll let you have selected artifacts on loan for a month. In return, we get the dinner invitations—'

'—And?'

'—We get fifteen of the *Polaris* artifacts at no cost prior to the auction. We'll take a look and let you know what we want.'

'You know damned well I can't do that, Chase. I don't have that kind of authority.'

'Talk to Ponzio.'

'He won't agree. He'd think I've lost my mind. So would I.'

'Windy, do I need to remind you that Survey is getting an *outstation* from us?'

'That was a gift. No strings, remember? You can't start trying to deal for it now.'

'Okay. That's fair enough. Not very appreciative, but fair.'

'Look, Chase, I tell you what I'll do. I'll give you first crack at the artifacts. A preauction sale. You can take a look at the stuff, and if we can agree on a price, you're in business.'

'A reasonable price,' I said.

'Yes. Of course. We wouldn't try to take advantage of Rainbow.'

'Windy, you know as well as I do there'll be an initial explosion in prices, then they'll settle down.'

'I'm sure we'll have no problem on that score. But I won't be able to see my way clear to make fifteen available.'

'How many did you have in mind?'

'Two.'

Bargaining room. I looked appropriately shocked. 'I beg your pardon?'

'Two. Two artifacts. That's the absolute best I can do.'

We went back and forth and finally settled on six.

After she was off the circuit, I brought up the Memorial Wall in the Rock Garden, which is located behind Survey's administrative center. It's a tranquil place, a glade, with a loud brook, a few stones left over from the last ice age, a wide range of flowering plants, and the wall itself. It's separated from the rest of the grounds by a line of galopé bushes, so that you get a sense of being in a forest. This is the memorial set aside for those working under Survey's auspices who have given their lives "in the service of science and humanity." There are more than a hundred names, covering almost two centuries, carved into the wall, which is really a series of shaped rocks.

The *Polaris* passengers and their captain are there, of course. Whenever more than one person is lost in a single incident, the names are grouped and placed alphabetically, with the date. That put Chek Boland at the head. Maddy was listed third. There'd been a twelve-year delay before they were officially added to the roll call of lost heroes. The ceremony had been, at long last, an official recognition of their deaths. A concession.

Windy had called me on my day off. Afterward, I arranged to meet Alex for lunch. I wanted to tell him that we had an inside track for some of the *Polaris* artifacts, but I saw right away that he was distracted. 'You okay?' I asked.

'Fine,' he said. 'I'm fine.'

He listened while I explained what the deal was, and he nodded and looked pleased. 'When do we get to see them?'

'She's making an inventory available. Visuals. So we can look at them at our leisure.'

'Good,' he said. 'I have something else.'

'I thought you might.'

We were in Babco's, on the Mall. Out back, in the courtyard, overlooking the Crystal Fountain. It was supposed to be a mystical place. If you'd lost your one true love, you tossed in a few coins, concentrated, and he would come back into your life. Assuming you wanted him to.

'I've been thinking,' he said, 'that Rainbow could expand into a new field. Something no one's ever done before.'

'And what might that be?'

'Radioarcheology.'

'What's radioarcheology?' I asked.

'We deal in antiquities. We collect, trade, and sell all kinds of dishware, pottery, electronic equipment. You name it.'

'Right,' I said.

He looked at me, and his eyes glowed. 'Chase, what is an *antiquity*?'

'Okay. I'll play your game. It's an object that has an identifiable history. From a remote period.'

'Isn't that redundant?'

'Well, maybe. What else did you want to know?'

'You said *object*. Are you implying that an antiquity has to be physical, in the sense of something you can hold in your hands?'

'Only the ones that lend themselves to selling.' Traditions, stories, customs were all antiquities of a sort.

'Has to be physical for us to sell it?' he said.

'Of course.'

'I'm not so sure. I think we've been missing something.'

'How do you mean?'

Sandwiches and drinks showed up.

'What about transmissions?' I must have looked baffled. He smiled. 'We already use radio broadcasts to locate things. That's the way we found the *Halvorsen*.'

48

The *Halvorsen* was a corporate yacht whose captain and passengers had died back at the turn of the century when the ship was fried by a gamma ray burst. We'd found and tracked their Code White. It was a quarter century old by the time we ran it down. It was the last transmission, but it gave us a vector. It wasn't much, but it turned out to be enough. We tracked it back, calculated for drift, and there was the *Halvorsen*. Okay, it wasn't quite that easy, but it worked.

'I'm not talking about using transmissions to find things,' he continued. 'I mean collecting them for their own value.'

I took a bite from my sandwich. It was cheese and tomato. 'Explain,' I said.

He was delighted to oblige. Nothing made Alex happier than enlightening the slow-witted. 'Six hundred years ago, when the Brok terrorists were trying to bring down Kormindel, and it looked as if the entire population was on the edge of panic, Charles Delacort broadcast his famous appeal for courage. *"More than our lives are at stake, my friends. It is our future through which these lunatics wish to drive a stake. We must hold fast, for ourselves, for our children, and for everyone who follows after. Generations unborn will remember that we took a stand."* Remember?'

'Well, I don't exactly remember, but I know about it, sure.' At the critical moment, Delacort rallied the nation. Today, every schoolkid is familiar with the appeal. 'I'm still not following.'

'It's lost, Chase. The appeal. We don't have it anymore. We know what he said, but we don't have the actual broadcast. But it's out there somewhere. We know approximately when it happened, so we know where it can be found. What stops us from going out, tracking it down, recording it, and bringing it back? Intact. All we have to do is get in front of it, and we can recapture one of our great moments. What do you think such a recording would be worth?'

A couple of quegs flapped past, landed in a tree, and turned their attention to the fountain. Someone had thrown bread into it.

Quegs are not shy. They sat for a minute or so, then launched themselves, flew over our heads, splashed down, and began feeding.

'It's a nice idea, Alex, but a broadcast doesn't last that long. Not nearly. There's nothing out there to recover except a few stray electrons.'

'I've done some research,' he said.

'And?'

'The Delacort Address was forwarded to several off-world sites. That means directed transmissions. Not broadcasts. Add the kind of power they used during that era, and the transmissions might still be recoverable.'

'Is there a way to pin down the transmission vectors?' Worlds and bases move around a good bit.

'We have the logs,' he said. 'We know exactly when the transmissions were made. So yes, it should be possible to work out the direction.'

I was impressed. It sounded plausible.

'There's a lot of history out there,' he said. 'Brachmann's Charge to the Dellacondans. Morimba holding the fort against the religious crazies on Wellborn. Arytha Mill's address at the signing of the Instrument. Damn, we don't even have that one *written* down. But it all went out in directed transmissions, and in every instance we can nail the time.'

'We might be able to do it,' I said. 'I don't think anyone's ever considered the possibility before.'

He looked pleased with himself. 'Something else.'

'Okay.'

'There's a lot of entertainment out there, too.'

'You're talking about holodrama.'

'I'm talking about a substantial portion of broadcast arts over the last few thousand years. Most of it, or at least much of it, was packaged and forwarded to orbitals and ships and everything else. It's all out there. You want to hear Paqua Tori, we can get her for you.'

'Who's Paqua Tori?'

'The hottest comedienne on Toxicon during the Bolerian Age. I've heard her. She's actually pretty funny.'

'Does she speak Standard?'

'Not hardly. But we can do translations, and keep her voice and mannerisms.'

'Tastes change,' I said. 'I doubt there'll ever be a wide audience for antique comedy. Or drama, or whatever.'

'Sophocles still plays.' He was all smiles. 'As soon as we get this *Polaris* business taken care of, we'll look into some antenna enhancement for *Belle*.'

3

Antiquities are . . . remnants of history which have casually escaped the shipwreck of time.

—Francis Bacon,
The Advancement of Learning

We received our invitations to the banquet and auction the day after I spoke with Windy. Later in the week, she called again. *'Chase, I wanted to let you know we've put together a reception tomorrow evening. There'll be some VIPs on the premises.'*

'Okay.'

'At eight. We'd like you and Alex to come and be our guests. You could look over the stock at the same time.'

'That's very kind of you.' Alex liked events. Especially something like this. It meant free food and drinks. And he'd inevitably come away with a new client or two. 'Thanks, Windy,' I said. 'I'll have to check with the boss, but I suspect we'll be there.'

Then she surprised me. *'Good. Something like this wouldn't be complete without Rainbow. Come fifteen, twenty minutes early, okay? I'll meet you in my office. And by the way, I'll need your birth date. And Alex's.'*

'Why?'

'Security.'

'Security?'

'Yes.'

'You think we might try to steal the artifacts?'

'Of course not.' She arched an eyebrow. 'You wouldn't, would you?' And then a grin. 'No. It has nothing to do with that. But I can't talk about it.'

'Why not?'

The eyebrow went up again. 'I can't tell you that, either.'

The *Polaris*, of course, was old news. It had happened long before I'd been born, and the story had an unreal aura about it. It almost suggested the existence of a supernatural power out there somewhere, something capable of invading a sealed ship before an alarm could be sent. Something able to shut down the AI. A force that stole humans for purposes of its own. It sounded too much like a fable, like something that had happened outside history. I had no more idea what might have occurred on board than anyone else did. But because the events as reported seemed to defy explanation, I was convinced that the report was in some way simply *wrong*. That something had been left out. Or added in. Don't ask me what.

I'd done some boning up on the incident after Windy told me about the auction. Aside from the disappearance of the people inside, there was something else that was very odd. When Miguel Alvarez went on board, the AI was not operating. The *Polaris* had sustained no damage, hyperlight communications worked fine, and all systems were functional, except that the AI was down. It appeared, Alvarez testified during the hearings, that it had simply been turned off. Tests indicated it had stopped functioning within minutes after that last transmission had been sent. *Departure imminent.*

Alex had also become interested. Usually, his juices only got flowing when there was money to be made. But the *Polaris* was something different. He commented that shutting down the AI eliminated the sole witness the investigators might have had.

He wanted to know how one did that. How did you turn off an AI?

'The easiest way,' I said, 'is simply to tell it to shut itself off.'

'You can do that?'

'Sure. It's done all the time. The AI records everything that happens on the bridge, in storage, and in the engine compartment. And maybe one or two other areas. If you want to have a conversation on the bridge, but you don't want a record kept, you tell it to shut down.'

'How do you turn it back on?'

'Sometimes there's a key word. Sometimes a switch.' We were standing on the porch outside the Rainbow office, which was located on the ground floor of Alex's country house. It was raining, a cold, driving rain that beat against the trees. 'But that's not what happened on the *Polaris*.'

'How do you know?'

'If you tell an AI to deactivate, it retains a record of having received the direction. When the *Polaris* AI was turned back on, a few minutes after Alvarez had boarded, it recalled no such instruction. That means somebody disconnected it manually.'

'Is there any other possibility you can think of? Anything that might account for the shutdown?'

'A power failure would do it. Ships are required to have backup power sources, but those regs aren't enforced now, and probably weren't enforced in 1365. But we know nothing like that happened, because the *Polaris* was still powered up when the *Peronovski* reached her.'

'So how do you explain it?'

'Somebody physically turned it off. Disconnected one of the circuits. Then he, or she, must have reconnected it later, because everything was where it should be when the *Peronovski* found them.'

'You're telling me that if they reconnect, that doesn't start up the AI automatically?'

'No. You have to use the enabling switch.'

'Why would an alien force go to the trouble to do that?'

'Well, the theory about the alien force is that it just threw up a field of some sort, and that shut her down.'

'Is that possible?'

'I guess *anything's* possible. If you have the technology.'

After locating the *Polaris*, the *Peronovski* had stayed in the area three days but found nothing. A salvage vessel arrived several weeks later and brought the *Polaris* home. After an intensive examination produced no explanation, Survey mothballed her, pending future investigations. In 1368, the ship was sold to the Evergreen Foundation. They changed its name to the *Sheila Clermo*.

I talked with Sabol Kassem, who'd made a study of the case. Kassem was at Traeger University in the Sunrise Islands. He'd done his doctoral thesis on the *Polaris*.

'According to the archives,' he told me, 'people riding the *Clermo* were "uncomfortable" aboard her. Didn't sleep well. Heard voices. There were reports of restless electronics, as if Madeleine English and her passengers were somehow trapped inside the control units. Marion Horn rode on the ship while he was in the process of making his architectural reputation, and he swore he always had the feeling he was being watched. "*By something in pain.*" And he added, "*I know how that sounds.*"' Kassem was seated on a bench in front of a marble facade, on which was engraved TRUTH, WISDOM, COMPASSION. He looked amused. 'The most famous – or outrageous – claim came from Evert Cloud, a merchandising king who was one of Evergreen's top contributors. Cloud claimed to have seen a phantasmic Chek Boland standing by the lander. According to Cloud, the spectre pleaded with him to help it escape from the *Polaris*.'

When I passed all that on to Alex, he was delighted. 'Great stories,' he said. 'They'll do nothing but enhance the value of the artifacts.'

Sheila Clermo, by the way, was the daughter of McKinley Clermo, the longtime guiding force behind Evergreen's environmental efforts. She died at fourteen in a skiing accident.

Jacob put together a pictorial history of Maddy English. Here was Madeleine at age six, with ice cream and a tricycle. And at thirteen, standing with her eighth-grade class in the doorway of their school. First boyfriend. First pair of skis. Maddy at eighteen, playing chess in what appeared to be a tournament. Jacob found a partial recording of *Desperado,* in which, during high school, she played Tabitha, who loved, alas, too well.

He showed me Maddy at flight school. And at Ko-Li, where she qualified for superluminals. There were dozens of pictures of her certification, standing proudly with her parents (she looked just like her mother), celebrating with the other graduates, gazing over the training station just before her final departure.

I knew the drill pretty well. I'd been through Ko-Li myself, and, though it has evolved and adjusted during the seventy-odd years since it counted Maddy among its graduates, it is still, in all the ways that matter, unchanged. It is the place where you are put to the test and you discover what you can do and who you are.

It's fifteen years since I went through, and I grumbled constantly while I was there. Two-thirds of my class flunked out. I understand that's about average. The instructors could be infuriating. Yet my time there set the standard for me, for what I've come to expect of myself.

I'm not sure any of that makes sense. But had I not graduated from Ko-Li, I would be someone else.

I suspect Maddy felt the same way.

There was a picture of her with a middle-aged man at Ko-Li. They were standing in front of Pasquale Hall, where most of the simulations were conducted.

The man looked very much like Urquhart!

'As an adolescent,' said Jacob, *'she was something of a problem. She hated school, she was rebellious, she ran off a couple of times, and she got involved with the wrong people. There were some arrests, and her parents could do nothing with her. Urquhart met her when he toured a juvenile incarceration facility. They were*

already talking about a partial personality reconstruction. He was apparently impressed by something he saw in her, persuaded the authorities he'd take responsibility for her. And he did. It was a bumpy ride, but he got her through high school. A few years later she completed her degree work, and eventually he got her the appointment to Ko-Li.'

He ran a clip. Maddy on a ship's bridge being interviewed for a show to be presented at the Berringer Air & Space Museum: *'I owe everything to him,'* she said. *'Had he not come forward, God knows what would have happened to me.'*

The Department of Planetary Survey and Astronomical Research was a semiautonomous agency, one-quarter supported by the government and the rest by private donation. In an age when disease was rare, the great majority of kids had two parents, and everybody ate well, there were few charities for those who enjoyed helping out, which seems to be a substantial fraction of the population. Makes me hopeful for the future when I think about it. But the point is that social conditions meant there was lots of money available for kids' athletic associations and research organizations. Of those, none was quite as visible or romantic as Survey, with its missions into unexplored territory. There are tens of thousands of stars in the Veiled Lady alone, enough to keep us busy well into the future. And, if the history of the last few thousand years is any indication, we'll probably keep at it indefinitely. It's always been an effort that engages the imagination, and you never really know what you might find. Maybe even Aurelia, the legendary lost civilization.

Survey was controlled by a board of directors representing the interests of a dozen political committees and the academic community and a few well-heeled contributors. The chairman, like the director, was a political appointee, rotated out every two years. He, or she, had a nominal scientific background but was primarily a political animal.

Survey's administrative offices occupied six prime acres on the north side of the capital, along the banks of the Narakobo. Its operational center was located halfway across the continent, but it was in administration that policy decisions were made, where the missions were approved, and the choices taken as to where they would go. It was where technical personnel were recruited to man the starships and researchers came to defend their proposals for missions. There was also a public information branch. The latter was the unit Windy worked for, the people who were running the auction.

Survey had moved its headquarters about three years earlier from a battered stone building in center city to its current exclusive domain. Alex liked to think it had something to do with a resurgence of interest in heritage, sparked by his work on the Christopher Sim discoveries; but the truth was that a different political party had come to power, promises had been made, and real estate is always a good showpiece. But I'd never tell him that.

As requested, we showed up fifteen minutes early and were conducted into Windy's office by a human being rather than the avatar that usually got the assignment if you weren't somebody they especially cared about. Windy was in a white-and-gold evening gown.

I should comment that Alex always knew how to dress for these occasions, and – if I may modestly say – I looked pretty good myself. Black off-the-shoulder silk, stiletto heels, and just enough exposure to excite comment.

I got a knowing smile from Windy, who made a crack about the hunting available that night. Then she was all innocent modesty while Alex fondled her with his eyes and told her how lovely she looked.

The office was illuminated by a single desk lamp. She might have turned up the lights, but she didn't. Everybody looks more exotic when you can't see too well. 'Who gets the proceeds?' Alex asked, when we'd settled into chairs. 'From the auction?'

'Not us,' she said.

'Why not? Where's it go?'

'Survey is funded by the Council.'

'I understand that. But the *Polaris* was Survey's baby. It's your equipment. Your mission. Anyhow, the bulk of the funding comes from private sources.'

Windy sent out for a round of drinks. 'You know how it is with government,' she said. 'In the end, they own everything.'

Alex sighed. 'So what's the occasion for the party? Who's in town?'

She had a malicious smile for that one. 'The Mazha.'

He did a double take.

I probably did, too. 'He's a thug,' I said. That got me a warning glance. Don't make waves.

The Mazha was the ruler of Korrim Mas, an independent mountain theocracy on the other side of the world. It was one of those places that never changed, that hung on generation after generation no matter what was happening around it, that steadfastly refused to seek admission to the Confederacy, largely because they couldn't meet the democratic requirements.

They believed that the end of the world was imminent and that the claim that humans had originated elsewhere was a lie. They denied the existence of the Mutes, insisting there were no aliens, and if there were, they wouldn't be able to read minds. The population lived reasonably well except that some of them disappeared from time to time, and nobody ever criticized the authorities. It was the oldest continuing government on Rimway. It had always been an autocratic state of one kind or another, its people apparently incapable of governing themselves. Every time they got rid of one dynasty, another bunch of gangsters took over.

'He's a head of state,' Windy said. She waited for a response, got none, and went on. 'He'll be arriving shortly. When he gets here, they'll show him to the director's suite in Proctor Union. We'll be there, along with the other guests. And, if he's not averse, we'll wander over and say hello.'

'Good of him,' I said. 'What if *I'm* averse?'

Alex sent another cease-and-desist signal. 'Why are we involved?' he asked. 'Is he here to see the artifacts?'

'Yes. And to be seen at a Survey event.'

I commented that I thought he didn't believe that starships existed.

'You'll have to ask *him* about that.' She grinned, refusing to take umbrage. I knew her pretty well, and she would have skipped it herself had she been able. But Windy's loyal. And she liked her job. 'Actually, Alex, he's heard of you. When the director mentioned you'd be here, he asked explicitly to be introduced.'

The drinks arrived. A sea spray for Alex, red wine for Windy, and dark cargo for me. Windy raised her glass. 'To Rainbow Enterprises,' she said, 'for its unwavering efforts in the search for truth.'

That was a little bit much, but we played along. I guess we needed a change of subject anyhow. I drank mine down and would have liked a refill, but I wasn't sure I wanted to slow down my reflexes on a night when I was going to meet the most murderous individual on the planet.

The bureaucratic workings, however, made the decision for me. A second round arrived. And I took the lead this time: 'To the passengers and captain of the *Polaris,* wherever they are.'

Alex drained his, then stood, examining the glass. 'I assume we've given up. Is there any kind of effort at all still being made to find out what happened?'

'No.' Windy drew the word out. 'Not really. There's an ad hoc committee. But it's not going anywhere. They'll respond if anything turns up. And every once in a while somebody writes a book, or does a show on it. But there's no concerted effort. I mean, Alex, it's been a long time.' She put her glass down. 'When it happened, they sent the entire fleet out there. To Delta Karpis. They searched everywhere. Checked everything they could think of for light-years in all directions.'

'With no result whatever?'

'Zip.'

'Was there never any indication at all,' I asked, 'what might have happened?'

'No. They never found anything.' She glanced down at a bracelet. 'We better get going. He's on the grounds.' She got up and opened the door for us.

I hesitated. 'I'm not sure I want to socialize with this guy,' I said.

Alex was on his feet, straightening his jacket. 'You don't have to be nice to him, love,' he said. 'He's not going to be interested in us.'

Windy stood by the doorway. 'I understand how you feel, Chase. I'm sorry. I'd have warned you, but they swore us to secrecy. There are too many people around who'd like to kill him. The Mazha.' Through her windows, I could see a pair of skimmers coming down onto the grounds. 'But I'd be grateful if you came. You'll brighten the place up.' She smiled. 'And how often do you get to meet a bona fide dictator?'

'That's a point.' I glanced at Alex.

'It's all in the interests of diplomacy and science,' he said, pushing me gently before him.

4

Everyone should have an opportunity to party with a tyrant.
Inevitably, he dances well.

—Tasker LaVrie

The artifacts were in the auditorium on the ground floor of Proctor Union, one level down from the director's suite. Proctor Union is a large, rambling structure, part administrative offices, part museum, part conference center. It was located beyond the western loop of the Long Pool, which was actually an elongated figure eight, the infinity symbol.

Ordinarily we could have descended from Windy's office and gone directly through a connecting corridor, under the waterway, but everything was closed off as a security measure. So we bundled up and went out through the front door. Windy led the way. The night was damp and blustery, and the moon was a luminous blur in a churning sky. The people loose on the grounds had their heads bent and were hurrying along. No casual strollers that night.

We crossed the Long Pool on one of its several bridges. There was no sign of the quocks, which usually flocked there at this time of year.

Windy pulled her coat tightly around her. 'A lot of VIPs will be here,' she said. She began rattling off names and titles. Senators and judges, CEOs, and lawyers. 'The movers and shakers of this town.' Meaning, of course, since Andiquar was the world capital, movers and shakers on a very large scale. 'When they heard the Mazha was coming, they all wanted to join the party.'

These were the same people who'd be attacking him and talking about morality on the talk shows the next day. I didn't say anything. Just kept walking.

'There won't be a large crowd, though,' Windy continued. 'The invitations went out at the last minute.'

'Security again?' asked Alex.

'Yes. His guards don't like long-range plans.'

'I guess not.'

Proctor Union was the administrative center of the complex, designed with a swept-back, ready-to-launch appearance. Rooftops rolled away in several directions, but all were angled to give the impression that the structure was aimed at the far side of the Narakobo. The river itself, visible through a line of trees, was dark and brooding. There was something unsettling about that night, some whisper of approaching catastrophe that was getting mixed up with the elements.

Two of the Mazha's security guards were standing silent and watchful outside the front entrance. You couldn't have mistaken them for anything else. Their clothes weren't quite right, although they must have been trying to blend in. But a thug is a thug. Their eyes swept across us, and one whispered into a bracelet. Perfunctory smiles appeared as we approached, and somewhere in the strained silence we identified ourselves and received permission to proceed.

'I don't guess,' said Alex, keeping his voice low, 'they think we're very dangerous.'

'You were preapproved,' Windy said. We climbed the twelve marble steps onto the portico.

Doors opened, and we went into the lobby. We got rid of our wraps, turned into the main corridor, and saw that the event had already spilled out into the passageway. A couple of guests saw us, saw *Windy*, and came over to say hello. Windy did introductions, and we traded small talk before moving on.

'I *am* surprised,' said Alex, 'that he'd be here, of all places. Doesn't a facility dedicated to science compromise his religious position?'

'I think it's just a role he plays,' she said, 'for the folks back home. He couldn't be that stupid and hold on to power.'

A couple of people who I assumed belonged to Windy's office were recording everything. 'But they'll see all this,' I said.

'There'll be a different story in Korrim Mas. The faithful will hear how he came to stand up to the infidels.' She laughed. 'Mustn't take these things too seriously, Chase.'

Blue-and-gold bunting decorated the walls. 'His national colors?' asked Alex.

'Yes.'

We turned through a set of double doors into the reception room. There were maybe thirty people inside, glasses in hand, enjoying the evening. I recognized a couple of senators, and the executive science advisor, and several academics. And, of course, Dr Louis Ponzio.

He broke away from the group he was with and came over, letting us see how pleased he was that we'd arrived. 'Alex,' he said, offering his hand, 'good to have you on board for the occasion. Did Windy tell you about our guest?'

'I'm looking forward to meeting him,' said Alex.

He obviously couldn't remember who I was, although he pretended to. Windy reminded him as surreptitiously as she could. 'His Excellency is especially anxious to meet you both,' he said.

I didn't know about Alex, but I was pretty sure I'd feel just as happy if His Excellency had no clue who I was. Or where I could be reached. 'Why is that?' Alex asked.

'He approves of the work you've done. You shook the historical establishment to its roots a few years ago. You provided him with ammunition.'

Alex frowned. 'Forgive me, Dr Ponzio, but I'm lost. Ammunition to do what?'

'To demonstrate to his countrymen that acquired knowledge is a slippery thing. That one can never be too sure of what the facts really are. It fits in with his position that they are best off if they simply rely on the sacred scriptures. And on him.' He must have seen how Alex was taking all this because he laughed and clapped him on the shoulder. 'It's all right, Alex. Had it not been you, it would have been someone else. Eventually the truth would have come out. You can't hide things forever, you know.' A brunette in green and white raised her hand slightly, caught Ponzio's eye, and nodded. 'He's here,' the director said. Immediately, the noise in the room subsided, and people moved toward the walls and faced the entrance.

We heard doors open and close. Then voices filled the corridor. And laughter.

The Mazha swept into the room like a tidal wave. Three or four aides and a couple of security people accompanied him. The other guests fell back, regrouped, and finally moved tentatively forward. Dr Ponzio was, as far as I could tell, the only person there who stood his ground. He offered a polite smile and a bow to the dictator. 'Your Excellency,' he said, 'it's an honor to meet you. We're delighted to have you with us this evening.'

I'd seen his picture, of course. But pictures don't always prepare you for the real thing. I was expecting him to look like Dracula. But it didn't turn out that way.

He was shorter than I'd expected. Not quite average height. Black hair, clean-shaven. He looked a little heavier in person. He wore a white jacket and dark gray slacks. Medals and ribbons clung to the jacket, and a red sash was folded over his right shoulder.

He returned the director's bow, said something I couldn't hear, and offered a hand. Ponzio clasped it with great respect and let go quickly.

Celebrity gets you forgiven for anything. Here was a guy with blood on his hands, whole tubs of it, and he was being welcomed like somebody who'd just made a major medical contribution.

His propaganda machine always claimed that his victims were killers and rebels who wanted to destabilize Korrim Mas. Or the Faith. That they were the worst kind of miscreants. That they were extremely dangerous, and that they thought nothing, if given the opportunity, of shedding innocent blood. The Mazha had no choice but to send them, however reluctantly, to the Almighty. It might have been less cruel to use mind-wipe technology, but there was a religious prohibition against that.

After a while, he advanced on us, turned to me, mentally licked his lips, and took my hand. I could see that he knew precisely what I was thinking and that he didn't care. He had the gaze of a sixty-volt laser. 'Ms Kolpath,' he said, bowing slightly. 'It is always a pleasure to meet one so beautiful. And talented. I understand you are a pilot.' He actually sounded sincere. And damned if the son of a bitch couldn't make himself likable.

Already he knew more about me than Dr Ponzio did. 'Yes,' I said, trying not to wilt under the attention, trying not to say it was really nothing, anybody could pilot a superluminal. There was something about this guy that made you want to abase yourself. 'I'm responsible for the *Belle-Marie,* Rainbow's corporate vessel.'

He nodded. His next comment was directed at Alex, but he kept me squarely in his sights. 'Lost in the sky with one so lovely,' he said. 'It takes the breath away.' He considered the sheer rapture of it all. 'And I must say,' he continued, 'that it is an honor to meet the man who wrung the truth from the stars.' So help me, that's exactly what he said. '. . . *Wrung the truth from the stars.*' And if you're thinking none of this sounds much like Dracula, I'd agree. He wasn't tall. Wasn't overbearing. Wasn't quietly sinister. None of the stuff you normally associate with intimidation. And he wasn't intimidating. I kept thinking he seemed like the sort of guy you'd want to have over for dinner. 'I understand,' he said, with a bare trace of an accent, 'that you have recently scored still another coup.' Someone put a glass of wine in his hand.

'The Shenji outstation,' Alex said. 'You are quite well informed.'

'Ah, yes,' he said. 'Would that it were so.' He raised the glass. 'To the outstation. And to the man who engineered its recovery.' He barely sipped the wine, held it out without taking his eyes from Alex, and let go of it. An aide was on the spot, made the save, and handed it off to someone else. 'We are indebted to you, Mr Benedict.'

'Thank you, Excellency.'

My pulse was up, and I was thinking that being lost in the sky with this guy would not be the way I wanted to spend a weekend. And yet—

'I would have preferred,' said the Mazha, still looking at Alex, but speaking to me, 'that we might have the opportunity to spend some time together. Unfortunately, at the moment I have obligations.'

'Of course,' said Alex, who saw exactly what was going on and made points with me by not volunteering anything.

Still, I'd be lying if I said I wasn't a bit flustered by all the attention. I found myself imagining how it would feel to be in his arms, on a moonlit balcony overlooking the sea. To make the situation complete, Windy looked annoyed. I had the feeling she was staring straight into my head.

'Perhaps, Alex, you might find your way clear to visit me in the Kaballahs.' The chain of mountains that was home to Korrim Mas. 'And when you do I hope you will bring your beautiful associate with you.' His eyes found me again.

'Yes,' Alex was saying. I suspected he was having a hard time suppressing a smile. But he looked absolutely correct. 'I'd like very much to do that when occasion permits.' And, to me: 'Wouldn't we, Chase?'

I was standing there like a dummy, wondering why I'd been running around with Harry Lattimore. But that's another story. 'Yes,' I said, with more enthusiasm than I'd intended.

'Good.' The Mazha turned to an aide. 'That's settled then. Moka, get contact information.'

And he was gone, headed toward a group of politicians, which opened to receive him. Moka, who was a giant, collected Alex's code, smiled politely, and rejoined the dictator.

I should mention that, although I can hold my own with other women, nobody's going to mistake me for a former beauty queen. Nevertheless, during the next few minutes, those eyes rotated back to me several times. Reflexively, despite everything, I returned a smile. Couldn't help it. Alex watched the byplay and made no effort to conceal his amusement. 'Caught your heart, has he?' he asked.

The Mazha seemed right at home. Whatever else he might have been, he was a consummate politician. He had a broad, warm smile for everyone. If I'd met this guy on the street, my first impression would have been that he was a thoroughgoing charmer, in the best sense of the word. Since that night, I've never entirely trusted my judgment.

Meantime we circulated. There was much shaking of hands and a flood of introductions. Let me present the commissioner of the waterworks. And this is Secretary Hoffmann. And Professor Escalario, who did the dark matter work last year. Jean Warburton, who's special aide to the chief councillor. Dr Hoffmann, the official record holder as the person who has traveled farthest from the Confederate worlds.

Windy took us aside before we went into the exhibition room. 'Alex,' she said, 'the Mazha will probably be buying some of the artifacts, too.'

'Anyone else?'

'No.'

'You're kidding? All this political clout walking around, and you're not letting them in the door?'

'The media will be at the auction tomorrow.' She lowered her voice. 'I don't think anybody here, other than you and probably the Mazha, really cares about the artifacts themselves. What they want is to get their pictures taken during the bidding, contributing money to a popular cause, then probably giving the item itself to a museum back home. We told them there'll be lots of press coverage tomorrow. That's what they want.'

'That surprises me.'

'They're all political critters, Alex. One way or another.'

The Mazha had an appetite for liquor, and he loved a good laugh. You could hear him throughout the hour or so that we wandered around the reception room and the lobby, chuckling, unrestrained, his eyes illuminated. I began to suspect I'd get an invitation before the evening was over. His security detail strolled about with glasses in their hands, but I don't think they were drinking anything hard.

Then, with a bit of fanfare, Windy's people got everyone's attention and opened the doors to the exhibition hall. We looked in at a series of long tables supporting hundreds of *Polaris* items, articles of clothing, pressure suits, cups, glasses, spoons, boots, and an array of electronic devices. There were a chess set, game pieces, playing cards (with the ship's insignia embossed on their backs), and even a crystal containing musical recordings made by Tom Dunninger. (A data card stated that Dunninger had been an accomplished musician.) Most of the items were sealed inside display cases, each accompanied by an inventory number.

The walls were hung with banners portraying Maddy English and her passengers. There was Nancy White tromping through a jungle somewhere, and Warren Mendoza bent over a sick child. Martin Klassner sat beside a sketch of a galaxy. Garth Urquhart talked with journalists on the steps of the capitol. Chek Boland was done in silhouette, apparently deep in contemplation. Maddy was in full uniform, gazing serenely out across the room. Finally, Tom Dunninger, in a print of the famous painting by Ormond, standing in a graveyard at night.

The Mazha, leading the way, paused to take it all in. Then he glanced back at Alex. Obviously, he'd been briefed about who else was enjoying the benefits of the preauction special.

Once in the room, he turned his attention exclusively to the items on display. Other people, for the most part, laughed and talked in his wake, paying little attention as they filed past the tables. But he walked slowly, absorbing everything that lay around him. Occasionally he spoke to an elderly aide, who nodded and, I thought, recorded his comment. Or perhaps the catalog number.

Some of the items were imprinted with names. A light gray shirt was marked with the initials *M.K.*, and a carryall wore a metal tag reading WHITE. The ship's jumpsuits were dark blue, with *Polaris* shoulder patches. Each patch contained the ship's registry, CSS 117, and its logo, a single star set above an arrowhead. Three of them were available, with the names *Warren*, *Garth*, and *English* stenciled in white letters above the right-hand breast pocket. The captain's own jumpsuit. 'What do you think?' Alex asked me.

'It's just the thing,' I said, mentally checking off a client. 'Ida would be thrilled.'

He signaled Windy. She complimented him on his taste, used her card to open the display case, and removed the jumpsuit. She handed it to a young man standing nearby. He placed it in a container, and we moved on.

The Mazha signaled that he would take Urquhart's suit. 'The ship's emblem is clever,' he said to no one in particular. When one of the politicians trailing in his wake asked him to explain, he looked surprised. 'Polaris was Earth's north star at the beginning of the age of expansion, Manny,' he said. 'Thus the lone star. And, of course, the compass needle started out as a metal bar and gradually morphed into an arrow.'

So much for religious fervor.

There was a jacket with a pocket patch reading DUNNINGER, a comm link with Boland's initials, and a paper notebook with Garth Urquhart's name on the brown leather cover.

Several pressure suits had been hung near the wall. One of

them read CAPTAIN across the left breast. Madeleine's gear again. Maddy, as she was known. A certified interstellar captain, single, beautiful, everything to live for. Where had she gone?

Alex was studying a gold chain bracelet with NANCY engraved on the connecting plate. 'How much?' he asked Windy. She consulted her inventory. Enough to buy a good-sized yacht. He turned to me. 'For Harold,' he said. 'What do you think?'

Harold was one of Rainbow's charter clients. He'd become a friend over the years. He was a good guy, but his tastes were limited. He liked things that sparkled, things he could show off, but he had no real sense of historical value. 'It's lovely,' I said. 'But I think you could make him happy for a lot less.'

'You underestimate him, Chase.' He signaled Windy that we'd take it. 'He has the gavel that was used in the first trial in his hometown. And he owns a circuit board from the Talamay Flyer.' The first overwater antigrav train in the Parklands. The Flyer had made its initial run more than three hundred years ago between Melancholy Bend and Wildsky. The trip was still a subject of legend, a race against Suji bandits, a cyclone, and, finally, an apparently lascivious sea serpent.

Windy passed the bracelet to the retainer and Alex decided the time had come to negotiate for more selections. 'Winetta,' he said, 'I have several people who would love to have items from this collection—'

She looked pained. 'I wish I could help, Alex. I really do. But the agreement is six. I'm not authorized to go any farther.'

'We're more than willing to pay fair prices, Windy. I shook hands with your dictator. And Chase made a play for him. That should be worth something.'

She pressed her lips together, imploring him to keep his voice down. 'You have my gratitude, Alex. Really. And you, too, Chase.' That seemed below the belt. 'But there's no negotiating room.'

'You could say you had to make the commitment to get me over here.'

'Look.' She sighed. 'I'll toss in an extra one. Make it seven. But that's all.'

'Windy, look at all this stuff. Nobody'll ever miss it. I need twelve pieces. You have enormous influence here, and it would mean a lot to me.' He actually managed to look downcast. I knew the routine. I'd seen him in action too often. He was good. He always made you feel sorry for him. 'How many times have I spoken to audiences here about the Christopher Sim thing?'

'A lot,' she admitted.

'Have I ever declined an invitation?'

'No,' she conceded, 'you haven't.'

'Have I ever charged a korpel?'

'No.'

'It must all have been volunteer work?'

'Yes, Alex, it was all volunteer work.'

'You bring other speakers in at a hundred per. Benedict does it free.'

The reason for that, of course, was that Benedict saw his appearances at Survey as an important channel for meeting and impressing prospective clients. Windy's eyes slid shut. She was no dummy, and she knew the routines, too. But she didn't want to offend him.

'You run the place, Windy. Everybody knows that. Whatever decision you make, Ponzio will go along with.'

'Nine,' she said, finally. 'And so help me, Alex, that's it. *Fini. Completo.*'

'You're a hard woman, Winetta.'

'Yes, we can all see that.'

He smiled. 'We'll try to get by. And thanks. I'm grateful.'

She looked at him sideways. 'When I get fired, Alex, I hope you can find room for me at Rainbow.'

'Windy, Rainbow will always have a place for someone with your talents.'

There were countless items, tableware, safety goggles, VR bands, towels, washcloths, even a showerhead.

'Windy,' I said, 'where are the ship's logs?'

She looked around, checked her pad. 'Over in the corner.' She indicated the rear of the room. 'But we're holding them back.'

'Why?'

'Actually, we're not putting everything up for sale. We're saving a few items for the *Polaris* exhibition.'

It turned out they were withholding some prime stuff. In addition to the logs, there was Martin Klassner's leather-bound copy of Sangmeister's *Cosmology,* with comments penned in the margins, many of them believed to have been done during the flight (according to the data card); Garth Urquhart's notes, which had allowed his son to complete the memoirs of his political years, published a decade after his disappearance as *On the Barricades*; and Madeleine English's certification for interstellars. There was also a picture of the pilot and her passengers taken on the space station just prior to departure on that final flight. Copies of the picture, a data card said, would be available in the gift shop the next day. Alex picked up a glass imprinted with the ship's seal. It was long-stemmed, designed for champagne. For celebrations. 'How do you think this would look in the office?' he asked.

It was gorgeous. Arrowhead. Star. css 117. 'You could never drink from it,' I said.

He laughed. The glass went into the container, and we moved on.

He found a command jacket that he liked. It was Maddy's, of course, blue and white, with trimmed breast pockets and a *Polaris* shoulder patch. He asked my opinion again.

'Absolutely,' I said.

He turned to Windy. 'Why weren't the personal items returned to the families?'

We'd stopped beneath the banner depicting Nancy White. Even in that still image, she was a woman on the move, her eyes penetrating the jungle, while she listened, perhaps, to the rumble of a distant waterfall. 'Quite a woman,' said Windy.

'Yes. She was.'

'The personal stuff was retained during the investigations. But they went on for years. Until recently, they'd never really stopped. At least not officially. I guess Survey just never got around to giving the stuff back. The families probably forgot about it after a while, or lost interest, so it just remained in storage.'

'What would happen if the families came forward now?'

'They no longer have a claim. They get seventeen years, after which the items become Survey's property.' She looked down at a pendant. 'Another reason they weren't anxious to return this stuff was the possibility it might be contaminated in some arcane way. With a virus or maybe a nano.'

'A nano that makes people disappear?'

She softened. 'What can I tell you? I wasn't there. But they must have been desperate for some kind of answer. They put everything into safekeeping, assuming that eventually something might be needed. I don't guess it ever happened. They even sterilized the hull, as if a plague might somehow have caused the problem.'

'And eventually they sold the ship.'

'In 1368. To Evergreen.' Windy sounded unhappy. 'Evergreen got a bargain price. The *Polaris* became the *Sheila Clermo,* and last I heard she was still hauling engineers and surveyors and assorted VIPs around for them.' She smiled and checked the time. Got to move on. 'Now,' she said, 'what else would you like to look at?'

We picked up a leather-bound Bible with Garth Urquhart's name on the inside title page. And a plaque commemorating the eight earlier missions of the *Polaris*. Koppawanda in 1352, Breakmann in 1354, Moyaba in 1355. That was a Mute world. Or at least, it was in their sphere of influence.

'They thought they'd found a white hole,' said Alex, reading my mind.

Windy smiled. 'Now *that* would have been earthshaking.' But they don't exist. Theoretical figments. White holes sound good, sound like something that should be there because they'd add a lovely symmetry to cosmic processes. But the universe doesn't pay much attention to our notions of esthetics.

Other destinations were listed, all places they'd named as they arrived, usually after one of the passengers. Sacarrio, whose sun was going to go supernova within the next ten thousand years; Chao Ti, once thought to be a source of an artificial radio signal; Brolyo, where a small settlement had taken root and prospered. The mission durations had extended as long as a year and a half.

I was headed toward a notebook, which, according to the attached certificate, had belonged to Nancy White. Its contents, to respect her privacy, had been deleted. That, of course, considerably reduced its value. But it was good to know there was still some integrity in the world. Alex lowered an eyebrow and went instead for a vest. It was the one Maddy could be seen wearing in some of the pictures from the flight. 'Priceless,' he said, shielding the remark from Windy.

'That's seven,' I told him.

Before we'd arrived, he'd remarked that the items connected with Maddy would be especially valuable. I had my doubts. 'She was carrying celebrities,' I told him. 'Historical figures.'

'Doesn't matter,' he said. 'The captain is the tragic figure in this. Add to that the fact that she's beautiful.'

'White looked pretty good.'

'White didn't lose her passengers. Take my word for it, Chase.'

He'd always been right before on such matters. So we added one of her uniform blouses (there were two available), and paused over a dark green platinum etui decorated with flowers and songbirds. It came with a certification that it had been the personal property of Madeleine English. Alex picked it up and opened it. Inside were a pen, a comb, a wallet, a string of artificial pearls, a set of uniform bars, and two pairs of earrings. 'This all included?' he asked Windy.

She nodded. 'It had cosmetics in it, too,' she said. 'But they were rotting out the interior.'

They agreed on a price that I thought was high, but it was a nice package, and Alex smiled benignly, the way he did when he wanted you to think he'd paid too much and was already having regrets. He gave it to Windy, and she handed it over to the aide, who showed us that we'd used up our allotment.

We wandered through displays of furniture and equipment across the back of the room. The captain's chair, a conference table, display screens, even a vacuum pump. VR gear. But these kinds of items, except the chair, were impersonal and would provoke less interest.

'You got the pick of the lot,' Windy said. She looked as if she meant it.

When we left, the Mazha was in the process of examining a wall plaque depicting the ship's schematic. 'How many is *he* getting?' I asked.

She cleared her throat. 'They didn't put a limitation on him.'

'That doesn't seem fair.'

'He's a head of state.' She allowed herself a smile. 'When you take over a government, we'll do the same for you.'

We headed finally into an adjoining room, followed by the young man with the case. He wasn't much more than a kid. Nineteen, at most. While Windy tallied up the bill I asked him where he was from.

'Kobel Ti,' he said. West coast.

'Going to school here?'

'At the university.'

While we talked, Alex transferred payment. The aide told me how happy he was to have met me, made a self-conscious pass, and handed over the items. I decided it was my night.

Windy gazed down at the case and asked whether we wanted her to have it sent over to the office. 'No,' Alex said, 'thanks. We'll take it with us.'

I noticed the Mazha leave the exhibition room, surrounded by his people, and pass quickly into the corridor. He looked worried.

We were starting for the exit when a security guard appeared in midair. A projection. *'Ladies and gentlemen,'* he said, *'we've received a warning that there may be a bomb in the building. Please evacuate. There is no cause for alarm.'*

Of course not. Why would anyone think there was cause for alarm? Suddenly I was being swept along by Alex. He had me in one arm and the container in the other. Windy, trailing behind us, called out that she was sure there was a mistake somewhere. Who would put a bomb in Proctor Union?

It became a wild scramble. The exit was through a doorway that would accommodate no more than three people at a time. A few of the less mobile ones went down. Alex told me gallantly to have no fear, and when we stopped to try to help a woman who had fallen, the crowd behind us simply pushed us forward. I don't know what happened to her.

'Stay calm,' the projection was saying. Easy enough for him. He was probably in another building.

The crush in the passageway was a nightmare. People were yelling and screaming. I was literally carried through the front door without my feet touching the ground. We exploded out onto the portico. Alex briefly lost the case, and he risked getting trampled to retrieve it.

Security officers kept us moving. *'Please stay well away from the building,'* they were saying. *'Keep calm. There's no immediate danger.'*

Nobody needed persuading. The crowd was scattering in all directions by then.

The security force directed the flow toward the bridges across the Long Pool. But they'd already jammed up as we came down the stone steps. So they changed tactics and moved the rest of us across the face of the buildings, out past the wings. I noticed Ponzio ahead of me. Windy, to her credit, was one of the last people to come out through the doors. And she barely got clear before Proctor Union shuddered and erupted in a fireball.

5

These watches and books and blouses are all that are left of the lives of their owners. It is the reason they are precious, the reason they have meaning. In most cases, we do not know the details of the person whom they served. We do not know what he looked like, or what color his eyes were. But we know he lived as surely as you and I do, that he bled if injured, that he loved the sunlight. One day, in another spot, others may congregate to gaze in awe at my shoes, or the chair in which I will sit this evening. It is why such things matter. They are simultaneously the link that binds the generations, and the absolute proof, if we needed it, that someone lived here before who was very much like ourselves.

—Garth Urquhart,
from the dedication of the Steinman Museum

The warning had come just in time. It helped that everything in the place was flame-resistant, so after the initial blast there was no fire. Nevertheless, it was a bad moment. The blast knocked us all off our feet. Hot debris rained down on us. A big piece of something hissed into the Long Pool, and a statue of Reuben Hammacker, one of Survey's founding fathers, was decapitated.

Emergency vehicles arrived within minutes and began picking up the injured. Other units showed up and sprayed water or chemicals on what remained of Proctor Union. A large cloud of steam formed overhead. I heard later that the Mazha was bundled into his skimmer and lifted away within seconds. We didn't know what kind of condition he was in, but at that point no one was thinking much about him.

The building was demolished. A smoking ruin. My first thought was that there had to be ten or twenty dead. We staggered around in a kind of daze. Everyone was in shock. I'd twisted a knee at some point during the panic and collected a couple of burns. Nothing major, fortunately, but it hurt. Alex complained that his jacket was torn, something I really needed to hear. He seemed otherwise okay. When I got myself together I went looking for Windy. But the place was boiling with confusion, people wandering around screaming and crying, searching for friends, trying to figure out a way to get home, asking one another what had happened.

I couldn't find her, although I found out later she was okay. Knocked down by the blast, but she came away with a few cuts and bruises and a broken ankle. One of the rescue workers corralled me and asked if I was all right and when I told her I was fine she insisted on looking in my eyes and the next thing I knew I was being loaded into a skimmer along with several others, and we were hauled off to a hospital.

They did an exam and told me everything was superficial, don't worry, gave me some painkillers, and suggested I have someone come get me.

Alex had followed the emergency vehicle, and he came to my rescue. While he filled out the forms, I talked on the circuit with a trim, blond, impeccably dressed man who identified himself as an agent from the NIS. Wanted to ask about the explosion. What did I recall?

'Just the bang,' I said.

'You didn't see anyone suspicious?' He was good. He operated in low key, and he seemed sympathetic.

'No.'

'*Are you okay, Ms Kolpath?*'

'Just bumps and bruises,' I said.

'*Good. Did you happen to notice whether anyone left early?*'

What the hell. 'We were all leaving a bit early.'

'*I mean before the warning.*'

'No,' I said. 'I wouldn't have noticed. I wasn't really paying attention.'

Alex signed me out of the casualty ward. They insisted on putting me in a wheelchair, and helping me get to the pad, where I was loaded into the company skimmer.

'Assassination attempt?' I asked.

'That's what they're saying.'

'That's pretty vicious,' I said. 'They were prepared to take out all those people just to get him.'

'Don't be too harsh on them. The guy needs killing.'

'But *I* don't.'

'Look at it this way, Chase. It's a major break for us.'

I must have stared at him. 'Have you lost your mind, Alex?'

'Think about it a minute. Rainbow now owns the only surviving artifacts from the *Polaris*. Other than the ship itself.'

'Well, good for us.'

We lifted off the rooftop, turned west, and headed for my place. 'I'll take you home. Then, if you want, I'll get us something to eat.'

It was late, well after midnight, but I suddenly realized I hadn't had much dinner, and, in spite of everything, I was hungry. 'That sounds good,' I said.

'Take the next couple of days. Stay off the knee until you're feeling okay.'

'Thanks. I will.'

'You can conduct any business that comes up from your place.'

'You're the world's greatest boss.'

He smiled. 'Kidding.'

We passed over Lake Accord. I saw a boat down there, lit up,

81

having a party. 'All that security,' I said. 'I wonder how they got the bomb past the guards.'

'They didn't have to. Whoever did it planted it in the storage area. On the lower floor, under the auditorium. The media are saying they came in the back way.'

'They didn't have the back sealed off?'

'Apparently not. They'd blocked off the stairways. You could get into the lower floor, but you couldn't get up to the auditorium. As it turned out—'

'—It didn't occur to anyone somebody might bomb the place?'

He fought back a yawn. 'When's the last time you heard of anybody bombing a *building*? With *people* in it?'

'Do we have any idea who's responsible?'

'I'm sure they know. How many people in Andiquar want to kill the Mazha?' We were approaching the far shore of the lake. He lapsed into silence. I'd taken one of the painkillers at the hospital, and a feeling of general euphoria was settling over me.

We started down.

'There were several bombs,' he said.

'Several?'

'Four, they think. Whoever did it was taking no chances on missing the Mazha.'

'Except that the police found out before the blast.'

'They got a call.'

'Damned lucky. If the things had gone off three minutes earlier—'

'They were planted directly under the exhibition area.'

'Isn't this the second assassination attempt against him?'

'*Third*. There've been three in the last six months.'

Ponzio sent flowers, his regrets, and best wishes for my speedy recovery. The message was handwritten, which, of course, is *de rigueur* on these occasions. He was happy to report that no one had been killed, although there were a few serious injuries.

At about the same time, Survey announced that the entire

Polaris collection had been destroyed. Reduced to rubble. That wasn't quite true, of course. Alex had the nine artifacts we'd purchased.

I got checked by my doctor, and the brace came off a couple of days later. The burns were gone by then, so I was feeling pretty good. Alex came by with dinner, and we talked a lot about crazy people with bombs, and how no doubt I could return to the office in the morning.

That evening, after Alex had left, I received a call from Windy. She was still hobbled, but she assured me she'd be fine, told me she'd heard I'd been carted off as well, and wondered how I was.

'Just a bent knee,' I said. 'It's okay.'

'*Good. I hope you managed to salvage your purchases.*'

'Yes. Fortunately, we got everything out.'

'*Glad to hear it. Thank God something survived.*' She looked genuinely relieved.

'It's a major loss,' I said. 'I hope when they catch these people they hang them up by their toes.' I knew that when they were caught we'd wipe their minds and reconstruct their personalities. I'll confess I was never a fan of letting criminals off like that when they did horrendous stuff. The bombers, whoever they were, tried to kill the Mazha and had no compunctions about blowing up a lot of strangers because they were standing too close to the target. I was in favor of taking them up a few thousand meters and dropping them into the ocean. But, of course, that's not civilized. It seemed grossly unfair to respond to what they did by giving them a couple hundred and a fresh start. Which is what mind wipes amounted to.

'*I understand completely, Chase.*' Long pause, which told me this was about more than the state of my health. '*I wonder if we might talk about the artifacts for a moment.*'

'Of course,' I said. 'The media are saying everything was destroyed.'

'*Unfortunately, that's correct.*'

'I'm sorry to hear it.'

'Yes. It's *thrown a wrench into our plans.*' She was in her office, behind a desk covered with folders, chips, books, and paper. A sweater had been laid across it. She was getting ready to go home. I was the last piece of business for the day. '*Chase,*' she said, '*you understand that the situation has changed dramatically.*'

'I beg your pardon.'

'*Survey would like to buy back the artifacts we sold Rainbow. To return your money. With a generous bonus.*'

'Windy, I don't really have authority to return them. They don't belong to me.'

'*Then I'll talk to Alex.*'

'That's not what I mean. We've promised them to clients.' She hesitated. '*You know we were planning a* Polaris *exhibit. A full-scale model of the ship's bridge. Avatars. People would be able to sit and talk with Tom Dunninger, or Maddy English, or whomever. We had the Urquhart holo,* Last Man Standing. *Some of the Nancy White programs. Actually, a lot of planning and preparation has gone into it.*'

'And without a few artifacts, you don't think it'll work.'

'*Exactly.*'

'Windy, I doubt the artifacts would make all that much difference. But I'll pass your request along to Alex. I'm pretty sure, though, he'll feel compelled to decline. I think you're underestimating the public. Set the exhibition up the right way, get your PR people on it, and it'll do fine.'

I could see that she'd not expected anything more. She simply nodded. '*I'm glad you're feeling better, Chase,*' she said, and blinked off.

And we had better not need any more favors from Survey.

Over the next few days, several of the Mazha's countrymen living locally were rounded up and questioned, but no arrests were made. It was Andiquar's worst criminal act in living memory. For the first time in my life, people were calling for a return to the death penalty. The public's blood was up. We needed to send a message.

The Mazha's government apologized and promised to send money to the victims and underwrite reconstruction of Proctor Union. I was surprised to receive a call from the Mazha himself, now safely back in his mountain retreat (or maybe not so safe). He'd seen my name among the injured. Was I healing well? Would I recover completely?

It was an odd feeling, to sit there on my sofa, in my own living room, talking with the world's most feared human being. *'I wanted to apologize for the imbecility of the would-be assassins,'* he said. *'They lack a basic sense of decency.'*

'Yes,' I said.

'We tried to be careful. But one can never be certain about the lengths to which these fanatics will go.'

'I know. You're absolutely right, Excellency.'

'Be assured, Chase, that we know who is behind this, and we are in the process of seeing to it that they will harm no one else.'

'Yes. Good. I've no sympathy for them.'

'As you should not.' He was in a leather chair, wearing black slacks and a white pullover. A gold chain hung around his neck, and he wore a gold bracelet on his right wrist. He looked quite dashing. *'But I'm pleased to discover that your injuries are superficial.'*

'Thank you.'

'I was worried.'

It occurred to me I hadn't inquired about him. 'You look well, Highness. I assume you were not harmed?'

'No. Thank you. I came away untouched.' The wall behind him was filled with books. *'I wanted to extend an invitation to you and to Alex to visit Korrim Mas as my guests. We have excellent accommodations, and I can assure you that you would find it an enthralling experience.'*

Okay. I know what you're thinking. That I was sitting there making nice with a guy who does mass executions and runs torture chambers. But he'd been polite to *me*, so I found it impossible to say what I really thought. I told him I appreciated the offer, but that I was soon to be married, and that I was unfortunately quite busy. I considered suggesting that, after the ceremony, my husband and I would be delighted to accept his kind offer, but it occurred to me he might say yes, by all means, let's have both of you to my mountain retreat.

'*May I ask whether the fortunate man is Alexander?*'

'No,' I said. 'My fiancé is a person I've known for a long time.'

'*Excellent.*'

'He's a good man.' Dumb.

'*Well, Chase,*' he said, '*please accept my best wishes for a long and happy future. And congratulate the lucky groom for me.*'

'I will. Thank you.'

'*I'll arrange to extend the invitation again, perhaps when life settles down a bit.*'

Rainbow had some decisions to make. We'd taken orders from nine clients and come away with a total of nine artifacts. If that sounds like good planning, it wasn't. Two, the command jacket and the glass, were reserved for the office. Of the remaining seven, Nancy White's gold bracelet would go to Harold Estavez. Maddy's blouse was headed for Marcia Cable, a longtime and valued client. And her jumpsuit was earmarked for Ida. Vlad Korinsky, a philosophy professor at Korchnoi University, would get the plaque, with its history of prior missions. Maddy's etui and its assorted contents would go to Diane Gold. That left only Urquhart's Bible and the vest to be divided among the four remaining aspirants.

'We have an obligation to keep our commitments,' I told Alex. 'You have enough for everybody. Forget about keeping stuff ourselves.'

'I *like* the idea of having some of it in the office,' he said. 'Reminds us what we're about.'

'Of course it does. But that's not the point.'

I could see he was not going to be moved. 'There's really no compelling reason to give it up, Chase. Everybody knows what happened. We have forty messages telling us our clients are glad we walked away okay. Nobody even knows, except a couple of people at Survey, that any of the artifacts survived.' He was sitting by the window, drinking something that reflected the sunlight. 'So that'll be the reason we have to disappoint a couple of them. They'll get over it. Hell, they'll appreciate the fact that we were almost killed trying to fill the order. We've already taken care of five of them. It seems to me it's easy enough to assign the Bible and the vest, and call the two who are left to pass along our apologies. Couldn't possibly have foreseen anything like this, terrible waste of excellent merchandise, thanks for your interest, sorry we couldn't oblige, maybe next time, et cetera.'

'And what happens the next time they call the office and see Maddy's jacket framed on the wall? Or the glass?'

'That's simple enough. We'll put them both out of visual range.'

'Isn't that defeating the purpose of having them here?'

He cleared his throat. 'We're just determined to throw up roadblocks this morning, aren't we?'

After we decided how the artifacts would be distributed, he made the calls himself to the two who weren't getting anything. I'll give him that. I've worked for people who wouldn't have hesitated to saddle the help with delivering the bad news. He called from the living room, seated on his sofa, the view of the Melony behind him. (He traditionally did things that way. I called from the office; he called from the sofa.) And he was good. He described the carnage, how horrified he'd been, how unfortunate that so much had been lost. He phrased everything carefully and told the truth, more or less. (Because he knew that eventually the truth would come out.) He'd managed to rescue a handful of objects, but unfortunately not the one he'd earmarked for the client, blah, blah, blah. He hoped next time that we'd all be more fortunate. And he would, of course, find a way to make it up.

It's okay, Alex, both clients said. Not to worry. I know how these things can be. Thanks for trying.

When he'd finished he flashed a satisfied smile at me. I told him I was embarrassed for him. That earned another grin, and he turned the pleasant task of notifying the successful aspirants over to me.

I called each, described the event, and showed the prizes to their new owners, the captain's vest to a laughing Paul Calder, the plaque to a stoic but obviously delighted Vlad Korinsky.

The vest was accompanied by a mounted picture of Maddy wearing it. Calder raised a fist in triumph. He'd wanted to pilot interstellars, but he suffered from defective color vision and could never qualify. It's a foolish requirement, actually, because corrective action can be taken, but the rules say your eyes have to meet the standards on their own.

Diane Gold beamed when I showed her the etui. We couldn't have done better, she said. Gold was an architect, an extraordinarily beautiful woman, but one with whom I suspect no man would want to live. She gave a lot of directions, always knew a better way to get things done, and started wearing on you five minutes after she walked in. She was personally angry with the bombers, who might have destroyed her etui and, incidentally, could have killed me. 'Death's too good for them,' she said.

The Bible went to Soon Lee, a book collector and a wealthy widow who lived on Diamond Island. Marcia Cable wasn't home when I called, but she got back to me, breathless, within the hour.

'You got a uniform blouse,' I told her. 'Maddy's.'

I thought she was going to collapse.

The most melancholy moment came when I showed Ida Patrick the jumpsuit. She listened and swayed a little and asked what else had been in the exhibition. 'Glasses and books,' I said. 'Flatware and jackets. There were two other jumpsuits.'

'*Whose?*' she asked.

'Urquhart's and Mendoza's.'

I could almost feel her physical presence in the room. The color drained from her face, and I thought for a moment she might be having a heart attack. '*And they were destroyed in the bombing?*'

'Yes.'

'*Barbarians,*' she hissed. '*Don't have enough common decency to do the assassination responsibly. I don't know what the world's coming to, Chase.*'

*   *   *

In its own way, each of the artifacts was intriguing, and I enjoyed having a chance to spend time with them while preparing them for shipment to their new owners. The one that was most fascinating was Garth Urquhart's Bible. It had gold trim, was well-worn, and it pages were filled with notes that were sometimes mournful and invariably incisive. Urquhart, whose public persona had suggested a relentlessly optimistic man, showed some doubts about where we were going. In Genesis, beside the passage, 'Be ye fruitful, and multiply; bring forth abundantly in the earth, and multiply therein,' he commented: *We've done that. Resources soon will start to become scarce. But it's okay. At the moment we have what we need. Our children, however, may be another matter.*

That was a fairly bleak appraisal. But there was a degree of truth to it. Toxicon and Earth and a couple of other Confederate worlds were suffering from crowding.

I spent an hour or so with it, and, had I been able to keep one of the objects, that would have been my choice.

Some of his comments were sardonic. 'I am going the way of all the earth,' from the Book of Joshua, was accompanied by his scrawled notation, *As are we all.*

'His family,' Alex said, 'didn't really want him to make the flight because they thought it was dangerous. Deep space, unknown country.'

'He should've listened.'

'Originally there were only to be two ships going to Delta Karpis. Then somebody at Survey, apparently Jess Taliaferro, the operations chief, got the idea of a VIP flight. Send out a few people who had made extraordinary contributions. Recognize their accomplishments by providing the show of a lifetime.'

'It must have seemed like a good move at the time,' I said.

'They had people come in for the launch and make speeches. They even had a band.'

'How old was Urquhart?'

'In his sixties.' Still relatively young. 'He had one son.'

In Ecclesiastes, 'Be not righteous overmuch,' Urquhart had written, *All things, even virtue, are best in moderation.*

'He served two terms on the Council,' said Alex. 'One of the best we had, apparently. But he was defeated in 1361. It seems he wanted people to stop having babies.'

I showed him the passage in *Genesis.*

Alex nodded. 'I'm not surprised. He was concerned about unrestrained population growth. You don't see it here, of course, but there are a lot of places that have serious problems. He grew up destitute in Klymor. His closest boyhood friend developed anemia and never really recovered, his mother died in childbirth when he was four, his father drank himself to death. Read his autobiography when you get a chance.'

And St Luke: 'Out of thine own mouth will I judge thee.' *A caution to authors. And politicians.*

In the Book of Ruth, he'd marked her famous promise: *Whither thou goest, I will go; and where thou lodgest, I will lodge . . . .* Under the circumstances of his disappearance, an eerily appropriate line.

'He made a lot of enemies in his time,' Alex said. 'He didn't like special interests. He couldn't be bought. And he apparently couldn't be intimidated.'

'Sounds as if he should have been chief councillor.'

'He was too honest.'

I was still turning pages. 'Here's another one from St Luke: "This night thy soul shall be required of thee."' He'd underscored the passage but left no comment. I wondered precisely when he'd done that.

'One of his biographers,' said Alex, 'quotes him as telling Taliaferro that having the opportunity to watch a sun get destroyed had forced him to think how different the scales were between human and cosmic activity. Given time, he'd said, who knew what Delta Kay might have produced?'

6

We have a clear obligation to Madeleine English and her six passengers to seek the truth and not to rest until we find it.
—From the founding documents of the *Polaris* Society

Garth Urquhart had piqued my curiosity. I looked through the record and watched him in action during his years as a senator and later on the Council, watched him campaign for himself and for others, watched him accept awards for contributions to various humanitarian efforts, watched him lose an election because he refused to budge on principle.

In 1359, six years before the *Polaris*, he'd been invited to address the World Association of Physical Scientists. He'd taken advantage of the opportunity to sound a warning. 'Population continues to expand at a level that we cannot absorb indefinitely,' he said. 'Not only here, but throughout the Confederacy. At current rates of growth, Rimway will be putting a serious strain on planetary resources by the end of the century. Prices for food and real estate and most other commodities continue to rise while demand increases. But there's a limit, and beyond that limit lies catastrophe. We do not want to repeat the terrestrial experience.'

It hadn't happened. Technological applications in agriculture and food production had combined with a growing tendency to keep families small. The so-called 'replacement' family had become the norm not only on Rimway, but through much of the Confederacy. The general population had increased, but by no more than two or three percent.

If he was wrong in his predictions, Urquhart was nevertheless an able speaker. He was persuasive, passionate, self-deprecating. 'Too many babies,' he'd said. 'We need to slow down a bit. And let nature catch her breath.'

Corporate Rimway had wanted a growing population precisely because it brought rising prices. And they'd gone after him with a vengeance. 'Urquhart Doesn't Like Children!' became the battle cry of his opposition in 1360. Organizations like Mothers Opposed to Urquhart arrived on the scene. He refused to back down, and he was beaten.

My kind of guy.

I shipped everything off to the new owners, except the vest and the etui. Calder and Gold lived nearby and preferred to come to the Rainbow office to pick up their prizes.

Under the circumstances, Alex could have renegotiated the prices with his clients. Everything had multiplied several times in value as a result of the attack. But he charged only his cost plus the usual commission. Ida responded with a bonus that didn't begin to cover the new value of the jumpsuit. Alex tried to refuse it, but she insisted. 'We did the right thing,' Alex commented afterward. 'We held no one up even though the opportunity was there, and nobody would have blamed us.' Of course, Rainbow's demonstrated integrity wouldn't hurt its reputation in the least.

Marcia Cable sent us a recording of herself appearing on a talk show in her area, showing off Maddy's blouse. She was literally glowing.

Meantime Alex found some assignments for me and sent me off around the globe to represent the company in a couple of auctions, to do some negotiating with a few Neeli who had found some curiosities in the Neeli Desert, and to fill in for him at the annual World Antiquities Convention. I was gone ten days.

When I got back, I heard there'd been talk that Survey would make an effort to restore some of the artifacts damaged in the explosion. But there's an odd thing about antiquities and damage. If you have, say, a vase that's been scorched by a laser, and it happened during the useful days of the vase, it might actually enhance the value of the object. Especially if we know whose troops were firing the lasers and who was holding the vase. There's nothing quite so priceless as a pistol that came apart while its heroic owner, say Randall Belmont, was using it to fend off the Hrin during the Last Stand. (The pistol exists, as you probably know, but I doubt there's enough money on the planet to buy it.)

But inflict the damage *after* the object is recovered from the soil, maybe by a careless archeologist cutting too close to it, and the value does a crash dive.

So the attempt went nowhere. Shortly after the restoration rumor first surfaced, Survey announced that it was abandoning the effort. And a few days later, the entire lot of mangled pieces was sold for a song.

Harold Estavez was delighted with White's bracelet.

He was tall, solemn, a man for whom a smile seemed painful. An initial impression suggested he'd never learned to enjoy himself during a long life. He was overcast and gloomy, always awaiting a storm that never arrived, convinced the worst would happen. Alex told me that Estavez felt he'd lost the one great love of his life. I suspected every other woman in the area would have bolted as well.

'Sorry to hear about it,' I said.

'A half century ago. He never got over it.'

However that might have been, I had the pleasure of watching him light up when he received the bracelet.

He called us as soon as the box arrived, and he unwrapped it in our presence. Until that moment he didn't know precisely what he'd gotten. (He'd shushed me when I tried to tell him what we were sending.) But his eyes went wide when he saw gold. And wider still when he saw the engraved name on the bracelet.

Nancy.

By that time, we were getting calls from all our clients, almost everyone on the list. Everybody was interested in the *Polaris*. They'd all heard we'd salvaged some artifacts. Was there perhaps a piece available?

Terribly sorry, we told them. Wish we could oblige.

I was glad we kept the jacket and the long-stemmed glass. Alex told me he'd intended to get something for me, too, and if I liked the glass, he'd be willing to part with it. But I could read the nonverbals. He wanted me to decline. I'd have loved to have it at home in my den. But better, I thought, was to have the boss feeling indebted to me. So I told him it was okay, keep it, think nothing of it. I'd see it every day anyhow. He nodded, as if he were doing me a favor by retaining it.

The ship's registry number, css 117, had been retired ten years after the incident. No future vessel would ever be so designated. Nor, I suspected, would there be another *Polaris*. The people who name superluminals aren't superstitious. But why tempt fate?

Alex bought a lighted display case for the jacket, which went into a corner of the office, near a cabinet and away from the imager. I folded and refolded it until it looked the way it should, with Maddy's name (which was sewn over the left-hand breast pocket) visible. We closed and locked the case, and stood for a minute or two admiring our new possession.

But where to put the glass? We needed a place where it couldn't be knocked over and wouldn't get dusty. And where there'd be at least a degree of security.

Bookshelves were built into two of the walls. There was also a Stratemeyer antique bookcase, a half century old, that Alex had inherited from his uncle. It had glass doors and could be locked. 'Yes,' he said. 'It's perfect.'

Not exactly. We had to move it out of range of the imager, so we found ourselves rearranging most of the furniture in the office. But when we were done, it looked good.

Alex stood back to admire the arrangement, opened the bookcase doors, made room on the top shelf, and handed the glass to me to do the honors.

Later that afternoon I got a call from Ida. *'Check the news on sixteen, Chase,'* she said. *'There's a weird piece about the Polaris.'*

I asked Jacob to take a look, and moments later a man and woman materialized in the office. The woman was Paley McGuire, who was one of CBY's reporters. They were standing beside five packing crates on the dock at Skydeck. A ship's hull protruded into the picture, its cargo doors open.

'—In orbit around the sun, Mr Everson?' Paley was asking.

'That's correct, Paley. It seemed the appropriate way to handle this.' The crates stood higher than he did. But they were, of course, in low gravity. Somebody picked one up and carried it through the cargo doors.

'But what's the point?' she asked.

Everson was about twenty-five. If you could overlook his age, he had a scholarly appearance, reinforced by a black beard. He was conservatively dressed. Gray eyes, a deportment that suggested maturity beyond his years, and the long thin hands of a pianist. *'In a sense,'* he said, *'these objects are almost sacred. They should be treated with respect. That's what we're doing.'*

'Jacob,' I said, 'what's in the boxes? Do you know?'

'One minute, ma'am, and I'll review the program.'

Paley watched another one get hauled away. *'How far out will you be going before you jettison them?'*

'One doesn't jettison this kind of cargo,' he said. *'One releases it. We'll lay it to rest.'*

'Chase,' said Jacob, *'the crates contain the debris from the bombing at Survey.'*

'You mean the artifacts?'

'Yes. What is left of them.'

95

'So how far,' asked Paley, 'will you go before you release them?'

'Just to the moon. We're going to leave Skydeck when it lines up with the sun. When the moon lines up with the sun, that is. That'll happen tonight. About 0300 up here. We'll still be on this side of the moon when we let everything go.'

'Mr Everson, I understand the containers will be going into a solar orbit.'

'Not the containers. We're keeping the containers. Only the ashes will be released—'

'Ashes?'

'We thought it appropriate to reduce everything to ashes. But yes, they'll be in solar orbit. Their average distance from the sun will be eleven point one million kilometers, which is one percent of the distance they were from Delta Kay when they were last heard from.'

McGuire turned and looked directly at Chase. 'So there you have it, folks. A final farewell to the seven heroes of the *Polaris*. Sixty years later.'

I called Alex in. Jacob patched on the beginning, which consisted of no new information, and ran the program again. 'You ever hear of this guy?' I asked, when it was finished.

'Never. Jacob, what do you have on Everson?'

'Not much, Alex. He's independently wealthy. Born on Toxicon. Has been on Rimway six years. Owns an estate in East Komron. He runs a school of some sort up there. Morton College. It's a postgrad school for high-IQ types. Not married. No known children. Plays competitive chess. Apparently quite good. And he's on the board of directors of the *Polaris Society*.'

'The *Polaris* Society? What's that?'

'It's a group of enthusiasts. Branches around the world. They stage a convention in Andiquar every year. It's traditionally on the weekend after the date that the *Polaris* was scheduled to arrive home.'

'Which is—?'

'This weekend, as it happens.'

*   *   *

96

I asked Alex offhandedly whether he'd be interested in going. It was intended as a joke, but he took me seriously. 'They're all crazy people,' he said.

Actually, it sounded intriguing, and I said so. 'They have panels, entertainment, and it might be a chance to meet some new clients.'

He made a face. 'I can't imagine any of *our* clients showing up at something like that. But you go ahead. Have a big time.'

Why not? I went to the Society's data bank and read about them. It didn't take long before I decided Alex was right; they were fanatics. The descriptions of the convention made the point: They read pseudoscholarly articles to each other; they played games based on the *Polaris;* they debated the finer points of the incident, whether the onboard lander had been disabled (some swore this had been the case); whether the AI had been a late substitution for the original system; whether the Nancy White who got on board was not the real Nancy White but an evil twin of some sort, and the real one had been living all these years in New York.

They were meeting for three days at the Golden Ring, a midlevel hotel downtown. I showed up the first evening, just as they were getting started.

The Golden Ring is located in the park district. Beautiful area, a patch of forest filled with streams, cobbled walkways, fountains, granby trees, and statuary. It was cold, and the fountains had been turned off. A brisk wind was blowing out of the north.

I went into the lobby, paid my admission fee, got a badge with my name on it, collected a program schedule, and took the elevator up.

Several meeting rooms had been set aside on the second and third floors, and events seemed to be running simultaneously in all of them. I stopped at the bar, picked up a drink, and looked around to see if I recognized anyone. Or, maybe closer to the truth, if there was anyone who might recognize *me*. Walking into a convention of this sort is a bit like showing up at a meeting of astrology buffs or the Gate Keepers (which, if you haven't been paying attention, claim to have the truth about the next world), or that reincarnation group, Onward. But I was surrounded by strangers, so I figuratively pulled up my collar, and stopped outside an open door that said ALIEN WIND PANEL.

There weren't more than about fifteen people in the audience, maybe a quarter of the room's capacity. But it was early yet; people were still coming in. 'The alien wind,' one of the panel members was saying, 'was more like a gale. It blew through the ship. It was able to do so because it consisted of antiparticles. They don't interact with regular particles; therefore, the hull doesn't present a barrier.' The speaker was well along in years, dignified, the kind of guy you might have mistaken for a physician, almost persuasive. But I knew just enough science to know he was talking nonsense.

The audience seemed to take him seriously, though. At least seriously enough to agree or, in some cases, to try to refute the argument. One energetic woman protested vehemently that such a thing could not happen, and the debate wandered into talk about electrons and properties of space curvature and momentum.

The topic was, I thought, appropriately named. I moved down the corridor to the next room.

They were discussing whether one of the human worlds, most probably Toxicon, had sent a mission to co-opt the *Polaris,* grab the passengers, and put them to work in a secret project. An elderly woman whom everyone called Aunt Eva pointed out that the passengers included two medical researchers, a cosmologist, a science popularizer, a politician, and a psychiatrist. The politician and the cosmologist were retired. What sort of project would require the services of such a diverse group?

The answer came back that the kidnappers only wanted Dunninger and Mendoza. The neurobiologists. Did the audience know they were working on life extension?

Of course it did.

Somebody pointed out that the way to find the culprits was to look for a world whose politicians had stopped ageing.

The most popular explanations inevitably involved aliens. It provided an easy response to all difficulties. If there was a threatening alien presence, and the ship was ready to jump into Armstrong space, why didn't it do so? Answer: The aliens had a device that prevented it. Why didn't Maddy send a Code White? Same answer.

What were the aliens up to? There was widespread disagreement. Some thought they wanted a few humans to dissect. Others, that they were measuring human capabilities. That was why they'd selected this particular mission, with its all-star passenger list. That notion led to a whole other line of thought: that the aliens lived unknown among us and might take us at any time. That they looked like humans, but inside one would find a heart of darkness.

Some pursued a culinary argument, that the aliens merely wanted to find out whether we were digestible. Or tasty. Apparently, judging by the fact there'd been no incidents since, we did not suit their palate.

Dr Abraham Tolliver read a paper arguing that the *Polaris* was indeed seized by an alien force, that the Confederacy and the Mutes had been aware of the existence of this force since pre-Confederate times, that the long on-again, off-again conflict between humans and Mutes was a hoax. What was actually happening, he said, was that both species recognized the presence of a lethal threat 'out there somewhere,' and that the war had been trumped up between two allies to mask an arms race that would provide for the day when the attackers actually came.

The *Polaris* had its historians as well as its speculators. I wandered into a panel titled 'Why Did Maddy Become a Star-Pilot?'

The credit, or the blame, was laid on her father's shoulders. Maddy was one of six kids for whom the bar was set high, for whom no accomplishment was ever sufficient to merit praise. The father, who had the unlikely given name Arbuckle, was a small-town merchant who was apparently unsatisfied with his own life and consequently sought to taste success through his children, three of whom eventually needed psychiatric help.

One panelist thought Maddy had chosen her field in a failed attempt to satisfy him. (He was reported to have told her, at the graduation ceremony, that she should keep striving, that she could do better.) Another panelist thought she'd done it in order to get as far as possible from him.

Tab Everson was at the convention. He was scheduled to give a presentation, so I went. When he was introduced, he received loud applause for having given proper disposition to the remnants of the *Polaris* artifacts.

He thanked the audience and explained that he had been aboard the *Polaris* a couple of years earlier. 'They call it the *Sheila Clermo* now,' he said, 'but we all know what's really inside the Foundation trappings.' He talked about Evergreen, which specializes in adapting crops and vegetation for use in off-world settlements, and in environmental pursuits. He had pictures of the CEO who had bought the ship, of the young *Sheila,* of the interiors, of the ship itself as it left dock on the day he'd visited. No theories anywhere, just a tour. He was in fact one of the more effective presenters of the evening.

A young woman on a panel titled The Grand Illusion insisted she'd seen Chek Boland less than a year earlier. 'It was right here, beneath the statue of Tarien Sim at the White Pool. He was just standing there, gazing across the gardens. Last summer. Last summer, it was.

'When I tried to talk to him, he turned away. Denied everything. But I'd know him anywhere. He's older, of course. But it *was* him.'

Then there was the Black Ship session, with four panelists and a crowded room. The panelists were described by the moderator as various sorts of experts on the *Polaris*. Apparently all had published something on the subject, which seemed to be the prerequisite for being recognized as an authority.

Each made a brief statement. In essence, two of them maintained there *had* been a black ship; the others insisted there had not.

'What's a black ship?' I whispered to a young man next to me.

The question seemed to startle him. 'The conspirators,' he said.

'What conspirators?'

'It's the ship that took them away. Maddy and the passengers.'

'Oh. Toxicon again?'

'Of course not.' He might have been annoyed because I'd become a distraction to the quarrel that was breaking out in the front of the room.

A man who looked and talked like a lawyer had the floor. 'The Trendel Commission,' he was saying, 'ruled that out at the time. During the incident, no interstellar was unaccounted for.'

The idea seemed to be that a small private group, with the connivance of one of the persons on board the *Polaris,* had arrived in the neighborhood and succeeded in gaining entry before anyone realized their purpose. The intention was to demand ransoms for the return of the passengers. Because of their celebrity, the payoff would have been substantial.

The problem with this theory was that no ransom demand had ever been received. But that could be explained, too. The victims were taken aboard the other ship, awaited their chance, and stormed the bridge. In the ensuing melee, the black ship was damaged and was floating through Armstrong space, where it could never be found. An alternate theory was that during the fighting, one or more of the kidnap victims had been killed, thereby making it too risky to return the others. Again, there was a difficulty with both scenarios: No ship had gone missing during the target period.

A woman wearing a gold scarf was trying to shoot down that objection. 'All it needed,' she said, 'was for somebody to gundeck the data. Damn, why is everyone so blind?'

So the debate went round and round.

At the height of all this, Cazzie Michaels showed up. He came in and sat down beside me, but I didn't notice he was there until he reached over and tugged on my arm. 'Hi, Chase,' he said.

Cazzie was an occasional client. He had a passion for anything that came from the preinterstellar period. Which was to say, terrestrial artifacts. There just aren't many of those around anymore.

I smiled back and, to my horror, he told me *we'd* straighten everything out about the black ship, and rose to be recognized. The moderator addressed him by name.

'Frank,' he said, 'we have Chase Kolpath with us.' I cringed. 'She pilots superluminals, and could probably settle some of these questions.'

'Good.' Frank looked at me and canted his head. Cazzie kept urging me to stand, and there was nothing for it but to comply. 'Ah,' he said, 'is that true, Chase? You're a pilot?'

'Yes,' I said. To my surprise, I got a round of applause.

'Chase, help us here. Is it possible to assign limits to where starships can be at any given time?'

'Even with the quantum drive,' I said, 'there are limits. But during the period you're talking about, they were much more pronounced. Then, government and commercial carriers were required to send movement reports to the controlling station every four hours. If a report went missing, alarms went off. So they always knew where you were. Private vehicles – and there just weren't very many of those – could participate if they wanted. Some did, some didn't.

'So it's easy enough to rule out the vast majority of the fleet. With the ships that are left, you can look at their ports of call and determine whether it was possible for any of them to get close to the target area. My understanding about the *Polaris* incident is that Delta Karpis was too far, and the commission was able to eliminate any possibility of another ship.'

The audience stirred. Someone said, 'I told you so.'

One session employed an avatar of Jess Taliaferro, the Survey operations chief who had organized the mission. He talked about how pleased he'd been at the opportunity to give something back to Klassner and the others, how carefully they had planned every-thing, and how devastating the news had been.

I was standing beside an elderly couple loaded down with items from the souvenir shop. They had books, chips, a model of the *Polaris,* a *Polaris* scarf, and pictures of Maddy and her passengers.

I said hello, and they smiled. 'I remember when it happened,' the man said, trying not to drop anything. 'We didn't believe it. Nobody did. Thought the early reports were mistaken. That they'd turn up belowdecks or something.'

The formal part of the presentation ended. It had been almost over when I walked in. 'Unfortunate man,' said the woman.

She meant Taliaferro. 'I suspect,' I said, 'the experience marked him the rest of his life.'

She had gone gray and seemed frail, yet she possessed a robust-ness of spirit that flashed in her eyes. 'Of course,' she said. 'Look at what happened to him afterward.'

'What happened afterward?' I asked.

Both seemed surprised at the question. 'He disappeared, too,' she said. 'Never got over the shock, I suppose. Two, three years afterward he walked out the front door of Survey's operations center, and nobody ever saw him again.'

They'd opened the floor for questions, and the audience couldn't resist asking where Taliaferro had gone that afternoon fifty-seven years ago. '*It was a bright summer day,*' the avatar said. '*Nothing out of the ordinary had been happening. I cleared off my desk, cleared* everything, *which was unusual for me. So it was obvious I knew that would be my last day on the job.*'

'So what happened to you, Dr Taliaferro?' asked a man in front.

'*I wish I knew.*' The avatar had Taliaferro's personality, and whatever knowledge the data systems had been able to load into him, and whatever Taliaferro himself had chosen to impart. '*But I honestly have no idea.*'

There was a collector's room, filled with books about the event, *Polaris* uniforms, models, games, pictures of the captain and passengers. And there again was Ormond's painting of Dunninger gazing across the country graveyard. Several dealers had lines of clothing emblazoned with the ship's seal. The most interesting item, I thought, was a set of four books certified as being from Maddy's personal library. I'd have expected treatises on navigation and superluminal maintenance. Instead, I saw Plato, Tulisofala, Lovell, and Sim's *Man and Olympian*. There was more to the lady than a pilot's license and a pretty face. Had the asking price been reasonable, I would have picked them up.

My sense of the convention was that the attendees treated the entire business as a means of escape rather than a serious exercise. They weren't really as caught up in the historical *Polaris* as they would lead an outsider to believe. Rather, it was a means to make the universe a bit more mysterious, a bit more romantic, and maybe a lot less predictable than it actually was. I concluded that nobody there really believed in the alien wind. But it charged them up to pretend, for a few hours, that it just might have happened that way.

The evening was mostly hyperbole. It was part celebration, part speculation, part mythmaking. And part regret.

7

The wind passeth over it, and it is gone. . .

—Psalms,
CIII

The *Polaris* convention provided just what I needed: a rationale to get away from my usual routine and an evening so full of whimsy and nonsense that it became pure pleasure. When the scheduled presentations ended, the attendees threw a round of parties that extended well into the night. I got home close to dawn, slept three hours, got up, showered, and staggered over to the office. It was my half day, and I knew I could make it through to lunch. But I hoped nothing would come up that would require me to think clearly.

More calls were coming in, mostly from people outside our regular circle of customers, asking what *Polaris* artifacts we possessed, querying prices or, in some cases, making offers. The word had gotten around.

The bids were, I thought, on the high side. Even accounting for the loss of the rest of the exhibition. But Alex nodded sagely when I reported the numbers to him. 'They'll be through the roof before it's over,' he said. 'By the way' – he looked innocently at the ceiling but couldn't restrain a smile – 'how'd it go last night?'

'It went fine.'

'Really? What did they decide about the *Polaris?* That the ghosts got them?'

'Pretty much.'

'Well, I'm glad you enjoyed yourself.' He saw that I wanted to ask something. 'What?' he said.

'You're sure you want to hang on to these?' I was talking about the jacket and the glass. 'We could get a lot for them. Guarantees your bottom line for the quarter.'

'We'll keep them.'

'Alex, this is a period of peak interest. I agree that they'll go still higher, but that's probably a long time away. In the short term, there could be a falloff. You know how these things are.'

'Keep them.' He walked over and looked at the glass, which was front and center in the bookcase.

Next morning, CBY announced that the Mazha had been assassinated. Apparently by his son. With a knife, while the guards watched.

'Just as well,' Alex commented. 'Nobody's going to miss him.'

I hadn't said anything about the call. It was embarrassing to have been a social contact of sorts with a monster. But when the news came, I told Alex everything that had happened.

'You must have made an impression,' he said.

Despite myself, I was sorry for him.

Alex was a good boss. I was responsible for day-to-day operations, and he left me to take care of things without trying to give a lot of directions. He spent most of his time entertaining clients and sources, but he always made it a point during the middle of the week to pull me out of the office and take me to dinner.

A couple of days after the convention, we went to dinner at Molly's Top of the World, which is located at the summit of Mt. Oskar, the highest peak in the area. He was excited because he'd located an early-German coal stove. The thing was worth a fortune, and the owner needed the money and wanted to make a quick sale. Usually, we simply put buyers and sellers together, but the price was so good, Alex was thinking of buying the unit himself.

We spent the hour talking about stoves and European antiques. He solicited my opinion, and I told him sure, buy it, what can we lose? The decision made, we fell into small talk. It was late when we finished, and normally he'd have taken me home, but I had work to do, so we rode back to the office.

The house had originally been a country inn, a solitary structure built atop a low-rise. It had catered to hunters and travelers until Alex's uncle Gabe bought it and had it refurbished. Alex spent much of his boyhood in it. In those early days it had been surrounded mostly by forest. There's an ancient graveyard just off the northwestern perimeter. The markers and the statuary are worn smooth from the centuries. Older boys had told Alex the occupants went wandering at night. 'There were evenings,' he said, 'if I was alone in the house, I hid behind a sofa.' That didn't sound at all like the Alex I knew.

Gabe had fought a long, and ultimately losing, battle against development. He'd been something of a fanatic on the subject, and he would not have approved of the surfeit of neighbors the house had acquired over the years, or the loss of large sections of forest.

It was a glorious house, four stories and lots of windows overlooking the Melony. Furnished in the reserved traditions of the previous century. Rooms everywhere, several with VR, another with workout gear, another with a squabble table, another for sitting and watching the river go by. Some rooms were held aside for visitors, and others were pressed into service to store the occasional pieces of other civilizations that Gabe had brought back from his travels.

It was completely out of sync with the other houses in the neighborhood, which were modern, sleek, utilitarian, no space wasted. Practical. Land was at a premium outside Andiquar, and you didn't find many houses that weren't part of a designed community. You'll understand then that the country house stood out. You could see it from a couple of klicks away when approaching from the city. Except, of course, at night.

We passed over the Melony, adjusted course, slowed, and drifted down through the treetops.

It was about an hour after sunset. The moon was down, but the stars were out in force. The house, and the landing pad, normally lit up as we approached, but on that evening they remained uncharacteristically dark.

Alex jiggled his comm link. 'Jacob,' he said, 'lights, please.'

No response.

'Jacob?'

We eased gently to the ground.

'I don't think he's there,' I said, as the engine stopped, and the skimmer's exit lights winked on and threw shadows along the front and side of the house. The cabin doors opened, and a cool breeze blew through the aircraft.

'Stay put,' said Alex. He climbed out.

The area was crowded with other houses. They pushed up to the edge of the low stone wall that marked the northern and eastern perimeters of Alex's property. They were all illuminated, so whatever was going on, it wasn't a general power failure.

The landing pad is in a slight depression. Once you're down you can only see the upper stories. He started up the incline toward the front door. I got out and fell in behind him. I'd never seen the place completely dark before. Burglars are virtually nonexistent nowadays, but you never really know. 'Careful,' I said.

The walkway was chipped stone. It crunched underfoot, and we could hear a mournful wind moving through the trees. Alex kept his ID remote in his ring. He strode up the front steps and pointed it at the door. It opened. But slowly. The power was low.

He pushed through. I hurried up beside him and grabbed his wrist. 'Not a good idea.'

'It's okay.' He waved me back and walked into the living room.

The lights tried to come on but faded almost immediately. 'Jacob,' he said, 'hello.'

Nothing.

Starlight came through the windows. He had an original piece of art, a Sujannais, hanging over the sofa. I was relieved to see it was still there. I stuck my head in the office. Maddy's jacket remained folded inside its display case. And the *Polaris* glass was in its accustomed place among the books. Had there been a burglar, they should have been the first things taken.

Alex came to the same conclusion. 'I think Jacob just went down,' he said. 'There's no sign of a break-in.'

'Did Jacob ever do a blackout before?'

'No. But AIs go down all the time.'

Actually, they almost never do.

He looked past me into the kitchen. 'Maybe you should wait outside, Chase. Just in case.' He opened a cabinet door, fumbled around, and produced a lamp.

Jacob's internals were located inside a wine cabinet in the dining room. A red warning light was blinking.

The power came by way of a laser link through a dish on the roof. I went outside, far enough away from the house that I could see past the overhang. The receiver was missing. I found it on the ground in back. The base was scorched where someone had cut it down.

I told Alex and suggested he get out of the house. 'Just a minute,' he said. He can be frustrating at times. I went in and dragged him out. Then I called the police.

A woman's voice responded. *'Please give your name,'* she said, *'and state the nature of the emergency.'*

I complied and told her that we'd probably had a burglar.

'Where are you now?'

'In the garden.'

'Stay there. Do not go inside. We're on the way.'

We watched the front door from a safe distance, back within running range of the skimmer, so we could jump aboard and skedaddle if we had to. But the house stayed quiet, and after a few minutes lights appeared overhead. A police cruiser. My link chimed. *'You the lady who called?'*

'Yes.'

'Okay, ma'am. Please stay well away from the house. Just in case.' The cruiser assumed station directly overhead.

Alex and I had talked before about security at the office. But burglaries were so rare as to be almost unheard-of, and Alex couldn't be bothered upgrading his alarm system. 'But I guess I've learned,' he said. There'd been two break-ins in the area over twelve years, and he'd been the victim of both. 'We'll do something about it this time.'

'Mr Benedict,' said the voice from the cruiser, *'we've scanned the house. It's clear. But we'd prefer you don't go inside just yet.'*

The police drifted down and landed beside the skimmer. There were two officers, male and female, both tall, neatly pressed, courteous. The male, who had dark skin and enormous shoulders and a vaguely northern accent, took charge. He questioned us about what we knew, then they went inside while we waited. After about ten minutes we were invited in, but told not to touch anything. 'They used a laser on your dish,' the male said. 'Took you right off-line. You're on backup power.' He was middle-aged, had been on the job awhile, and obviously thought citizens should take better care of their property. Maybe invest in decent security systems. I could see it in his eyes. He had thick arms and a heavy black mustache. 'We found a set of footprints that we followed out to the road. But after that—' He shrugged. 'Whoever did it must have worn a suit. He left nothing we can trace.'

'I'm sorry to hear it.'

'Have you noticed any strangers in the area? Anyone behaving oddly?'

Not that either of us could recall.

'Okay, why don't you folks look around? Let's find out what's missing.'

* * *

110

The thieves had taken Alex's collection of Meridian coins – about two thousand years old but not particularly valuable – and a few first editions. Nothing else seemed to be gone.

The officers linked Jacob to a portable power source, and the lights came back on. Alex activated him and asked what he remembered.

'Have I really been off-line?' he said. *'It appears I've lost two hours, forty-six minutes.'*

'Not that long after we left,' said Alex.

We watched while the AI produced pictures of the missing books and coins. The officers asked about estimated value, and they seemed to have an idea how the thieves would get rid of the property. 'Anyone who's shown an unusual interest in any of this stuff?' the female asked. She looked puzzled.

We couldn't think of anyone other than Alex who had even seen the coins during the last year, although they'd been in plain sight in one of the upstairs rooms. As to the books, everybody knew about them, but they, too, weren't all that valuable.

'Mr Benedict,' said her partner, 'am I safe in assuming that you have some jewelry on the premises?'

'Yes, I do. But it's still there. I checked it.'

'Anything else you'd describe as a likely target for thieves?'

He thought it over. 'Just the collectibles. Fortunately, it doesn't look as if they knew what they were doing.'

'You mean they missed the good stuff.'

'That's exactly what I mean. There are other things, a lot easier to carry than books, that they might have taken.' There was, for example, a Kulot bowl and a recorder from ancient Canada, both in the living room, and in the study a necklace worn at the beginning of the century by Anya Martain. Not to mention the *Polaris* glass and Maddy's jacket. All in plain sight.

'Odd,' he said.

Alex shrugged. 'If they were smart, they wouldn't be thieves.'

The intruder had cut through the back door, which would have to be replaced. The male took a deep breath, suggesting a world-weariness. 'You have the nicest house in the neighborhood, Mr Benedict. If a thief is going anywhere, he's coming here.'

'I guess.'

He slapped the cover shut on his notebook. 'I think that's about all we can do for now. If you find anything else we should know, get in touch.' He handed Alex a crystal. 'Here's a copy of the record, with your case number.'

Alex managed a smile. He was not happy. 'Thanks.'

'No trouble, Mr Benedict. We'll keep you informed. You can keep the generator until you get up and running again.' They wished us good evening and got back into the cruiser. 'I don't think you need to worry,' he said. 'They never come back. But keep your doors locked anyhow.'

I went out onto the roof, hauled the dish back up, reset it in its housing, taped it down, and was gratified to see that it worked. 'It should be all right for tonight,' I said. 'We'll want to get somebody over in the morning to take a look at it.'

We sat down and began running pictures of the house, room by room, on a split screen, as it had been at the beginning of the day, and as it was now, to see whether we'd missed anything. But everything looked unchanged. Cushions were arranged as they had been, kitchen chairs were in the same positions, a cabinet door left half-open in the dining room remained half-open. 'It doesn't look as if they were very serious,' he said.

'Maybe they'd just started when we arrived and scared them off.'

'That can't be. Jacob says he was down well over two hours.'

'Then they must have known exactly what they wanted.'

He frowned. 'The coin collection and *The Complete Fritz Hoyer*?'

'Yeah. I don't understand it either.'

The kitchen before and after flashed on the wall screen. The dining area. The living room.

The living room had four chairs, a sofa, a bookcase, and side and coffee tables. A book lay open on one of the chairs. The drapes were drawn. Vina, the pagan goddess of the Altieri, stood fetchingly atop a globe representing the world, her long arms outstretched. The book was *My Life in Antiquity,* and it was open to the same page in both displays. Pictures were distributed around the walls. These were of Alex's father (whom he had never known) and Gabe, of Alex and some of his customers, and a couple of Alex and me.

Finally, he sighed, told Jacob to shut it down, and we took to wandering through the house, studying drapes and windows and tables and bookshelves. 'They went to a lot of trouble,' he said. 'There must have been a reason.'

So much of the stuff should have begged to be taken, onyx religious figurines from Carpalla; a ninth-century drum from the obscure rhythm group, Rapture; a set of eight-sided dice from Dellaconda. 'Don't know,' he said. 'Makes no sense.' We gave up finally, went back to the office, and sat down.

We sat there for a couple of minutes in puzzled silence. It was late, and I was ready to go home. He was looking at Maddy's jacket.

'Gotta go, boss,' I said, getting to my feet and pulling on my coat. 'Tomorrow comes early.'

He rose also, nodding, but paying no attention. Instead he walked over to the case holding the jacket, stared at it for a minute, and tried the lid. It was still locked.

'You look surprised,' I said.

The lock was electronic, designed to keep children or idle adults from handling the contents. It wasn't the sort of thing that would have deterred a burglar. He opened it and pursed his lips. 'They've been into it,' he said.

You already know the angle of the imager didn't give us a picture of the jacket as it had appeared earlier. But it was still folded. It looked okay to me. 'Alex,' I said patiently, 'if they'd done that, they wouldn't have gone to the trouble to put it back. And relock the case.'

'You got me there, love.' He grimaced. 'This *is* different from what it was, though. Look at Maddy's name.'

It had been clearly visible before. It still was, actually, but it was partially around the fold. 'This isn't the way it was,' I said.

'No. They took it out, refolded it, and put it back.'

'That can't be right. Why would a thief do that?'

'Why would a thief leave the jewelry? Or the Sujannais?' He walked over to the bookcase, turned its light on, and looked at the long-stemmed glass. The lock was an old-fashioned one requiring a metal key. It could have been opened, but, unlike the display case, not without breaking it. 'It hasn't been touched,' he said.

Advanced Electronics showed up next day, shook their heads a lot, and wondered that we'd left so much to chance. 'Well, no more,' they told us. 'From now on, anybody tries to knock out your dish, you've got a serious backup. Anybody manages to break in, Jacob will call the police, and the intruder will be lying on the floor when they get here.' They collected the police generator and announced they'd return it.

That was the day we started the paperwork to implement the idea about doing some radioarcheology. But Alex was distracted by the break-in. 'We better assume,' he said, 'that they got into the records.'

'Did you ask Jacob whether he can make a determination as to whether that happened?'

'He says he has no way of knowing. So we have to assume the worst.'

'Okay.'

'Chase, we need to inform everyone with whom Rainbow has done business recently, say, the last two years, that the details of all transactions have been compromised and may be in the hands of thieves.'

While I was taking care of it, he went to lunch with someone, and I got a call from Fenn Redfield. Fenn was a police inspector, and also a friend. He'd handled the original burglary years before. *'When you get a chance, Chase,'* he said, *'you and Alex might want to drop by the station.'*

'Alex isn't here,' I said. 'He's off working with a client.'

'Then yourself will do fine.'

Fenn has an unusual history. In another life, literally another life, he'd been a small-time thief, apparently not very competent. In the incident that ended that career, the owner of a house he was burglarizing walked in on him. There was a struggle, the owner got pushed through a second-floor window and died of his injuries. Fenn, who had a different name in those days, was caught leaving the premises. The jury found him guilty, a fourth conviction. The judge pronounced him incorrigible and a danger to society, so they'd done a mind wipe and a personality adjustment. Nobody in Fenn's new life is supposed to know that. *He* didn't even know it. He received a new identity, a new address halfway across the country from where the crimes occurred, a new set of memories, and a new psyche. Now he had a wife and kids and a responsible job. He worked hard, seemed to be competent, and showed every sign of enjoying his life.

I knew all this because the victim's sister was a Rainbow client. She'd wanted the killer dead, and she'd shown me pictures from the trial, and there was Fenn. Incredible. I pointed out to her that the killer *was* dead, as surely as if he'd been dropped in the ocean.

But I've never said anything to anyone, not even Alex. And I doubt this memoir will ever be published. In any case, I won't allow it until I'm sure it can do no harm.

I thought his summons meant they'd caught the intruder. Probably trying to break into someone else's place.

The police office is located on the lip of a ridge about a kilometer away from the country house. The day was unseasonably warm, so I decided to walk over.

It's an old run-down stone building, a former courthouse, with a lot of space in back and upstairs that they'd sealed off because they had no use for it and wanted to avoid the expense of climate control.

The front looks like a neglected thirteenth-century portico. Lots of fluted columns, curving steps, and a fountain that doesn't work anymore. A bit pretentious for a police station. I climbed the steps and went in. The officer on duty showed me directly into Fenn's office.

Fenn was short and heavy, with a voice down in the basement somewhere. Off duty, he enjoyed a good party, a good joke, good VR. But when he put the badge in his pocket, his personality changed. Not that he became unduly formal, but anything not related to the business at hand was clearly perceived as inconsequential.

He had large jaws, riveting green eyes, and a talent for making people feel that everything was going to be all right. A plastene bag stood on the floor at his feet. 'Don't know what we're coming to, Chase,' he said, looking up from a document and waving me to a seat. 'Getting so people's homes aren't even safe anymore.'

He lifted himself out of his chair, came around in front of the desk, and used it to prop himself up. The office was small, with a single window looking out on the house next door. The walls were covered with awards, commendations, pictures of Fenn standing by a police cruiser, Fenn shaking hands with important-looking officials, Fenn smiling broadly as someone pinned a set of bars on his shoulders. A blackened Fenn carried a child out of a disaster site.

'Did you catch them?' I asked.

He shook his head. 'No. Afraid not, Chase. Wish we had. But I *do* have good news for you.' He reached down beside the couch, picked up the bag, and held it out to me.

It was the coins.

'That was quick,' I said. 'Where'd you find them?'

'They were in the river.'

'In the river?'

'Yes. About two klicks downstream.'

116

The satin-lined container that had housed the collection was ruined. But the coins were okay.

'A couple of kids were making out on a landing. Skimmer comes by, swings low over the river, and drops *that* and the books. Everything was in a weighted sack.' He produced one of the books. It was a soggy mess. I couldn't even read the title.

'I don't get it,' I said. 'Why steal stuff, then throw it in the river? Were they worried about getting caught?'

'I have no idea. It happened the same night they were taken. Next day, the boy came back to the spot with a sensor.' He examined one of the books under a lamp, holding it carefully as if it were something unclean. 'He thought it was strange, and he called us. This one' – he consulted his notes – 'is *God and the Republic*.'

'Yep. That's one of ours.'

'Leather cover.' His jaw muscles worked. 'I don't think it's of much use now.' We sat staring at one another.

'Sounds as if somebody has a grudge,' I said.

'If they did, Chase, Alex wouldn't have had a house to come home to.' He ran his fingers through his hair and made a series of pained faces. 'It doesn't make a lot of sense. Are you sure nothing else is missing?'

'How do you mean?'

'Sometimes thieves really want an ID, but they take other stuff so the owner doesn't notice right away. That way they can go on a spree.'

I looked down at the bracelet that carried my data disk and thought about it. 'No,' I said. 'We checked that possibility last night. Did the kids get a look at the skimmer?'

'It was gray.'

'That all?'

'That's it. They didn't get the number.' He squinted at one of the coins. 'Where's it from?'

'Meridian Age. Two thousand years ago.'

'On Rimway?'

'Blavis.'

'Oh.' He put it back. 'The inspecting officer told me there were other valuables that the thieves missed.'

'That's correct.'

'And that some of them were out in the open.'

'That's true, too. You've been over there, Fenn. You know what it's like.'

The green eyes narrowed. 'You and your employer need to get serious about security.'

'We already have.'

'Good. It's about time.'

I thought we were ready to change the subject. 'By the way,' I said, 'have you made any progress toward catching the people who planted the bomb at Proctor Union?'

He grunted. 'It's not my case. But we'll get them. We're checking out every Kondi in the area.' *Kondi* was a disparaging term for anyone from Korrim Mas. His lined face acquired a bulldog look. 'We'll get them.'

'Good.'

'The bomb was homemade. From chemicals available over the counter. And insecticide.'

'Insecticide? Can you really make a bomb out of that?'

'Yes, indeed. And it packs a wallop.'

I sent the boy who'd found the package in the river a couple of rare coins, and judging from his reply, he was smart enough to understand their value. A few days later Fenn confessed they were having no luck tracking down the thieves, and he said that we'd have to be patient, that eventually they'd make a mistake, and he would catch them. What he seemed to be saying was that the police were waiting for them to burgle somebody else.

At about the same time I got a call from Paul Calder. He materialized in the office, wearing a gray military-style jacket over a blue shirt. He was outside on his veranda. '*Chase,*' he said, '*I wanted you to know how much I appreciated your getting Maddy's vest for me.*' He'd already thanked us. That, and the fact that he looked embarrassed, told me something had happened. '*I'm sending you another four hundred.*'

'Was there something else you wanted to buy?'

'No. Call it a bonus.'

We'd already been paid. 'That's generous of you, Paul. But why?'

He was about average height, a bit overweight. He wore an unruly black beard in an effort to appear intellectual, but he just looked unkempt. Calder was afflicted with runaway piety. Lots of references to the Almighty. '*I really liked that vest.*'

I noted the past tense. 'What happened to it?'

Another grin. '*I got an offer I couldn't refuse.*'

I believe, had he been physically in the room, I'd have throttled him without a second thought. 'Paul,' I said, 'tell me you didn't sell it.'

'*Chase, they doubled my money.*'

'*We* would have doubled your money. Damn it, Paul, I told you that thing was worth a lot more than you'd paid for it. Do you still have it in your possession?'

'*He picked it up this morning.*' I sat there shaking my head. He cleared his throat and pulled at his collar. '*I know what you said, about what it was worth, but I thought you were exaggerating.*'

Paul's money was inherited. He'd never known what it took to create wealth, so he'd never taken it seriously. Money was just something he spent when a whim took him. More or less, I thought, the way he took his religion. There was a superficiality to it. Lots of *Bless you's* and *God willing's* but I never got the sense he thought in serious terms about what a Creator might be like. Or what the implications were. Nevertheless, he was a difficult man to stay angry with. He literally cringed while waiting for me to react. So I calmed down. 'Any chance you can cancel the deal?'

'No,' he said. '*I wrote a receipt, took the money, and gave it to him.*'

'No escape clause?'

'What's an escape clause?'

I found myself thinking about the thief poking around in the Rainbow data banks. 'Paul,' I asked, 'how'd he find out you had it?'

'Oh, that's no big deal. Everybody knew. I didn't make a secret of it. And anyway I took it with me the other day to the monthly meeting of the Chacun Historical Association.'

'How'd they react to it?'

'They loved it. Friend of mine even brought a sim of Garth Urquhart.'

'Paul, the person who bought it, did you know him? Prior to the purchase?'

'No. But he was at the meeting.' He tried grinning again. *'Little guy. Name's Davis.'*

'Okay. Thanks for letting me know.'

'I'm sorry if I upset you. Selling it seemed like the right thing to do.'

'Maybe it was. I'm not upset, Paul. You doubled your money so I guess you came out of it all right.' I thought about returning the bonus he was sending us, but there was really no point in that. I'd just earned it.

I stared at the empty space Paul's image had occupied. How could he be so dumb? But there was nothing to be done about it.

Even though we were no longer involved with *Polaris* artifacts, I was still curious about the incident itself. I began to think I'd never rest easy until I could at least construct a rational sequence of events that could have resulted in the disappearance of Maddy and her passengers. 'Jacob?' I asked. 'Is there a visual record of the *Polaris* departure?'

'Checking.'

While he looked, I went to the kitchen and got a cup of tea.

'Yes, there is. Do you want me to set it up?'

'Please.'

The office morphed into a Skydeck terminal. And they were all there. Maddy and Urquhart, Boland, Klassner (looking barely alive), White, Mendoza, and Dunninger. Along with a crowd of about fifty people. And a small band. The band played a medley of unfamiliar tunes, and people took turns shaking hands with the voyagers.

Martin Klassner was propped against the back of his seat, talking to a rumpled man, whom I recognized immediately as Jess Taliaferro, the Survey director who'd organized the mission and had himself eventually disappeared. It was an odd scene, Klassner and Taliaferro, two men who'd walked into the night on different occasions, and never been seen again. Klassner's lips barely moved when he talked, and his hands trembled. I wondered that they'd send a man so obviously ill on such a journey. There was a physician on one of the accompanying ships, but that hardly seemed sufficient.

Nancy White stood near a souvenir shop. She was trim, attractive, dressed as if she were headed out of town for a holiday. She was talking quietly to a small group, one of whom was a tall, dark-complexioned, good-looking guy, who looked worried. '*Her husband, Michael,*' said Jacob. '*He was a real estate developer.*'

Urquhart was surrounded by journalists. He was smiling, holding up his hands, no more questions, folks, I really need to get on board, okay just one more.

Chek Boland was flanked by two women. '*He's been described as the man who solved the mind-body problem.*'

'What's the mind-body problem, Jacob?'

'*I'm not clear on it myself, Chase. Apparently it's an ancient conundrum. The issue seems to revolve around the nature of consciousness.*'

I thought about asking him to explain, but it sounded complicated so I let it go. Tom Dunninger and Warren Mendoza were holding forth for another group near the ramp. '*The one next to Dunninger,*' said Jacob, '*is Borio Chapatka. Ann Kelly's there, too. And Min Kao-Wing—*'

'Who are they?' I asked.

'*At the time, they were the major biomedical researchers.*'

There was a fair amount of gesturing and raised voices. Whatever they were talking about, it was loud and open to debate. Ann Kelly appeared to be making notes.

Madeleine English, crisp and blonde and very efficient, came out of a side passageway with a tall man. He was a looker. Big, red hair, dark eyes, and a faintly lascivious smile. Probably a few years younger than she was. *'That's Kile Anderson,'* said Jacob. *'He's a journalist. Assigned to Skydeck. It's how he met her.'*

'This was her boyfriend?'

'One of them.'

Boland looked up, straight across the terminal at me, almost as if he knew I was there. He had classic features, with dark bedroom eyes. One of the women with him looked familiar. *'Jessica Birk,'* said Jacob. She'd later become a senator.

Birk eventually detached herself and wandered through the boarding area, taking a couple of minutes with each of the passengers, giving the journalists a clear shot whenever possible, shaking hands with all. *Good luck. Enjoy the flight. Wish I were going with you.*

Maddy disappeared with her male friend up the tunnel leading to the ship. Moments later he came back down alone, looking forlorn. He surveyed the people around him, shrugged, and walked off.

Klassner, assisted by Taliaferro, got to his feet and started for the ramp. Several of the onlookers crowded around to shake his hand. I could read their lips. *Good luck, Professor.*

Klassner smiled politely, and said something.

Nancy White joined them and gave him her arm to lean on. Taliaferro answered a call on his link. He nodded, said something, nodded again. Looked at White. Sure, she told him, go ahead.

He looked apologetic. I could make out *Something came up. Have to go. Sorry.*

He made a quick round of the other voyagers, wished them luck, then was pushing through the crowd. Within moments he'd disappeared down the concourse.

There was an announcement that the *Polaris* would be departing in ten minutes, please board, and everyone began moving toward the ramp, saying their good-byes, waving for the cameras. A journalist cornered Boland, asked a couple of quick questions, *What do you expect to see out there?*, and *As a psychiatrist, will you be more interested in the reactions of the other passengers than you are in the collision itself?* Boland answered as best he could. *I'm on a holiday. You don't get to see something like this very often.*

One last round of farewells, and they drifted into the tunnel, all smiles.

8

The investigation into the circumstances surrounding the loss of the *Polaris* passengers and its captain continues, and we will not rest until we are able to deliver a full and complete explanation. God willing, we will know everything before we are done.

—Hoch Mensurrat,
Spokesman for the Trendel Commission

Rainbow Enterprises does not deal in run-of-the-mill antiquities. We trade almost exclusively in items that can be defined as having historic value. We aren't the only business of our kind in Andiquar, but if you're serious, we're the ones you want to talk to.

A couple of days after Calder let the vest get away, I received a call from Diane Gold. She was furnishing a house that she'd designed. Getting ready to move in with her third husband, I think it was. The house was on top of a hill on the western edge of the city, with a view of Mt. Oskar, and she was trying to establish a Barbikan theme. You know, flashy drapes and carpeting, lots of cushions and throw rugs, and wooden furniture that looks as if it's about to take flight, everything contrasted against period artwork, with its exaggerated sense of the ethereal. I've never cared for the style myself. It seems to me to be pure shock value, but then I have an old-world taste.

Could I put her in touch with somebody who could supply the art? Some figurines, two or three vases, a couple of paintings? She was relaxed in an armchair.

Whenever Diane's image showed up, I felt a surge of envy. I am by no means hard to look at, but she played in a higher league than the rest of us. She was the sort of woman who made you realize how dumb men could be, how easily they could be manipulated. Blond, blue eyes, classic lines. She managed to look simultaneously attainable and beyond reach. Don't ask me how, but you know what I mean.

'Sure,' I said. 'I'll put together a catalog and send it over this afternoon.' In fact, I could have produced the catalog on the spot, but that would leave her with the impression there was no personal input on my part.

'*I appreciate it, Chase,*' she said. Her hair was cut in the San Paulo style, just touching her shoulders. She was wearing a clingy white blouse over dark green slacks.

'I'm happy to help.'

She lifted a cup, drank from it, and smiled at me. '*Chase, you really must come out to the house sometime. We'll be having a party for Bingo at the end of the month. If you could make it then, we'd be delighted to see you.*'

I had no idea who Bingo was, other than that he was not the third husband. He sounded like a pet. 'Thanks, Diane,' I said. 'I'll try to be there.'

'*Good. Plan on staying the weekend.*' When Diane Gold threw a party, it tended to be a marathon event. I was busy and wanted to break away, but you can't just do that with clients. 'What did you decide to do with Maddy's etui?' I asked.

'*I haven't decided where to put it yet. I was going to set it in the dining room, in the china closet, but I'm afraid the kori will knock it over.*' For anyone unfamiliar with Rimway, a kori is a

126

feline, greatly favored by pet owners. Think of it as a cat with the attributes of a collie.

'We don't want that.'

'*No. By the way, I have an odd story to tell you.*'

'I'm all ears.'

'*I won a cash prize last week. Two-fifty.*'

'For what?'

'*That's what makes it odd. They said it was from the Zhadai Cultural Cooperative. For my work on the Bruckmann Tower.*'

'Congratulations.'

'*Thank you. They called, a woman who described herself as the executive assistant, to tell me about it. Her name was Gina Flambeau. She made an appointment, came out to the house, and presented me with the award and the cash.*'

'It's nice to be appreciated, Diane.'

'*Yes, it is. She told me how much they admired my work, not only on the Bruckmann, but some of the other stuff as well.*'

'So what's the problem?'

'*Doesn't that strike you as an odd way to present a trophy? I mean, usually, you get invited to a banquet, or at least a lunch, and they give it to you there. In front of an audience. Everybody gets some publicity out of it.*'

I didn't know. I'd never received an award. At least not since the sixth grade, when I got a certificate for perfect attendance. 'Yes,' I said, 'now that you mention it, it does seem a bit out of the ordinary.'

'*I got curious, so I looked into their award history.*'

'They usually throw banquets?'

'*Invariably, dear.*'

'Well, it looks as if they've changed their policy.' I tried laughing it off and made an inane remark about how banquet food generally tastes insipid anyhow.

'*There's more to it. I called them, Chase, on the pretext of saying thanks to the president of the Cooperative. I met her once, years ago. She, uh, didn't have the faintest idea what I was talking about.*'

'Are you serious?'

'Do I look as if I'm making this up? Moreover, she said there's no Gina Flambeau in the organization.'

'Uh-oh. You check your account?'

'The money's there.'

'Well, I'd say you're ahead on this one.'

'I have a plaque.' She asked her AI to post it for me and it showed up on the wall screen. It was an azure block of plastene. A plate read: *In Recognition of Outstanding Achievement in the Design and Construction of the Bruckmann Tower.* Et cetera. Done in traditional Umbrian characters.

'Looks official.'

'Yes. I showed it to the Cooperative president. That's her signature at the bottom.'

'What was her reaction?'

'She told me she'd get back to me. When she did, she apologized profusely and said somebody was apparently playing a practical joke. They had made no such award. She also told me that in her opinion I deserved to be noticed by the Cooperative, and I should be assured I was under consideration for next year.'

The sunlight angled through the big front windows and made rectangles on the carpet. I didn't know what to make of the story.

'I thought of it,' Diane said, 'because of your question about the etui. Gina Flambeau asked me about it. Said she'd seen I had acquired it, and wondered if I'd show it to her.'

'And did you?'

'Of course. That's the whole point of having it.'

'But she knew you had it? In advance of coming?'

'Yes.'

'How did she know?'

'Everybody knew, love. I gave a couple of interviews. Didn't you see them?'

'No,' I said. 'I must have missed them. What was her reaction?'

Diane shrugged. *'She was suitably impressed, I thought.'* She looked at me carefully.

'Did she actually handle it? Physically?'

'Yes.'

'She didn't do a switch, did she?'

'No. It's the same box.'

'How can you be so sure?'

'It was never out of my sight.'

'You're positive?'

'Absolutely. You think I'm an idiot?'

'You least of all, Diane. But put it somewhere safe.'

'Security's pretty serious here, Chase.'

'Okay. Let me know if anything happens.'

'If anything happens,' she said, *'they'll find bodies in the river.'*

When I mentioned the incident to Alex, he grew thoughtful. 'What was the name of the man who bought the vest from Paul?' he asked.

'That was the Chacun Historical Association.'

'What was the name of the representative?'

After a moment's thought I came up with it. 'Davis.'

'Call them. Find out whether there's a Davis on the membership list.'

'Why?' I said. 'What do we care?'

'Just do it, please, Chase.'

He wandered out of the room to tend the flowers in back. Alex was a botanist by inclination, and he had a wide array of hydrangeas and damned if I knew what else. I've never been big on greenhouses.

I called Chacun and got the AI. *'Why, yes, Ms Kolpath,'* he said. *'You're probably referring to Arky Davis.'* The voice was male, a measured baritone, the sort of voice you hear in drawing rooms out on the Point.

'Can you give me a code for him?'

'I'm sorry. But Association policy prohibits our giving out that kind of information. If you like, I can forward a message.'

'Please. Give him my name and code. Tell him I'd like very much to see the vest he just bought from Paul Calder. I'm hoping he intends to make it available for inspection by the general public. If so, I'd appreciate being informed.'

Davis didn't reply until late in the afternoon. *'I have to confess, Ms Kolpath,'* he said, *'that I'm not sure what we're talking about.'* His voice had a gritty quality.

He was seated in an armchair in a dark-paneled study. I could see drapes behind him and a couple of talba heads on the wall. A hunter. He was wide, with a large nose and a thick gray mustache. He wore a dressing gown (even though it was midmorning), and was sipping a purple-colored drink. *'I think there may be some confusion here somewhere,'* he continued. He was about eighty, and he looked *big*. It's always hard to tell a person's size when all you have to work with are virtuals. If you're comparing him to, say, custom-made furniture, you don't know where to start. But the way Davis straightened up in the chair, the way he shifted his weight, his whole demeanor told me he was not someone you'd think of as small. How had Paul described Davis? *A little guy*.

'I may have the wrong person,' I said. 'I was looking for the Mr Davis who bought a rare vest a couple of days ago from Paul Calder.'

He took a long pull at his drink. *'You're right. It wasn't me. I don't know a Paul Calder. And I sure as hell didn't buy a vest from anybody.'*

'He was at the last meeting of the Chacun Historical Association. Had the vest with him, I believe.'

Davis shrugged. *'I wasn't at the last meeting.'*

He was about to cut the link when I held up my hand. 'Is there anybody else in the organization named *Davis*?'

'No,' he said. *'We have thirty, maybe thirty-five members. But no other Davises.'*

'Something's going on,' said Alex. 'Get in touch with everybody who got one of the *Polaris* artifacts. Warn them to be careful.

130

And ask them to notify us if anybody they don't know shows undue interest.'

'You think somebody's trying to steal them?'

We were on the back deck, adjacent to the greenhouse. He'd been watching a couple of birds fluttering around in the fountain. 'I honestly don't know. But that's what it feels like, doesn't it?'

I dutifully talked with everyone. 'We don't know for sure that something out of the way is happening,' I told them. 'But take precautions to safeguard your artifact. And please keep us informed.'

Alex stuck his head in the door between calls. 'Got a question for you,' he said. 'The *Polaris* was a special trip to a special event. Every scientific figure on Rimway wanted to go. Yes?'

'That's the way I understand it, yes.'

'Why were there only seven people on board? The *Polaris* had accommodations for eight.'

I hadn't noticed. But he was right. Four compartments on either side of the passageway. 'Don't know,' I said.

He nodded, as if that was the answer he expected. Then he was gone again.

I had a few other duties to attend to, and they took me well into the afternoon. When I'd finished I had Jacob pull up the contemporary media accounts of the *Polaris* story. At the time, of course, it had been huge news. It dominated public life for months. The entire Confederacy was drawn into the search, largely because of a suspicion there was something hostile beyond known space. Entire fleets came from Toxicon, Dellaconda, the Spinners, Cormoral, Earth. Even the Mutes sent a contingent.

The general assumption seemed to be that Maddy and her passengers had been seized by *something*. No other plausible theory could be produced. And that meant that a force with extensive capabilities existed somewhere out there. And that it had aggressive inclinations.

For more than a year, the fleets spread out through the Veiled Lady, across thousands of star systems, looking for something, *anything*, that might provide a clue. For trying to help, the Mutes got attacked regularly by commentators and politicians. They were a silent species, endowed with telepathic abilities. That fact made a lot of people nervous, and, of course, they didn't look much like us. So they were accused of spying. As if they could get any useful information about Confederate defenses by going to Delta Karpis.

To a casual reader it sounds like a thorough search, but the reality is that the volume of space involved was so large that it couldn't be adequately examined in a year's time with the resources available. In fact, they wouldn't have come anywhere close. Meanwhile, the hunt cost money, and gradually the public lost interest. In the end, the seven victims were simply written off and declared dead.

For as long as anyone could remember, people had thought of the wilderness beyond the known systems as human territory by implied right, by default, to be claimed when we got around to it. Even the discovery of the Mutes, and the on-again off-again conflict with them, hadn't altered that. But the *Polaris* incident made the outer darkness really *dark*. We were reminded that we didn't know what was out there. And, in Ali ben-Kasha's memorable phrase, we suddenly wondered whether we might be on somebody's menu.

All that has long since gone away. There were no subsequent disappearances, no encounters with the suspect *alien wind* by the research ships that continued to push deeper into the unknown, no indication of a dark genie. And people forgot.

Alex came inside, sat down beside me, and watched the reports as Jacob posted them. 'All that effort,' he said. 'And they never found anything.'

'Not a hair.'

'Incredible.' He leaned forward, frowning. 'Chase, they examined the *Polaris* when it came back. And they didn't see anything unusual. If something hostile wanted to get into the ship, the captain or the passengers had to *let* it in, right? I mean, can you get through an airlock if the people inside don't want you to?'

'Well,' I said, 'you can't really lock the outer hatches. If someone, or some*thing*, gets to the hull, he can let himself in. Although you could stop that easily enough if you wanted to.'

'How?'

'One way is to pressurize the airlock. Then the outer hatch won't open no matter what.'

'Okay.'

'Another way would be to accelerate. Or slam on the brakes. Either way, the intruder goes downtown.'

'So for something to get in, the people inside *had* to cooperate, right?'

'Or at least not take action against it.'

He sat for several minutes without saying anything. Jacob was running a report from the team that had investigated the interior of the *Polaris* after it had been returned to Skydeck. *No indication occupants were at any time in distress.*

No sign of a struggle.

No evidence of hurried departure.

Clothes, toiletries, and other items present suggest that when personnel departed, they took with them only what they were wearing.

Open copy of Lost Souls *in one of the compartments and half-eaten apple in the common room imply ship was taken completely by surprise. Book is believed to have belonged to Boland. Towel found in the washroom had Klassner's DNA.*

'I wonder who directed the search,' he said.

'Survey did.'

'I mean, *at* Survey.'

'*Jess Taliaferro*,' said Jacob.

Alex folded his hands and seemed lost in thought. 'The same guy who disappeared himself.'

'Yes. That *is* an odd coincidence, isn't it?'

'They never found him either.'

'No. He left his office one day, and nobody ever saw him again.'

'When?' he asked.

133

'Two and a half years after the *Polaris*.'

'What do you think happened to him, Chase?'

'I have no idea. Probably a suicide.'

Alex considered the possibility. 'If that *is* what happened, would it have been connected with the *Polaris*?'

'I wouldn't be surprised. The common wisdom is that Taliaferro was distraught by the disaster. He dreamed up the idea to send a group of VIPs out to watch the event, to accompany the research ships. He knew Boland and Klassner personally. They were both past chairs of the White Clock. Of which he was a contributor and fund-raiser.'

'The old population-control group,' said Alex.

'Yes.' I told Jacob to shut down. He complied, the curtains opened, and bright, dazzling sunlight broke into the room. 'When the search found nothing, according to Taliaferro's colleagues at Survey, he got depressed.' I could see it happening easily enough, the idealistic bureaucrat who had lost a ship's captain and six of the most celebrated people of the age and couldn't even explain what had happened to them. 'I've been reading about him. After the *Polaris*, he used to go to Carimba Canyon sometimes and just stand out there and watch the sun go down.'

Alex's eyes had become hooded. 'He might have jumped into the Melony. Been carried out to sea.'

'It could have happened that way.'

'But there wasn't a suicide note?'

'No. Nothing like that.'

'Chase,' he said, 'I wonder if I could persuade you to do me a favor?'

Georg Kloski had been with the team of analysts that went over the *Polaris* when it was brought back. He had to be older than he looked. He could have passed for a guy in his midforties, but he was at least twice that age. 'I work out,' he said, when I commented on his appearance.

He was about medium size and build, affable, happily retired on Guillermo Island in the Gulf. I introduced myself, told him I was collecting information for a research project, which was true enough, and asked whether I could take him to lunch. It's always more convenient, of course, to ask questions over the circuit. But you can get a lot more out of people if you treat for tea and a steak sandwich.

He said yes, of course, he'd never decline lunch with a beautiful woman. I knew right away I was going to like this guy. I flew down next morning and met him at a waterfront restaurant. I think it was called the Pelican. There are, of course, no pelicans on Rimway, but Georg (we got quickly to a first-name basis) told me the owners were from Florida. Did I know where Florida was?

I knew it was on Earth somewhere, so I guessed Europe and he said close enough.

He lived alone. Some of his grandkids were nearby on the mainland. 'But not too close,' he said with a wink. His hair was thick and black, streaked with gray. Broad shoulders, lots of muscle, a helping of flab. Good smile. Every woman in the restaurant seemed to know him. 'I was mayor at one time,' he said, by way of explanation. But we both knew there was more to it than that.

So we sat for the first few minutes, getting acquainted, listening to the shrieks of seabirds. The Pelican was located off a stone walkway that ran along the waterfront. The island has a much balmier climate than Andiquar. Hordes of people in beachwear were strolling past. Kids trailed balloons and some folks rode in motorized coaches. Guillermo was popular because it had real thrill rides, glider chutes, tramways, boat rides, a haunted house. It was a place for people who wanted something a bit more challenging than the virtuals, which induced the same heart-stopping effects, but were always accompanied by the knowledge you were actually sitting in a dark room, perfectly safe. Which some folks thought took the edge off things.

From the Pelican we could see a parachute drop.

'It was a terrible time,' he told me, when I finally steered the conversation around to the *Polaris*. 'People didn't know what to think.'

'What did *you* think?' I asked.

'It was the lander that really threw me. I mean, it would have been easy enough to imagine that they'd all decided to go for a joyride somewhere and gotten lost, or hit by an asteroid. Or something. At least it would have been a theoretical possibility. But the lander was still moored in the launch bay. And that last message—'

'—*Departure imminent*—'

'—*Imminent*. It still sends a chill down my back. Whatever happened, happened very fast. Happened within the few seconds between the time she sent the message and the moment she'd have initiated the jump. It's as if something seized them, shut them down, cut off their comms, and took the people off.'

The sandwiches arrived. I tried mine, chewed on it for a minute, and asked whether he had any ideas at all how it could have happened, other than superior technology.

'Look, Chase,' he said, 'it has to be something out there way ahead of us. I mean, on their own, it wouldn't even have been physically possible for them to leave the immediate area of the ship. Not without the lander. Maddy had four pressure suits on board. They were still there when the *Peronovski* arrived on the scene.'

There was a tourist artist out on the walkway, sketching a young woman. She wore a wide-brimmed straw hat and smiled prettily for him. 'Georg,' I said, 'is it possible there could have been some kind of virus or disease that drove everyone insane?'

Two young women in see-through suits strolled past. Followed by a couple of guys. 'Shocking what people wear these days,' he said with a smile. His eyes never left the women until they disappeared past the window. 'Anything's possible, I suppose. But even had something like that happened, had they been rendered incompetent by a bug of some sort that subsequently became undetectable to the cleanup crew, so what? It still doesn't explain how they got off the ship.'

The tea was good. I listened to the roar of the surf. It was solid and real and reassuring.

'No,' he continued. 'The suits were still there. If they went out one of the airlocks, they were either already dead, or they died a few seconds later. You ever been on a ship, Chase?'

'Occasionally.'

'The outer hatch won't move until the air pressure in the airlock goes to zero. Anybody trying to leave who doesn't have a suit is going to be in pretty bad shape before the door even opens. But let's say he holds his breath and doesn't mind that things get a little brisk. He jumps out. It's a good jump. Say, a meter a second. The *Peronovski* gets there six days later. How far away is the jumper?'

'Not very far,' I said.

He pulled a napkin over, produced a pen, and started scribbling. When he'd finished he looked up. 'I make it at most five hundred eighteen kilometers. Round it off to six hundred.' He tossed the pen down and looked at me. 'That's easily within the search range of the *Peronovski's* sensors.'

'Did they do a search?'

'Sure. They got zero.' He sighed, and I wondered how many times he'd thought about this during the past sixty years, whether he'd ever been free of it for a full day. 'If I hadn't lived through it, I'd say that what happened to the *Polaris* wasn't possible.' He ordered a lime kolat and sat staring at the window until it came.

'When they brought the ship back,' I said, 'did you find anything you hadn't expected to? Anything out of the ordinary?'

'No. Nothing. Their clothes were all there. Toothbrushes. Shoes. I mean, what it looked like was that they'd all stepped out for a minute.' He leaned over the table. His eyes were dark brown, and they got very intense. 'I'll tell you, Chase. This was all a long time ago, but it still scares me. It's the only really spooky thing I've seen in my life. But it makes me wonder if sometimes the laws of physics just don't apply.'

Georg looked like a guy who ordinarily enjoyed his food. But he only nibbled at his sandwich. 'We spent weeks inside the ship. We pretty much stripped it. Took everything out and labeled it and sent it to the lab. The lab didn't find anything that advanced the investigation. Eventually, they put the stuff in a vault somewhere. Later the Trendel Commission came in and sorted through it. I was there for that, too.'

'Don't take this the wrong way, but how thorough were you?'

'I was only a tech. Fresh out of school. But I thought we were reasonably thorough. The commission brought in outside people so nobody could claim cover-up. I knew one of the investigators they brought in. Amanda Deliberté. Died early. In childbirth. You believe that? She's the only case of a childbirth fatality we've had during the last half century. Anyhow, Amanda wasn't given to screwing around. But they didn't find anything more than we did. I'll tell you, Chase, there was nothing there. Whatever happened to those people, it happened fast. I mean, it had to, right? Maddy didn't even have time to get off a Code White. Not a blip. People talk about some sort of alien whatzis, but how the hell could they get through the airlock before she'd sent off an alert?' He tried the drink and looked at me across the top of the glass. 'I've never been able to come up with any kind of explanation. They were just *gone,* and we didn't have any idea, any at all, what had happened to them.'

I watched a couple of people seated against the wall trying to mollify a cranky kid. 'Your team took everything out of the *Polaris,* right?'

'Yes.'

'*Everything?*'

'Well, we left the fittings.'

'How about clothes? Jewelry? Books? Anything like that get left behind?'

'Yeah. I'm sure we left some stuff. We were looking for things that would have thrown some light on what happened. Look, Chase, it's been a long time. But we wouldn't have left anything of consequence.'

9

The disappearance of Jess Taliaferro embodied more than simply the loss of a supremely competent administrator. It would perhaps be an exaggeration to describe him as a great man. But he was the sort of person who works behind the scenes to make great men (and women) possible. We tend to overlook him, because he never aspired to political office. He never won a major award. He did not show up on the newscasts, save as the spokesman for a befuddled Survey when seven people walked off the *Polaris* into oblivion. But he was an inspiration and a bulwark to all of us who wanted to provide a better life and a brighter future for everyone.

—Yan Quo,
Taliaferro: The Gentle Warrior

Alex told me to take the next day off to compensate for the travel, but I went in anyhow that afternoon. When I got there, he was looking at screens filled with information about Jess Taliaferro.

The onetime director is the subject of three major biographies. He has appeared at least tangentially in dozens of histories of his era. I'd thumbed through much of the material by then. It was not that he was a towering political or scientific figure, or that the

Department of Planetary Survey and Astronomical Research broke new boundaries during his thirteen-year tenure at its helm. But he seemed to know all the groundbreakers of the era. He was constantly in the company of councillors and presidents, major show business personalities, Galaxy prizewinners, and other newsmakers. But more important from my point of view was that he seemed to be a man of iron principle. He was a champion of humane causes. Take care of the environment. Arrange things so nobody gets too much power. Make sure we educate, rather than indoctrinate, our kids. Find a way to establish a permanent peace with the Mutes.

He was unstinting in his exertions, and he never backed away from a fight. He supported efforts to reduce government corruption, to achieve stable populations on the worlds of the Confederacy, to reduce the power of the media, to control corporate thieves. He battled developers who were willing to destroy archeological sites and pristine wilderness. He did what he could to protect species in danger of extinction.

He, Boland, and Klassner were close allies in these culture wars. 'People never appreciated him,' one biographer observed, 'until he closed up his office that last evening, said good night to his staff, and walked away from the world.'

In those days, Survey was located in Union Hall, an old stone building that had once been a courthouse. When Taliaferro was ready to go home, his skimmer routinely picked him up at the rooftop pad. But on that final day, he instructed his AI that he would be dining out and that he'd call for transportation if and when he needed it.

With whom was he planning to eat?

'*Nobody knows,*' said Jacob. '*When investigators tried to figure out what had happened, they discovered he'd pretty much cleaned out his bank accounts, except for a modest sum that eventually went to his daughter, Mary. His only child, by the way.*'

'What about his wife?'

'*He was widowed. She died young. Boating accident. According to friends, he never stopped mourning her. But there was another woman later in his life.*'

'Who was that?' asked Alex.

'*Ivy Cumming. She was a physician.*'

'How much money did he have?'

'*Millions.*'

That surprised Alex. 'Where'd it come from?' he asked.

'It was old money,' I said. 'His family'd been wealthy for generations. When its resources came under his control he began using it to support various causes. He seems to have been utterly unselfish.'

I had dinner with a friend, went home, and decided to take a whack at the Taliaferro avatar. I'd seen it briefly at the *Polaris* convention, of course, when I didn't even know who he was. Now I had a few questions.

There's always a problem, of course, with an avatar. It looks like the person it's representing, but you know it's really just a projection backed by a data retrieval system. People trust data retrieval systems, though, and the avatars look absolutely real. They're convincing, so everyone has a tendency to take these things at their word, when in fact all the information is based on the input provided by the subject himself, which is to say it's somebody putting his best foot forward. And there might be additions by interested persons with agendas of their own. Consequently, they're no more reliable than the subject himself might have been. If you're approaching one of these conversations to learn something rather than to be entertained, you have to bring along a healthy skepticism.

Jess Taliaferro appeared standing on a rocky beach. He was a small man, middle-aged, with fading auburn hair that would not stay down and eyes that seemed a bit too far apart. He had too much stomach and not enough shoulder. When he moved, as he did constantly during our conversation, he was awkward, weaving from side to side in a flatfooted manner. There was much of the camaroo about him, the big southeastern bird that one finds waddling along shorelines looking for stranded sealife. He was quite ordinary in appearance. I would not have thought of him as a driving force. But there you are. You just never know.

'Hello, Ms Kolpath,' he said. '*You were at the convention, I believe.*'

'Yes, I was. I enjoyed your presentation.'

'*Very kind of you.*' He stopped by a stone bench, facing out to sea. It seemed to be the only structure in the area. '*May I?*' he asked.

'Please,' I said.

He sat down. '*It's lovely here at night.*' He was dressed in the antique manner of his era, colorful shirt, wide-open collar, cuffed trousers, a rakish blue hat with a tassel.

'Yes,' I said.

'*How may I help you?*'

How, indeed? A long wave broke and rolled up the beach. 'Dr Taliaferro, please tell me about yourself. What you care about. What you're proud of. How you felt on the day the *Polaris* set out. What you think happened.'

'*About myself?*' He looked surprised.

'Yes,' I said. 'Please.'

'*Most people want to hear about the* Polaris. *Not about me.*'

'You know why.'

'*Sure. But it's as if I never did anything in my life except send those people to Delta Kay.*'

He talked about his family, his dreams, his years of service to Survey.

'Did you ever have any indication at all,' I asked, 'that there might be somebody else out there, other than the Mutes?'

His eyes slid shut. '*No,*' he said. '*Oh, look, we knew there would be other sentient life somewhere. We've always known that. The universe is just too big. It happened twice that we knew about, so we understood that it necessarily existed elsewhere. Once you had that much, once you knew it wasn't the result of some virtually impossible combination of events, then there had*' *to be others. Had to be. The real question was whether they were scattered so far in time and space that we would never encounter another in the lifetime of the species.'*

There were lights moving at sea.

'An intersection seemed so unlikely that we never seriously considered it. I mean, we had a policy in place, guidelines on what to do if anyone actually saw another ship out there. But we never believed it would happen. And we certainly assumed that if it did, the aliens would not be hostile. Cautious, perhaps, but not hostile.'

'Why not? The Mutes are hostile.'

'They're hostile because there was a series of incidents at the beginning, when we first discovered each other, that created conflict. It was mishandled on our end, and to a degree, on theirs. I don't know. Maybe it wasn't anybody's fault. People were surprised by an unprecedented situation and they reacted badly. Some of it's in the genes. We can't stand to be near them. Have you ever been close enough to a Mute to feel the effect?'

He wasn't simply talking about their mind-reading abilities, but the fact that they touched something revolting deep in the bone. It was hard to say why; they were humanoid. But people reacted to them the way they did to large spiders, or snakes. Add to that the knowledge that, in their presence, your brain lay open to the sunlight. That you had to struggle not to think of anything that would embarrass you. That the creature knew more about you than you did because all the walls were down, all the rationalizations and pretensions set aside. They knew, for example, precisely how we reacted to them. It made diplomacy difficult.

'No, I've never seen one.' There weren't many of them running around inside the Confederacy. They didn't like us very much either. 'Are you sure they weren't involved?' I asked.

'We looked into it. You know, of course, they'd have to come through the Confederacy to get to Delta Karpis. Or go exceedingly far out of their way.'

'Is that the only reason?'

143

'Not at all. Things had been quiet between them and us for a long time when the Polaris happened.' He rubbed the back of his neck and looked up at the moon. It wasn't Rimway's moon. Too big, and hazy with atmosphere. In fact, it had oceans. 'We couldn't see any motive they'd have to kidnap the people on the Polaris. Certainly none worth risking war over. We talked to some of them. I personally talked with a representative.' He made a face at the memory and tried to shake it off. 'He said they had nothing to do with it. I believed him. And I've seen no reason to change my mind.'

'Why would you take his word? There don't seem to be any other likely suspects.'

'Because whatever else you want to say about them, Chase, they are notoriously poor liars.'

'Okay.'

'Furthermore, I couldn't see how they could have accomplished it. They couldn't have approached the Polaris without being seen. Had that happened, Maddy would surely have sounded the alarm. We'd have known.'

'Afterward,' I said, 'you mobilized everything you had to look for them.'

'Yes. In fact, a sizable portion of the Confederate navy went out and conducted the search. And, although we didn't encourage anybody, at least not officially, a lot of corporate and even some private vessels helped. The hunt went on for more than a year.'

'I assumed there'd been a campaign to get everyone involved.'

'We didn't need a campaign. You don't know what it was like at the time. People were scared. We thought something new had shown up. Something with hostile intentions and advanced technology. Something completely different. It was almost as if we'd discovered a supernatural entity. It was so bad there was even talk of an alliance with the Mutes. So a lot of corporate types sent their ships out. Became part of the effort.' He moved some sand around with his feet. He was wearing sandals. 'It generated good publicity for them. For the corporations.'

'And never a sign of anything at all out of the ordinary?'

'That's correct. We never found anything.'

One of the vents came on and delivered cool air into the room. We sat quietly, listening to it. It was reassuring, evidence that basic physical law still ruled. 'Dr Taliaferro,' I said, 'do you have a theory? What do you think happened to them?'

He considered it. *'I think they were taken,'* he said finally. *'By whom, or for what purpose, I don't know.'*

His bench was placed just beyond the reach of the incoming tide. We watched a wave play out and sink into the sand. 'Why was there an empty compartment on the *Polaris*?'

'You mean, why were there only six passengers instead of seven?'

'That's the same question. But, yes.'

'That's easy to explain. The eighth compartment was reserved for me. I'd intended to go.'

'For you?' He nodded.

'You were fortunate. Why did you change your mind?'

'Something happened at the office. I just don't know what it was. I was never informed. I, the avatar. Whatever it was, it was serious enough that I felt constrained to cancel out of the flight.'

'It was at the last minute.'

'Yes. We were literally boarding the Polaris.'

I pressed for an explanation, but he insisted he had none. Whatever it had been, Taliaferro had kept it to himself. And I recalled seeing the director leaving early at the Skydeck launch. 'Dr Taliaferro, how about your disappearance? Why would you have walked off the way you did?' I should mention that it was a rhetorical question. No answer would be forthcoming. *This* Taliaferro was a construct of what was known of the man. It was, in effect, only his public persona. I wasn't disappointed.

'It is strange, isn't it?'

'Yes. What do you think?' Might as well push the point. I'd heard the question asked at the convention, and he'd offered no explanation. But the atmosphere was better on that beach, alone and in casual surroundings as opposed to the clamor in the meeting room.

'I have to think I met with foul play. There were people who would have liked to see me dead.'

'For example?'

'Barcroft. Tulami. Yin-Kao. Charlie Middleton, for God's sake. They're too numerous to name, Chase. But it's all in the record. Easy enough for you to find, if you're really interested. I stepped on a lot of toes in my time.'

'Any who might have been willing to take your life?'

He thought about it. *'No,'* he said. *'I wouldn't have thought so. But it appears someone did me in.'*

'When you were at the convention, you mentioned that you'd cleared off your desk that last day. You said that was uncharacteristic.'

'Did I say that?'

'Yes, you did.'

'I may have exaggerated. For effect. I mean, you appear at a convention, there's always a little show business involved, right?'

'And you removed everything that was in your accounts.'

'Yes. Well, that does sound as if I was thinking about leaving.'

'Any chance you might have committed suicide?'

'I had everything to live for. A good career. I was still relatively young. Only in my sixties. In good health. I was in a position to help a number of causes that needed assistance.'

'Which causes?'

'At the time, I was active in efforts to improve public education. And I was helping the Kern Group raise money.' The Kern Group was a nonprofit organization that sent volunteers and supplies to places like Talios, where famine was common. (Talios, of course, was not on Rimway. Not many people ever miss a meal on Rimway.) *'And I'd recently met a woman.'*

Ivy Cumming. After Taliaferro's disappearance Ivy waited a few years before giving up and marrying an academic. She eventually gave birth to two children, and was herself still alive.

'No,' he said. '*I was ambushed. I understand how it looks, about the bank accounts. But I still don't think I'd have gone voluntarily.*'

I'd dropped by Windy's apartment shortly after the bombing to see how she was doing. By then she was on her way to recovery. The day after I talked with Taliaferro's avatar, Alex announced he thought it incumbent on him to pay a visit.

'Why?'

'Because,' he said, 'I want to reassure myself she's okay.'

'She's fine.'

'I should let her see I'm concerned.'

'We sent her flowers. I stopped by. I can't see there's much point. But if you really want to—'

'Civic obligation,' he said. 'It's the least I can do.'

So we went. She was almost completely recovered by then, and the only trace of the injury was a blue cane left in a corner of the office. From her window, had she been so minded, she could have watched construction bots clearing off the last of the debris of what had been Proctor Union.

We'd brought candy, which Alex presented with a flourish. He could be a charmer when he wanted. She was receptive, and you would have thought they were the best of friends. There was no sign of the annoyance I'd seen over our refusal to return the artifacts.

We talked trivia for a few minutes. Windy had gone back to playing squabble, which required good legs. And gradually we worked around to our real reason for coming. Alex segued into it by mentioning that he'd just finished Edward Hunt's *Riptides*, a history of the various social movements of the last century. An entire chapter was dedicated to Taliaferro. 'Did you know,' he asked innocently, 'that he was supposed to be on the *Polaris*?'

'Oh, yes,' she said. 'That's right. If you look at the pre-op passenger manifest, you'll see his name.'

'What happened?'

147

'Some last-minute thing. I don't know.'

'The last minute—'

'They were loading up and getting ready to leave.'

'And you have no idea at all why he backed out?'

'No. The story was that he got a call, some sort of problem at the office. But I don't know the source. And you won't find it recorded anywhere.'

'Were there any problems at Survey at the time? Something so serious that he'd have canceled out?'

She shook her head. 'There's nothing on the logs for that date. There *were* calls to Skydeck during the departure, but nothing official. It was all just to wish everyone good luck.'

'Maybe it was personal,' I said.

'He told Mendoza it was a call from the office.' She was bored with the subject. 'Of course, it could have been personal. Could have been something they were just relaying. Does it matter?'

'Do we know,' Alex persisted, 'whether he returned to the Survey offices that day?'

'The day the *Polaris* left? I really have no idea, Alex.' She tried to look as if her head was beginning to hurt. 'Look,' she said, 'we have no record of the call. And it was all a long time ago.'

I asked Jacob what we had on Chek Boland.

Boland's specialty was the mind-body problem, and his tack had been that we'd always been deceived by the notion of duality, of body and soul, of the mind as an incorporeal entity distinct from the brain. Despite thousands of years of evidence to the contrary, people still clung to the old notion.

Boland had done the breakthrough work, mapping the brain, showing why its more abstract functions were holographic rather than embedded in a specific location. Why they were part and parcel of the way a brain was supposed to function.

Boland had been the youngest of Maddy's passengers. He had dark eyes and looked like one of those guys who spent two or three hours at the gym every day. I watched him in the visual

148

record, watched interviews, presentations at luncheons, watched him accept awards. The Penbrook. The Bennington. The Kamal. He was self-deprecating, easygoing, inclined to give credit to his colleagues. It appeared that everybody liked him.

Despite his accomplishments, he seems to be best known as the onetime mind-wipe expert, who worked with law enforcement agencies for thirteen years to correct, as they put it, persons inclined to habitual or violent criminal behavior.

Eventually, he resigned, and later he became an opponent of the technique. I found a record of his addressing a judicial association about a year after he'd terminated his own law enforcement career. *'It's akin to murder,'* he said. *'We destroy the extant personality and replace it with another, created by the practitioner. We implant false memories. And no part of the original person survives. None. He is as dead as if we'd pushed him out of an airlock.'*

But he'd spent thirteen years performing the procedure. If that was the way he felt, why did he not resign sooner?

'I thought it was useful work,' he said in an interview. *'It was satisfying, because I felt I was removing someone's felonious characteristics and replacing them with inclinations that would make him, and everyone who had to deal with him, happier. I was taking a criminal off the streets and returning a decent, law-abiding citizen. It was painless. We reassured the victim that everything would be fine, and he would be back out in the world again by dinnertime. That was what I told them. Out by dinnertime. And then, God help me, I took their lives.*

'I can't answer the question why I was so slow to accept the reality of what I was doing. If there is a judgment, I hope I'll be dealt with in a more lenient manner than I have dealt with others. I can only say now that I urge you to consider legislation banning this barbaric practice.'

10

She crash-landed among the classics, and never fully recovered.

—Bake Agundo,
Surfing with Homer

A day or two after I'd looked through Boland's background, we took several clients to dinner. When it was over, and they'd left, Alex and I stayed for a nightcap at the Top of the World. We were just finishing when I got a call from Marcia Cable. *'Chase, you told me to get in touch if anything unusual happened about Maddy's blouse?'*

We were sitting looking out over the vast tableau that Andiquar presents at night, the sky teeming with traffic, the two rivers filled with lights, the city aglow. 'Yes,' I said, not quite focused yet. 'What's going on?'

'There was a guy just left here who came to look at it. It was the damnedest thing.'

'How do you mean?' I asked. Alex signaled for me to turn up the volume so he could hear.

'He told me he wanted to buy it. Offered a barrel of money. Damned near three times what I paid for it.'

'And—?'

'I'm not sure whether I'd have sold it or not. I'll be honest, Chase. I was tempted. But after he looked at it he changed his mind.'

Marcia came from money. She'd gone to the best schools, married more money, was a skilled equestrienne, and specialized in taking over failing companies and turning them around. She had red hair, dark eyes, and a low tolerance for opposing opinions.

'He withdrew the offer?' I said.

'Yes. He said it wasn't quite what he expected and that he'd decided it wouldn't go well with his collection after all. Or words to that effect. Thanked me for my time, turned around, and left.'

Alex said hello and apologized for breaking in. 'Marcia,' he said, 'you say he looked at it. Did he handle it?'

'Yes, Alex. He did.'

'Any chance he could have done a switch?'

'No. After what Chase told me, I never took my eyes off him. My husband was there, too.'

'Okay. Good. What was his name?'

She paused, and I heard the bleep of a secretary. 'Bake Toomy.'

Alex shook his head. The name was not familiar. 'Did you ask how he came to know you had the blouse?'

'I think everybody knew. I told most of my friends, and I was on the Terry MacIlhenny Show with it.'

'That's the one you sent us?' I said. I'd noticed it in the queue, but hadn't really gotten around to watching it.

'Yes.' She was trying to decide whether she should be worried. 'I was wondering if he was trying to pin down where we keep it. Maybe he's going to try to steal it.' I told Alex, out of range of the link, that I hoped we weren't getting people upset for no reason. 'I asked him,' Marcia continued, 'if he knew you, Alex. He said he did.'

'What did he look like?' Alex asked.

'He's a young guy. Not very big. Midtwenties. Auburn hair cut short. Sort of old-fashioned style.'

'Did he leave contact information?'

'No.'

'Okay. Marcia, I have a favor to ask.'

'Sure. Alex, what's this about anyhow?'

'Probably nothing. Just that somebody's showing unusual interest in the *Polaris* artifacts. We don't know what's going on. But if you hear from him again, try to find out where he can be reached and get in touch with us. Right away.'

Young. Not very big. Midtwenties. Auburn hair cut short. Old-fashioned style.

'Maybe he's legitimate,' I said. 'Just wanted to look and changed his mind. No big deal about that.'

A call to Paul Calder confirmed that Davis, the purchaser of Maddy's vest, fit the description of Bake Toomy. It seemed to be the same person.

Marcia lived in Solitaire, on the northern plains. Paul was a local. 'Whoever this guy is,' Alex said, 'he gets around.' He instructed the AI to check the listings in Solitaire for anyone named Toomy. 'Can't be many,' he said. 'The population's only a few thousand.'

'Negative result,' said the AI.

'Try the general area. Anywhere within a six-hundred-klick radius.'

'I have eighteen listings.'

'Anybody named Bake, or any variation like that?'

'Barker.'

'Any others?'

'Barbara. But that's it.'

'What do we have on Barker Toomy?'

'He's a physician. Eighty-eight years old. Attended medical school—'

'That's enough.'

'Not our guy, Alex.'

'No.'

'Bake Toomy might be unlisted.'

'He might. But that would be unusual for a collector. Or a dealer. Check our clients. You won't find any of them who aren't listed.'

'Alex,' I said, 'you think this is the same guy who did the break-in?'

'I don't think it's much of a leap.'

'I wonder if he's connected with the woman who gave the bogus award to Diane?'

'I suspect so. Maybe not directly, but they're after the same thing.'

'Which is—?'

'Ah, my sweet, there you have hold of the issue. Let me ask a question. Why did our intruder find it necessary to open the display case, but not the bookcase?'

I watched a taxi rise past the window and swing out toward the east. 'I have no idea. Why?'

'Because the glass was in the bookcase. And you can't hide anything in a glass.'

'You think somebody hid something in one of the artifacts?'

'I don't think there's any question about it.'

I was trying to digest it. 'Then the thief took the coins and books—'

'—As a diversion.'

'But why not *keep* them? It's not as if they weren't valuable.'

'Maybe he didn't know that,' he said. 'Maybe he doesn't know anything about collectibles.'

'That can't be,' I said. 'This whole thing is about collectibles.'

'I don't think it is. This whole thing is about something else entirely, Chase.'

We sat looking at one another. 'Alex, if there'd been something in the pockets of the jacket, Maddy's jacket, do you think we'd have noticed?'

'Oh, yes,' he said. 'I always inspect the merchandise. I even

154

examined it for the possibility that something had been sewn into it. In any case, we know they didn't find what they wanted at the house, or they wouldn't still be hunting for it.'

My apartment building is a modest place, a privately owned three-story utilitarian structure that's been there a hundred years. It has four units on each floor and an indoor pool that's inevitably deserted in the late evening. We came in over the river and drifted down onto the pad. I heard music coming from somewhere, and a peal of laughter. It seemed out of place. We sat in the soft glow of the instrument lights. 'You looked through the Bible?' he said.

'Yes. There was nothing there.'

'You're sure?'

'Well, I didn't check every page.'

'Call Soon Lee and ask her to look. Let's be certain.'

'Okay.'

'And talk to Ida. She has the jumpsuit, right?'

'Yes.'

'Tell her to look in the pockets. And check the lining. Let us know if she finds anything. Anything at all.'

I opened the door and got out. Something flapped in the trees. Alex joined me. He'd walk me to the door and see that I got safely home. Ever the gentleman. 'So who,' I asked him, 'had access to the artifacts? Somebody at Survey?'

He pulled his jacket around him. It was cold. 'I checked with Windy a day or two after the burglary. She insists they'd been secured since the Trendel Commission, until the vault was opened a few weeks ago and they were inventoried for the auction. That means, whatever they're looking for, it had to have been placed during the period of time between the opening of the vault and the attack. Or during the first months of the investigation, in 1365.'

'There's another possibility,' I said.

He nodded slowly. 'I didn't want to be the first to say it.' Someone on the *Polaris* might have left something.

*　　*　　*

155

Soon Lee called to report there was nothing in the Bible. She said she'd gone through it page by page. There was no insert of any kind, and she could find nothing written on its pages that seemed out of place. Ida assured me there was nothing hidden in the jumpsuit.

The only thing we had in our inventory with a direct connection to any of the *Polaris* victims was a copy of Pernico Hendrick's *Wilderness of Stars*. It had once belonged to Nancy White. I had some time on my hands, so I dug it out and began to page through it. It was a long history, seven hundred-plus pages, of environmental efforts undertaken by various organizations during the sixty years or so preceding publication, which took it back to the beginning of the fourteenth century.

There weren't many notations. White was more inclined to underline sections that caught her interest and draw question or exclamation marks in the margins. *Population is the key to everything*, Hendrick had written. *Unless we learn to control our own fertility, to stabilize growth, all environmental efforts, all attempts to build stable economies, all efforts at eliminating civil discord, all other courses, are futile.* Three exclamation marks. This was the precursor to a long series of citations by the author. Despite advanced technology, people still bred too much. Hardly anybody denied that. The effects were sometimes minimal: There might be too much traffic, not enough landing pads. At other times, states collapsed, famines struck, civil wars broke out, and off-world observers found themselves unable to help. *It doesn't matter how big the fleet is, you can't ship enough food to sustain a billion people.* The book detailed efforts to save endangered species across the hundred worlds of the Confederacy, to preserve the various environments, to husband resources, to slow population growth. It described resistance by government and by corporate and religious groups, the indifference of the general public (which, Hendrick maintains, never recognizes a problem until it's too late). He likened the human race to a cancerous growth, spreading through the Orion Arm, infecting individual worlds. More exclamation marks.

It was hair-raising stuff, and somewhat overheated. The author never settled for a single adjective where two or three could be levered in.

But the book was well thumbed, and it was obvious that Nancy White was more often than not in agreement. She quibbled now and then on factual information and technical points, but she seemed to accept the conclusion: A lot of people died, or were thrust into poverty, and kept there, for no very good reason other than that the species couldn't, or wouldn't, control its urge to procreate.

I showed it to Alex.

'The guy's an alarmist,' he said. 'So is she, apparently.'

I stared at the book, depressed. 'Maybe that's what we need.'

He looked surprised. 'I didn't know you were a Greenie wacko.'

I was on my way home the following day, approaching the junction between the Melony and Narakobo Rivers when Vlad Korinsky called. Vlad owned the *Polaris* mission plaque. Ultimately, I thought it might prove to be the most valuable of the artifacts that survived the explosion. There was no way to know where it had actually been located in the ship, but if Maddy had adhered to tradition, it would have occupied a prominent position on the bridge. Vlad was a traveler and adventurer. He'd been to Hokmir and Morikalla and Jamalupé and a number of other archeological sites on- and off-world. His walls were decorated with pictures showing him standing beside the shattered ruins of half a dozen ancient civilizations. He'd had a little too much sun over the years, and the winds of a dozen worlds had etched their lines into his face.

He was shopping. Refurbishing his den. He'd been looking through our catalog. Was there anything new in the pipeline?

'You called at exactly the right moment, Vlad,' I said. 'It happens that I can put my hands on a comm link from Aruvia. Four thousand years old, but it's in excellent condition. It was lost during the Battle of Ephantes.'

We talked it over, and he told me he'd think about it. I knew his tone, though. He was hooked, but he didn't want to look like an easy sell.

I liked Vlad. We'd been out together a few times, in violation of the general principle that you don't get involved in personal entanglements with clients. Alex knew about it and looked pained whenever Vlad's name came up. But he didn't say anything, relying, I suppose, on my discretion. Or good sense. I hope not on my virtue. *'How are you doing, Chase?'* he asked.

He sounded worried, and I figured out why he'd really called. 'Good,' I said. 'I'm doing fine.'

'Good.' A sprinkle of rain fell across the windscreen. *'You have anything yet on the guy who's trying to steal the artifacts?'*

'I didn't say anyone was trying to *steal* them, Vlad.'

'The implication's clear enough.'

'Actually we're not sure what's happening. We just want you to be careful.'

'Well, I wanted you to know there've been no strangers around here.'

'Good,' I said.

'If I see anybody, I'll let you know.'

It was my night, I guess. When I got home the AI told me that Ida Patrick was on the line.

Ida was the sort of middle-aged, well-educated, precise woman you might find playing orinoco and sipping fruit juice on weekday afternoons down at the club. Nothing roused her indignation quite like improper behavior. For Ida, the world was a clean, well-lighted place, decorum the supreme virtue, and anyone who was uncomfortable with those standards should simply apply elsewhere. Her indignation had soared when I suggested there might be a thief abroad. Nevertheless, she loved intrigue.

'Chase,' she said. *'I've had a call.'* She dropped her voice conspiratorially.

'About the jumpsuit?'

'*Yes.*' She drew out the aspirate.

'From whom?'

'*He said he was an historian. He tells me he's writing a book about the* Polaris, *and wanted to know if he could take a look.*'

'What's his name?'

She consulted a piece of paper. '*Kiernan,*' she said. '*I think the first name was Marcus.*'

Marcus Kiernan. I ran a quick search.

Two Marcus Kiernans came back. One was halfway around the globe; the other was in Tiber, which was twenty klicks west of Andiquar, close to Ida's residence. The local one had written two popular histories, both on famous disasters of the last century. *Palliot* reconstructed the loss of the celebrated airship that went down in 1362, taking with it 165 passengers, including the literary giant Albert Combs; and *Windjammer* traced the disappearance of Baxter Hollin and his show business passengers, who sailed into the Misty Sea in 1374 and vanished without a trace. The second Kiernan was seventy.

'What's he look like, Ida?'

'*Reddish hair. Good-looking. Young.*'

'How tall is he?'

'*I can't tell. I haven't seen him in person. On the circuit he looks about average.*'

'When's he coming?'

'*Tomorrow evening. At seven. He wanted to come tonight, but I told him I was busy.*'

We checked out the other Marcus Kiernan, just to cover our bases. Despite the name, it turned out to be a woman.

We could have simply alerted Fenn. But Alex wanted to see who this individual was and hear what he had to say. 'For the moment,' he told me, 'there might be more to this than Fenn would be prepared to deal with.'

Ida lived alone in a magnificent old-world house outside Margulies, on Spirit Lake, eighty kilometers west of Andiquar. The house had directional windows and a domed roof and a wraparound upper deck. A glass tower guarded the eastern wing. Inside, the furnishings were eclectic. Whatever caught her eye. A modern split-back chair sitting next to an Altesian sofa and a mahogany table. It wasn't the kind of décor I'd have wanted, but in Ida's house it seemed correct.

Alex had arranged to have a replica of the jumpsuit made up, and we brought it with us. He handed it to Ida, who compared it with the original. 'Marvelous,' she said. 'Can't tell one from the other. Do you expect him to try to grab it?'

'No.' Alex sounded reassuring. 'I don't think anything like that will happen. But if he does, don't try to stop him.'

'Is he dangerous?' she asked.

'I'm sure he's not, Ida. Chase will be with you, though, so you'll be safe.' (Yes, indeed!) 'And I'll be right behind the curtains. The thing you should be aware of, though, is that he isn't who he says.'

'Are you sure?'

'Well, let me put it this way: If he's the person we think he is, he uses a different name every time we hear from him.' He suggested she have the AI make a visual recording of the entire conversation.

We had decided that Alex should stay out of sight because of the possibility our visitor would know him. He was a public figure and easily recognizable. So it came down to me, which was probably just as well.

Ida appeared to be having second thoughts. 'What *do* you expect him to do?'

'I think he'll look at the jumpsuit, tell you how much he admires it, and possibly make an offer.'

'If he does, how do I respond?' Her voice suggested she was getting seriously into the spirit of the occasion.

Alex thought it over. 'I'd like you to tell him thanks, but you can't accept it. The jumpsuit isn't for sale.'

'Okay.' We went into the study, opened the glass cabinet in

which she kept Maddy's suit. As at our place, Maddy's stenciled name was prominently displayed. She removed it and inserted the substitute, arranging it as lovingly as if it were the original. 'This is exciting,' she said.

She folded the original carefully and put it inside a chest under a quilt. 'Actually, I'm disappointed you don't think he'll try to grab it and run.'

'I'm sorry,' Alex said. 'Maybe we could persuade him—'

'—In case he tries anything,' she continued, 'I'm equipped with sonosound.'

'Isn't that illegal?' he asked. Her AI could take down an intruder with a directed sonic strike. It had been known to be fatal, and owners had been charged with manslaughter.

'If there's a problem,' she said, 'I'd rather be the one in court answering the charges.'

Marcus Kiernan descended onto the pad promptly at seven in an unpretentious gray Thunderbolt. A three-year-old model. The kids who'd seen our stuff get dropped into the river hadn't gotten a good look at the skimmer because it was dark. But they'd said it was gray.

I watched the cabin hatch open, watched our guy literally bounce out. He looked around at the manicured grounds and the lake, and started up the brick pathway to the house.

Ida and I had returned to the living room and were seated beneath some artwork by a painter I'd never heard of. Alex retreated behind the curtains. The AI, whose name was Henry, announced that Dr Kiernan had arrived. Ida instructed Henry to let him in, the front door opened, and we heard him enter. He traded comments with the AI, then came into the room.

He wasn't as tall as I am. In fact, I'm taller than a lot of guys. But Kiernan didn't reach my ears. He looked clean-cut and law-abiding, someone you could instinctively trust. My first thought was that we'd been wrong about him, that this was not the man we were looking for. But then I remembered how I'd liked the Mazha.

Kiernan reminded me of somebody. I couldn't think who. He had an ingenuous smile and amicable green eyes, set a bit far apart. 'Ms Patrick,' he said, 'good evening. This is a lovely house.'

Ida extended her hand. 'Thank you, Doctor. Chase, this is Dr Kiernan. Doctor, Chase Kolpath, my houseguest.'

He bowed, smiled, and said how pleased he was to meet two such beautiful women at the same time. I reacted about the way you'd expect. And I got an association with the *Polaris* convention. He'd been there, but I still couldn't place him.

We shook hands and sat down. Ida served tea, and Kiernan asked me what I did for a living.

'I pilot superluminals,' I said, deciding that my connection with antiquities would be best left unmentioned.

'Really?' He looked impressed. 'That must mean you've been all over the Confederacy.'

He was smarter than I was. I realized it immediately, but it didn't help. I started rattling off names of ports of call, trying to impress him. And I knew that Alex, listening behind the curtains, would be sneering. But I couldn't help myself. And when he nodded and said, yes, I've been there, some beautiful places, have you seen the Loci Valley, the Great Falls, I began to feel a connection with him.

I wouldn't want you to think I get swept away by every good-looking young male who shows up. But there was something inherently likable about Kiernan. His eyes were warm, he had a great smile, and when anyone spoke to him, he paid strict attention.

'So tell us about the book,' said Ida, who was also impressed, and was making surreptitious signals to me, indicating no, this guy is a sweetheart, he just couldn't be up to any harm.

'The title will be *Polaris*,' he said. 'I've interviewed over a hundred people who were connected with it in one way or another.'

'And do you have a theory as to what happened?' she asked.

He looked nonplussed. 'Everybody has a theory, Ida. Is it okay if I call you Ida?'

'Oh, yes, by all means, Marcus.'

'But what happened out there isn't the thrust of the book.'

'It isn't?' she said.

'No. In fact, what I'm doing is examining the political and social consequences of the event. For example, did you know that spending on armaments during the eight years following the incident increased twelve percent? That formal attendance at religious worship around the globe went up by almost a *quarter* during the next six months? Twenty-five percent of three billion people is a substantial number.'

'It certainly is.'

'The statistics elsewhere in the Confederacy were similar.'

'That doesn't mean,' I said, 'that the *Polaris* had anything to do with it.'

'I don't think there's any question it was a reaction to the *Polaris*, Chase. The public mood changed during that period. You can document it in a lot of ways. People began storing food and survival equipment. There was a surge in the sales of personal weapons of all kinds. As if you could fight off an advanced alien technology with a scrambler.' A smile touched the corners of his lips. But there was something sad about it. 'Even the Mutes were affected, though to a lesser degree. Some aspects of the reaction were only temporary, of course. But even today ships going beyond the bounds of known space frequently take a small armory with them.'

We gabbled on for about half an hour. Finally, Ida apologized that we were taking so much of his time and no doubt he'd like to see the jumpsuit.

'It's a pleasure, ladies,' he said. 'But yes. I would like to take a look, if I may.' We got up and headed for the study. Alex would have to watch the rest of the show on a monitor. He'd be only a room away if needed, but everything seemed under control.

We walked down the long central hallway, Ida in front, Kiernan bringing up the rear. The passageway was lined with original oils, mostly landscapes, and he stopped twice to admire the work and compliment Ida on her taste. He seemed quite knowledgeable, and Ida was clearly struck by him.

Eventually we reached the study, and she told Henry to unlock the display cabinet.

'You keep it *here*,' he said, 'in this room? I assumed you'd have it inside a vault somewhere.' It was a joke, but his tone suggested he was serious. *It's precious. Take care of it. There are unprincipled persons about.*

'Oh, it's perfectly safe, Marcus.' She opened the top of the case and removed the duplicate jumpsuit, lifting it by the shoulders and letting it fall out full length. It was dark blue, the color of the sea at night. The *Polaris* patch was on the left shoulder, and ENGLISH stenciled in white over the right-hand breast pocket.

Kiernan approached it as one might a relic. 'Magnificent,' he said.

Unaccountably, I felt a pang of guilt.

He reached out with his fingertips and touched it. Touched the embroidered name.

ENGLISH.

Maddy. I think, in that moment, I understood why passengers riding the *Sheila Clermo* felt the presence of Mendoza and Urquhart and White and the others. And especially Maddy. Poor tragic Maddy. Nothing worse can happen to a captain than to lose the people who travel with her, who depend on her to bring them safely through whatever obstacle might arise. Ida must have felt it, too. Her eyes were damp.

Kiernan stood as if drawing strength from the garment, and finally he took it in his own hands. 'I can hardly believe it,' he said.

'Marcus,' I asked, 'have you been on board the ship?'

'The *Clermo*? Oh, yes. I've been on it.' His expression changed, became troubled. 'Years ago.'

'Is something wrong?'

'No. I was just thinking that Survey should never have sold it.'

'I agree,' said Ida, with indignation.

'It's of immense historical value.'

I looked at the jumpsuit. And at him. He had to raise it a bit to keep it off the floor. Maddy had also been taller than he was.

We all gazed at it. At the smooth dark blue cloth, at the shoulder patch, at the pockets. Six in all, breast pockets outlined in white trim, back and cargo pockets plain.

'Nothing in them, I suppose?' he said.

'No,' said Ida. 'I should have been so lucky.'

Casually, as if it were an afterthought, he looked. Opened each pocket and peeked in, smiling the whole time, saying how you never know, shaking his head sadly that no scrap of *Polaris* history had drifted forward inside the suit. He had me almost believing it was the original. 'Pity,' he said, when he'd finished. 'But it's enough that we have this.' He refolded the jumpsuit and gave it back. 'Thank you, Ida.' He looked at the time. 'It's gotten late. I really must go. It's been a pleasure to meet you, Ida. And *you*, Chase.'

He started toward the door.

'You've come a long way, Marcus,' said Ida. In fact we weren't at all sure how far he'd come. 'Can I offer you anything before you leave?'

'No,' he said. 'Thank you, but I really must be on my way.'

Bows to both of us, and then we were all walking toward the front door. It opened, and he swung out into the sunset, waved, climbed aboard his skimmer, and rose into the evening sky.

I collected the duplicate jumpsuit, and I was putting it carefully into a plastene bag when Alex charged into the study. 'Let's go,' he said.

'Where?'

'Ida.' He beamed at her. 'You were exquisite.' And, glancing at me, 'Both of you.' We were headed toward the front door. 'Thanks, Ida. I'll get back to you. Let you know what happens.' He took the duplicate jumpsuit and put it under his arm. If nothing else, we had 'Kiernan's' DNA.

We paused in the shelter of the house to watch the skimmer

moving out over the treetops. Gave it a moment to get clear. 'He seems like such a nice young man,' said Ida.

When we thought it was safe to do so, we climbed into our own vehicle. 'What's the plan?' I asked him.

'Let's see if we can find out where he lives.' We lifted off, and Alex opened a link to Ida. 'Probably best, Ida,' he said, 'if you don't mention this to anybody.'

'*Why?*' she asked.

'Just a precaution. Until we find out what it's about.'

'*What do you want me to do if he contacts me again—?*'

'Let us know right away.'

'And keep the doors locked,' I said.

I asked Alex whether he thought she was actually in any kind of danger. 'No,' he said. 'Kiernan got what he wanted—'

'—An opportunity to search the jumpsuit—'

'Exactly. There's no reason for him to come back. But it's just as well to be safe.'

'Your notion that they're looking for something—'

'Yes?'

'—Looks as if it's on target.'

We could see Kiernan in the fading sunlight, headed east toward Andiquar. 'Follow it,' he instructed the AI. We rose above the trees and began to accelerate. He turned in my direction. 'What did you think of him?'

'Actually, he seemed like a nice guy.'

He smiled. 'I'm willing to bet you and Ida were just talking to the man who set the bombs at Proctor Union. Or knows who did.'

I had to run that through a second time. 'What makes you say that?' I asked. 'Why would Kiernan try to kill the *Mazha*?'

'He didn't.'

'I'm sorry, Alex; I'm not following the conversation.'

'What I'm saying is that he took advantage of the Mazha's presence to destroy the collection and make it look like something else.'

That was hard to believe. 'You don't think it was an attempt to take him out?'

'No, I don't. And they got away with it, Chase. The investigators are looking for an assassin. Not a *Polaris* conspirator.'

'But I still don't see—'

'They didn't want anyone to realize what was really happening. They don't want people asking a lot of questions. It was a perfect opportunity. They find out the Mazha's visiting, and nobody is surprised when assassins try to finish him off.'

'That's incredible. But why? If there's something they're trying to find, why destroy everything?'

'Maybe they just want to be sure that whatever's there—' He hesitated.

'—Doesn't fall into somebody else's hands,' I finished.

'Yes. Now think about the bombs again.'

'They turned the artifacts to slag.'

'It's obvious Kiernan doesn't know where to find the thing he's looking for. It might have been in Maddy's jacket. Or in her jumpsuit. Or in her blouse.'

'It's always Maddy,' I said.

'That might be an illusion. Most of the stuff we took from the exhibition belonged to Maddy. So we need to withhold judgment a bit.'

The sky was getting dark. Below us, lights were coming on. 'But what could it be?' I asked.

'I don't know.'

'How'd they find out the Mazha was coming? There must be a leak someplace.'

'I suspect there were leaks in a lot of places. Organizations like Survey aren't used to keeping secrets. That's why he came with a small army of bodyguards.' He jabbed an index finger at Kiernan's aircraft. 'They didn't want to kill anyone, so they called in the bomb threat minutes before it went off.'

'It was a close thing.'

'Yes. Whatever they're looking for, they're willing to risk killing a few people if that's what it takes to find it. Or to make sure no one else does.'

'Hey, that means Tab Whatzis-name is involved.'

'Everson.'

'Yes. Everson.' The guy who'd bought the debris, incinerated it, and launched the ashes toward the sun.

'Are we beginning to see a pattern?'

'But what could be that important?'

He looked at me. 'Think about it, Chase.'

'The *Polaris*. There's something that would tell us what happened.'

'That's my guess.'

'You think somebody wrote a note? Left a message of some sort?'

'Maybe. It may not be that clear-cut. But there's something that somebody's afraid of.'

'It doesn't make sense,' I said. 'Even if there had been some sort of conspiracy, everybody who could have been involved in it is long dead or out of power.'

Kiernan was still headed east. We were gaining on him, trying to get closer without being spotted. 'Let's go to manual, Chase. Move up, but stay in traffic.'

I disabled the AI and activated the yoke. 'We're in legal jeopardy here,' I said. Going to manual wasn't strictly an offense, but God help you if you did it and then got involved in an accident.

'Don't worry about it,' he said.

'Easy for you to say.'

Kiernan's Thunderbolt joined the east-west stream along 79, over the Narakobo. It was the middle of the week; traffic was moderate and moving steadily. 'I still think we should call Fenn,' I said.

'What do they charge him with? Fondling Maddy's jumpsuit?'

'At the very least, they ought to be able to bring some sort of charges against a man who wanders around the countryside gaining entrance to people's homes while using false identities.'

'I'm not sure that's illegal,' he said. 'Anyhow, all it would do is let him know we're onto him. If we want to find out what this is about, we need to give him a chance to show us.'

Ahead, we could see the lights of Andiquar on the horizon. The Thunderbolt rolled into the northeast corridor and headed toward the estuary.

'He's going out to one of the islands,' I said.

The night was alive with moving lights. Aside from the air traffic, some were on the river, others on the walkways. Compared to most Confederate capitals, Andiquar is a horizontal city. There are towers at its four corners, and the Spiegel and Lumen towers downtown, but otherwise the tallest buildings run to about six stories. It's a beautifully designed amalgam of parks and piers, monuments and elevated walkways, fountains and gardens.

It was a cold, still evening, no wind, the moon not yet up. We passed a hot-air balloon.

'Late in the season for that,' said Alex.

Kiernan was staying with the flow, doing nothing to draw attention to himself as he passed over Narakobo Bay and headed out to sea. There are hundreds of islands within an hour's flying time of Andiquar, and in fact they hold almost half the capital's population.

As we drew abreast of the city, we started picking up heavy traffic. 'Let's get a bit closer,' said Alex. Most of the aircraft were running between altitudes of one and two thousand meters. The long-range stuff was higher. I dropped down to about eight hundred and moved in behind the Thunderbolt.

'Good,' said Alex.

I should have realized immediately something was wrong because a sleek yellow Venture that had been down at the same altitude now pulled up behind us.

Alex hadn't noticed. 'He's talking to somebody,' he said.

'You mean there's someone else in the skimmer?'

'No, I don't think so. He's on the circuit.'

The Venture swung to starboard and began to crowd me.

Alex's attention was riveted on the Thunderbolt. 'I'd love to hear what he's saying.'

The hatch on the Venture popped open. That never happens in flight. Not ever. Unless somebody wants a clear shot. 'Heads up, Alex—!'

I swerved to port but it was too late. There was a flash of light, and, in that instant, I felt the downward jolt of normal weight slamming back, and we began to fall.

Alex yelped. 'What are you doing?'

I tried accelerating to provide more lift for the wings. Skimmers, of course, are designed to function with antigrav pods. During operation, the aircraft weigh about eleven percent normal. So it doesn't take much wingspan, or much thrust, to keep them airborne. Consequently, the wings are modest, and the vehicles are slow. You're not going to get past 250 kph with any of them. And that's just not enough to keep you in the air when you're carrying full weight.

We were sinking toward the ocean. I fought the controls but couldn't get any lift. 'Going into the water,' I told him. 'Get ready.'

'What happened?'

'The Venture,' I said. It was accelerating away, pulling out of the traffic as we fell.

A male voice broke in over the circuit: *'You okay in there? We saw what happened.'*

And another, a woman: *'Try to get down. We'll stay with you.'*

I got on the link to the Patrol. 'Code White,' I told them. 'I'm in free fall.' That wasn't quite true, but it was close enough.

The surface looked dark, cold, and hard. 'Hang on,' I said.

We got a voice from the Patrol. *'I see you.'* I love how those guys keep calm when somebody else is falling out of the sky. *'We are en route.'*

I didn't have enough velocity even to get the nose up. 'Try to keep loose,' I told Alex. He managed to laugh. I had to give the guy credit.

Water can be hard. We blasted down, bounced, flipped, turned sideways, and crashed into a wave. The roof tore away. Skimmers are routinely driven by AIs, and they never collide, either with each other or with anything else. Furthermore, the lighter they are, the more efficiently they run. Consequently, they're not built to withstand impact. Even the seat belts are intended only as a precaution against rough weather.

Water poured in on us. I had a glimpse of lights, then we went under. I could feel myself rising against my harness.

I checked what was left of the overhead to make sure we had clear passage to the surface. When I saw that we did, I released my restraints, but held on, and twisted around to see how Alex was making out. At that moment, the power failed, and the lights went off.

He was struggling with his belt. He didn't know where the manual release was. That was no surprise; he'd probably never had to use it before. It was located in the center of the aircraft on the board between the seats. But I had to push his hand out of the way to get at it. It was a bad situation because at that moment he thought he was going down with the skimmer and was fumbling desperately and in no mind to accept help. I literally had to rip his hand clear before I could thumb the release. Then I pushed him up. He went out through the top, and I followed.

The Patrol picked us up within minutes and wanted to know what had happened. I told them. An unknown person in a late-model yellow Venture had taken a shot at us. Apparently she had hit the antigrav pods.

'You say *she*. Did you know who it was?'

'No idea,' I said.

The interviewing officer was a woman. We were seated on the deck of the rescue vehicle. 'Why would she do that?'

'Don't know,' I said. 'No idea.'

'But it *was* a woman?'

'I think so.' Not much help there.

We were both drenched and shivering with the cold and

wrapped in blankets. They gave us coffee. When the Patrol officer allowed us a moment alone, Alex asked whether I'd thought to rescue the duplicate jumpsuit.

'No,' I said. 'I thought you had it.'

He looked at me and sighed.

11

He looks here, he looks there, he looks, by heaven, everywhere. He searches the dark corners and all the shadows,
behind the doors, and down in the cushions.

—Chen Lo Cobb,
'I Put It Here Somewhere,' from *Collectibles*

When Fenn caught up with us, he was indignant. How could we
not have confided in him? We were at the country house the morning
after we got dunked, and the police inspector was on the circuit.
He was parked behind his desk, a glowering angry bulldog, while
I wondered what had become of the light-footed thief he had been
in that earlier life. '*You could have gotten yourselves killed.*'

'We didn't think it was dangerous,' Alex protested.

'*Ah*,' he said. '*You've got someone stealing artifacts, and you
didn't think it would be dangerous.*'

'He wasn't actually *stealing* artifacts.'

'*Why don't you tell me precisely what he* was *doing?*'

So Alex explained. Someone looking at objects salvaged from
the *Polaris*. Searching through them, actually. Changing his name
from place to place. A woman involved too. One Gina Flambeau.
We showed him pictures of Kiernan at Ida's house.

173

'*Is Flambeau the woman who was driving the other vehicle?*'

'Don't know. But she was doing the same thing as Kiernan. Trying to get a look at a *Polaris* artifact. In her case by pretending to give one of our clients a monetary award.

'*Pretending?*'

'Well, the client *did* get the money. But that's not the point.' It all sounded lame. Except that someone had tried to kill us.

Fenn was reluctant to believe the Survey attack was anything other than an assassination attempt. There had, in fact, *been* a plot to kill the Mazha while he was in Andiquar. Members of two independent groups had been arrested. They'd denied everything, and both were telling the truth. To the authorities that simply meant there was a third group. Or a lone rider.

'*There's one thing about it that's strange, though,*' said Fenn. '*The experts tell me these people don't like to use bombs for assassinations. In Korrim Mas they're considered too impersonal.*' His voice dripped sarcasm. '*The correct way to do an assassination is with a knife or gun, up close. Lots of eye contact. Anything else is unsporting.*

'*There are rules.*' He couldn't resist laughing. '*In any case, I'm glad you're both okay. This is what happens when civilians get involved in these things. I hope next time, we can see our way clear to do it by the book.*'

He looked directly at me, as if it were my responsibility to look after Alex.

Alex, without hesitation, said, 'Absolutely.' Something in his voice implied that, had I not been along, he'd have gone to the police forthwith. He even looked over at me as if suggesting that Fenn knew very well how it had happened.

'*Did you get their number?*' the inspector asked.

'We have the Thunderbolt.'

'*But not the Venture?*'

'It happened too fast.'

More disapproval. '*Okay, let's see who the Thunderbolt belongs to.*'

*   *   *

When he got back to us, late that afternoon, he was frowning. *'It was leased,'* he said.

'By whom?' Alex asked.

He was looking at a data card. *'According to this, by* you, *Chase.'*

'Me?'

'That your address?' He showed me the document.

I don't have to tell you it was unsettling that these people knew where I lived. That during the entire conversation at Ida's place, Kiernan had known exactly who I was.

'We talked to the leasing agency. It was picked up three days ago. The description of the lessee fits your boy Kiernan. But he had identification that said he was Chase Kolpath.' He settled back into a frown.

'Maybe,' said Alex, 'you should switch to a gender-specific name. *Lola* would be nice.'

'It's not funny, champ.'

'Anyhow, we're working on it. I'll let you know when we find him.' He took a notebook out of his pocket and studied it. *'It looks as if they used an industrial beamer on you. Took the pods off, and part of the right wing. You're lucky to be here. One of the other drivers saw it all. She didn't get the hull number either. But you were right about the woman driver. Young, apparently. Black hair.'*

'You'll want to check with the leasing agencies,' Alex said.

'Good idea. I'd never have thought of doing that myself.' Alex mumbled an apology, and Fenn continued. *'I don't think it'll take long before we get a handle on this.'*

'Good.'

'You say you got this guy's DNA on a jumpsuit?'

'It went down with the skimmer,' I said.

'Was it bagged? The water's not that deep at the crash site. We can send the diver back down.'

Alex shook his head. 'We didn't seal the bag,' he said.

He was back next morning. *'Good news. We got both fingerprints and DNA off the front door at the Patrick estate. Kiernan's real*

175

name, we think, is Joshua Bellingham. Name mean anything to you?'

Alex glanced at me, and I shook my head no. 'We never heard of him,' he said.

Fenn checked his notebook. *'Bellingham was an administrative officer at ABS, Allied BioSolutions, which manufactures medical supplies. People there say he's a hard worker, good at his job, never in trouble. Nobody knows much about his social life, and he doesn't seem to have a family.*

'He's lived in the area for just under five years. Has no criminal record, at least not as Joshua Bellingham.'

'You say you *think* that's his real name?'

'Well, it's an odd business. Prior to the time he arrived at ABS, Bellingham doesn't seem to have existed. There's no record of his birth. No ID number. We checked the employment application he filled out for the job. The work history is fabricated. They never heard of him at the places he claimed were former employers.'

'So ABS never checked them?'

'No. Employers usually don't bother. Most companies do a personality scan. Tells them if you're really reliable. If you know what you're talking about. They don't need much more than that.'

'Are you going to arrest him?'

'We'd like very much to talk to him. So far, we don't know that he's broken any laws. But, for the moment, he's missing. Hasn't reported for work since the day you saw him. Hasn't called in.'

'He's not at home, either?'

'He lives on a small yacht. The yacht's gone.'

'So who is he really?' That should have been an easy question to answer. Everyone was in the data banks.

'Don't know, Alex. He might be from Upper Pisspot or some such place. There are a few countries that don't subscribe to the registry. Or he might be an off-worlder. But we've got his picture on the hot board, so as soon as he walks in front of one of the bots, or gets spotted by a patrol, or by an alert citizen,

176

we'll be in business.' Which I suspect translated to as soon as he walked into police central and gave himself up.

Despite his casual manner with Fenn, Alex had been visibly shaken by the incident. I guess I was, too. When somebody tries to kill you, you tend to take it personally, and it changes your perspective on a lot of things. He returned to his old work habits, which is to say he was out enjoying the nightlife with the clientele when he wasn't wandering around in the greenhouse. But he was quieter than usual, more subdued, almost somber. We didn't talk about it much, probably because neither of us wanted to reveal the degree to which we were bothered by the experience and by the probability that there was still a threat out there. He spent a lot of time looking out windows. Fenn installed something he called an early-warning system at both my apartment and at the country house. It was just a black box with its own power unit that he tied into the AI's. It would monitor all visitors, block doors, disable intruders, notify police, shriek, and generally raise hell if anybody tried anything. It was probably the end of privacy. But I was willing to make the trade to sleep peacefully.

The day after the black boxes were installed, Fenn called again to report that they'd tried to locate Gina Flambeau, the woman who'd visited Diane Gold to present her with her award, apparently for the sole purpose of inspecting Maddy's etui. *'There's no such person,'* he said. *'At least, not one who fits the description.'*

'Did you try for a DNA sample?' Alex asked. 'She handled the etui.'

'You mean the little jewel box?'

'Yes.'

'Half the people in the village have handled it.'

Every time I thought about Marcus Kiernan, I got an echo from the convention.

The people who belong to the *Polaris* Society refer to themselves as Polarites. That's not an entirely serious appellation, of course.

But it fits the mood of things. The head Polarite was a woman from Lark City whom I couldn't reach. Out of town. Doesn't take a link with her. Doesn't care to be disturbed, thank you very much.

The number two Polarite was an electrical engineer from Ridley, which is about ninety kilometers down the coast. I called him and watched his image gradually take shape along with a burst of starlight. I'm always a bit suspicious of people who use special effects in their communications. You talk to somebody, it should be a conversation, not showbiz. He had narrow eyes, wore a black beach jacket, looked generally bored. Better things to do than talk with you, lady. *'What can I do for you, Ms Kolpath?'* he asked. He was seated in a courtyard in one of those nondescript polished tan chairs that show up on front decks everywhere these days. A steaming drink stood on a table beside him.

I explained that I'd been to the convention, that I'd enjoyed it, and that I was doing research for a book on the Society and its contribution to keeping the *Polaris* story alive. 'I wonder,' I said, 'if an archive of this year's meeting is available?'

His demeanor softened. *'Have you actually published anything?'*

'I've done several,' I said. 'My last was a study of the Mazha.'

'Oh, yes,' he said.

'The title is *The Sword of Faith*.'

'I've seen it,' he said solemnly.

'It's been well received,' I said. 'Now, I was wondering whether you have an archive I could look at?'

'We always put one together for the board.' He had a raspy, high-pitched voice. The kind you associate with somebody who yells at kids a lot. *'It helps with planning next year's event. Did you just want to see the one from this year? We have them going back to the beginning of the century.'*

'At the moment, I only need the current one.'

'Okay. I can take care of it.' Delivered with a sip of his brew.

A few minutes later I was fast-forwarding my way through the convention. I skipped the stuff I hadn't seen during my original visit. I dropped in on the alien wind panel again. Saw myself. Moved on to the Toxicon kidnap plot. Watched the man who'd been on board the *Polaris* after it became the *Sheila Clermo*. And there he was! Kiernan was sitting six rows to my rear on the left. Almost directly behind me. But I couldn't recall having noticed him back there. I associated him strongly with the convention, but there was a different version of him at the back of my mind.

Alex asked me to get Tab Everson on the circuit. Everson was the man who'd reduced the artifacts to ashes and put them in solar orbit. 'What do we want to talk to him about?'

'The *Polaris*,' he said. 'I think he'll be receptive.'

He was right. Everson's AI at Morton College put me through to a private secretary, a gray-haired, efficient-looking woman. I identified myself and explained why I'd called. She smiled politely and asked me to wait. Moments later she was back. *'Mr Everson is busy at the moment. May I have him return your call?'*

'Of course.'

Alex told me that when the call came, he wanted me to sit in, using an offstage chair. Everson would not know I was there. An hour later he was on the circuit.

Tab Everson was president of a food distribution firm, although his primary interest seemed to be Morton College. The data banks put his age at thirty-three, but he looked ten years younger. He was casually dressed, white shirt, blue slacks, and a checkered neckerchief. A windbreaker embossed with the name of the college hung on the back of a door. His office was filled with mementoes from the school – awards, certificates, pictures of students playing chess and participating in seminars and standing behind lecterns. He was a bit more than average height, with black hair and piercing gray eyes. *'I've heard a lot about you, Mr Benedict,'* he said. He was seated in an armchair framed by a picture window. Outside, I could see a hilltop and some trees. *'It's a pleasure.'*

Alex had taken the call in the living room, as was his custom when representing the corporation. He returned the greeting. 'You may know I'm an antiquities dealer,' he said.

Everson knew. *'Oh, I think you're a great deal more than an antiquities dealer, Mr Benedict. Your reputation as an historian precedes you.'* Well, that was a bit much. But Alex accepted the compliment gracefully, and Everson crossed one leg over the other. *'What can I do for you?'* he asked.

There was a maturity about this guy that belied his age. He leaned forward slightly, conveying the impression he would be intrigued with whatever Alex was about to say. Yet he managed to signal that time was a factor and that a long interview was not in the cards. Say what you have to say, Benedict, and stop taking my time. I had the feeling he knew why we were there. Which put him a step ahead of me.

'I was struck by your disposal of the *Polaris* artifacts,' said Alex.

'Thank you, but it was the least I could do.'

'I didn't mean it as a compliment. It must have occurred to you that, even in their condition after the explosion, they might have retained some value to historians. Or investigators.'

Everson let us see he had no sympathy with that view. *'I really can't imagine what an historian might have hoped to find among them. And the debris would not have engaged any collector's interest. Not in the condition it was in. Did you by any chance see what was left of the artifacts? After the bombing?'*

'No. I did not.'

'If you had, Mr Benedict, you'd not need to raise the issue. By the way, I understand you were there that night.'

'Yes. It wasn't a pleasant evening.'

'I would think not. I hope you weren't injured.'

'No. I came away fine, thank you.'

'Excellent. These madmen.' He shook his head. *'But they did eventually get the thugs, didn't they? Or did they?'* He allowed himself to look momentarily puzzled. *'I don't know what's*

happening to the world.' He got up from the chair. Well, terribly sorry. Have to get back to work. *'Was there anything else?'*

Alex refused to be hurried. 'You obviously have had some experience with antiquities.'

'Well, in my own small way, perhaps.'

'Anyone who deals with them learns quickly the value of anything that links us to the past.'

'Yes.'

'Would you explain, then, why you—?'

'—Why I reduced everything to ashes before releasing it into orbit? In fact, you're asking the same question again, Mr Benedict, and I will answer it the same way. It was out of respect. I'm sorry, but that will have to suffice. It is the only reason I have.'

'I see.'

'Now, perhaps I may ask you a question?'

'By all means.'

'What is it you really want to know?'

Alex's face hardened. 'I think the bombs at Survey were aimed at the exhibition, not the Mazha.'

'Oh, surely that can't be—'

'A few nights ago, there was an attempt to kill me and an associate.'

He nodded. *'I'm truly sorry to hear it. Why would anyone do such a thing?'*

Whatever else he might have been, he wasn't a good actor. He was hiding something. At the very least, prior knowledge of the attempt on our lives.

'I think there's something in the exhibition that somebody finds threatening.'

'Sufficiently threatening to kill for?'

'Apparently.'

He looked shocked. Then insulted. *'And you think—'*

'—I think you know what it is.'

He laughed. *'Mr Benedict, I'm sorry you feel that way. But I have no idea what you mean. None whatever.'* He cleared his throat. Departure imminent. *'I wish I could help. But unfortunately I can't. Meantime, if you really believe I'd do something like that, I suggest you go to the authorities. Now, if you'll excuse me, I must get back to work.'*

'Why did we do that?' I asked.

'This guy is part of it, Chase. I wanted him to know we understand that. It lets him know that if anything happens to us, somebody will be around to ask more questions.'

'Oh, well, that's good. It could go the other way, too.'

'How's that?'

'They dumped us in the sea to stop us from following Kiernan home. But if you're right, you may have persuaded Everson that we're getting too close to whatever it is they're hiding and that they have no choice but to get rid of us. And do it right this time.'

That possibility seemed not to have occurred to him. 'He wouldn't be that foolish, Chase.'

'I hope not. But the next time we decide to do something that puts both our lives on the line, let's talk about it first.'

'Okay.' He looked sheepish. 'You're right.'

'You really have no doubt about it, do you? That Everson's involved?'

'None.' He headed for the coffee. 'I've been in touch with Soon, with Harold, with Vlad. Nobody's been to visit them. No one's interested in the stuff they have.'

'The plaque, the Bible, and the bracelet.'

He gave me his victory smile. 'Am I right?'

'None of them have places where you could hide anything.'

'Exactly.'

'Except maybe the Bible.'

'You can stash a piece of paper in the Bible. Other than that, it doesn't work very well.'

'So it's not a note. Not a message.'

'Not a note, anyhow.'

'Whatever it was, it probably got blown up,' I said. 'Ninety-nine percent of the artifacts got taken out by the blast.'

We wandered out onto the deck, which was heated and enclosed. The wind blew steadily against the glass. 'Not necessarily,' he said.

'Why do you say that?'

'They would have searched the debris before they burned it. They didn't find what they were looking for.'

'If that's the case, why did they burn everything?'

'Call it an abundance of caution. But I think we can assume that, whatever it is, it's still out there.'

Maddy's jacket and the ship's glass remained in the office. I got up and walked over to them. The *Polaris* seal, the star and the arrowhead, seemed almost prophetic, somehow to predict the destruction of Delta Karpis by the superdense projectile that had lanced into its heart, that had shattered it and charged on.

Next day, we heard from Fenn again. He looked tired. I remembered his telling me once that police officers were like doctors: They shouldn't work on cases in which they had a personal interest. '*I need to speak with Alex,*' he said.

I hadn't seen him all morning, but I knew he was in the house. The *Polaris* business was beginning to weigh on him. I was pretty sure he was sitting up half the night trying to construct a workable explanation.

The problem was that he was letting the company slide. He was doing the social stuff okay, but he also was responsible to scan the markets to see what was available, what might be coming on-line, what was worth our time. I couldn't do that. I didn't have the background. Or his instincts. My job was communicating with the clients on administrative details and keeping them happy. But without Alex bringing stuff on board our bottom line was beginning to look vulnerable.

Jacob told me he was out back. 'Tell him Fenn's on the line.'

Minutes later he wandered into the office. '*You look exhausted,*' the inspector told him.

'Thanks,' he said. 'You look pretty sharp yourself.'

'*I mean it. Chase, you need to take better care of him.*'

'What can I do for you, Fenn?'

'*We know who was driving the Venture.*'

Alex came to life. 'Good man. Who is the bitch?'

'*Gina Flambeau.*'

'Okay. No surprise there. You have her in custody, right?'

'*Not exactly. She's gone missing.*'

'She's missing, *too*?'

'*Yep. Without a trace.*'

'How'd you find who she was?'

'*We had her description from Diane Gold. There aren't that many Ventures in the Andiquar area, so on a hunch that Flambeau would turn out to be the person who attacked you, we pulled out pictures of all the young women owners and lessees who fit the general description and showed them to Gold.*'

'What do we know about her?'

'*Her real name's Teri Barber. She's a schoolteacher. Twenty-four years old. Born off-world. On Korval.*'

'We were taken out by a *schoolteacher*?' I said.

He shrugged. '*She came to Rimway four years ago. According to her documents she's from a place called Womble. Graduated from the University of Warburlee. With honors. Majored in humane letters.*'

I couldn't restrain a laugh.

They ignored me. Alex said, 'You think she might have gone home?'

'*We're looking into it.*' Korval was a long way off, literally at the other end of the Confederacy. '*There's no record that a Teri Barber went outbound over the last few days, but she could be traveling under a different name.*' An image took shape off to one side of Fenn's desk. Young woman, black hair cut short, good features, blue eyes, red pullover, gray slacks. Alex came to attention.

'She has an exemplary record as a teacher, by the way. Everybody at the school says she's a princess. The kids, administration, they all love her. They think she walks on water.' He braced his chin on the palm of his hand. 'The Venture's leased. Long-term. The leasing company has the same address we do.'

It was hard not to stare at the raven-haired woman. I could see why everybody – at least all the males – had such good things to say about her. She reminded me of Maddy. She had the same charge-the-hill, no-nonsense look. Not quite so pronounced, maybe, but then she was considerably younger than Maddy had been.

'Our best guess is that Barber waited near Ida Patrick's house to make sure Kiernan wasn't followed. They knew you folks were on their track. The fact that Kiernan used Chase's name to rent the skimmer tells us that much.' He frowned. 'I'd guess that was intended to send you a message to back off.'

Alex was silent for a moment. 'Barber gave that an exclamation mark,' he said at last. 'Fenn, when you catch her, I'd like very much to talk to her.'

'We can't allow that, Alex. Sorry. But I'll do this much: When she explains what's going on, I'll pass it to you. Now, there's one more thing.'

'Name it.'

'We've locked down her quarters. It occurs to me there might be a connection somewhere we're not aware of. I'd like to have you, and maybe Chase, too, take a virtual tour of her place. You might see something that'll help.'

It's always struck me as odd that despite the vast range of building materials available, people still prefer to live in houses that look as if they're made of stone, brick, or wood. They rarely are, of course. Haven't been for millennia in most places, but it's hard to tell the difference. I suppose it's something in the genes.

Teri Barber had lived in a log-style home atop a wooded hill on Trinity Island, about four hundred kilometers southeast of Andiquar. Big enclosed deck, looking out over the sea. A place where the wind blew all the time. There was a landing halfway down the hill, connected by a creaky wooden staircase on one side with the house and on the other with a pier. The yellow Venture waited on it. A few meters away, a canoe rested in a rack at the edge of the pier.

'*Rental property,*' said Fenn.

Alex was visibly impressed. 'Where did she teach?' he asked.

'*Trinity University. She taught the basic syntax course for first-year students. And classical literature.*'

We went down to the pad and inspected the Venture. It was sleek, with swept-back lines. Ideal vehicle for kids, except that it was pricey. 'Any sign of the laser?' Alex asked.

Fenn shook his head. '*No weapons of any kind on the premises or in the vehicle.*' The dock rose and fell. '*We aren't finished with it yet, but it doesn't look as if it's going to tell us much.*'

We looked inside the Venture but saw no personal belongings. '*This is the way we found it,*' Fenn said. '*She didn't leave anything.*'

We went back to the house. Two rockers and a small table stood on the deck. A stack of cordwood was piled against the wall. On one side of the house you could see a stump she apparently used as a chopping block.

The place was well maintained. It was one of those two-story big-window models from the last century. Something about it suggested fourteenth-century sensibilities. Maybe it was the big porch and the rockers.

'She live here alone?' asked Alex.

'*According to the rental agent, yes. She's been here four years. He didn't get up here that often, but he said there was no sign of a live-in boyfriend, or anything along those lines. He also said he didn't realize she was gone.*'

186

The scene changed, and we were inside. My impression of an antique atmosphere was confirmed by the interior: The furniture was immense: a padded sofa big enough for six; two matching chairs; and a coffee table the size of a tennis court. Thick forest green curtains were drawn over the windows. You sank into the carpets. Quilts were thrown across the sofa and one of the chairs.

'How long has she been missing?' Alex asked.

'We're not sure. The school was on a semester break. Nobody can recall having seen her for about a week.' He glanced out the window. *'Nice place. I understand they have a waiting line if it becomes available.'*

'You think she might be coming back?'

'I doubt it.' He tugged at his sleeves. *'All right, this is obviously the living room. Kitchen's over there, on the other side of the hallway. Washroom through that door. Two bedrooms and another washroom upstairs. Everything pretty well kept.'*

'But only one person living here.'

'She has money,' I said.

'That's what's strange. We checked her finances. She's comfortable but not well-off. This apartment is an extravagance. Unless—'

'She has accounts under other names,' said Alex.

There were several prints on the walls. An old man deep in thought, a couple of kids standing on a country bridge, a ship gliding past a ringed planet. *'It's a furnished unit. Everything belongs to the owner. She left clothes and some assorted junk. But no jewelry. No ID cards.'*

'She knew when she left,' Alex said, 'that she wasn't coming back.'

'Or that that there was a chance she wouldn't, and she wanted to be ready to run.'

Her bedroom was in the back of the house, overlooking the ocean. It was cozy, dark-paneled walls, matching drapes and carpet. The bed was oversized, with lots of pillows. It was flanked by side tables and reading lamps. A couple of framed pictures stood atop a bureau: Barber laughing and having a good time

187

with a half dozen students; Barber posing with a male friend on the front steps of what was probably a school building.

'Who's the guy?' I asked.

'Hans Waxman. Teaches math.'

Alex took a close look. 'What's he have to say?'

'He's worried about her. Says she's never done anything like this before. Just taken off, I mean. They've had an on-again, off-again relationship over the last year.'

'And her students like her, you say?'

'Yeah. They say she was a good teacher. Nobody seems to know anything about her personal life. But they really like her. They couldn't understand why we were interested in her.'

'Did you tell them?'

'Only that we wanted to talk to her because we thought she might have been a witness to an accident.'

The guest bedroom was a bit smaller, with a view of the chopping block. A chair, a table lamp, a picture of Lavrito Correndo leaping across a stage.

'Anything ring any bells?' Fenn asked.

'Yes,' said Alex. 'What's missing?'

'How do you mean?'

'Your office has pictures of your entire career, from when you first started. At the house, I can walk around and see pictures of your wife and kids, of you on the squabble team. Even, if I recall, of me.'

'Oh.'

'She has pictures,' I said, pointing to them.

'Those are from last week. Where's her past?' Alex held up his hands as though the apartment were empty. 'Where was she before she came to Trinity?'

An ornate mirror hung over the sofa. The drapes were pulled back, and sunlight poured in through a series of windows.

'How about you, Chase? See anything?'

'Actually,' I said, 'yes. Let's go back downstairs.' There was a dark blue quilt thrown over one of the chairs. Embroidered in its center was a white star inside a ring. It had to be handwoven, and it looked as if it had been around awhile.

'*What is it?*' asked Fenn.

'Who do you think owns the quilt? The landlord?'

'*Why do you ask?*'

'It has a connection with somebody who pilots superluminals.'

Fenn squinted at the quilt. '*How do you know?*'

'Look at the seal. Here, let me show you.' I killed the picture, and we were back at the country house. I touched my bracelet to the reader. The screen darkened, and my license appeared on it: . . . *That Agnes Chase Kolpath is hereby certified to operate and command superluminal vessels and vehicles, class 3. With all responsibilities and privileges appertaining thereto. Witness therefore this date* – Signatures were attached.

'*Agnes?*' Alex said. 'I didn't know that was your given name.'

'Can we proceed?' I asked.

They both laughed.

The background symbol on the document was, of course, Diapholo's ring and star. 'It's named for the fourth-millennium hero,' I said. 'He sacrificed himself to save his passengers.'

'I know the story,' said Alex. 'But I don't think the design is quite the same.'

'The style has changed over the years.' I returned us to Barber's living room and adjusted to a better angle on the quilt. 'This is pretty close to what it used to look like.'

'When?'

'Sixty years ago. Give or take.'

'So who could the pilot have been? Her grandfather?'

I shrugged. 'Anybody's guess. But the quilt looks like an original. Does it belong to her or the landlord? And you might have noticed Barber looks a lot like Maddy. Maybe they're related.'

Fenn called again that afternoon. He'd talked with the landlord. The quilt belonged to Barber. He also reported that the Teri Barber who graduated from the University of Warburlee was not the same Teri Barber who'd been teaching the last few years at Trinity.

Superluminal certification records showed no listing for anybody named Barber. So Alex and I fed her image to Jacob. 'See if you can find anyone,' I told him, 'who has or had a license who looks enough like her to be a relative.'

'*That's fairly vague,*' he complained. '*What are the search parameters?*'

'Male and female.' I looked at Alex. 'You think she might actually have been born in Womble?'

'Probably not. But it's a place to start.'

'How far back?'

'All the way. The certification design's been around awhile.'

'Anywhere over the last sixty years,' I told Jacob. 'Born in, or lived in, Womble. On Korval.'

'*Looking,*' he said.

'Take your time.'

'*Of course this is very nonscientific. It calls for an opinion.*'

'I understand.'

And, after a few moments: '*Negative search.*'

'You don't need to find a duplicate,' I told him. 'Anybody who looks remotely like her would do.'

'*There are no persons, male or female, licensed to operate interstellars, who at any time lived in Womble on Korval.*'

'Try the same search,' said Alex. 'But go planetwide.'

He produced three pilots, two male, one female. I didn't think any of them looked much like Barber. '*It's the best I can do.*'

'Proximity to Womble?' asked Alex.

'*Closest one is eight hundred kilometers.*'

Detailed information on the families was blocked under the privacy laws. 'Doesn't matter,' Alex said. 'I don't think Teri Barber exists. Let's try something else. Same search, substitute Rimway. The Associated States.'

I wondered whether Fenn would institute a search of college

yearbooks from, say, 1423 to 1425. 'She had to graduate from somewhere.'

'The database would be pretty big,' said Alex. 'Anyhow, who says she had to graduate from somewhere?'

'*I have a hit*,' said Jacob. '*A female pilot.*'

'Let's see her, Jacob.'

She *looked* like Teri Barber. She was wearing a gray uniform and her hair was brown instead of black. But the certificate was dated 1397. Thirty-one years ago. 'She's a pretty good match,' Alex said. The woman would now be in her midfifties. Barber was no more than twenty-five.

'What's her name?' I asked.

'*Agnes Shanley.*'

'Another Agnes.' Alex smiled. Not a real smile. More like a reflexive one. 'Did Agnes have any daughters?'

'*It doesn't say. She married in 1401. To one Edgar Crisp.*'

'Do we have an avatar for her?'

'*Negative.*'

'How about a locator? Can we talk to her?'

'*Yes*,' said Jacob. '*Her file's been inactive for twenty-five years. But I have a locator code.*'

'Good. On-screen, please.'

'We should pass it to Fenn,' I said.

Alex ignored me. He does that when he doesn't want to deal with me. But I wasn't so sure I wanted to get directly involved again. This was precisely the sort of behavior that had gotten us into trouble already.

'If we tell Fenn,' Alex said, apparently judging that the silence between us had become strained, 'he'll shrug and say the fact that she looks like Barber is irrelevant. I can hear him now: You look through every pilot certified worldwide over the last sixty years, of course you'll find someone who looks like her.'

'Actually,' I said, 'that's a pretty strong argument.'

He laughed. 'You have a point.'

'I still think—'

'Let's just stay with it for a bit. I want to know what's so important that somebody tried to kill us.' I heard anger in there somewhere. Good for him. Alex had always seemed to me to be a bit too passive. But I wondered if we weren't picking a fight with the wrong people. I get a little nervous around bomb throwers. He turned back to the AI. 'Jacob, see if you can get me on the circuit to Agnes Shanley Crisp.'

Jacob acknowledged. I got up and wandered around the room. Alex sat listening to the birds outside. They were especially noisy that afternoon. Then Jacob was back: *'Alex,'* he said, *'it appears the code is not currently in service.'*

12

There's a lot to be said for doing a disappearance. You bamboozle the bill collectors, upset the relatives, rattle the local social group, and give them all something to talk about. It's an easy way to become a legend. And it feels good. I know because I've done it several times myself.

—Schaparelli Cleve,
Autobiography

Alex had some questions to ask Hans Waxman, the math teacher. But Waxman didn't know us and would probably be reluctant to talk to strangers about his girlfriend. So we looked for a better way.

Waxman ate breakfast most mornings at a quiet little place called Sally's, just off the northern perimeter of the Trinity University campus. Several days after we'd toured Teri Barber's apartment, I arranged to be waiting for him.

I'd selected a table near the front window. Alex waited in a park across the street, relaxing on a bench, trying to look inconspicuous. I wanted Waxman to be able to see the passing traffic, so I put my hat on the chair that had its back to the window. I set my reader on the table and brought up *The Mathematical Dodge*. It's a collection of puzzles and logic problems, and I made sure I angled it so he could see the title as he came in the door.

He arrived at his usual time, looking thoughtful and distracted, his mind presumably on that morning's classes. He was, as they say in the girls' locker, a juicy piece – tall, blond, nice jaw. Looked even more congenial in person than he had in the picture. We made eye contact and I smiled and that was all it took.

He came over, shuffled his feet a bit, and said hello. 'I see you enjoy doing puzzles,' he added.

'Just a hobby.' My. He *was* attractive. In an innocent sort of way. The kind of guy you don't see around much anymore.

I'd ordered a fruit plate with hot chocolate. The chocolate arrived while he was considering how to pursue the gambit. I decided to save him the trouble and held out a hand. 'Jenny,' I said.

The smile widened. It was a shy grin, made all the more appealing in a guy who should have been able to get anybody he wanted. 'Nice to meet you, Jenny. My name's Hans. May I join you?'

The truth is I started regretting the lie before I delivered it. Alex had instructed me to avoid using my name, but I was thinking, yes, he was a bit young for me, but what the hell. Now, with the deception, he was forever off-limits. 'Sure,' I said.

He picked one of the remaining chairs, with the window view that I wanted him to have, and sat down. 'Are you a teacher, Hans?' I asked.

'Yes. Math. How did you know?'

I nodded toward the book. 'Most people would take no notice.'

'Oh.' The smile widened. 'Am I that obvious?'

'I wouldn't put it that way. But we're close to the school, and you look as if you belong—' I stopped, canted my head, and let him see I was impressed. 'I don't think I'm getting this right.'

'It's okay, Jenny. Thank you. In fact, I have a class in forty-five minutes.' He ordered eggs and toast, and I asked where he was from. He started talking about far-off places. My fruit dish showed up, and things went swimmingly. He wondered what I did for a living.

I admitted to being a financial advisor finishing a vacation on Trinity. 'From Wespac,' I said. Wespac was safely in the middle of the continent. 'Going home tomorrow.'

His face dropped. He looked genuinely distressed, and I have to confess I was charmed. 'I'm sorry to hear that,' he said. 'It would have been nice to be able to get together again. Assuming you'd have been willing.' He picked up the menu but didn't look at it. 'Are you by any chance free this evening? I'd love to take you to dinner.'

I hesitated.

'There are some excellent restaurants on the island. But you know that.'

'Yes. I do. And I wish I could, Hans. But I'm committed.' Sweet temptation. I would have enjoyed doing it and letting the rest of the evening play out as it would. It wasn't a reaction I usually had with strangers, even handsome ones. I was thinking, though, that it would be a way to get back at Barber. Take her guy and show him the time of his life. But that would have been an indecent way to treat Hans.

'What's funny, Jenny?'

'Nothing, really,' I said. 'I always meet the good-looking guy as I'm headed out of town.' I let him see I wasn't entirely joking.

I steered the conversation back to teaching, to his passion for mathematics, to his frustration that his students rarely recognized the elegance of equations. 'It's as if they have a blind spot,' he said.

'How long have you been at Trinity, Hans?' I asked.

'Six years. Ten if you count my time as a student.'

'I have a friend who teaches here. In the literature department.'

That got his attention. 'Really? Who?'

'Her name's Teri.'

He smiled. 'I know her,' he said. Noncommittal.

'I'd expected to surprise her, but she seems to have gone off somewhere.'

His eggs came. He tried one, commented how good it was, and bit into the toast. 'She left the island. I don't know where she is.'

'You mean, since the accident?'

'You know about that?'

'I know a skimmer went into the ocean. The police were looking for her. They think she saw it happen.' I paused. 'I hope she's okay.'

'So do I. I don't know the details. But I think the police believe she was responsible for it.'

'I heard the same thing. But I don't believe a word of it.'

'Neither do I.' He shrugged it off.

Sally's was automated. Our bot showed up and refilled my hot chocolate. 'Hans,' I said, 'I got the impression last time I talked to her, a few days before the accident, that something was on her mind.'

His gaze met mine. Steady. Worried. 'Me too. She's been down a bit lately. Depressed.'

'It was unlike her in the old days. She was always upbeat.'

'I know.'

'Any idea what it might be about?'

'No. She wouldn't tell me anything. Denied anything was wrong.'

'Yeah. That's what she told me, too. I wonder what happened?' I was trying to be casual, yet sound concerned. Not easy for somebody whose acting skills are pure wood.

'Don't know,' he said.

'How long has she been like that?'

He thought about it. 'A few weeks.' He made a guttural sound. 'I hope she's okay.'

I wanted to bring the *Polaris* into the conversation, but couldn't think of an indirect way to do it. So I just blurted it out: 'She used to be fascinated by the *Polaris*.'

'The ghost ship, you mean?' he asked. 'I didn't know. She never mentioned it.'

I wasn't quite finished with my meal, but I moved the plate

off to one side. That was a signal to Alex, who was armed with a projector.

'It was a strange business,' I said. I went on for a minute or two in that vein, recounting the many times I'd heard Teri wonder aloud what had happened to the people on the mission. Meantime, Marcus Kiernan's simulacrum, projected by Alex, came strolling along the sidewalk. In full view of Hans. Of course, there was no way for Hans to know it wasn't actually Kiernan himself out there. The simulacrum stopped just outside the door to study the menu.

Hans was pointed directly toward the window. Couldn't have missed him. But he gave no sign of recognition. He simply went on quietly eating his breakfast. He did not know, and had never seen, Marcus Kiernan.

After Hans left for his classes, I strolled outside and went across the street into the park.

Alex was waiting. He'd heard the conversation on my link. I detailed my impressions for him while he sat casually, watching a couple of toddlers riding swings under their mother's supervision. It seemed to me we hadn't learned anything helpful. Other than that he didn't know Kiernan.

'I'm not so sure,' he said.

'In what way? What else do we know now that we didn't know before?'

'He said the change in her mood began a few weeks ago. That puts it about the time Survey announced it would auction the artifacts.'

That night I was at home reading a mystery when Alex called. '*I found something in the archives,*' he said.

He sent it over and stayed on the circuit while I dimmed the lights, put on my headband, and looked at it.

We were inside a paneled room. Book-lined walls. Bokkarian artwork. Flowers. Old-fashioned furniture. Lots of people milling around, shaking hands, embracing. I saw Dunninger. And Urquhart. 'Where are we?' I asked.

'University of Carmindel, the evening before the Polaris *flight.'*

'Oh.' I spotted Nancy White in a corner of the room. And Mendoza. And there was Maddy, striding among the giants like a goddess.

'They held a celebration for everyone associated with the Polaris *the night before they left.'*

Mendoza was talking with two women. *'The younger one,'* said Alex, *'is his daughter.'*

Jess Taliaferro was engaged in an animated conversation with a man whose dimensions dwarfed him. A Tupelo. Connections somewhere with a low-gravity world. Taliaferro himself was smiling, nodding, looking earnest. Obviously feeling good. He was well turned out for the occasion: blue karym jacket, white neck-piece, gold buttons and links.

'Martin Klassner's over by the table.'

Klassner sat beside a middle-aged woman and a little girl. The little girl was playing with a toy skimmer. Zooming it around and landing it on Klassner's arm. He seemed to be enjoying the attention.

'He was pretty sick,' Alex said. *'I'm not sure what it was.'*

'Bentwood's,' I told him. It was ironic that Klassner would be traveling with two of the great neurological research people of the age, but no one could do anything for him. Bentwood's, of course, is beaten now. You go down to the clinic, and they give you a pill. But then—

'The woman is Tess, his wife. And the little girl is a grandchild.' Tess looked worried.

Chek Boland stood in a small mixed group near a window. *'The caption indicates those are all people from the literature department. One of them, the one in the white gown, is Jaila Horn. A major essayist in her time.'*

'I never heard of her.'

'It says she's pretty much forgotten today. Only read by scholars. She was planning to write about the collision. About Delta Kay. She saw lots of analogies between what was going to happen to the

*star and what institutional authority does to individual freedom.
Or something like that.'*

'She didn't go?'

'*She was on the* Sentinel.'

Nancy White had been cornered by a group of young people who, I suspected, were graduate students. White had managed several careers. One of them consisted of doing shorthand biographies of the great scientists. But her most famous work was *Out of the Trees,* an attempt to reconstruct the early progress of knowledge. Where was the first evidence that we'd begun to believe that the universe worked according to a system of laws? Who had first realized that the cosmos was not eternal? Why did people instinctively resist the notion? How had scientists first come to understand the implications of the quantum world? Who had first understood the nature of time?

Well, I didn't understand the nature of time. And neither did anybody I could think of.

Occasionally I was able to make out a comment. '*Wish I were going with you.' 'Is there any danger?' 'Not going to happen again within traveling range probably, for a hundred thousand years.'*

'Is there a point to all this?' I asked. It felt like a rerun of the other farewell, on Skydeck.

'*Let me fast-forward.'*

He rippled through, and the celebrants raced around the room at a ferocious rate, gulping down drinks and raiding the snack table. Then he returned to normal, and they were saying goodbye, moving toward the doors. Final shaking of hands. Tell your brother I said hello.

White extricated herself from her attending party and circled the room, nodding, accepting embraces. 'Is that her husband at her side?' I asked.

'*The big one?*'

'Yes.'

He nodded. '*They've been married nineteen years. His name's Karl.'*

Dunninger and Mendoza carried small crowds with them as they passed out of the room. Maddy English waited near the bar, talking earnestly with a red-haired olive-skinned man. '*Sy Juano*,' Alex said. '*He's a financial manager, it says here.*' It seemed as if she smiled past him, her thoughts concentrated elsewhere. The conversation seemed to be ending. Juano was nodding yes, then he leaned over and kissed her. She looked a bit reluctant.

The picture went off, and the AI brought the lights up. 'Well, that was interesting,' I said.

Alex looked at me as if I were the slow kid in the classroom. '*You didn't notice?*'

'Notice what?'

'*Teri Barber.*'

'I'm sorry?'

'*I thought you'd pick her out right away.*'

'Teri Barber was there?'

'*Well, not Barber herself. It might have been Agnes.*'

I had no idea what he was talking about. 'Where?' I asked.

'*Take another look.*' He told Jacob to rerun the last two minutes. Dunninger and Mendoza and their satellites trying to squeeze through the door. Maddy allowing Juano to kiss her. He hung on, chastely pressing his cheek against hers, as if he knew they were in the center of the picture.

'Freeze it,' I said.

'*Well, what do you think?*'

I stared at Maddy. At the same blue eyes, the perfectly sculpted jaws, the pert nose, the half smile playing about the full lips. A few more lines. Otherwise – 'Yes,' I said. 'If she were younger, they'd be very close.'

'*Make her twenty-three, Jacob. And change her hair color. Go with black.*'

Her features softened. The intensity gave way to a leisurely innocence. The creases that were just appearing on her brow and at the corners of her mouth went away. The skin around the jaws tightened.

Add the black hair, shorten it.

'*You thought Teri Barber resembled Maddy?*' he said.

Well, I'd been right. She *was* Maddy. They were identical.

The record said that Madeleine English had never borne a child. But there was an army of nieces and cousins, and when we looked through the pictures of current family members, we found three who resembled Teri Barber and seemed to be about the right age. One in particular, Mary Capitana, was a dead ringer. But Mary was a medical intern at a Kubran hospital in the middle of the Western Ocean, and the other two also had careers that would have prevented their living on Trinity Island in their spare time.

We couldn't find any record on Agnes Lockhart Shanley prior to her superluminal certification in 1397. Whatever she'd told the board about her background was subject to privacy laws. Her only known address was in a resort town with the ominous name Walpurgis, eleven hundred kilometers up the coast. She'd left there two decades ago, in 1405, according to the data file. After which there was no further record.

Current residence was unknown.

Walpurgis is one of those places that was bypassed in the boom of the last ten years. For whatever reason – you'd have to find a sociologist to explain it – the crowds have abandoned the northern coastal resorts for the islands.

Not that the area is poor. But when Alex and I got there it looked as if most of the inhabitants lived off the minimum subsistence income and didn't do much else. The center of town was anchored by large crumbling hotels built in the last century, a few restaurants done up in gaudy colors, and some sporting palaces. A plethora of walks and ramps overlooked the ocean, and the entire south side was dedicated to a vast warpark, which had probably gone bust when big-time gaming faded a few years ago. Nothing was moving in its streets.

We were riding Rainbow's new skimmer, purchased to replace

the one that had been lost. It located Shanley's old address and brought us down onto a public pad near a fading, two-story house on a corner near the western edge of town. An elderly woman with a white dog was coming out of a store, her arms filled with packages. A few kids were playing in a nearby schoolyard. Otherwise, there was no sign of life.

'This place has seen better days,' said Alex.

Well, I thought, so have we all.

Lawns were overgrown and full of weeds. The houses leaned in one direction or another. Creepers were strangling the trees, and it didn't look as if anyone had touched the hedges for years. It was a gray, dismal day, threatening but not delivering rain, and we could see lights in most of the windows. A cheer went up from the schoolyard. Kids are amazing. Feed them, give them a toy, and they never notice the wreckage around them.

The walkway wound past the school and a run-down park with climbing bars and a ball field. The house Agnes and her husband had lived in stood near a cluster of stacia trees. It was green and white, but the colors had faded. The front porch sagged, the shutters needed replacing, and a post light leaned at an unseemly angle.

'Yes?' said the AI as we approached. 'May I be of assistance?'

The front door was big, heavy, and scored by too many years of wind and sand. 'Yes,' Alex said. 'My name's Alex Benedict. I'd like very much to talk with the occupant. I'll only take a moment of his time.'

'If you'd care to state your business, Mr Benedict, I'll inform her.'

'I was admiring the house. I'm interested in a possible purchase.'

'One moment, please.'

'You have no shame,' I said.

'What do you suggest? Tell him we're here to ask questions about a missing starship captain?'

'I could see you living here.'

'It's a nice out-of-the-way place.'

'That's true.'

202

Alex stepped down off the deck and looked up, pretending he was inspecting the roof. Abruptly the door opened and a tired-looking woman in her fifties appeared. She looked suspiciously from one of us to the other. In this part of the world, visitors were never good news.

She resembled the neighborhood, listless, passed-by, dilapidated. In an age when no one is hungry, no one need go without shelter, and in which one need not even work if he, or she, chooses a life of leisure, I remain surprised that there are still people who seem unable to put their lives together. Or maybe the lack of necessity is the reason. 'Mr Benedict,' she said, throwing a suspicious glance my way, 'the house has not been put up for sale.'

'I'm interested, nevertheless.'

She studied us, decided she had nothing to lose, and stepped aside so we could enter. The interior was more or less what you would have expected: worn furniture, no curtains, bare floors. A few family pictures decorated the walls. Everyone was either very young or very old.

'My name is Casava,' she said. 'Casava Demmy.'

We completed the introductions, and Casava showed us around. The house was musty, but not disheveled. While we walked, we asked about the property. How much would she want for it? What kind of neighbors did she have? How long had she been living there?

'Eighteen years. It's a nice house. Needs some work, as you can see. But it's very solid.'

'I can see that. Yes.'

'Close to the beach.'

'Yes. It *is* quite nice. It looks as if the former owner took good care of it, too.'

'Yes, he did. Tawn Brackett. Good man, he was.'

'Before Tawn was here,' said Alex, 'a couple owned the house. Ed and Agnes Crisp.'

Casava's expression hardened. 'Is that what this is about?' she asked. 'The murder?'

Alex did a double take. 'What murder?'

She pressed her lips together and shook her head. 'It was supposed to have been an accident. But I doubt it.'

'Who got murdered?'

'Why, her husband. Ed.' She shook her head at the depravity of the world. 'You knew about the Crisps, but you didn't know what happened?'

'No. What happened?'

'He died in a fall. Off Wallaba Point. She was with him at the time. They'd only been married a few years.'

'Did you know her?' asked Alex.

Suddenly she looked reluctant. 'Just in passing,' she said.

Alex showed her his comm link. He transferred some funds. I couldn't see how much. 'What can you tell us about Agnes?'

She took a moment to retrieve her own link, which was in a table drawer. She checked her account, looked at both of us as if trying to decide what our interest was, and shrugged. 'Yes. I knew her. We were the same age. Dated some of the same men, in fact. Before she got married, of course.'

'Of course. Was she a friend?'

'I wouldn't go that far.'

'What kind of person was she? Why do you say she killed her husband?'

'It's a long time ago, Mr Benedict. I never really knew her that well.'

'It's okay,' he said. 'It won't go any further.'

We were back in the living room. She was looking closely at Alex, then she turned her gaze on me, and I could have sworn she was asking me whether she could believe Alex. I nodded yes, of course. 'I wouldn't want you to think,' she said finally, 'that I don't trust you, but a moment ago you were telling me you wanted to buy my house.'

We waited. A dog started barking outside.

'It just seemed strange. They went walking one night, and he didn't come home. I think she got tired of him.'

204

'Did she give you any reason to believe that?'

'She struck me as someone who'd get tired of any man pretty quick.'

'What else can you tell us?'

'She was a pilot of some sort. She had a pretty high opinion of herself. Thought she was better than everybody else. I was living over in Brentwood when she first came to town. I was at that time just out of school. We both belonged to a theater group. That's how I met her.'

'You did some shows together?'

'Yes. I had a good voice then.'

'Do you know what she piloted?'

'I was a singer,' she said. She listed a few of the shows she'd been in. We listened, tried to look impressed, and Alex asked his question again. 'Starships,' she said. 'Like I told you. She used to be gone for long periods of time. Off to the stars. She'd drop out of sight for months. Even after she got married.'

'Did they have any children?'

'No. No time for kids, I guess.'

'Did they have any family that you knew of?'

'I really don't remember, Mr Benedict. Actually, I'm not sure I ever knew.' She shook her head. 'The only thing I can tell you is that she was gone a lot. Then her husband died. And not long after that she took off for good, and we never saw her again.'

'But she sold the house first.'

'I guess so. I don't know.'

'Did she tell anyone she was leaving?'

'If she did, I didn't know about it.' She shrugged again. This time I thought I saw regret. 'Don't know what happened to her.'

'How long did she live in Walpurgis? Do you know?'

'I don't know,' she said. 'Maybe ten years.'

We went down to the city hall, logged in, and began scrolling through the public record.

The first item of interest was the dead husband. We found that easily enough in news accounts dated over a twelve-day period in late autumn, 1404.

CASINO EMPLOYEE FALLS TO DEATH FROM PRECIPICE

And, eight months later:

Police denied today they are working on the assumption that Agnes Crisp's disappearance is connected with the death of her husband last year.

There were pictures of Agnes, in uniform and in civilian clothes. Some wedding pictures. She and Ed made a handsome couple.

Ed had been a young worker at one of the casinos. The reports jibed with what Casava had told us. They'd gone out walking one night. To Wallaba Point. According to friends, they went there frequently. It was part of a workout routine. But on that particular evening Agnes admitted there'd been a quarrel. Apparently there was some pushing and shoving, although Agnes denied that she'd sent him over the edge. *'He lost his footing,'* she'd insisted. *'I loved him.'* Apparently the police uncovered no convincing evidence to the contrary. No arrest was ever made.

What had the argument been about?

'We were trying to decide about kids. I didn't think we were ready to do that because he didn't earn that much, and I'd have to give up my career.'

We checked the almanac. It had been a moonless night, dark and overcast.

Crisp had had the build of a moonball player. Young, athletic, good features. He wore his black hair cut short in the style of the day. He'd had dark, penetrating eyes, a broad forehead, dark skin. Neatly clipped beard and mustache. Was employed as a host at the Easy Aces Casino. He didn't look like the sort of person who would accidentally stumble off a cliff.

There was no avatar available.

Police had questioned Agnes for several days. People who knew them said there were no problems between them. They were good together, everyone seemed to think. (I wondered if anyone had questioned Casava.) Nevertheless, suspicions in the town ran high.

Ed Crisp reminded me of somebody.

'Again?' asked Alex. 'Who this time?'

I was running my interior catalog. Clients. Relatives. People from sims. 'James Parker,' I said. The actor.

'Everybody you see,' he said, 'reminds you of somebody else. He doesn't look at all like Parker.'

Actually he didn't. But there *was* someone. Well, I'd think of it later.

Casava and her husband had bought the house near the school in 1409. Brackett had picked it up three and a half years earlier.

The media archives revealed that, on a pleasant day in the late spring of 1405, eight months after Crisp's death, Agnes had sold her house, left Walpurgis, and not returned. No one knew where she had gone.

She'd bought the house in 1396. There was no mention of a former husband. Or of children. That seemed to suggest she was *not* Teri Barber's mother. It looked as if we were chasing the wrong rabbit.

'Maybe not,' said Alex. 'When people leave a place, they usually stay in contact with *somebody*. Right? A friend. Someone they'd worked with. Or people down at the club. Agnes did theater.'

'I don't—'

'People don't do theater without getting close to other people. Can't be done.'

'How do you know?'

He laughed. 'I don't. But I think it has to be true. Yet this woman stayed in touch with nobody.'

'Nobody that we know of.'

'Okay. Anyhow, what I was getting at: Who else did something like that?'

'You mean walked off and disappeared? Taliaferro. But that's an odd sort of link.'

'Odd ones are the best. Teri Barber would have been three or four at the time all this happened.'

'But we don't have a connection between Barber and Shanley. Other than that they look alike.' I began to suspect we were seeing patterns where none existed. There were all kinds of studies that showed people tended to find the things they looked for, even if some imagination was required.

Several weeks after Agnes had gone, there was a final piece of news:

Attempts to identify Edgar Crisp's family and notify them of his death have been unsuccessful. Crisp was a native of Rambuckle, in the Rigellian system. He came to Walpurgis in 1397.

'About the same time as Agnes,' I said.

'Yes.' Alex's brow furrowed. 'Why couldn't they locate his family?'

'I don't know. What are the rules on Rambuckle? I've never been there.'

'Maybe they don't maintain a directory.'

'I guess not.'

He was making faces, the way he always did when he was trying to puzzle something out. 'But I wonder whether we're looking at somebody else with a fictitious identity.'

'Oh, come on, Alex. If you were going to adopt a pseudonym, would you opt for *Edgar Crisp*?'

13

Stride the mountaintops and survey the world. But watch your step.

—Tora Shawn,
Firelight

In the data banks we found pictures of Agnes's home. It had looked pretty good at the turn of the century. It was smaller then. A wing had been added since, and that sagging front porch. One of the pictures, taken during a snowstorm, showed a glowing post light – the same one that now leaned sharply toward the walkway – and two people gazing out through the front window. Agnes and Ed? We couldn't tell. The illumination behind them didn't reach their faces.

The media stories described Agnes as a superluminal pilot and indicated she was often gone on long cruises. (In those days, of course, flights could take months. Or even years, if you could pile enough food on board.) They also mentioned that she'd captained the Echo flight. 'Incredible,' Alex said.

'Why?' I asked. 'What's an Echo flight?'

He took his time answering. 'You know the notion that the loss of the people on the *Polaris* was a supernatural event?'

'Yes.'

'In 1400, on the thirty-fifth anniversary of the mission, a few people belonging to the Arrowhead Club decided to reproduce the voyage, as nearly as possible.'

'What's the Arrowhead Club?'

'You know it as the *Polaris* Society today. It was a group of enthusiasts. They chartered the *Clermo* from Evergreen. The *Polaris*. What they wanted to do was to try to re-create the original circumstances to see whether the occult event would manifest itself a second time.'

Sometimes it's hard to believe the extent of human gullibility. I saw a report recently that more than half the population of Rimway believes astrology works. 'I remember hearing about it. The loony flight.'

'Then you know the rest.'

'Refresh my memory.'

'They rechristened the ship *Polaris*, held a launch ceremony, put six passengers on board, five men and a woman, and went shopping for a female pilot. I guess they wanted a Madeleine English look-alike. So they settled on Agnes.'

'Did they make her dye her hair?'

'Don't know. I guess their big problem was that they thought the occult event they were looking for was connected with the collision between the star and the dwarf. They thought it had released, as I recall, something called "psychokinetic energy." But they couldn't very well stage a second smash-up, so they had to settle for hoping that whatever had arrived in 1365 was still hanging around out near the collision site.'

'But this is what, thirty-five years later? The dwarf star was a long way off by then, and so was whatever was left of Delta Kay. Which, if I recall, was zip.'

'That's correct. But I guess they were nothing if not optimistic. They figured out where the debris from the destroyed sun would have gone, and, I suppose, where they could expect to find the spiritual forces. And that's where they went.'

'I don't understand what you're talking about, Alex.'

'Who does?'

'They must have had some money.'

'I assume.'

'So what were they hoping? That they'd all disappear, too?'

'They took six passengers, like the original flight. One of them was a spiritualist, who thought that if they burned the right sort of candles and set lasers at the right frequency, they would be able to control whatever appeared.'

'No drums?'

'Not as far as I know.'

'How come you know so much about this?'

Alex smiled. Man in charge. 'This kind of stuff fascinates me. And, from a professional perspective, it's significant. I always knew there'd be a pile of money to be made if Survey ever turned the artifacts loose. Even artifacts from the Echo flight command a decent sum.'

That brought up another issue. 'Why did Survey sell the *Polaris*? They must have realized it was going to be worth serious money one day.'

Alex closed his eyes and shook his head. 'It's hard to understand the bureaucratic mind, Chase. My best guess is that they knew it would take time for the ship to appreciate. And that means the sale gets made on somebody else's watch. Meanwhile the *Polaris* hangs around reminding everybody of the organization's most spectacular failure. Did you know people were actually afraid of it?'

'Of the ship?'

'Read the accounts. They were seriously spooked. If an other-world force could make the passengers disappear, what couldn't it do? Some people even thought that something might have come back with it.'

'So what happened on the Echo flight?'

'They supplemented the AI with black boxes, to record everything. In case it *did* happen again.'

'Because the AI had been no help on the original flight.'

'Right. The black boxes were supposed to have been specially designed to withstand supernatural forces. And continue recording. They were going to trigger and start transmitting as soon as anything out of the ordinary happened.'

'How'd they define that? "Anything out of the ordinary"?'

'I told you. The presence of psychokinetic forces. The Arrowhead got a lot of publicity, gave all kinds of interviews and whatnot, and took off.'

'And they didn't see anything,' I said.

'They claimed later there were apparitions. That several of the passengers from the original flight made appearances. I forget which ones. A couple of the Arrowhead people came back claiming they understood what had happened, but that humanity wasn't ready for the truth.'

'Sounds as if they were reading too much Stepanik Regal.'

'Yeah. There were stories that the apparitions begged for help. Floated through the ship. Nothing more than spectres. They also said that the candles and lasers kept infernal presences at a distance. There were even some pictures, I believe.'

'Pictures of what?'

'Haze, it looked like to me. Wisps of fog in the engine room. I remember one of them really looked as if it had eyes.'

We got names and addresses for neighbors who'd been around when Agnes was in town. We commandeered a booth on the first floor of the city hall and started making calls. I explained that my name was Chase Shanley, that I was a niece of Agnes Crisp, and that the family was still trying to find her. 'We haven't given up,' I told them.

'*She had a nice life here,*' one elderly woman said. '*She seemed to have enough money, she had a lovely house, and a good husband.*'

'She must have been very unhappy, though,' I said, 'when Ed was lost.'

Some said she hardly went into mourning at all. Others claimed she was distraught. A former casino employee who'd worked with Crisp told us she'd been hit hard by the experience. '*She loved Ed,*' he said. '*It was hard enough on her when she lost him. Then* the town turned on her and decided she'd killed him. The truth is that the town was jealous of her. She was a beautiful woman; she goddam flew starships. So, of course, they didn't like her. That's why she left. It didn't have anything to do with feeling guilty, which was what they were all saying. She just got fed up.'

In fact, everyone spoke well of her. That's what happens, I guess, when you claim to be a relative. We located a couple of former boyfriends, but both seemed reluctant to give details. 'I'm a happily married man,' one said. 'She was a nice lady, but that's all I know.'

Nobody remembered a daughter. 'She liked gardening,' a neighbor said. And she was a skilled chess player. Played down at the club. 'Beat everybody, I hear.'

'Was she capable of pushing someone off a cliff?' Those who knew her personally thought not. She was friendly, they reported. Kind to kids and dogs. She'd never hurt anybody. Although she might have been a bit standoffish. 'In what way?'

'Well,' one woman said, 'I always got the impression she thought she was kind of elite. But I never saw a serious flash of temper. Or got mistreated by her.'

No one had any idea where she'd gone.

Several believed she might have thrown herself off the same summit that had claimed her husband. The forest was thick at the base of the precipice. Police had looked, but some said not very thoroughly because they never subscribed to the theory.

'I don't believe it either,' said Alex.

Ed Crisp had fallen from a place called Wallaba Point. It was three kilometers northwest of Walpurgis, where the land rose sharply into the foothills of the Golden Horn, a range that comes in from offshore, arcs around the town, and runs southwest almost to the Gulf. There was a fence at the site when Alex and I visited it.

We got there in the early evening. It was cold and overcast, with a few flakes in the air.

I don't mind heights when I'm in an aircraft, but I always get a bit queasy on a stationary perch. It was all I could do to lean out over the fence and look down. The sun had just set. The foot of the precipice was buried in thick forest. There were a river, a few boulders, and, in the distance, a ramshackle shed. It wasn't really a long way down, but it was sheer and you were going to bounce pretty high when you hit bottom.

We paced back and forth, measuring possibilities, wondering precisely from which point Edgar had fallen. Even without the fence, which hadn't existed when the accident occurred, I couldn't see how a grown man in possession of his faculties could wander off the edge. The news accounts said no alcohol or drugs had been found. There were no trees near the summit, no bushes, nothing to disguise its existence. The woods ended about fifteen meters away.

'Couldn't happen,' I concluded.

Alex wasn't so sure. 'No moon. Acrimony in the air. She wants to keep her job. He wants kids. But he doesn't make much, and probably doesn't have much of a future. So it goes back and forth and he's not watching what he's doing.'

I didn't believe it. 'It's not possible.'

'Happens all the time, sweetheart.'

'It does *not* happen all the time.'

'Seriously, Chase, people get excited, and they can lose sight of everything. He's backing away from her, throws up his hands, trips on a loose rock, and over he goes.'

'I just can't see it. Nobody's that dumb.'

The hiking trail we were following ran right along the edge. If you decided to play tag up there, you'd back off a good bit, move back by the trees. Your instincts wouldn't let you do anything else. 'I think she killed him,' I said.

He nodded. 'You too? Why?'

'I think it's the only way it could happen. They come up here, maybe she'd discovered he'd been cheating, maybe she'd gotten tired of him. They're in, what, the third or fourth year of their marriage. That's about the time you find out whether you've got a real marriage or not.'

'When did you become an expert?'

'It doesn't take a specialist, Alex. We're talking about stuff every woman knows but apparently not many guys. If she did it, I doubt it had anything to do with whether they were going to have kids. Anyhow, she probably decided she had an easy way out, she was probably angry, or frustrated, so you get a quick push, and it's over. Who'd ever know the difference?'

We walked back through the woods to the skimmer. It felt good to get into the cabin, where it was warm. We were in a glade, about a half kilometer from the summit. Alex sat listlessly, not saying anything, just staring out at the trees. I felt it, too. There was something depressing about that windblown hilltop. 'It's the weather,' I said.

Alex made a rumbling sound in his throat. 'Louise,' he said, speaking to the AI, 'see what you can get on Edgar Crisp.' He'd left me to pick the name for the system, and I picked one at random that seemed warm, friendly, and nonthreatening. Alex wasn't overwhelmed, but he hadn't complained.

There wasn't much on Crisp. Birth. Death. Parents came to Rimway in 1391. Graduated from the Indira Khan Academy in Lakat, which was halfway across the ocean. Licensed to operate a skimmer 1397. Gained title to a skimmer 1398. Lived three years on Seaview Avenue in leased quarters before marrying Agnes. Employee of Allnight Recreation Services, the owner of the Easy Aces Casino. Died at twenty-eight.

That was it. Edgar's passage through the world had been unremarkable. He'd disturbed nothing, changed nothing, had only called attention to himself by the manner of his death. It was almost as if he'd never existed. I wondered who had attended his funeral.

'That's the way for most of us,' Alex said. 'Birth, death, and good riddance. The world takes no note. Unless you're lucky enough to overturn somebody's favorite mythology.'

I laughed. Alex was persuaded he'd achieved immortality by the Christopher Sim discoveries, and he was very likely right.

'Louise,' he said, 'check the graduation lists for the Khan Academy. Make it 1395 and 1396. See if an Edgar Crisp shows up.'

'You don't think the media had it right?' I said.

'Just following my instincts.'

Louise needed only a few seconds. *'Lakat does not subscribe to the registry.'*

'Is there any way to verify his background? Short of going there?'

'There is no off-line arrangement.'

A couple of kids wandered past with backpacks. Headed toward the Point. If they were planning on staying outside, it was going to be cold.

'Another one with no history,' I said. 'How'd you know?'

'I don't think it's a coincidence we keep running into people who come from places that don't maintain a register.'

I started the engine. 'You think any of these people are going to turn out to be who they say they are?'

'Don't know,' he said. 'What I'm wondering is where they're coming from.'

The Walpurgis Cemetery was less than a half hour's walk from the home once occupied by Agnes and Ed Crisp. It occupied roughly a square kilometer, mostly on gently rolling hillside. The markers, like the town, were old and worn. It wasn't used much anymore, because the local population had declined significantly and also because having one's ashes given to the winds or the sea is now generally favored over other forms of disposal.

We had heard that some of the graves went back eight hundred years, although we saw nothing that old. They were crowded together, three and four people in each plot, and I saw no part of the cemetery that wasn't lacking space. It was crowded, and the town was empty.

Markers were designed in a wide range of styles, depending mostly, I guess, on the wealth of the occupant and also, to some extent, on the era. Fashions come and go. Some were simple slates, set in the ground, with a name and dates. Others were larger, more elaborately carved headstones, expressing the sentiments of those left behind. *Beloved father. Left us too soon.* On some, the characters had become too smooth to read.

Statuary ranged from modest to elegant to overblown. Angels stood guard, a young boy cradled a lamb, biblical figures bowed their heads, doves flew.

It had gotten dark by the time we arrived. The snow had stopped, and the night was very still. I thought briefly of Tom Dunninger, who'd devoted his genius to life extension, who'd said he hated cemeteries, who was reported to have been on the track of a major breakthrough before he joined his colleagues on the *Polaris*. Well, Tom, nothing has changed. At best, people still live for maybe 120 or 130 years, tops, which is the way it's been for a long time. Dunninger himself was pushing it when he headed out to Delta Kay. A hundred twenty-something, as I recall. I could understand his interest. All of us would like to think there's a way of shutting down the ageing process, but if it hasn't been done by now, I suspected that meant it couldn't be done.

We walked among the headstones, exchanging irrelevancies, contemplating mortality, trying to keep warm.

Crisp's grave was in the fold of a hillock, his marker one of four clustered together. It was unpretentious, a white stone, engraved with his name and dates, and the legend *In loving memory*. Someone had planted a sabula bush beside the headstone. It wasn't much to look at in the face of approaching winter, but in the spring it would become a golden glory.

The ground was a bit worn. When the weather got warm, the grass would grow. 'I wonder who he is,' Alex said.

Back in the skimmer, Alex called Fenn, told him where we were and what we'd been doing, and asked whether he could get an exhumation order for Crisp.

I suppose I could say Fenn was reluctant. *Irritated* might be closer. '*You're not supposed to be involved in this,*' he said.

'I'm not breaking any laws, Fenn.'

'Whoever this is you're looking for, they're dangerous, Alex. Can't you just leave things alone?'

Alex was good. He was skilled at dealing with people, and his professional persona surfaced. 'Fenn,' he said, 'I don't think we've got the identity right on this guy. Find out who he is, and you might find out why somebody tried to kill us.'

'Oh, c'mon, Alex. A guy who died twenty years ago?'

'I think there's a very good possibility that all this is connected. Fenn, I don't ask for much—'

They went back and forth for a couple of minutes, Fenn growing less adamant. Finally, he began to cave. 'I would if I could, Alex. But you're talking about something that's really old news. What's your evidence?'

'There are too many people involved in this who seem to come and go without leaving tracks. Barber. Agnes, who may or may not be her mother. Crisp. Maybe even Taliaferro.'

'Taliaferro has a long history, Alex. He did not walk in out of nowhere.'

'No. But he walked off. And seven more people disappeared out of the Polaris. I think it would be helpful if we could find out who's in Crisp's grave.'

Fenn held up both hands, the way people do when they want you to calm down. Or when they're pretending you're hysterical. 'Look,' he said, 'Crisp died when? Fourteen oh-five? Oh-four? And nobody has seen Agnes Shanley since.' He pushed back in his chair. 'I'll pass along what you've told me to the jurisdiction up there. With a recommendation they take a second look at the case. Okay? Will that satisfy you?'

'Are they likely to take a look at the body?'

I could see him debating whether to tell us what he really thought. 'No,' he said at last. 'From their point of view, no matter who's in the grave, there's nobody to prosecute anyhow. So why bother?'

14

People should only die when they fall off bridges. Or swim with the sharks. No one's lights should go out because a clock hidden in his cells has struck midnight. We seem to have a notion that when nature decrees we self-destruct, it is somehow wrongheaded to do anything about it, and we should go contentedly to our graves. Me, I'm looking for a detour.

—Thomas Dunninger,
Right to Life

Nature cares only that you reproduce and rear the kids. After you've done that, get out of the way.

—Charmon Colm,
Chaos and Symmetry

Alex talked about digging him up ourselves. I don't know how serious he was, but I pointed out that there were severe penalties for grave desecration. And I wasn't sure what good it would do even if we *did* find out who was buried there. It was a guessing game. Alex admitted that. And he backed off the idea when I started suggesting what the headlines would look like.

ANTIQUITIES DEALER TURNS GRAVE ROBBER
BENEDICT CHARGED IN DESECRATION PLOT

Sitting in the skimmer on the perimeter of the cemetery, watching the moon drift through the sky, I found myself thinking of Tom Dunninger, who had dreamed of doing away with graveyards. Or, at least, of reducing the need for them.

We decided to stay over in Walpurgis. Most of the restaurants and the larger hotels were closed for the season, but we got a suite overlooking the ocean at the Fiesta and ate in the dining room, which was inauspiciously named Monk's. But the food was good, and a few other people drifted in, so we weren't completely alone.

I don't remember what we talked about. What I remember is that I kept thinking about the grave, and wondering whether it had been an accident or a crime of passion. Or whether it had been something else entirely: Had someone found it necessary, or expedient, to kill Ed Crisp? Had he known something?

I had trouble sleeping. I got up in the middle of the night and fixed myself a snack. The sky was full of gauzy clouds, giving the moon a halo effect. For reasons I don't understand, other than maybe because I associated him with graveyards, I called up Tom Dunninger's avatar, which materialized in the center of the room and said hello. He was tall, dark-skinned, with somber features and white hair. He didn't look like the kind of guy who enjoyed a good laugh.

I had settled onto the sofa, with a donut and coffee at my disposal. *'What can I do for you, Chase?'* he asked. He was impeccably dressed in creased slacks, a blue jacket, and a white shirt with a string tie.

The last update to the avatar had been made in 1364, a full year before the *Polaris* flight. This was a Dunninger whose face was lined with age. His knees appeared to be giving him trouble, and he grimaced as he sat down.

'Can we just talk for a bit, Professor?'

'*My time is yours,*' he said. He glanced around the room. '*A hotel?*'

'Yes.'

'*Where are we?*'

'Walpurgis.'

'*Ah, yes. The resort. You know, I don't believe I ever took a vacation. In my entire adult life.*'

'You didn't have time?'

'*Didn't have the interest.*' He smiled. '*I don't think I'd have enjoyed myself in these sorts of places.*'

'Probably not,' I said. 'Professor, you achieved a great deal during your lifetime, but you're best known for your pursuit of life extension.'

'*It's nice of you to say so, that I made some contributions. But I didn't manage the one that mattered.*'

'—Because people still get old?'

'*Yes. Because people are still betrayed by their bodies. Because they live only a relative handful of years before they begin to decay.*'

'But isn't that the natural way of things? What would happen if people stopped dying? Where would we put everybody?'

'*It's the natural way of things that people run through the forests of Earth, chasing deer and wild pigs, I would guess. And getting chased. And huddling around fires on nights like this. Is it as cold out there as it looks?*'

'Yes.'

'*Is that how you'd prefer to live your life? The way your distant ancestors did?*'

'I'm not much into hunting. No.'

'*Or being hunted. So the first argument is turned out of court. And you ask, what would happen if people stopped dying? I'd argue, to begin with, it's the wrong question. Rather, we need to know what would happen if people were able to retain youth and vigor indefinitely. I propose, to begin with, that we would remove, at a single pass, the bulk of human suffering. Not all of it, of course. It's beyond our power ever to do that. But if we can stop the automatic funeral, kill it dead in its tracks, if we can stop the slow degradation that leads eventually to the grave, we will have given the human race a gift beyond measure.'*

'Professor, a lot of people feel death is not necessarily a bad thing. That a life that goes on too long becomes terribly dull—'

'—*It only becomes dull because the body becomes stiff and fragile. Things break easily. The energy level declines.'*

'—That it becomes a burden both to the individual and to his family—'

'—*Again, because of weakness. Of course the extremely old are a burden. I proposed to prevent that very condition.'*

I hung in there as best I could: 'It might be that art arises from our sense of the transience of beautiful things. That death is part of what makes us human. That people need to get out of the way so their children can move on.'

'*Hogwash. Chase, you're babbling. All that is fine when you're talking in the abstract. Death is acceptable as part of the human condition as long as we mean somebody else. As long as we are only talking statistics and other people. Preferably strangers.'*

'But if you succeeded, where would we put everybody? We don't have limitless land space. Or resources.'

'*Of course not. There'd be a price to be paid. Humans would have to stop reproducing.'*

'They wouldn't do that.'

He smiled in a way that suggested he had heard all this before. '*You think not?'*

'I'm sure of it.'

'*Then I would put it to you that if you offer a young couple the choice between having children, or living forever in young bodies, never having to lose one another, that their response would not be the one you predict.'*

'You really believe that?'

'*I have no doubt.'*

'So we stop having kids.'

'We'd have a few. Have to have a few, to replace those lost in accidents. It would be necessary to work that out, but it would be only a detail.'

'What about evolution?'

'What about it?'

'The race would stop evolving.'

'That probably happened shortly after we climbed down out of the trees.' He sighed. 'Okay, that was over the top. But do you really believe that some far-off descendant of yours will be smarter than you are?'

Well, no. But I thought other people could stand a lot of improvement.

When I didn't respond, he plunged on: 'We have no obligation to give nature what it wants. Our obligation is to ourselves, to make ourselves comfortable, to provide the means to live fruitful lives, to eliminate the pain and degradation allotted to us by the natural order, to preserve individual personalities. As far as the evolutionists are concerned, if they like dying so much, let them volunteer to be carried out. If we truly want to see stronger bodies, genetic engineering can already take care of that. If we want smarter people, we have enhancement techniques.'

'I don't know, Professor. It doesn't seem right.'

'That's because people have been getting old and dying for several million years. We've gotten used to it. And like any other necessity imposed by nature, because we couldn't do anything about it, we pretend to approve. Wouldn't have it any other way. I've actually heard people – women, primarily – say they wouldn't want to live their lives again under any circumstances.

'But we don't like dying. That's why we have religion. We've always tried to circumvent it, to tell ourselves that we're immortal. So we embrace physical death and at the same time pretend it doesn't happen.'

'Professor, somebody said the human race progresses one funeral at a time. People become less flexible mentally as they age. Wouldn't we end with a lot of elderly cranks in young bodies?'

'Oh, well, you have something there. There'd be some problems. Bosses would never retire. Never die. You get very little fresh talent. Funeral directors would have to branch out. Find another line of work. Politicians would try to hang on literally forever. But we've always shown ourselves to be an adaptive species. I think, for one thing, that if people did not have to face the ageing process, they'd be less likely to defend lifelong opinions. They tend to be crutches, principles people hold on to ever more desperately as the end approaches. But if no end is approaching—' He held out his hands, palms up. What could be more obvious? 'There would be a period of adjustment. But I think the end result would be more than satisfactory.'

'What happened to you?' I asked.

'How do you mean, Chase?'

'Most of us accept death and loss as the price we pay for our lives. What happened to *you*? Did you lose someone especially close?'

'Listen to yourself, child. Who has not lost someone especially close? A father, a sister, a daughter. A friend. A lover. We sit at memorial services and pretend they've gone into some sunny upland. We talk about the happy hereafter and how they're better off. We tell each other we are immortal, and that there is a part of us that lives on. But the truth, Chase, as everyone who's thought about it knows in his heart, is that dead is dead. Gone. Forever.

'You can see I'm not young. But if you want to know why I've worked on the problem, it's because I've watched too many people die. It's that simple. I want it stopped. And I saw a way to do it.' The room was illuminated by a single lamp. He gazed at it a long moment. 'We love the light,' he said.

'What's the stumbling block? I mean, I know we're able to get cells to reproduce indefinitely. That should mean virtual immortality, right? But it doesn't happen.'

'What's your background, Chase?'

'I sell antiquities.'

'Really?'

224

'Well, I also pilot superluminals.'

'Ah. Would you be interested in life extension for yourself? If I could offer it?'

'No. I'm satisfied with what I have.'

'A sensible position, my dear. But self-deluding. And ultimately dishonest.'

'I accept the terms on which I received my life.'

'Oh, Chase, you're beginning to sound shrill. You're still young. Give it time. Wait for the first effects of winter to settle in your joints. Feel the first flutter of your heart, the numbness in your fingertips, the growing chill deep in your stomach as the horseman gallops closer. And he is coming. At a gallop, as you'll learn. Youth is an illusion, Chase. We are none of us young. We are born old. If a century seems like a long time to someone like you, let me assure you that the annual round of seasons and holidays becomes a blur as the years pass.'

He was right, of course. None of us ever admits directly to wanting something we know we can't have. It doesn't matter whether it's a house, a lover, or avoiding getting old. We just go on pretending. 'Professor, am I correct in assuming that it's true you did not succeed?'

His eyes grew intense. 'Look at me,' he said. 'Do I strike you as a man with the secret of immortality?'

I said nothing and he broke into a broad smile. 'The problem is fundamental. It is not sufficient simply to cause cells to reproduce indefinitely. They must also communicate with one another.'

'Synapses.'

'Very good. Yes. Synapses. That capability is the very core of life. Brain cells collaborating to make a decision that it would be prudent to get out of the way of a flood. Digestive cells working cooperatively to extract nutrition from one's most recent meal. Cells in muscles taking directives from cells in nerves.

'When a human being reaches 125 or thereabout, cells simply cease talking with one another. For a long time we did not know why.'

'And we do now?'

'Ioline,' he said.

'That makes communication possible?'

'*That makes it* happen. *When the body's supply of ioline runs out, processes begin to break down. We tried to stimulate internal production, tried adding synthetic concoctions. Nothing works. Except for a very short time. There seems to be a clock, a timer, something that determines when the lights go out. It's called the Crabtree Limit.*' He launched into a detailed explanation, and I was lost from the start. But I listened closely, nodding occasionally as if I understood. When he'd finished, I asked whether he had any hope the problem could be resolved.

'*It has been the scientific grail for millennia,*' he said. '*Barcroft thought he'd solved it at the City on the Crag two centuries ago, about the time it was getting attacked by the Mutes. He was killed, and the lab destroyed. Nobody knows how close he might have been.*' His eyes clouded. '*Stupidity is always expensive.*' He stared past me, focusing on something I could not see. Then he shrugged. '*In the last millennium, Torchesky might have found a way to persuade the body to continue to manufacture ioline, and there was even talk that a few immortals were actually created. That they're still alive out there somewhere, hiding themselves from the rest of us. Legend, of course. The work was taking place in a politically unstable climate. A lot of people were frightened by what they heard he was doing. There was theological turmoil. Eventually he and his work were seized by a pious mob, and that was the last anyone ever heard of it. Or him.*

'*There've been other reports of breakthroughs, maybe valid, maybe not. But unfortunately nothing that's made an impact.*'

'Are you close?' I asked again.

'Yes,' he said. '*It's imminent.*'

Imminent. The word kept popping up.

It was time to go home.

We loaded up on sandwiches and coffee, checked out, and went up to the roof. It was another cold, overcast day, no sun, and maybe snow coming. We retrieved the skimmer and climbed in. Alex took the driver's seat. 'Louise,' he said, 'take us home.'

A sudden gust blew in off the ocean. There were only three other vehicles parked up there, which gives you an idea how busy the hotel was.

'Louise? Answer up, please.'

Nothing.

The AI lamp was dark. 'She's down,' I said.

Alex shifted his weight impatiently. He didn't have a lot of tolerance for glitches. Moreover, when one occurred, he always concluded it was somebody's fault. And, of course, never his. 'Brand-new vehicle,' he said, 'and trouble already.'

He tried the toggle, but there was no sign of activity. 'Probably a loose connection,' I said.

He grumbled. 'You always claim these things don't go down.' He switched over to manual and turned on the engine. 'We'll have to drive.' He extracted the yoke and engaged the pods. That always feels good, when nine-tenths of your weight drains off. There's another project that's been going on for a long time: trying to find a way to reduce antigrav engines to something you could wear, say, on your belt. If you could walk around all day feeling the way you do in a skimmer . . . But that's another one of those things that I doubt we'll ever see.

'We should take it back to them tomorrow,' he said. 'Get her repaired.' That, of course, would be my job.

He checked the screens for other traffic, touched the vertical thrusters, and we lifted off. I made a show of pulling on my harness to make sure I was securely belted. He grinned at me and told me to hang on. We swung around, passed over the edge of the roof, and turned south. The core thrusters fired, and we began to accelerate.

A couple of kids were walking on the beach. And somebody in the downtown park was flying a kite. Otherwise, Walpurgis might have been deserted.

If you had to drive, this was the kind of area you wanted to be in. There was nothing else in the sky, save a lone vehicle coming from the west. We soared out over the marshlands, which dominate the land immediately south of the city. A few klicks out, we passed into a gray haze. The sensors showed no traffic ahead, but I knew Alex didn't like driving when he couldn't see. So he took us higher, and we emerged into sunlight at about two thousand meters. A few minutes later, the clouds broke up and we glided out over Goodheart Bay. There were a few boats, and I thought I saw a long tentacle rise out of the water and slide back in.

I told Alex, and commented they better stay alert.

Alex enjoyed driving. He didn't get to do it often. But I think it made his testosterone surge.

The bay is big, 150 klicks before we'd hit land again, and Alex didn't seem disposed to talk, so I closed my eyes and let my head slip back. I was almost asleep when I realized my hair was rising.

'Something wrong,' I told him.

'What? You're not feeling well?'

'Zero gee.' That wasn't a good sign. 'We've lost all weight.'

He looked at the instrument panel. 'You're right. How's that possible?'

'I don't know. What'd you do?'

'Nothing. Are we going down?'

'*Up*. We're going *up*.'

I know everybody reading this rides his or her skimmer around and never thinks much about the mechanics of it. As I always did prior to the incident I'm about to describe. The vehicles are usually equipped with two to four antigrav pods. The standard setting for them is .11 gee. You switch them on, eighty-nine percent of the weight cancels out, and you can lift off and go where you want. The way it works is that the pods create an antigrav envelope around the skimmer. The dimensions and arrangement of the envelope differ from one vehicle to another, but it's designed for economy: The envelope is no larger than necessary to ensure that the entire aircraft, wings, tail assembly, whatever, is enclosed. If you could see it, it would resemble a tube.

The pods can be dangerous, so to change the setting you have to open a black box located in the central panel and do it manually. Alex looked down at it. He didn't like black boxes. But he pulled the lid up, pressed the control square, and waited for the gravity to come back.

Nothing happened.

He tried again.

We were still going up.

I took a shot at it and got the same lack of result. 'It's not working,' I said. Alex made a face that told me that wasn't exactly news. I pried the face off the unit and pulled a couple centimeters of cable out of the system. 'It's been disconnected.'

'You mean deliberately?'

I thought about it. 'Hard to see how it could happen on its own.'

The skimmer was a dual, which is to say it had two antigrav units, both mounted beneath the aircraft, one just forward of the cockpit, one toward the rear between the cabin and the tail. The control cable, which I held in my hand, divided in two and linked into both pods. When I tugged again on the individual strands, there was still no tension. 'It's been disconnected at both ends,' I said. 'Or cut.'

'Can we fix it?'

'Not without getting under the skimmer.'

The color drained out of his face, and he looked down at Goodheart Bay, which was beginning to look pretty small. 'Chase,' he said, 'what are we going to do?'

We were passing three thousand meters, going up like a cork in a lake. 'Lower your flaps,' I said. 'And kick in the thrusters.'

He complied. We accelerated, and the rate of climb slowed. But it wasn't going to be nearly enough.

He got on the radio and punched in the Air Rescue frequency.

'Code White,' he said. 'Code White. This is AVY 4467. We are in uncontrolled ascent. Request assistance.'

A woman's voice responded. *'AVY 4467. Please state the nature of your emergency.'* I wondered if it was the same person we'd talked to last time we got in trouble. *'Be as specific as you can.'*

'I thought I just did that.' Alex's temper surfaced. 'The pods are on full, and I can't cut them back. We are stuck at zero gee. Going up.'

'AVY 4467, there is a manual control for the pods, usually located between the front seats. Open the—'

'Rescue, I've tried that. It doesn't work.'

'Understood. Wait one.'

Alex looked out at the sky, looked at me, looked at the black box. 'We'll be okay,' he said. I think he was reassuring himself.

We rose into a cumulus cloud, passed through, and came out the top.

'Four four six seven, this is Rescue. Assistance is on the way. ETA approximately thirteen minutes.'

We didn't have thirteen minutes, and we both knew it. We passed through four thousand meters. The numbers on the altimeter were blurring.

'Rescue, that will probably be too late.'

'It's our nearest aircraft. Hang on. We'll get to you.'

'Chase,' he said, 'help.'

Suddenly I was in charge. The only thing I could think of was *We could jump.* Get outside the bubble and the ascent would stop quickly enough. 'I don't see an easy way, Alex.'

Lines creased his face. 'Air's getting thinner.'

Skimmers are not designed for high-altitude flight. They have several vents, and if the oxygen gets scarce outside, the people inside are going to feel it. My head was beginning to hurt, and there was already pressure in my chest. 'Breathe faster,' I said. 'It'll help.'

I looked around the cabin. There was a time that these things carried parachutes or glide belts, but accidents were so infrequent that more people died from experimenting with the escape gear than from crashes, so it was eventually decided that it was safer in an emergency for ordinary citizens to ride the aircraft down. But that assumed the aircraft was *going* down.

'How about,' he suggested, 'we shut off the pods?'

'We don't have that option,' I said. 'They're on and disconnected, so they're going to stay on.'

We cleared five thousand meters.

'Well,' he said, 'if you've an idea, this would be a good time.' He was speaking more deliberately by then, inhaling and exhaling with every couple of words.

'You have any cable in this buggy?' I was climbing into the backseat, to get access to the cargo compartment. 'Something we can use for a tether?'

'I don't think so.'

I made a show of looking around, but I knew there was nothing like that.

'Okay,' I told him. 'Shut down the thrusters and take off your shirt.'

'I don't think we ought to be joking around.'

'Do it, Alex.' He complied while I opened the cargo compartment and found the tool box. I took out a pair of shears, a wire cutter, and the key. The key, of course, was a remote that would open panels on the bottom of the aircraft.

'What are you going to do?'

I pulled off my blouse. 'I'm going to try to give you back control of the pods. Or at least one of them.' He handed me his shirt, and I used the shears to cut it and my blouse into strips.

He demanded to know how I intended to do that. But we were a trifle short of time, and I was in no mood to go into a long explanation. 'Watch and learn,' I said.

I slipped the key into a pocket. Then I climbed back into my seat and tied the cloth strips into a line. I looped one end around my waist and tied the other end to my seat anchor. 'Wish me luck.' I opened the door, and the wind roared through the cabin. It was frigid.

Alex was horrified. 'Are you crazy? You can't go out there.'

'It's safe, Alex.' We were both shouting to get over the wind. 'It's zero gee out to a couple meters from the hull. All I have to do is not drift too far away.' Or get blown off. 'But I need you to keep us as steady as you can. Use the verticals if you have to, and hang on to the yoke. Okay?'

'No!' He pushed back in his seat. 'I can't let you do that.'

I was halfway out the door. 'It's not as dangerous as it looks,' I yelled at him. And damned sure less dangerous than doing nothing.

'No! You stay here. *I'll* go.'

We both knew he didn't mean it. In his defense, I'd argue that he thought he did, but I couldn't see Alex climbing outside an aircraft under any circumstances. Even on the ground I don't think he'd have tried it. Moreover, he didn't know what to do.

'It's okay,' I said. 'I can handle it.'

'You sure?'

'Of course. Now, listen: When the pods reactivate, these two lamps'll go on. But don't do anything until I'm back inside.' I was trying to hold the door open against the wind. 'If anything goes wrong—'

'What?'

'Nothing. Never mind.' He'd have no way out.

One section of the tether was midnight blue, composed of strips of the most expensive blouse I owned. I sighed and climbed out the door. The wind howled. I wasn't really prepared for it, I guess. It caught me and ripped me off the fuselage and tossed me partially outside the envelope. My weight came back and my lower limbs felt like a bag of bricks. The skimmer was still going up, and it dragged me behind it. I suddenly became aware that I was dangling several thousand meters in the air.

I hadn't thought things out very well. The tether was wrapped around my waist instead of under my arms, and when it snapped tight it knocked the wind out of me. I needed a minute to recoup. Then I began to haul myself back up the line, hand over hand. The drag was horrific, but I'd been smart enough (or lucky enough) to make the tether no longer than I had to. Had I been tossed completely outside the bubble, I'd not have been able to do it.

As I climbed, the antigrav field took hold of my hips and legs again, and my weight went away. I grabbed a tread, got onto it, and tried to catch my breath. I now had access to the underside of the aircraft. It hadn't been pretty, but I was there.

Each of the pods had an access panel. What I would have liked to do was open both panels and reconnect the control leads to the terminals. The forward pod was within easy reach. But the one toward the tail would be impossible to get to because the tread didn't extend that far. And I couldn't just float back there because of the wind. Nor would my tether have been long enough.

It was getting progressively harder to breathe. A darkness was beginning to gather around the edges of my vision. I took the key from my pocket, handling it carefully so the wind didn't blow it away, and punched the purple button. Both panels opened.

In the forward compartment, I could see the loose cable. It was simple enough: I hung on to a strut with one hand and reconnected it. (I'd brought the wire cutters in case I had to splice.) There was nothing I could do about the rear pod.

When it was done I closed the panels.

We were still going up, of course. We passed through another cloud, and for the moment I couldn't see anything except cumulus.

When we cleared I climbed back into the cabin, fell into my seat, and pulled the door shut. 'I've only got one light,' he said.

'That's because you've only got one pod,' I replied. 'It should be enough.'

He hit the button and the status lamp glowed green and we got some weight back. The rate of ascent began to slow. The rear of the skimmer went up, and the nose dipped. That figured since the tail still weighed nothing. Gradually we nosed over and continued to rise more slowly until we hit apogee. Then we began to fall.

'Okay.' I reset the black box to zero.

'What are you doing?' he asked. We were looking straight down at the ocean.

'Preventing a crash. If we jiggle it a bit on the way down, turn it on, turn it off, we won't hit too hard.'

'We're going to crash again?' he asked.

'Probably,' I told him. 'But the air's going to feel better.'

We drifted down the sky. Alex clapped a shaky hand on my shoulder and told me I'd performed like a trouper. Made him proud.

The Patrol appeared and moved alongside. The bay got closer, but only slowly. We were descending like a leaf, while the Patrol encouraged us and told us to keep at it. My heart settled back inside my ribs, and color returned to Alex's cheeks.

Alex tried to manage things to keep us out of the water, but the position the aircraft was in prevented any kind of maneuver except up and down. Forty minutes after we'd begun to fall, we hit the surface. But unlike last time we slipped gently into the waves. It was nice and gradual, and the people in the rescue vehicle actually cheered.

15

We have solved every major scientific problem except the one that matters most. We still die too soon. I propose to set a worldwide goal that a child, born before this decade has ended, may look forward to a life span counted in centuries.

—Juan Carillo,
Counsel General, Aberwehl Union, 4417 C.E.

I can tell you that your perspective changes on a lot of things once you get the idea that somebody's out to kill you. It's bad enough, I suppose, if you're caught up in a war, and they want to take you out because you're wearing the wrong uniform. But when the situation comes down to where you're a personal first-name up-close target, you just don't sleep so well anymore.

I was scared. I wouldn't admit it, especially since Alex was describing me to everybody he knew as a daredevil. 'You should have seen her climbing around out there,' he told Fenn. And Windy. And one of the guys I was dating. And probably every client within range. And everybody else who touched base with us over the next couple of days. 'She was outstanding.'

Oh, yes.

In any case, that was how, for the second time in two weeks, we went into the ocean. Well, into Goodheart Bay, actually. But that's a technical point.

We came out of it okay. Rescue pulled us from the water. The power went off in the new skimmer, and it headed for the same neighborhood where the other one was. We filled out another round of forms, answered more questions, probably made the patrol's list of people to look out for. One of the Rescue guys suggested that next time we drive over water, if we'd let them know in advance they'd keep a unit ready.

It was too much for Universal, Alex's insurance company, which informed him he was henceforth *persona non grata*. Me, I went down to Broughton Arms to buy a scrambler. I gave them my link, and they ran the record. When it cleared, I picked up a small nickel thirty-volt Benson. It was efficient-looking, shaped, of course, like a pistol, capable (according to the manual) of putting somebody on the ground for a half hour or so by knocking out his circuitry.

Scramblers could, of course, be manufactured to resemble comm links or compacts or virtually any other kind of metal object. But my philosophy is that if someone has a weapon pointed at him, he should know about it.

Fenn lectured us again. 'I wish you'd stop the nonsense,' he told us. 'Either stay home, where you're safe. Or clear out altogether until we settle this matter. Don't you have anything planned that would get you away from here for a while?'

Actually we did. But eventually we'd have to come back. And there was no reason to believe that Fenn would be any closer to a solution in six days or six months. The problem the police have is that there are almost no crimes. So when one happens, they're more or less at a loss. I doubt they can resolve anything unless they happen to be in the neighborhood when the lawbreaking happens, or the perpetrator makes the mistake of bragging to the wrong people. Or does something equally stupid.

'I have a couple of specialists,' he continued, 'who aren't doing a great deal at the moment. It might be prudent if I assigned them to look after you. But you'd have to abide by their judgment.'

Alex made a face. 'You mean bodyguards.'

'Yes.'

'That's really not necessary. We'll be fine.'

Speak for yourself, big fella. Fenn looked at me. Personally, I'd have felt more comfortable with a cop at my side. But I took Alex's lead. 'It's okay,' I said. 'I'll be careful.'

Fenn shook his head. 'I can't force you to accept them.'

'We haven't been in a situation,' Alex said, 'where having a bodyguard would have changed anything.' We were all sitting in the Rainbow office. 'Has the investigation been making any progress?'

'Of course,' he said.

'Did the exhumation order for Crisp go through?'

'Yes. I told you it would.'

'Are they going to dig him up?'

'No. They didn't even take it to a hearing. They told us the case was closed a quarter century ago.'

I took to reading and watching everything I could find about the *Polaris* and the people who had ridden her on that last mission.

Nancy White was possibly best known for her fireside forays into the natural world. Her living room (or the set, whichever it actually was) looked extraordinarily cozy, comfortable, snug. White customarily sat in an oversized armchair, in the soft glow of an antique lamp on a side table. She was usually sipping a drink and talking to the viewer in a tone that implied we were all good friends, enjoying an evening together. There was inevitably a storm beating at the window, sometimes thunder and lightning, sometimes heavy snow. But it added to the warmth and good feeling inside.

This was a living room, she liked to remind us in one of her signature comments, that looked out on the cosmos. *'Like your own.*' She specialized in drawing parallels between natural processes and the human condition. Nothing is forever, not even a black hole. Springtime on Qamara, a world with (as she put it) too much ellipse in its orbit, was brief and quickly buried beneath a years-long winter, but the flowers were all the more valued for that reason.

Early in each of the White conversations, we leave the living room and sail among galaxies, or watch the fierce harridans of Dellaconda glide through the valleys of that distant world, or plunge into the fiery interior of Regulus, or soar through the churning atmosphere of a newly born world. If there was a recurrent theme, it was the significance of the moment. Life is not forever. Take the cup and drink. Seize the day. Enjoy the jelly donut.

One of her more moving shows used the ancient outstation Chai Pong as its central symbol. During the golden days of the Kang Republic, twenty-six hundred years ago, several successive heads of state engineered a major push into the Veiled Lady. The Kang set themselves an ultimate goal of mapping the nebula, a task that would take centuries, even for an exploration fleet many times the size of the forty-plus ships they had available. But they made the commitment and devoted their wealth and energy to the enterprise. They built outstations (one of which was Chai Pong) and established bases and for centuries they moved among those far suns, discovering and recording living worlds, including the one at Delta Karpis. In a show recorded exactly one year before the *Polaris* departure, she observed that the Kang had established an outstation, since lost, somewhere in the Delta Kay region. (It was the Kang who initially found the incoming white dwarf and predicted the eventual collision.)

Locating another technological species had not been their stated mission. They simply wanted to know what was out there. The habitable worlds were too far to establish settlements, even had the Kang been of a mind to make the effort. But the point that

White stressed was that in all those years, amid all those missions, no living civilization was ever discovered.

'It has always been argued that placing ourselves at the center of creation is an act of supreme arrogance,' she said from the Chai Pong control room. 'But in a very real sense, it is nonetheless true that humans are central to the scheme of things. Cosmologists tell us that we cannot ask why the universe exists. We cannot ask about its meaning. These are misleading questions, they say. It exists, and that is the sum of all we know on the subject.' She stops at this point and lifts a cup to her lips. 'Maybe, in a narrow sense, they're right. But in a broader context, we can argue that all the workings of the cosmos seem designed to produce a conscious entity. To produce something that can detach itself from the rest of the universe, stand back, and appreciate the vault of stars. Birds and reptiles are not impressed by majesty. If we were not here, the great sweep of the heavens would be of no consequence.'

In the end the Kang, exhausted in spirit and treasure, abandoned their outstations, gave up, and went home.

Chai Pong orbited a rocky world in the Karaloma system. The platform, the world, and the system had been all but forgotten. 'Given enough time,' White said, 'it's what happens to us all.'

Alex had a combination den and workroom at the back of the house. He'd covered the walls with pictures of the *Polaris* passengers, all in settings that emphasized their humanitarian contributions. Warren Mendoza looking down a line of injured patients in a surgical hut on Komar during one of its endless guerrilla wars. Chek Boland helping give out coffee and sandwiches at St Aubrey's in a poor section of a terrestrial city. Garth Urquhart landing with a relief unit in a famine-stricken village in South Khitai. Nancy White helping rescue workers in flood-ravaged and disease-ridden Bakul, also in South Khitai. A middle-aged Martin Klassner sitting behind a set of drums for the Differentials, a group of scientists with, maybe, musical talent, in one of a series of fund-raising events for survivors of a civil war on Domino. And, of course, there was the celebrated picture of Tom Dunninger, gazing at sunset across the West Chibong Cemetery.

It was supposed to be a day off. I'd gone in to conduct some minor piece of business. Alex, seeing that I was staring at the walls, stopped what he was doing. 'It's common to all of them, isn't it?' he asked.

'You mean that they were all humanitarians?'

'They were all true believers.'

'I suppose you could put it that way. It strikes me that the people who make the contributions are always true believers.'

'That may be,' he said. 'But somewhere in the mix, people need to be pragmatic.' I asked what he was suggesting, but he just shrugged and denied any deep significance. 'I do have a surprise for you, though,' he said.

After what we'd been through, I thought I was about to get a bonus or a raise or hazardous duty pay. So it came as something of a disappointment when he handed me a headband. 'Jacob,' he said, 'show her.'

I was in a dining room, seated, facing the head table. It was a big room, and I saw the logo of the Al Bakur Hotel.

'Never heard of it,' I told Alex.

'It was torn down,' he said. 'Forty years ago.'

The attendees numbered about three hundred. There was a constant buzz of conversation, and the clink of silverware and glass, and I smelled lemon and cherries in the air.

A chime sounded and a heavyset middle-aged woman seated at the center of the head table stood and waited for the room to quiet. When she had everyone's attention, she welcomed the audience, told them how pleased she was to see the turnout, and asked the organization's secretary to read the minutes of the previous meeting.

Alex leaned in my direction. 'We don't need to see this,' he said. The speaker and the diners accelerated and blurred. He stopped it a couple of times, shook his head, and finally arrived at the place he wanted.

'. . . *featured speaker for the evening,*' the heavyset woman was saying, '*Professor Warren Mendoza.*'

'This is 1355,' said Alex, as applause broke out.

'*Thank you, ladies and gentlemen.*' A relatively young and slim Mendoza rose and took his place behind the lectern. The *Polaris* was still ten years away. '*It's my pleasure to be here with you this evening. I want to thank Dr Halverson for the invitation, and you folks for the warm reception.*

'*I won't mince words. I want you to know that you have my full support. There is no more important work being done today than the effort to stabilize population.*'

'It's the White Clock Society,' said Alex, keeping his voice low.

Bone white, I thought. And it keeps ticking. It counts the time left before Rimway's population outruns its resources to the degree that people begin to die in large numbers. Their slogan was on the wall behind Mendoza:

We Can, or Nature Will.

'*Unless we persuade people there is a problem,*' Mendoza was saying, '*we will never be able to arrange a solution. Despite all our technology, there are hungry children on Earth, disease-ridden adults on Cordelet, economic dislocations on Moresby. Members of the Confederacy, during the past ten years, have suffered literally dozens of insurrections and eight full-blown civil wars. All are traceable, either directly or indirectly, to scarcity of resources. Elsewhere, economies go through their standard cycles, taking wealth from all and impoverishing many. This isn't the way it was supposed to be.*'

'Am I hearing this right? This is the guy who's trying to extend life spans.'

'No,' Alex said. 'That's Dunninger.'

'But Mendoza was helping him.' I looked at Alex. 'Wasn't he?'

'Makes you wonder, doesn't it?'

Mendoza talked for twenty-five minutes. He used no notes, and he spoke with passion and conviction. When it was over, he got a standing ovation. I've never worried much about over-population, but I wanted to join the general cheering. He was good.

Alex shut the program down and picked up a folder, 'There's something else that's interesting. I've been looking into Taliaferro's career.'

'What have you got?'

He opened the folder. 'In 1366, a year after the *Polaris,* he conceived of, and pushed hard for, the Sunlight Project.'

'Which was what?'

'Accelerated educational opportunities for select graduate students. He made the project work, but in the long term it broke away from Survey and received direct government funding.'

'Why is it significant?'

'It became the Morton College.'

That afternoon, when I had some spare time, I had Jacob post the convention archive again. Alex told me I was consumed by the *Polaris.* He had room to talk.

I looked through it, thinking that if Bellingham/Kiernan had been there, then Teri Barber might have been present as well. That meant I had to look at everything this time, not just the events I'd attended. Barber was a distinctive woman and would have been easy to spot. But there was no sign of her.

Alex joined me, though, and we spent the day at it. He got interested in the convention itself, and we listened to parts of several presentations.

I remembered my impression that the attendees were people trying to escape the routine of life, to add a bit of romance, to reach out and touch a less predictable kind of world. I saw the guy who thought everyone from the *Polaris* was alive and well and hidden in the woods somewhere. And the woman who'd claimed to have seen Chek Boland by the White Pool.

And the avatar of Jess Taliaferro.

I'd seen it at the convention and spoken privately with it later. But I froze the image and looked at it again, at the auburn hair turning prematurely gray. At the awkward middle-aged body. At the slightly puffy features. 'Alex,' I said, 'who is that?'

Alex chewed his upper lip and jabbed an index finger at the image. 'Damn,' he said, 'it's Marcus Kiernan.' He tried to remember the alias. 'Joshua Bellingham.'

Fenn called. *'Alex, we don't have a DNA record for Teri Barber.'*

Alex frowned. 'I thought everybody local was on record.'

'Well, all the law-abiding types. We got a sample from her apartment, but there's nothing to match it to. And that's not all. There's nothing on Agnes either.' Someone caught his attention. He nodded and looked at us. *'Be right back.'*

'Well,' said Alex, 'now it's beginning to make a little sense.'

'What makes sense? You got this figured out?'

'Not entirely.' He lowered his voice. 'But it's a darker business than we thought.'

Fenn reappeared. *'We also ran an archival search on Crisp,'* he said. *'The results are just in.'*

'And?'

'Ditto.'

'No record?'

His large heavy features were creased. *'Not a thing. Other than what's known about his life at Walpurgis. It's as if he never existed prior to moving there. Alex, I don't know what's going on, but it looks as if it goes back a lot of years.'* He looked up again at another distraction. *'I have to go.'*

'Okay.'

'Look, I'm not sure what we're into. But I want you two to be careful.'

'We will.'

'I've talked to the people at Walpurgis. We're taking another run at the exhumation order. If we can find out who Crisp was,

243

maybe we'll get an idea why he fell, or was pushed, off the cliff.'

During the next several days I hardly saw Alex. Then, on a cold, frosty morning minutes after I'd arrived, he walked into the office, dragged me away from a conversation with a client, and hustled me into the VR room. 'Look at this,' he said.

Another party.

'This is about six weeks before the *Polaris*.' Mendoza was front and center, smiling and talking with a small group of men and women in formal clothing. They all had drinks in their hands, and banners hung from the walls proclaiming yushenko. 'It's the opening of the Yushenko Laboratory,' Alex said.

I must have looked puzzled.

'You never heard of it?'

'No.'

'No surprise, I guess. It went under seven years later when the financial manager ran off with the funds, and contributions subsequently dried up. But for a while it looked like a researcher's dream.' He pointed over my shoulder. 'There's Dunninger.'

We were on our sofa, in the center of the room, while the action swirled around us. Dunninger looked uncomfortable in formal wear. He stood near a long table, loaded with snacks. He also was attended by several people.

The sense of actually being present was undercut by the fact I could not hear what anyone was saying. We got a distant buzz of conversation, and occasionally it was possible to catch a phrase or two, but for the most part we were doing guesswork and trying to read nonverbals.

Mendoza seemed to be watching Dunninger. When Dunninger excused himself and left the room, Mendoza also broke away and arranged to be waiting for him when he came back. He took Dunninger aside and walked him back out into the corridor.

Just before they disappeared, Dunninger shook his head no, *vehemently* no.

They were gone about five minutes. When they returned, Dunninger was leading the way. He looked angry, and the conversation had apparently ended.

They were colleagues. Dunninger had been working almost four years at the Epstein Retreat. Mendoza, at Forest Park, had been the man against whom Dunninger bounced ideas.

Dunninger crossed the room, picked up his drink (which he'd left on a table), and rejoined his group. But he looked furious.

Alex brought us back to the office. 'What do you think?' he asked.

'Just a disagreement.'

'You don't think there was more to it than that? I thought it looked pretty serious.'

'I don't know,' I said. 'When you can't hear anything, it's hard to tell.'

Alex went through a series of facial contortions, puzzled, annoyed, sad. Then he exhaled. 'I think it was the last chance,' he said.

'For what?'

He looked up at the tall-stemmed *Polaris* glass in the bookcase. 'Answer that, and everything else might fall into place.'

Alex had dinner with potential suppliers that evening. When he's out entertaining, he always reroutes his link so that any call gets diverted to me. Which is okay, but there's no provision for me to reach him. His theory was that nothing could come up that I wasn't qualified either to handle or defer. I could have had it inscribed in bronze and put in the office. Company motto.

So it happened that, as I was getting ready to pack it in for the day, Jacob informed me that a gentleman was on the circuit asking to speak with Alex. *'Audio only,'* he said.

'Who is it, Jacob?'

'He doesn't seem to want to identify himself, Chase.'

Ordinarily, I'd have told Jacob to refuse the call. Sometimes we get contacted by unscrupulous types who have lifted something from a museum, or made off with it in some other dubious way, and they want to have us take it off their hands. It's a magnificent piece of work, they say. And you can't beat the price. These kinds of people always stay away from the visuals. Usually, though, they will give us a name. It just won't be the right one.

But in the present climate, I thought I should hear what it was about before terminating things. So I told Jacob to put him on.

'*Hello?*' The voice was subdued and anxious.

'Go ahead. This is Chase Kolpath.'

'*I wanted to speak to Mr Benedict.*'

'I'm sorry. He's not here. Can I help you?'

'*Can I reach him? It's important.*'

'I'm afraid not. I'd be happy to help if I can.'

'*Do you know when he'll be available?*'

'What's your name, please?'

I heard a distinct sigh. '*It's me, Chase. Marcus Kiernan.*'

That got my attention. 'Marcus, I'm sorry, but I really have no way to get to him. You'll have to talk to me.'

He took a deep breath. In the background, I could hear the buzz of conversation. He was in a public place, trying to ensure that we didn't track him.

'Mr Kiernan, are you still there?'

'*Yes.*'

'If you want to talk to someone, it'll have to be me. What can I do for you?'

'*Meet me.*' He said it a bit louder than necessary, as if he'd just taken a difficult decision.

'Why?'

'*I've something to tell you.*'

'Why not just tell me?'

'*I don't want to broadcast it.*' Another pause. '*Come alone.*'

'Why? Did you want another shot at me?'

'*That wasn't me.*'

'It was your girlfriend, Barber. What's the difference?'

'*Please,*' he said.

I let him wait while I listened to my heartbeat. 'All right,' I said.

'*Chase, if anybody's with you, I'll clear out.*'

'Where are you going to be?'

He thought for a moment. '*In the lobby of Barkley Manor. In one hour.*'

I don't know what kind of impression I make on people, but I don't like to think I look dumb. 'No,' I said. 'I'll be at the base of the Silver Tower in forty minutes. I'll wait five minutes, then I'm gone.'

'*I don't think I can get there in forty minutes.*'

'Give it your best.'

Andiquar is the Confederate seat of power, and the Hall of the People constitutes the visible symbol of its presence. It's a magnificent, sprawling, marble structure, four stories high, roughly a half kilometer long. At night, it's bathed in soft blue light. The flags and banners of the Confederate worlds snap along its front in the winds off the ocean, and thousands of visitors arrive every day to gawk and take pictures. At night, the dazzling light display draws even larger crowds.

The Council meets there; the executive offices are located symbolically on the lower floors; and the Court convenes in the eastern wing. A series of fountains feed the White Pool, which runs the length of the building.

The Archive, which houses the Constitution, the Compact, and the other founding documents, is adjacent the Court. At the opposite end of the White Pool stands the Silver Tower of the Confederacy. In the daytime, visitors can go inside the Tower and take the elevator to the top, where a balcony circles the building. There are substantial crowds at almost any hour. Which was why I'd chosen the location.

I called Fenn. He was out of the office. At home. I had the code for his place, but he'd not be able to reach the Tower in time. So I left a message for Alex, grabbed my scrambler and put it in my jacket, jumped into my skimmer – it was now the only one we had left – and took off. Then I started to call Fenn again. But I hesitated. He'd send somebody from the station and maybe scare Kiernan away.

In a crowd, on the ground, I should be reasonably safe. If it was a setup, I thought I'd taken the initiative away from him.

It was starting to snow as I lifted away from the country house. But traffic was light going downtown, and I made good time, dropping onto one of the capitol landing pads with ten minutes yet to get to the Tower.

I patted my jacket, reassured by the bulge. I wished I had something lethal, but you can't really get your hands on a serious weapon without going through a lot of red tape. If it came to it, though, the scrambler would put his lights out, and that would be sufficient.

In case you're wondering, I was qualified to use the weapon. I wasn't exactly an expert, but in my full-time piloting days there'd been places I'd gone that you didn't want to visit unarmed.

The snow had all but stopped. There hadn't been enough to get any accumulation, but it felt as if more was coming.

The landing pads are on the roof of the Archives. You ride down in an elevator and come out one of the ramps into Confederate Square, close to the statue of Tarien Sim. The usual sight-seers were thinning out, most headed for dinner, some just getting out of the weather. I hurried along the perimeter of the White Pool toward the Tower.

It was closed for the evening when I got there, but there were still people gathered around its entrance, looking up toward the illuminated balcony. It was an obelisk, not really all that high. Only a few stories, actually. But it was a brilliant piece of crafts-manship – reflective, seamless, polished. It had been erected more than two centuries ago as a tribute to the men and women who had come to the aid of the Dellacondans and their allies in the long war against the Mutes. That was the action that had led directly to the formation of the Confederacy, which marked the first time in its long history that the human family had stood united. Well, almost united. There were always places like Korrim Mas.

It occurred to me belatedly that I should have worn a wig, or done something else to change my appearance.

I scanned the crowd, looking for Kiernan. There was no sign of him, but I was still a few minutes early. I stayed close to a group of tourists who were gathered at the edge of the pool. They were mostly standing with their heads back, looking up. I did much the same, while trying to keep an eye on my ground-level surroundings.

I'd assumed coming out that I was reasonably safe. But I began thinking how easy it would be to pick somebody off at that location. There were lots of bushes and trees lining the pool, and still more scattered across the Square. Any of them could hide a sniper. For that matter there was nothing to stop a killer from walking up alongside me and using a knife. It would be over before I knew there was a problem.

So I kept my back to the pool, tried to watch the shrubbery, tried to watch everything.

A family of three paused in front of me and took pictures of the Tower. On the far side of the pool, someone squealed in delight, and I saw running kids.

It was past the designated hour.

If he'd been unable to get here, he would have called. Right? Tried to get a delay.

A security bot wheeled past.

An older man with three or four people in tow explained how young he had been when he'd first gone there, and how the city had changed since then.

A couple of lovers strode by, holding hands, absorbed in each other.

A skimmer drifted down, hovered over the pool, then hurried away. A couple of people tossed coins into the water and smiled at each other.

The crowd opened up a bit, but I still saw no sign of Kiernan.

A group of young boys, all about twelve or thirteen, invaded the area. A kuwallah team, judging by their jackets. Two men were with them. The kids charged to the front of the Tower, and one of the men tried to slow them down.

I imagined Kiernan speeding through the night, trying to get there before I left to tell me – what? That it had all been some sort of terrible mistake? Nothing personal, you understand.

Off to my right, in the direction of the Archives, someone screamed. I heard the sound of running, then spotlights began to come on. It was a frosty sort of illumination.

People were moving toward the Archives.

Whatever was happening, I decided it was prudent to stay clear, to remain where I was. Lights appeared in the sky and began to descend. Security bots hurried past and cleared a perimeter. Within minutes, emergency and police units had arrived.

Word got passed around that someone had fallen from the roof of the Archives. 'A man,' they said.

The emergency vehicles touched down. I threw caution aside and tried to get close. I arrived just in time to see somebody carried into a med unit. Moments later it lifted away.

Police officers fanned out through the crowd looking for witnesses.

Kiernan never showed up.

I wasn't entirely surprised when Fenn called in the morning to tell us about the man who'd been killed at the Archives. 'Identified him from Ida's pictures,' he said. 'It's Kiernan. The same guy. No question.'

Alex told him I'd been there. Fenn's expression hardened. *'You're not going to be satisfied until you get yourself killed, are you, Chase?'*

'I tried to call.'

'Next time try harder.'

'It won't happen again,' said Alex.

'You keep telling me that. I can't protect you if I don't know what's going on.'

I told him about Kiernan's call. He listened. Nodded. Scribbled something down. 'All right,' he said. 'Thanks. We've got his DNA, and we are working now on establishing who he is.'

'Good. Let us know, okay?'

'If you hear anything more from these people, anything, would you be good enough to contact me? Right away?'

16

We cannot excise death from the process. If we sincerely wish to keep grandparents and elderly friends, and eventually ourselves, in full flower for an indefinite period, we had best be prepared to give up having children. But do that, and the creativity and the genius and the laughter will abandon the species. We will simply become old people in young bodies. And all that makes us human will cease to be.

—Garth Urquhart,
Freedom Day Address, 1361

The AI at the Epstein Retreat, Dunninger's longtime lab, had been named Flash, after a pet retriever. Three days after the departure of the *Polaris*, campers had gotten careless. The timber was dry, a fire wasn't properly put out, and the woods caught. The lab was completely destroyed.

When we'd gotten tired trying to figure out what Kiernan had wanted to tell us, we went back to trying to decipher the nonverbal communication between Dunninger and Mendoza. Eventually we got around to looking at the news coverage of the fire.

The blaze was already out of control when the media arrived. The fire brigade was only a few minutes behind, but by then the area was an inferno.

Epstein was located on a bank of the Big River. The facility consisted of two white one-story mod buildings, the living quarters, and the laboratory. At one time they'd been a boating facility and restaurant. There'd been rumors that Dunninger had been close to a solution to the Crabtree problem, but I had trouble believing he'd have gone off to a distant star system if he'd been on the verge of making the greatest discovery in history.

The fire had completely engulfed the lab. The buildings themselves, of course, resisted the flames, but the forest came all the way out to the water, so everything around them had burned. Lab materials burst into flame, or melted. In the end, the Epstein structures still stood, charred and smoking, but nothing else survived.

There was no serious effort to save the facility. Apparently some private homes along the western rim of the valley had been in danger, and the firefighters went there first. By the time anyone got near the laboratory it was too late. Judging from what we learned of the blaze, it wouldn't have mattered in any case. There'd been a long drought, and the trees went up like tinder.

Flash was gone, too. The AI, not the dog. The core material for Dunninger's work on life extension, which he called, simply, the Project, had not yet been submitted for peer review. It was gone as well. Up in smoke, you might say. Had he maintained a duplicate data bank elsewhere? Probably. But no one knew where it might be, or how it might be accessed.

There were no fatalities during the incident, and most of the homes on the western perimeter were saved. The rescue services congratulated themselves, and the media reported how fortunate everyone was, how it could easily have been a disaster.

Alex wanted to hear how Dunninger had responded when he heard the news, but his reaction never made the public nets. We dug around and discovered that his response to the damage was listed in the Environmental Service archives. But to get into those we'd have to make application and provide an explanation for the request. 'We should take a run out there tomorrow,' he said. 'Get a look at the records.'

'Okay,' I said.

'Afterward we can go to lunch.' Alex enjoyed his lunches.

The Environmental Services Department is located along the perimeter of a preserve named Cobbler Green, about ten kilometers southwest of Andiquar. It's a quiet area favored in the daytime by young mothers and in the evening by lovers. Sable trees, flowering bushes, sculpted brooks, curving walkways, traditional and virtual statuary. The building itself is, in the spirit of the neighborhood, an unadorned two-story structure covered with vines.

We walked into the main lobby, which was manned by an auto-processor. '*Good morning,*' it said in a gender-neutral voice. '*How may I help you?*'

Alex explained that we wanted to see the *Polaris* record that would detail Thomas Dunninger's response to the news that his laboratory had been destroyed. 'Thirteen sixty-five,' he added.

'*Very good,*' it said. '*There is a corresponding archive. The application forms are displayed. Please use the designated headbands.*'

We sat down at a table, put on the headbands, and the applications appeared. We each completed one, citing antiquity background (whatever that might mean) as the purpose. A few minutes later, we were directed to an inner cubicle. A bored-looking middle-aged man in a Forestry Service uniform appeared and introduced himself as Chagal, or Chackal, or something like that. He directed us to a screen, told us to call him if we needed help, turned, and left. An access board powered up, and the screen turned on.

We got some numbers and a tag identifying the date and time of the desired communication. Fourth day of the flight, 1365, audio only. We listened to a station comm officer inform the *Polaris*, attention Dr Dunninger, that a forest fire had destroyed the Epstein laboratory. '*At this time,*' the officer said, '*reports indicate complete destruction of the facility. Nothing of value is believed to have survived other than the buildings, and they are damaged. This includes, unfortunately, the AI.'*

A reply came back two days later. It was Madeleine's voice: *'Skydeck, the news of the fire has been passed as you requested. If there's anything additional, please let us know.'* Then she signed off.

'That's it?' I asked.

Alex exhaled. 'Damn.'

'I thought he'd get on the circuit and demand details. How it happened. Whether there was anything at all left. Stuff like that.'

'Apparently not. Of course, *complete destruction* pretty much says it.' We got up and started for the door.

'So what now?' I asked.

'How far's Epstein?'

The Epstein Retreat had been located in West Chibong, in the north country. We booked a flight, left that evening, and got into Wahiri Central shortly after midnight. Not good planning. We checked into a hotel and set out the following morning in a taxi.

West Chibong is exactly what it sounds like: isolated, remote, one of those places where, once you get beyond the town limits, there's nothing for a hundred kilometers in any direction except mountains and forest. The Big River runs through the area, providing good fishing, according to the locals, and, of course, it features the Wainwright Falls.

Alex told the taxi to pass over the Epstein site. It didn't have any idea what he was talking about so he sighed and directed it instead to take us to Special Services, which housed Air Rescue, Forest, and Environment.

It was headquartered in a big, grungy, domed building downtown. Not exactly ramshackle, but close. The interior was impersonal, drab, damp, not a place where you'd want to work. I'd expected to find pictures of the rescue services in action, skimmers dropping chemicals on blazing trees, emergency technicians tending to victims, patrols chasing a runaway boat through rapids. But the walls were undecorated, save for a few dusty portraits of elderly men and women you probably wouldn't have wanted to have over for dinner. There'd been a time when I'd thought briefly about doing something like this for a living. The rescue services especially had always seemed glamorous. And it would have been nice to dedicate my life to helping people in trouble. But I either grew out of it or found out the pay wasn't very good.

'Yes, folks,' said an AI. 'What can I do for you?' Sexy voice. This was going to be a unit made up primarily of young males.

'My name's Benedict,' Alex said. 'My associate and I are doing research. I wonder if I could speak with someone for a few minutes? I won't take much time.'

'May I ask the subject of your research, Mr Benedict?'

'The forest fire in 1365.'

'That's a long time ago, sir. Just a moment, please. I'll see if the duty officer is available.'

The duty officer, despite my expectations, was a woman. She was a tiny creature, early thirties, brown eyes, brown hair. She wore the standard forest green uniform and looked happy to have visitors. 'Come on back, people,' she said, leading us down a passageway and into an office. 'I understand you want to talk about one of the 1365 fires.'

Uh-oh. 'You had more than one?'

She introduced herself as Ranger Jamieson. There was something irrepressible about her. I never saw her again after that interview, but to this day I remember Ranger Jamieson. And I've promised myself I'll find a reason to go back again one day and say hello.

She brought numbers up on her monitor. 'Looks like seventeen. Of course, that depends on how you define the term.'

'You had seventeen fires that year?'

257

She nodded. 'It's about average for this region. We only cover a narrow area, but we get droughts on a regular basis. It has to do with the winds. And we have lots of campers, some of them not too bright. We also get a fair number of lightning strikes. In summer or fall, it doesn't take much to start a blaze.'

'The one I'm looking for took out the Epstein Retreat.'

She looked blank. 'I beg your pardon?'

Well, there you are. We were assuming everybody on the planet knew about the Epstein lab, but as a matter of fact, a few weeks earlier I hadn't heard of it myself. Alex explained what it did, who'd worked there, what might have been lost. Its connection with the *Polaris* incident.

'How about that?' she said when he'd finished. 'I know about the *Polaris*. That's the starship that disappeared back in the last century, right?'

'The passengers disappeared. Not the ship.'

'Oh. Yes, of course. That was odd, wasn't it?'

'Yes, it was.'

'And they never figured out what happened?'

'No.'

Her eyes brushed mine. Okay, so she didn't exactly know about the *Polaris* either. That's not really big news in most people's lives. 'And you think there's a connection with the fire?'

'We don't know. Probably not, but the fire happened right after the *Polaris* left.' Alex gave her the specific date.

'Well, let's see what we have, Mr Benedict.' She sat down in front of a display. 'Thermal events, 1365,' she said. Data appeared, and she began running down the list with her index finger. 'You know, the problem here is that we've never kept very good records. Especially before 1406.'

'Fourteen oh-six?'

'Don't quote me.'

'Of course not. What happened in 1406?'

'We had a scandal and there was a reorganization.'

'Oh.'

She smiled. 'Well, here we are.' She studied the screen, brought up fresh displays, shook her head. 'I don't think we have anything that's going to be much help to you, though.' She got out of the way for us, and we looked through the data. It was all technical details, when the fire started, its extent, estimated property loss, analysis of the cause of the blaze, and a few other details.

'What exactly,' asked the ranger, 'did you want to know about the fire?'

What did we want? I knew Alex: He was operating on the assumption that he'd recognize it when he saw it. 'It says here the cause was careless campers. How much confidence would you have in that conclusion?'

She flicked back and forth in the record, and shrugged. 'Actually,' she said, 'not much. We always determine the cause of a fire. In the sense that we announce a cause. But—' She paused, cleared her throat, folded her arms. 'We're a little more exacting, now. In those years, if they had lightning on a given night, and later there was a fire, lightning was ascribed as the reason unless there was some specific circumstance indicating otherwise. You understand what I'm saying?'

'They made it up as they needed to.'

'I wouldn't want to put it quite that way. It was more like taking a best guess.' She smiled, carefully distancing herself from those long-ago rangers.

'Okay,' Alex said. 'Thanks.'

'I wouldn't want you to think that's the way we operate now.'

'Of course not,' said Alex. 'You wouldn't have any way of determining where the lab was located, I don't suppose?'

'I can ask around.'

'It was somewhere along the riverbank,' he said.

She brought up the same news report we'd looked at earlier and zeroed in on a river. 'That's the Big. It's about forty-five klicks northeast of here. I can give you a marker.'

The marker would allow the skimmer to find it. 'Yes, please.'

'Something else. There's a man you might want to talk to.

Name's Benny Sanchay. He's been around here a long time. Kind of a regional historian. If anybody can help you, he can.'

Benny was well into his second century. He lived in a small cabin on the edge of town, behind a cluster of low hills. 'Sure,' he said, 'I remember the fire. There were some complaints later that the rangers let the lab go. Didn't bother with it because they didn't think it was important.'

'Was it important?' I asked.

He squinted at Alex while he thought it over. 'Must have been. All these years later and here you folks are asking about it.'

Benny Sanchay was small and round. He was one of the few men I've seen who had no hair left on his skull. He wasn't given to shaving, and his eyes were buried in a mass of whiskers and wrinkles. I wondered whether he'd spent too much time looking into the sun.

He invited us inside, pointed to a couple of battered chairs, and put a pot of coffee on. The furniture was old, but serviceable. There was a bookcase and a general-purpose table. The bookcase was sagging under the weight of too many volumes. Two large windows looked out on the hills. The thing that caught my eye was a working range. 'That would be worth a fair amount of money,' Alex told him, 'if you wanted to sell it.'

'My stove?'

'Yes. I could get you a good price.'

He smiled and sat down at the table. There were pieces of notepaper stacked on it, a pile of crystals, a reader, and an open volume. *Down to Earth*. By Omar McCloud. 'What would I cook with?' he asked.

'Get some hardware, and your AI'll do it.'

'My AI?'

'You don't have one?' I said.

He laughed. It was a friendly enough sound, the kind you get when someone thinks you've deliberately said something silly. 'No,' he said. 'Haven't had one for years.'

I looked around, wondering how he stayed in touch with the world.

He glanced at me. 'I've no need of one.' He propped his chin on his elbow. 'Anyhow, I enjoy being alone.'

So we were in the presence of a crank. But it didn't matter. 'Benny,' Alex said, 'tell me what you know about the loss of the lab.'

'It's not good for you,' he continued, as if Alex hadn't spoken. 'You're never really alone if you've got one of those things in the house.' I got the sense he was laughing at us. 'What was it you wanted to know?'

'The lab.'

'Oh. Yes. Epstein.'

'Yes. That's it.'

'The fire was set deliberately. It started near the lab. They did it when the wind was blowing east.'

'You know that? Know it for a fact? That it was deliberate?'

'Sure. Everybody knew it.'

'It never came out.'

'It didn't become a story because they never caught anybody.' He got up, checked the coffeepot. 'Almost ready.'

'How do you know it was deliberate?'

'Do you know what was going on at the lab?'

'I know what they were working on.'

'Eternal life.'

'Well,' I said, 'I think they were talking about life extension.'

'*Indefinite*. That was the term they were using.'

'Okay. Indefinite. What are we getting at?'

'There were a lot of people who didn't think it was a good idea.'

'Like who?' I immediately began thinking about the White Clock Society.

He laughed again. His voice changed tone, and he began to sound as if he were talking to a child. 'Some folks don't think we were meant to live indefinitely. *Forever*. We had a local church

261

group, for example, thought what Dunninger was trying to do was sacrilegious.'

Now that I thought of it, I remembered having heard something about that. 'The Universalists.'

'There were others. I remember people coming in from out of town. They were doing meetings. Writing letters. Collecting signatures on petitions. Getting folks upset. I always thought that's why Dunninger took off.'

'You think he believed he was in danger?'

'I don't know whether he thought they'd try to kill him or anything like that. But they were trying to intimidate him, and he didn't strike me as a guy who stood up well to bullies.' He went back to the stove, moved the coffeepot around, decided it was okay, and poured three cups. 'And religious types weren't the only ones.'

'Who else?' I asked.

'Lamplighters.'

'The Lamplighters? Why would they care?' They were a service organization with outposts – that's what they called their branches – in probably every major city in the Confederacy. They were a charity. Tried to take care of people who'd been left behind by the general society. The elderly, orphans, widows. When a new disease showed up, the Lamplighters put political pressure where it did some good and made sure the funding got taken care of. Several years ago when an avalanche took out a small town in Tikobee, the local government moved the survivors out and arranged to get everybody patched up, but it was the Lamplighters who went in long term, took care of the disabled, spent time with people who'd lost spouses, and saw to it that the kids got their education. Urquhart and Klassner had been Lamplighters.

'Yeah, they did a lot of good,' said Benny. 'I'll give you that. But it's not the whole story. They can be fanatics if you get on their wrong side. If they decide you're dangerous, somebody who's going to pollute the streams, or you're fooling with something that could blow up, they could get pretty ugly.'

The coffee was good. The flavor was a little off what I was

used to, a little minty, maybe. But it was better than the stuff I got at home. Benny shook his head at the sheer perfidy of the Lamplighters and how people like us could not know them for what they really were.

He had to be exaggerating. I thought of the Lamplighters as people who were forever arriving on disaster scenes to pass out hot beverages and provide blankets.

'They sent representatives to the lab to ask Dunninger what they were going to do to prevent the human race from stagnating when people stopped dying.'

'How do you know, Benny?'

'Because they always made sure everything they did got plenty of publicity. And the other side got put in the worst possible light. They thought death was a good idea. Gets rid of the deadwood. So to speak. They actually said that. And when they didn't get anywhere with the lab they got on the media. For a while we had demonstrators out there.'

'At Epstein.'

'Yes.' He rubbed the back of his head. 'And then there were the Greenies.' People who worried about the effect of population on the environment.

'Other people said they'd have to do away with the minimum subsistence payouts, because the government wouldn't be able to afford to pay all the people who'd become eligible.

'It got so bad they had to hire security guards. At the lab.'

'Did you know any of them, Benny? The guards?'

He broke into a wide, leathery grin. 'Damn, Alex,' he said, 'I *was* one.'

'Really?'

'Oh, yes. I worked up there about six months.'

'So you knew Tom Dunninger.'

'I knew Mendoza, too. He was here a couple of times.'

'Did they get along?'

'Don't know.' His face scrunched up while he considered the question. 'My job was mostly outside.'

'How did Dunninger react to the opposition?'

'Well, he didn't like it much. He made some efforts to reassure everyone. Gave interviews. Even attended a town meeting once. But it seemed as if it didn't matter what he did, what he said, things just got worse.'

'How about Mendoza?'

'I don't know that he ever got involved with the demonstrators. No reason for him to. I mean, he was just in and out a couple of times.'

'Were there any incidents while you were there? Anybody try to break into the lab?'

He swung his chair around, pulled a hassock forward, and put up his feet. 'I don't think anybody *ever* actually got into the lab who shouldn't have been there. Not while I was there, anyhow.' He thought about it. 'They got close. Right up to the doors a couple of times. People sticking signs under my nose. Making threats.'

'What kind of threats?'

'Oh, they were saying they'd close the place down. It got so that Dunninger wouldn't go into town. We did his shopping for him. But conditions never really got completely out of hand. The idiots came and went. Sometimes for whole weeks we wouldn't see anybody. And then they'd start showing up every day.'

'The police must have been involved.'

'Yes. They made some arrests. For trespassing. Or making threats. I really don't remember the details.' He squinted. 'People can really be sons of bitches when they want to.'

'What'd you think about it?'

'I thought the protestors were damned fools.'

'Why?'

'Because anybody who knew anything understood he wasn't going to succeed. We weren't intended to live forever.' He thought about it. 'On the other hand, if somebody actually figured out how to do it, I sure wouldn't want to see anybody stop him.'

*   *   *

Twenty minutes later Alex and I were drifting over the Big River searching for the Epstein ruins that the marker said were down there. It turned out there weren't any. Benny had warned us there'd be nothing left, but we thought he was exaggerating, that there'd be *something*, a scorched wall, a few posts, a collapsed roof.

The trees came out to the river's edge. They were relatively new growth, the older trees having been destroyed in the fire. There were still signs of destruction, fallen trunks, blackened stumps, but whether they were from the 1365 fire, or another one, there was really no way to know. Nor, I suppose, did it matter.

'Look for a bend in the river,' Benny had told us. 'You can see a small island out there with a lot of rocks piled on it. The lab's located just west of the bend, on the south bank.'

We found a few pipes sticking out of the ground, some buried paving, and the remnants of a power collector submerged in heavy brush. That was all.

The river was wide at that point. The island with the rocks would have taken a few minutes to swim to. I stood on the bank and wondered how the past sixty years might have been different had the fire of 1365 not happened.

17

People seem to be hard-wired to get things wrong. They confuse opinion with fact, they tend to believe what everyone around them believes, and they are ready to die for the truth or whichever version of it they have clasped to their breasts.

—Armand Ti,
Illusions

'I think,' Alex said, 'it's time we paid a visit to Morton College.' We were in our hotel suite at West Chibong.

'Everson's place?'

'Where else?'

'But if you're right about Everson—'

'—I am—'

'—Wouldn't that be taking a horrendous chance?'

'Staring back at the Gorgon,' he said. 'Chase, we'd be safer there than we are here.'

That hardly put me at ease. 'What makes you say so?'

'Everson knows we wouldn't go out there without informing someone. He wouldn't want us to turn up dead or missing when we were known to be visiting the college.'

'Okay. That makes sense.'

'When can we be ready?'

'This afternoon,' I said reluctantly. 'I have some work to do.'

'Let the work go. See if you can arrange transportation as early as possible. It's a long run, and I'd like to get there today.'

'If you want.'

'All right.' I waited for him to say something more. But he turned on his heel and started for the door.

'Alex,' I said, 'are we actually going to inform someone?'

'Jacob will. If we don't come back.'

'And what will we be looking for?'

'I want to confirm an idea.'

Morton College is located in the Kalo Valley in the far northwest, almost on the ocean. It's a cold, bitter climate, forty below on a pleasant day, with winds ranging to seventy kilometers per hour. There aren't many mountains, but the land is broken up by ridges, gullies, rills, and chasms. There's a huge waterfall in the area that, were it in a more hospitable place, would have been a major tourist draw.

The nearest town is Tranquil, a village with a population at that time of six hundred. Census figures revealed that people had been leaving Tranquil at a steady rate for about thirty years. The town was originally a social experiment, an attempt at an Emersonian lifestyle. It worked for about three generations. Then people apparently started getting fed up. I asked Alex if he knew why, and he shrugged. 'One generation's ideals don't necessarily fit the kids,' he said.

The college was six kilometers northeast of Tranquil. It occupied a substantial tract of land, maybe twelve acres, most of it wilderness. There was a complex of four buildings, all in the ponderous, heavy style of Licentian architecture. Lots of columns, heavy walls, curved rooftops, and a sense that the buildings would last forever. The grounds were buried by unbroken snow, so we knew the facility was tied together by passageways.

According to the data file, Morton College presently had eleven students. And a dean, whose name was Margolis. It limited itself to postgraduate work, and granted doctorates in humane studies, in biology, physics, and mathematics.

Despite what we'd been led to expect, the day was bright and warm. Well, warm in a cold, crackling way, in the sense that you knew it could have been a *lot* colder. An energy collector on the main building was aimed at the sky. We could see lights in some of the windows.

But there was no pad. Presumably it was under the snow.

'*Hello,*' said a cheerful female voice on the link. '*Are you looking for something?*'

'I was hoping,' Alex said, 'we might come by for a visit. My name's Benedict, and I was considering making a donation.'

'Alex,' I told him, covering the link, 'if Everson is involved, these people know your name. Maybe it would have been a good idea not to tell them who you are.'

'Give them credit, Chase,' he said. 'As soon as we walk in the door, they'll know.'

'*That's very kind of you, Mr Benedict,*' said the voice on the circuit, '*but donors usually proceed through Mr Everson. If you want to give me contact information, I'll see that he gets it.*'

'I understand that. But we were in the area, and I haven't really made a decision yet. I hoped you might allow me to take a look at the school.'

'*Just a moment, please.*'

We circled for several minutes before the voice came back. '*Professor Margolis says he can't spare much time. He'll meet you at the ramp.*'

The snow cover north of the complex broke open. Two doors rose into the air, the snow slid back, and we were looking into an underground pad. We descended and eased down past several meters of snow. The doors closed overhead, and we were in. 'That was easy,' I said.

The space was bigger than it looked from the air. Two other skimmers were parked, one on either side. We climbed out, and the voice told us to exit to our right. A door swung back, revealing a tunnel. More lights came on.

Margolis was the teacher you always wanted to have. Congenial smile, right-to-the-point attitude, a voice like water running over rocks. He was about seventy, with a shock of prematurely white hair, a neatly clipped beard, and sea blue eyes. His right hand was wrapped in a protective sheath. 'Broke it in a fall,' he explained. 'You get old, you get clumsy.' He looked at me. 'Don't ever do it, young lady. Stay right where you are.'

The place was paneled with light-stained wood. There was a bust of the dramatist Halcón Rendano, and another of Tarien Sim, and a couple of paintings of people I didn't recognize. It was the sort of room in which you instinctively lowered your voice.

He indicated chairs for us, introduced himself, and asked whether we would like some refreshment. Coffee, perhaps?

That sounded good, and he whispered an instruction into his link, and lowered himself into a hardwood chair, the least comfortable-looking chair in the room. 'Now, Mr Benedict,' he said, 'how may I be of service?'

Alex leaned forward. 'You can tell me a little about the facility, if you will, Professor. How it works. What the students are doing, and so on.'

Margolis nodded. Pleased to be of service. 'We are strictly an independent-study institution. We take students whom we perceive to be especially gifted, we provide the best mentors, and we, I suppose you would say, turn them loose.'

'I assume the mentors are not physically present.'

'No. That's correct. But those who are part of the program make themselves available on a preset schedule. We try to provide an atmosphere that fosters development. Talent mingling with talent, we find, often produces spectacular results.'

'Synergy.'

'Precisely. We give our students a place to live, where they can congregate with others like themselves, where they have access to unlimited academic resources. Our objective is that they have the opportunity to communicate with the best minds in their fields of interest.'

'Is there any charge to the individual student?'

'No,' he said. 'We are completely funded.'

A bot rolled in with the coffee and pulled up in front of me. There were two cups, both inscribed Morton College, with a coat of arms. I took one, and the bot proceeded to serve Alex.

'Freshly brewed,' said Margolis.

After the cold air in the landing portal, it was just what I needed.

'I'm interested,' Alex said, 'in some of the collaborating mentors. Who's participating?'

A broad smile appeared on Margolis's weathered face. This was a subject he enjoyed. 'There are quite a few, actually, depending, of course, on who is currently enrolled at Morton. We have Farnsworth at Sidonia Tech, MacElroy at Battle Point, Cheavis at New Lexington. Morales at Lang Tao. Even Hochmyer at Andiquar.'

The roll call was unfamiliar to me, but then I really didn't follow the academic world very closely. Alex seemed to be impressed. I decided I should make a contribution, and cast about for an intelligent question. 'Tell me, Professor,' I said, 'the college seems so small. Wouldn't it be more efficient to specialize in, say, the humane arts? Or in AI technology?'

'We don't strive for efficiency, Ms Kolpath. At least not in that sense. In fact, with a worldwide faculty from which to draw, we have no need to limit ourselves. Here at Morton, we remain open to a wide range of fields. We recognize the contributions made by science, which improves our lives, and by the arts, which *fill* our lives. We have numbered among our students physicists and pianists, surgeons and dramatists. We set no limits to human endeavor.'

'Professor,' Alex asked, 'what was the Sunlight Project?'

The smile broadened. 'You're looking at it. It was the

271

inspiration for what we've become, a way to provide for able minds to develop. It was the way we started, and it has changed very little.'

'Over sixty years. I'm impressed.'

'Over ten thousand years, Mr Benedict. We like to think of Morton as a direct descendent of Plato's Academy.'

'Would it be possible,' asked Alex, 'to speak with some of the students?'

'Ah. No, I am sorry, but they're at study. We never interrupt them, save for an emergency.'

'I see. Admirable custom.'

'Thank you. We try very hard to ensure the best possible atmosphere conducive to—' He hesitated.

'—Learning?' I suggested.

'—Perhaps rather to *creation*.' He laughed. 'Well, I know how that sounds. Can't help it sometimes. But so often we perceive learning as an essentially passive exercise. Here at Morton, we have no interest in producing scholars. We're not trying to assist people to appreciate Rothbrook and Vacardi. We want to find the *new* Rothbrook.'

Rothbrook had been a mathematician of note in the last century. But I couldn't tell you why. Vacardi's name rang a bell, but I had no clue why he was important, either. It struck me that Morton would never have let me in the door.

'Could we possibly tour the facility?' asked Alex.

'Of course,' he said. 'It would be my pleasure.'

For the next twenty minutes we wandered through the complex. Doors opened as we approached. Here was the community room, in which the students spent much of their leisure time. 'We encourage social development,' Margolis said. 'There are too many examples of potential greatness unrealized because an inability to interact with other persons created roadblocks. Hasselmann is a good example.'

'Of course,' said Alex.

And this was the gymnasium. With its attendant pool. One

student was in the water, doing laps. 'Jeremiah just came to us this year,' said Margolis. 'He's already done some interesting work in time/space structure. He operates on a different schedule from the rest of the world.' He seemed to think that was something of a joke, laughed heartily, and looked disappointed when we didn't react accordingly.

And our library. And our lab.

And our holotank. 'Used more frequently for exercises, but occasionally for entertainment as well.'

A young woman appeared. Redheaded. Quite formal. She smiled apologetically. 'Excuse me,' she said. 'Professor, Jason Corbin is on the line. He needs to talk with you. Says it's very important.'

Margolis nodded. 'That's the Education at Sea program.' He shook his head. 'They're always having problems. But I'm afraid I'll have to break off. It's been a pleasure talking with you both. I hope you'll come back and see us again when perhaps we're not quite so rushed.' He looked at the redhead. 'Tammany will show you out.'

And, that quickly, he was gone.

Tammany apologized. 'Things are always a bit frantic here,' she said.

We ate in Tranquil at the Valley Lunch. It was the only eatery in town, a small place with small windows overlooking a row of dilapidated buildings. There were other customers, and they all came in wearing heavy jackets and boots.

A bot took our orders, and while we waited Alex got up and walked over to the service desk, where he engaged the attendant in conversation. She was about fifty, probably the owner. They talked for a couple of minutes, and he fished a picture out of his pocket and showed it to her.

She looked at it and nodded. Yes. Absolutely. No question.

When he came back, he told me there really *are* students at Morton.

'Did you doubt it?' I asked.

'I heard voices upstairs,' he said. 'And there was the kid in the pool. But I wasn't sure they weren't putting on a show for us.'

'If you're thinking that way, Alex, how does *she* know they're students?'

'Well, she doesn't, actually. At least, she doesn't know they're *students*. But there are warm bodies in the place.' Our sandwiches came. He took a bite. 'I want to check to see if the scholars he named are really at the places he says they are, and if so whether they're actually part of the program.'

'Why are you so suspicious about the place, Alex? If it's not a school, what else could it be?'

'Let it go for a bit,' he said. 'Until we're sure.'

Irritating man. 'All right,' I said. 'Whose picture were you showing her?'

He pulled it out of his jacket. I'd caught enough of a glimpse to know it was a male, and I thought it might turn out to be Eddie Crisp. Don't ask me why; my head was beginning to spin. But it was a stranger. Lean, average looks, early twenties, brown wavy hair, brown eyes, friendly smile, high forehead.

'One of the students?' I asked.

'She's seen him. But she doesn't think he's a student.'

'An instructor, then?'

'I assume. Though probably not this semester.'

'Who is he, Alex?'

He smiled at me. 'Don't you recognize him?'

More guessing games. But yes, I *did* know him. 'It looks like a young Urquhart,' I said.

On the way home, he spent his time with a notebook. We'd been aloft less than an hour when he told me the guest professors were where they were supposed to be. 'Proves nothing, of course.'

He buried himself in the data banks, while I slept. Shortly before we were scheduled to arrive in Andiquar, he woke me. 'Take a look at this, Chase.'

He turned the notebook so I could see the screen:

MAN KILLED IN FREAK SKIMMER ACCIDENT

Shawn Walker, of Tabatha-Li, near Bukovic, died today when the antigravity generators on his skimmer locked at zero, causing the vehicle to become weightless, and to rise out of the atmosphere into the void. It is believed to be the first accident of its kind.

Walker was retired, a former employee of Cyber-Graphic, and a native of Bukovic. He is survived by his wife, Audrey, and two sons, Peter, of Belioz, and William, of Liberty Point. There are five grandchildren.

The report was dated 1381, sixteen years after the *Polaris*.

'It is,' he said, 'the only instance I can find of this sort of incident. Other than our own, of course.'

'But Alex,' I said, 'this is forty-five years ago.'

'Yes.' His eyes narrowed.

'So where's Bukovic?'

He commented that it was nice to be getting back where the weather was decent, then responded: 'It's on Sacracour.'

'You're not suggesting we want to go there?'

'You got anything hot pending?'

'Not exactly. That doesn't mean I want to go for another trip. Off-world.'

'I think it would be prudent to get out of range of the psychos anyhow for a bit.' He blanked the screen and looked meaningfully at me. 'CyberGraphic's specialty was AI installation and maintenance.'

'Okay.'

'The corporation doesn't exist anymore. They created a series of maladjusted systems, were responsible for some elevator accidents, of all things, and went bankrupt in an avalanche of lawsuits. That was about fourteen years ago.

'What's fascinating is that Shawn Walker was the technician on board the *Peronovski* when it went to the aid of the *Polaris*.'

He looked at me as if that explained everything. 'Audrey, the widow, is still alive. She remarried and was widowed again. She's still in Tabatha-Li.'

'I don't want to sound unsympathetic, but why do we care?'

And there came that self-indulgent smile, as if he knew something I didn't. He's maddening when he's like that. 'Reports at the time,' he said, 'suggested Walker's skimmer had been sabotaged.'

'Did they catch anybody?'

'No. Nothing ever came of it. People who knew him claimed he had no enemies. Nobody could think of anyone who wanted him dead.'

I read the story again. 'Let's go talk to the lady.'

18

A secret may sometimes be best kept by keeping the secret of its being a secret.

—Henry Taylor,
The Statesman

We did the research. Shawn Walker had done well with Cyber-Graphic, but had been forced out in what the industrial reports described as a power grab in 1380, a few months before his death, and fifteen years after his historic flight with the *Peronovski*. There'd been some suspicion that his untimely end was connected with events at the corporation, but no charges had ever been filed.

His wife Audrey married again several years later. The second husband was Michael Kimonides, a chemistry professor at Whitebranch University. He'd died eight years ago.

We let Fenn know where we were headed, and received his heartfelt wish that we stay away until he was able to complete the investigation. He told us, by the way, that they had found no record on Kiernan. '*Why am I not surprised?*' he grumbled.

Earlier I said that traveling around the local galactic arm was just eye-blink stuff. And that's true, up to a point. But the generator has to charge before you make the transit. That takes time, at least eight hours for *Belle,* and maybe a lot more depending on how far you're going. And, of course, you always give yourself plenty of leeway at the destination so you don't arrive inside a planetary core. Twenty million klicks is the minimum range. I'm inclined to increase that by fifty percent. So that means at least four or five days transit time.

The quantum drive has been a godsend for Alex, who used to get deathly ill during the jump phases with the old Armstrongs. It was a major problem because the nature of his work required him to travel extensively. I wouldn't go so far as to say he enjoyed it during the time I'm describing, but heading out at least no longer involved him in minor trauma.

While we waited for clearance to depart skydeck, Alex settled in the common room, which was located immediately aft the bridge. When I went back after setting up, he was scribbling notes to himself and occasionally consulting his reader.

'Maddy,' he said, by way of explanation. 'She's central to this whole thing.'

She'd begun her professional career as a fleet pilot and had taken out a Mute destroyer during an engagement near Karbondel. She'd been decorated, and when it turned out that the strike had taken place shortly after a cease-fire had gone into effect, nobody had cared. The Mutes, after all, had initiated the attack. At least, that was the official version.

She had apparently been an independent spirit. Didn't like having to deal with superior officers, and had left at the end of her obligated time to become a freelancer. She'd hired out to corporate interests, but got bored hauling passengers and freight between the same ports, and finally, at Urquhart's urging, signed on with Survey. It didn't pay as well, but it meant flights into places no one had ever gone before. She liked that.

Sacracour orbited the gas giant Gobulus, which was 160 million kilometers from its swollen red sun. The sun was expanding, burning helium, and would, during the next few million years, swallow its four inner worlds, one of which would be Gobulus, its rings, its vast system of moons, and, of course, Sacracour.

The planet's biosystem was eight billion years old. It featured walking plants, living clouds, and, arguably, the biggest trees on record, skyscrapers twice the size of Earth's Sequoias. Martin Klassner had predicted that humans would eventually learn to juggle stellar development and would stabilize the local sun. Sacracour would be forever.

The first settlers had been members of a religious order. They'd built a monastery in a mountain chain, called it Esperanza, and they were still there. And prospering. Some of the prime scholars and artists of the past few centuries have made it their home, including Jon Cordova, who, by many accounts, is the greatest of all playwrights.

Most of the planet's contemporary inhabitants – there are fewer than three hundred thousand altogether – live along a seacoast that's usually warm and invigorating. Lots of beach and sun. Great sky views. They haven't yet achieved tidal lock, so if you time things right you can sit out on the beach and watch Gobulus, with its rings and its system of moons, rise out of the ocean.

The hitch was that the section of seacoast to which we were headed was experiencing mid-winter.

The orbital transport brought us down to Barakola in Bukovic at night in the middle of a sleet storm. We were on the near side of Gobulus, facing away from the sun, and the gas giant itself had set an hour earlier. The darkness was almost absolute. We rented a skimmer, checked in at our hotel, changed clothes, and headed for Tabatha-Li.

It was an island, home to Whitebranch University, two hours from the hotel. We outran the storm and the clouds and sailed out under a canopy of moons and rings. Directly ahead of us, just off the horizon, we saw an oscillating blue star.

'What is it?' asked Alex.

'It's Ramses. A pulsar.'

'Really? I've never seen one before. It's a collapsed star, right? Like the one that hit Delta Kay?'

'More or less,' I said.

It dimmed and brightened. Dimmed and brightened. He didn't approve. 'Having that thing in the sky all the time would give you a headache.'

Tabatha-Li was quaint, quiet, and old-fashioned, but not in the way Walpurgis had been. This was last-century style with money. The island was a favorite location for retired technocrats and government and media heavyweights. This was one of the places local interviewers visited when they wanted commentary on some contentious political or social policy.

Audrey Kimonides, the former Audrey Walker, lived in a luxurious turtle-shell house on the north side of the campus. There was stone art on the lawn and a Marko skimmer by the pad. Audrey did not want for resources.

Icicles hung from the roof and the trees. Snow was piled up everywhere. Lights were on inside and out. Audrey had known we were coming, and the front door opened before we were on the ground.

If you're visiting a centenarian, you expect to see someone who's come to terms with mortality and exhibits a degree of composure and resignation. It's never expressed, of course, but you can see it in the eyes and hear it in the voice, a kind of world-weariness, a sense of there being nothing left that can yield a surprise.

Audrey Kimonides, on the contrary, was a bundle of barely suppressed energy. She strode purposefully out the front door, a book in her left hand, a wrap thrown around her shoulders. 'Mr Benedict.' She exhaled a little cloud of mist. 'Ms Kolpath. Do please come inside. You didn't pick the right time of year to come visiting.' She led the way back, warned us that the house was full of drafts, and settled us in front of a fire. 'May I get you something to fight off the cold?' she asked.

'By all means,' said Alex, warming to her immediately.

She broke out a decanter of dark red midcountry wine and, when Alex offered to help, insisted he sit and relax. 'You've had a long flight,' she said. 'I'll take care of it.' She popped the cork, filled three glasses, passed them around, and offered, as her toast, 'The world's historians, who never really get things right.'

She beamed at Alex to let him know that she understood exactly who he was and that she admired people who upset applecarts. 'Mr Benedict,' she continued, 'it's such a pleasure to meet you. And Ms Kolpath. The two of you. Here at my home. I can hardly believe it. I can't tell you how much I would have given to have been with you when you made your discovery.'

She was a trim woman, not tall, with startling blue eyes and the erect posture of someone half her age. Her hair was white, but her voice was clear and vibrant. She put the decanter on a coffee table, where we could all reach it, and sat down in an armchair. 'I assume you wanted to ask me about Michael.'

Michael was the second husband, known for his work on the Columbian Age. 'Actually,' Alex said, 'I was interested in Shawn.'

'Shawn?' She looked at me for confirmation. *No one's ever really interested in Shawn.* 'Well, of course. What did you want to know?'

There were pictures atop a bookshelf and on a side table. An audacious-looking young Audrey and a dreamy-eyed Shawn Walker. And a much older Audrey with another man, formal, white whiskers, officious-looking. Kimonides.

'I was wondering if you'd tell us about him, what kind of work he did?'

'Certainly,' she said. 'It's simple enough, I suppose. He designed, installed, and maintained AIs. He worked thirty years for CyberGraphic before starting his own company. But I assume you know that.'

'Yes.'

'May I ask why you're interested? Is there some sort of problem?'

'No,' said Alex. 'We're trying to figure out what happened to the *Polaris*.'

She needed a moment to process that. 'Shawn always wondered about that himself.'

'I'm sure.'

'Yes. Odd thing, that was. I never understood how it could happen. But I don't see how I can help.'

'Good wine,' I said, to ease the pace.

'Thank you, dear. It's from Mobry.'

I doubt either of us had any idea what or where Mobry was, but Alex nodded sagely. 'Ms Kimonides—' he said.

'Oh, please, do call me Audrey.'

'Audrey, yes. Shawn was on the *Peronovski*.'

'That's right. First ship on the scene. He and Miguel Alvarez – Miguel was the captain – were the ones who found the *Polaris*.' She looked momentarily regretful. 'Everybody knew about Miguel Alvarez, of course. The captain. But if you're the number two guy, nobody notices.'

'Did he ever talk to you about it? Did he tell you what happened out there?'

'Alex, he told the world. If you're asking me whether he said things in private that he didn't reveal to the commission, the answer's no. Except his personal feelings.'

'How did he feel?'

'*Spooked* would probably be the appropriate word.' I could see her looking back across the years and shaking her head. 'It was an unnerving experience. He knew Warren personally, you know.'

'Mendoza?'

'Yes. They were close friends. They grew up together. Stayed close all that time.' Her eyes slid shut, then opened again. 'Poor Warren. In the early days we used to socialize with them. He and his wife, Amy.'

'Did Shawn know anybody else on the flight? Did he know Tom Dunninger?'

'Not really. We met him once. But I wouldn't want to say we really *knew* him.'

'Audrey, I don't like bringing up a painful memory, but there was some suspicion that Shawn's death wasn't an accident. What do you think happened?'

'It's not a problem, Alex. I got past it long ago. I assume you want to know whether I think he was murdered?'

'Do you?'

'I don't know. I honestly don't know.'

'Who stood to gain by his death?'

'No one that I know of. May I ask what this could possibly have to do with the *Polaris*?'

'We're not sure it has anything to do with it. But a couple of days ago, someone sabotaged the antigravity pods in our skimmer. Very nearly killed us.'

Her eyes got wide, and she looked over at me, then at something far away. 'Well, isn't that strange? I'm so glad you're both all right.'

'Thank you.'

'You were luckier than Shawn.'

'I was fortunate to have this young lady along,' said Alex, giving me full credit. Deservedly, I suppose. He described what I'd done, embellishing it substantially so it sounded as if I'd been doing handstands on the wings.

When he finished she refilled our glasses and offered a toast to me. 'I wish you'd been with Shawn,' she said. A tear rolled down her cheek. 'It got a lot of coverage here, naturally.' I could see her replaying old memories. 'And you think there's a connection with Shawn's death.' The lines around her eyes and mouth deepened. 'But surely—' She thought better of what she was going to say and let it go.

Alex wrote something in a paper notebook. He often took notes when he dealt with clients. He'd learned long ago to avoid recording whole conversations, because it had the effect of making people reluctant to speak. 'Had there been any indication your husband was in danger? Any threat? Any warning?'

She sipped her wine and placed the glass, still half-full, on the table. 'No. Nothing like that. There was just no reason I knew of that anyone would have wanted to harm him.'

'Audrey,' I said, 'forgive me for asking, but if there had been a problem, would he have told you?'

That prompted a hesitation. 'Earlier in our marriage, he would certainly have said something. During the later years' – her brow wrinkled, and she looked uncomfortable – 'he never gave me reason not to trust him, Chase. He was a decent man. But I did feel he had secrets.'

I thought she immediately wished she could recall the remark. But it was too late, and she only shrugged.

'About the problems at CyberGraphic?'

'No. Not really. I knew about those. They were all trying to get control of the operation, three of them, and I'm not sure Shawn was any better or worse than the others. Not that they were vile, or anything like that. They were all just competitive. Opportunistic. Money and power were important to them.' Her eyes met mine. 'You know what I mean, dear.'

'Yes,' I said, not sure what she was suggesting.

'Audrey,' said Alex, 'what made you think he had secrets?'

She sat back and thought it over. 'He changed,' she said.

'In what way?'

'It's hard to put a finger on.'

'Did he not confide in you as much as he had?'

Those blue eyes became suddenly suspicious. 'Is any of this for publication, Alex?'

'No, ma'am. Listen, somebody tried to kill us. We think it's the same somebody who blew up the exhibition at Survey last month. And it might be the same somebody who arranged Shawn's accident. If I may ask, where were you and your husband based when the *Polaris* incident occurred?'

'We were at Indigo.'

'But, of course, he wasn't with you when the *Polaris* docked there on its way to Delta Kay.'

'No. He'd been gone for a couple of weeks. On the *Peronovski*.'

'This change in attitude, did it occur after the *Polaris* incident?'

She thought about it. 'It's hard to remember, but yes,' she said finally.

Alex nodded. 'How long were you at Indigo?'

'Three years. The standard tour.'

'Audrey, how would you describe those years?'

Her eyes brightened. 'That was a good time. Best years of my life.'

That surprised me. 'Most people don't much care for duty on the outstations,' I said.

Audrey glowed. 'We were a small group, the technical support people. We shared the same interests, and we all got along quite well. No, they were good days.'

'Not like here?'

'Well, not like the corporate world. At Indigo, he was isolated from the movers and shakers. Out there we were together, and there was no one else there except friends.'

Alex made another notation in his book. 'You left there in 1366?'

'Yes.'

'The *Polaris* and the other two ships docked at Indigo on the way out to Delta Kay. A year earlier.'

'Yes, that's right.'

'You remember it, then?'

'Oh, yes. It was a major event. Six celebrities on the *Polaris*. Everybody was excited. They did interviews. People went down to the dock hoping to see one or another of them. It became a holiday.'

'Did you see Mendoza during that time?'

'Yes. We had lunch together, as a matter of fact. At dock-side, I believe it was. They weren't in port long. Hardly a day, as I recall.'

'Was he excited about going to Delta Karpis?'

She frowned. 'I don't know. He seemed kind of quiet that afternoon.'

'Was that unusual?'

'Yes, I thought so. I'd always found him outgoing. Nonstop jokes. Everything was funny to Warren.'

'But not that day?'

'No. I thought at the time that he was overawed by the nature of the mission.'

'That might explain it.' Alex looked thoughtful.

She got up and went over and poked the fire a couple of times. 'I had a renaissance sandwich. Funny how you remember something like that. Renaissance and iced tea. And bamberry sauce. I don't know why it sticks in my mind. Maybe because as it turned out, I never saw Warren again.'

'They left next day?'

'First thing in the morning. I went over and watched them shove off.'

'Was there anything unusual about your conversation with him?'

'Not that I can recall.'

'Were there any contacts at all between your husband and Warren? Any messages pass between them?'

'I don't think so. At least nothing that Shawn ever mentioned.'

'Audrey,' I said, 'how did your husband react when you first heard what had happened to the *Polaris*?'

'Well, understand he was out on the *Peronovski*. He'd been gone a couple of weeks. They were on their way to some place or other, I really don't remember where, but it was Shawn's job to calibrate the AI. That's what he did, design and smooth out the AIs. At that time the company had been marketing a new system, or upgrading an old one. I'm not sure which. I'm trying to remember the name. Sailor. Voyager. Something like that.'

'Mariner,' I suggested.

'Yes. That's it. He took it out to run tests.'

'Mariner,' I said, 'became a precursor for the Halo series.' Belle was a Halo.

'So how'd he react?'

'I used to hear from him every day or so. When the news

first got to him, he sent me a message and told me he was sure everything would be okay. He said it was probably just a communication breakdown.'

'When they found the *Polaris*, did he continue to keep you abreast of things?'

'No. Captain Alvarez ordered him to stop all personal communications. I received a notification to that effect from the comm center telling me I wouldn't hear any more from Shawn for a while.' She smiled. 'It was very upsetting. They told me Shawn was okay, but we all knew something terrible had happened.'

'How long was it before they revealed that the passengers had been lost?'

'Three or four days, I think.'

Alex finished his wine, and put the glass down. 'What can you tell me about your husband, Audrey?'

'What's to tell? He was a good man, mostly. He was a good father.'

'How many children did you have with him?'

'Two. Two sons. They're both grandfathers now. He worked hard, Alex. He was a good provider. Liked to play simulated war games with the boys. They went on sometimes for weeks.' She smiled. 'I was just out of high school when I met him.'

'Love at first sight?'

'Oh, yes. He was the handsomest man I've ever seen.'

'I don't know how to ask the next question.'

'It's all right. He never cheated. Never showed any interest in other women.'

'No. That's not really where I was headed. Was he honest in his dealings with other people?'

'Why, yes. Of course.'

'Could he be bought?'

'To do something dishonest? No, I don't think so.'

Alex showed her pictures of Agnes Crisp, Teri Barber, and Marcus Kiernan. 'Do you by any chance know any of these people?' he asked.

She studied them and shook her head. 'No, I've never met any of them.' She focused on the two women. 'They look a lot alike. Styles are different, hair color. But aren't they the same person?'

Alex said no, he didn't think so. 'I wanted to thank you for talking to us,' he said, 'and for the wine.'

We came out the door, stood a moment in the cold air, then walked between the banks of snow and got into the skimmer. We lifted off and headed out to sea. 'Okay,' I said, watching the lights of Tabatha-Li recede. 'What was that all about?'

'Shawn Walker was killed because he knew something.'

'What did he know?'

'Let me ask you a question first,' Alex said. 'What can you tell me about the *Peronovski*?'

'Class II freighter. Sheba model. Obsolete. They don't build them anymore.'

'There were two people on board, Alvarez and Walker. How many people could the *Peronovski* support?'

'It had two cabins topside, and, as best I can recall, two below.'

'Damn it, Chase, I didn't ask about cabins. How many *people*?'

'No need to get excited,' I said. 'It was designed to accommodate three passengers plus the captain. Four in all. The rule of thumb is that your life support can normally handle fifty percent more than the official capacity. That makes six maximum.'

'What happens if they go for more than that?'

'Brain damage,' I said. 'Not enough air. Why? What are you thinking?'

Alex was staring down at the sea. 'I think I know *why* it all happened. What I'm trying to figure out is *how*.'

'Tell me why.'

'I think Dunninger had the formula he was looking for. I think the other five passengers were involved in a conspiracy to see that it never saw the light of day.'

'That can't be right,' I said. 'Those people were heavyweights. They weren't going to get involved in a kidnapping.'

'You want me to play Mendoza's address to the White Clock Society again? You've heard what they think. All five were committed to the idea that most human misery is in a direct cause-and-effect relationship with overpopulation. And here's a guy who's going to prevent people from dying? Who's going to see that the population of the Confederacy goes up by hundreds of millions every year?'

'So they kidnapped Tom Dunninger? And Maddie?'

'They kidnapped Dunninger. That's why they destroyed the Epstein lab. To get rid of everything. To ensure nobody else could repeat the work.'

'But why do something so complicated as the *Polaris*? If they were going to kidnap him and burn the lab, why not just do it?'

'Because, first, they knew they'd get caught if the authorities began investigating a kidnapping. It would have resulted in a massive manhunt. And, second, because they didn't want people to know that Dunninger was on the right track. Everybody assumed then, as they assume now, that it can't be done. So what they needed was an elaborate illusion. The Delta Kay business provided the perfect opportunity.'

'My God, Alex. You really think it happened that way?'

'I have no doubt.'

'But where'd they go? How'd they manage it?'

'I don't know. I thought at first they might have come back on the *Peronovski*. With Walker's collusion.'

'That's not possible.'

'Even with extra air tanks installed?'

'It would have been difficult. And Alvarez would have had to be in on it, too. Not to mention a couple of technicians.'

'Too many outside people.'

'I agree. They'd never have been able to keep it quiet.'

When we got back to the hotel, they had us sign a statement that we wouldn't go onto the beach for the next few nights because it was the mating season for the yoho and if we did go out and something happened, we would not hold the hotel liable.

'What,' I asked Alex, 'is a yoho?'

We were in the lobby. The snow had stopped, and the sea was gray and misty. 'I don't think we want to know,' he said.

19

It (the pulsar) is like those of us who seek final answers from the sciences: It casts its beams wildly about in all directions, but they touch nothing, reveal nothing, and in the end they lead only to confusion.

—Timothy of Esperanza,
Journals

It became an interesting evening. The snowstorm renewed itself and turned into a howling blizzard, there was an earthquake warning at about the time we were going to bed, and a few hours later they evacuated the hotel because a yoho got into the building.

The yohos, it turned out, were arthropodic creatures with a taste for people. Fortunately, they only showed up five days out of the year, which coincided with their breeding season, and on those occasions they rarely left the beach. After an hour standing in the snow, we were informed by management that the yoho had gone, everything was okay, and we could go back in. When we got to our suite, we inspected it carefully and locked the doors.

The quake hit shortly after we got back inside, but it amounted to nothing more than a series of moderate tremors. By then I had no interest in turning off the lights, so I went into the sitting room and spent time with Alex, who was engaged in a VR conversation. He handed me a headband. I put it on, and Chek Boland's avatar appeared. He was relaxed on a beach in a collapsible chair, wearing khaki shorts and a pullover and a wide-brimmed hat to keep the sun off. There was no ocean visible, or audible, however. The beach went on forever.

'. . . *one son,*' he was saying. '*His name was Jon. He was twenty at the time of the* Polaris.'

'What happened to your marriage, Dr Boland? If you don't mind my asking.'

'*I think Jennifer and I got bored. That's inevitable in any long-term relationship.*'

'You don't really believe that?'

'*I'm a psychiatrist. I see it all the time.*'

Alex was nothing if not traditional about such matters. He allowed his expression to reflect his disapproval of the comment, as if he were talking with a real person. 'I read somewhere,' he said, 'that sixty percent of all marriages endure. That they stay together.'

'*They tolerate each other, usually from a sense of duty. To the kids, generally. To their vows. To an inability to inflict pain on someone they think loves them.*'

'You're pretty pessimistic about the institution.'

'*I'm a realist. Long-term marriage is a trap that has survived from our beginnings in the forest, when it was the only way to guarantee species survival. That is no longer the case. Hasn't been for thousands of years.*'

'Then why has it survived?'

'*Because we've invested it with so much mythology. It's the sanctum sanctorum of adolescent giddiness. It is the sentence we impose on our lives because we watch too much romantic drama. And maybe because people are too scared of being alone.*'

'Okay.'

'*Was there anything else you wanted to talk about?*' He glanced down at his arm and made a face. '*Getting burned,*' he said. A new shirt appeared, with longer sleeves.

'Yes. There is something more.' In the background I could see a gathering dust storm. It's the sort of thing that some folks use not too subtly to suggest they have more important things to do than continue the conversation. But this was an avatar. Boland, I decided, had had a sense of humor. 'You were a crusader,' continued Alex. 'You gave time and energy to all sorts of causes.'

'Nonsense. I made an occasional contribution. No more than that.'

'You supported sweeping changes in education.'

'We've never known how to ignite a thirst for knowledge in our kids. Individual parents sometimes figure it out. But the institutions? They've been an unmitigated disaster for as long as anyone can remember.'

'You were a spokesman for Big Green.'

'People on Rimway don't notice yet the damage they're doing. But spend a few weeks on Earth. Or Toxicon. Now there's a world that's well named.'

'You were an advocate for population control.'

'Of course.'

'Is there really a population problem, Doctor? There are hundreds of summer worlds out there, with hardly anybody living on them. Some are empty.'

'Where are we now?'

'Sacracour.'

'Ah. Yes. A perfect example of your point. As of the last census, there are two hundred eighty-eight thousand six hundred fifty-six persons living on Sacracour. Almost all of them are concentrated along the eastern coast of one of its continents.'

'If you say so.'

'Three other major land masses, including a supercontinent, are virtually empty.'

'That's exactly my point.'

'The population on Earth is currently eleven billion. Plus or minus a few hundred million. They are pressed very hard.'

'But we could move them elsewhere. We have options.'

'Yes, we do. But moving whole populations to even the friendliest of worlds is not one of them.' His features hardened. 'Do the math, Alex. Do the math.'

'You're talking about resources to move people?'

'Of course.'

'So we dedicate everything we have to the operation.'

It was time for me to break in. 'There aren't enough ships, Alex,' I said. 'No matter what, there aren't enough ships.'

'The young lady is right. There are currently one thousand sixty-four superluminals in the Confederacy, with an average passenger capacity of twenty-eight people. Three will accommodate more than a hundred; many, as few as four. In fact, if you use the entire fleet, you still don't have enough capacity to move thirty thousand people. Assuming you make a round-trip every week with everything you have, which would be pushing it, you might be able to transport one million five hundred sixty thousand people a year. Round it off to one point six million.

'Toxicon's population growth is less than one percent. That shows restraint. But it still comes to five million births annually. So the population of Toxicon produces people three times faster than the entire fleet could haul them away.'

Alex could see he'd lost that argument. 'You're also opposed to reconstructing personalities.'

'Yes.'

'But that's what you did for a living. For almost eight years. And not just for criminals.'

'I believed in it at first.' He stopped, as if to think what he wanted to say. 'Alex, some of my patients were so fearful of the world around them that they couldn't get through their lives.'

'Fearful of the world around them? What does that mean?'

'It means they were afraid they'd fail. Or be rejected. They thought they might simply be inadequate. Drugs could be made to work for some. But there were others whose psyches were too delicate, and some, too twisted.'

'Suicides waiting to happen?'

'Or criminal or other types of antisocial behavior.' His eyes closed, and for a moment he said nothing more. Finally, he looked up. 'I wanted to give them decent lives. I wanted to take away the fear, to give them reason to respect themselves. I wanted them to be proud of who they were. So I changed them. Made them better.'

'Except—'

'Except that I came to realize that the person who emerged from the treatment was not the person who came to me for help. The old memories were gone. The former life was gone. The person behind the eyes was a stranger. I could have given my patients new names, and they would not have known the difference.'

'But if these people were miserable—'

'I did not have license to impose a death sentence!' His voice shook. 'But that was what I did. In more than a hundred cases. And that doesn't count the assorted killers, kidnappers, thieves, and thugs I was called on to treat.' He delivered the final word with venom. 'There has to be a way to untangle even the most diseased psyche. To keep the essence of the individual while softening the more abrasive qualities.'

'But you never found it.'

'No.'

'Why did you make the flight on the Polaris?'

His mood changed. 'How could I not? Who'd want to miss a show like that? Moreover, if you want the truth, I was pleased to be associated with Mendoza and White and Urquhart and the others.'

The records showed that Boland had kept his avatar current. The last update had been from Indigo, just before the Polaris left on the final leg of the mission. So I felt free to ask how things had gone up to that point.

He smiled. 'On the first leg of the flight, we were like kids.'

'You mentioned kidnapping a moment ago. Did you and your colleagues plan to kidnap Tom Dunninger?'

'Ridiculous.'

'Had he planned such a thing, would Dr Boland have informed you?'

'No,' he said. *'It would have been imprudent.'*

We left Sacracour, as we came, in the dark. It would be another nine hours before Gobulus rose, and eleven or twelve before the sun showed up. We were loaded with local treats, more desserts than I should have been eating. We were still getting snow and strong winds. The local authorities put out a traffic advisory, suggesting everyone stay put, but we didn't want to miss the ride up to the orbiter, or we'd be stuck another thirty hours. So we left the hotel on schedule. The flight was uneventful, and we caught the shuttle with time to spare.

It was a fifty-minute run up to the orbital dock, where we got our departure time (which would be four hours later), boarded the *Belle-Marie*, unloaded the bags, showered, and went back to the concourse for dinner.

We ate too much and finished off with a couple of drinks. By then it was almost time to go. We returned to the ship, and I went onto the bridge to do my preflight. I can't tell you that I actually saw a problem, but Belle seemed to be slow posting the status for some of the systems. I wasn't sure whether it was my imagination at work. But I asked her if anything was wrong.

'No, Chase,' she said. *'Everything's fine.'*

Well, okay. The numbers all checked out, and I informed operations that we were ready to leave. 'At your discretion,' as the line goes.

They told me to stand by. There'd been a delay of some sort getting a freighter loaded. *'You'll be a few minutes late,'* they said.

I went back and talked to Alex. I don't remember what about. He was distracted, and I knew he was thinking about Shawn Walker and the *Peronovski*. We waited a half hour before Ops cleared us for departure.

'Lock down, Alex,' I told him. Moments later the green light came on, signaling he was secure. 'Okay, Belle,' I said. 'Let's head out.'

I always enjoy casting off the umbilicals and getting under way. Don't ask me why. It's not as if I'm anxious to get to the next port, but I like the feeling of leaving things behind. First it's the station, then the blue globe of the world itself starts getting smaller. And eventually even the sun winks out. I tied the engines into the quantum generator so it would begin charging. We'd need nine hours to store sufficient energy to make the jump to Rimway.

Quantum technology had taken the tedium out of long-range flight. But it had also eliminated most of the romance. It was all very simple now. And almost too quick. You wanted to go from Rimway to East Boston, you ate a couple of meals, watched a VR, maybe napped a bit, and when the lamps came on indicating the system was sufficiently charged, you pressed a button. And there you were. You needed a few days after you got to the target system to make your approach. But basically, it was an eyeblink. The range was limited only by the strength of the charge you could pack into the system.

People had once complained that the Armstrong engines, with their ability to tunnel through linear space, had resulted in our losing track of how truly big the Orion Arm was. And how far from home the Veiled Lady really was. Now, you were in and out. Virtually teleported, with no sense of having gone anywhere. Distance, range, deep space, the light-year, had all gone away. And as it always seems to be with progress, you pay a price. The price might be in reduced safety, or in social dislocations, or, as was the case with the quantum drive, in losing touch with reality.

I turned the conn over to Belle and wandered back into the common room with Alex. That's a joke, really. Belle did pretty much everything in flight. I was there in case of emergency.

I wasn't looking forward to going home. It had been nice to be away from Rimway and feel safe again. Given my way, I'd have opted for an old-fashioned long flight this time. I felt secure inside the metal cocoon. I'd even have considered staying on at Sacracour, despite the blizzards and the quakes and the yohos. At least you could see the yohos coming.

Alex settled in for the evening, reading more about Madeleine English. 'She left no avatar,' he said, tapping the display. 'She was an ordinary pilot with an adequate work record.'

'*Adequate* is about the best you can do,' I told him. 'It means you always got where you were going with a minimum of fuss, and you never lost either people or cargo.'

She'd been running missions for Survey six years by then. Her biographers – there were four – noted that she'd had several lovers, including the best-selling novelist Bruno Shaefer. She'd been born in Kakatar and shown an early interest in spacecraft. Her father was quoted as saying somewhere that it was her love for the superluminals, and the intervention of Garth Urquhart, that saved her. 'Otherwise,' he commented, apparently not entirely kidding, 'it would have been, for her, a life of crime.'

She'd piloted the T17 Nighthawk against the Mutes and qualified for superluminals at twenty-three. That wasn't the record for youngest certification, but it was close.

There were pictures of her in uniform, in evening gowns, in workout gear. (She'd apparently been a fitness nut.) There were pictures of her at the beach, at various monuments, at Niagara Falls, at Grand London Square, at the Tower of Inkata, at the Great Wall. Here she was in cap and gown. There, in the cockpit of her T17. She stood with various groups of her passengers after she'd joined Survey. There were pictures of her with Urquhart, with Bruno Shaefer beside a publicity still for one of Shaefer's books, and with Jess Taliaferro at a banquet somewhere.

She'd never married.

Usually, when people talked about the *Polaris,* they talked about the Six, Dunninger and Mendoza, Urquhart, Boland, White, and Klassner. But I suspected, when they thought about it, they fixated on Maddy. Of them all, she was the one who came away seeming unfulfilled.

'What do you think about her?' Alex asked.

That was easy. 'She was okay. Apparently Survey thought so, too. They trusted her with six of the most celebrated people in the Confederacy.'

Alex was looking at the picture of her in uniform. Blonde hair cut short, startling blue eyes, lots of intensity. 'She took out a Mute destroyer,' I said. 'Riding a fighter.'

'I know.' Alex shook his head. 'I don't think I'd want to fool around with her.'

'Depends what you mean.'

He sighed. 'Women are all alike,' he said. 'You think we're all obsessed with sex.'

'Who? Me?' We were still almost eight hours from jump. And we were figuring four and a half days from home. We sat and talked for a bit, then I decided I'd had enough for the day. I took the reader to bed, but I was asleep fifteen minutes after I crawled in.

I'm not sure what woke me. Usually, if there's any kind of problem, Belle won't hesitate to let me know. The result is that the pilot of a superluminal can sleep soundly, secure in the knowledge that the helmsman will not doze on duty. But Belle hadn't spoken; nevertheless, I lay staring up at the overhead, listening to the silence, knowing something had happened.

Then I became aware of the engines. They were becoming audible. And changing tone. The way they did when running through the last moments before making a jump.

AIs do not make jumps on their own. I twisted my head and looked at the time. We were back on ship time, which was Andiquar time. It was a quarter to four in the afternoon, but the middle of the night to me. And two hours before we were scheduled to transit.

'Belle,' I said, 'what's going on?'

'*I don't know, Chase.*' She appeared at the foot of my bed. In her *Belle-Marie* work uniform.

'Belay the jump.'

'I don't seem to have control over the displacement unit.' She meant the quantum engines, which were continuing to rev up. We hadn't had time to take on enough of a charge to get to Rimway, but that wouldn't prevent us from leaving the immediate area and going *somewhere*. It just limited the options.

'Try again, Belle. Belay the jump.'

'I'm sorry, but I'm unable to do so, Chase.'

I was out of the sack by then, charging into the passageway. I banged on Alex's door and barged into his compartment. It took a moment to get him awake.

'Jump coming,' I said. 'Heads up.'

'What?' He rolled over and tried to look at the time. 'Why the short warning? Isn't it too early?'

You could feel the pressure building in the bulkheads. 'Get hold of something!' I told him. Then the lights dimmed. Quantum jumps are accompanied by a sense of sudden acceleration, only a few seconds long, but enough to do some serious damage if you're caught unaware. I heard Alex yelp, while I was thrown back against a cabinet. I saw stars and felt the customary tingling that accompanies passage between distant points.

The lights came back up, full.

Alex had been tossed out of bed. He got to his feet with a surge of intemperate remarks and demanded to know what we were doing.

'I don't know yet,' I told him. 'You okay?'

'Don't worry about me,' he said. 'The bone'll set in a few days.'

I scrambled onto the bridge. 'What happened, Belle?'

'I'm not sure, Chase,' she said. *'The clock seemed to be running fast.'*

'And you weren't aware of it?'

'I don't monitor the timers, Chase. There's never been a need to.'

Alex appeared at the hatch.

'Okay, Belle,' I said. 'I want to know precisely what's going on.

And while you're trying to figure it out, let's open up and see where we are.'

Somewhere, thrusters fired. The ship moved. Began to rotate. I grabbed hold of the side of my chair. Alex was thrown off-balance, staggered across the bridge, and finally went down in a heap. 'Belle,' I said, '*what* are you doing?'

There were more bursts. The prow was rising, and we were swinging toward starboard.

'Belle?'

'*I don't know,*' the AI said. '*This is really quite extraordinary.*'

Alex got to the right-hand seat and belted in. He threw a desperate look at me.

'Belle,' I said, 'open up. Let's get a look at the neighborhood.'

Still nothing.

'Okay, how about the monitors then?' I was striving to keep my voice level. Don't alarm the passengers. Never sound as if you've lost control of events. 'Let's see what the telescopes have.'

The screens remained blank.

'Belle. Give us the feed from the scopes.' I dropped into my chair and belted down.

'*There's a break in the alignment, Chase.*' Her voice was flat. Detached. '*I can't get a picture.*'

'Where?'

'*Main relay.*'

'Damn you, Belle,' I said, 'what's Walt Chambers's real name?' Walt Chambers was a client we'd carried a couple of years earlier while he was researching ruins on Baklava. He'd been with a group of academics, and his name was Harbach Edward Chambers. But he didn't like *Harbach*. He looked a lot like Walter Strong, the old horn player. He'd claimed the name *Walt* during adolescence, and it stuck. He'd traveled with us, and Belle knew him.

'*Searching,*' she said.

'Search, hell.' I opened the data flow panel. System status seemed normal. 'Belle,' I said, 'take yourself off-line.'

The main engines fired a short burst, then shut down. There

followed a series of volleys from the attitude thrusters. Up, down, port, and back to center. We were aligning ourselves on a new course.

'I'm sorry, Chase. I don't seem to be able to do that.'

'Hey,' said Alex, 'what's going on?'

'I'm working on it.' The port thrusters fired. 'She's changing our heading.'

'Why?'

'Damn it, Alex, how do I know?'

I was suddenly aware I was floating. My hair drifted up, and I was rising against the seat belts. The ship's rotational motion stopped, and the main engines came back on. We began to accelerate. At maximum thrust.

'Gravity's off,' Alex said. 'You okay?'

'I'm fine.' I tried to take Belle off-line, but nothing happened.

'You're giving us a hell of a ride, Chase.'

'It's not me.' The engines shut down again and the gee forces went away. The ship became dead quiet, and a series of status lamps began to blink. 'Son of a bitch,' I said. 'I don't believe it.'

'What's wrong?'

'Belle's dumping our fuel.'

'My God,' he said. 'All of it?'

I tried again to wrestle control away from her. The fuel status lamp went to amber, then to red, then to bright scarlet.

I released my harness and got over to the maintenance panel.

'What are you going to do?' Alex demanded.

'For a start, we're going to disable her.' I opened the panel.

'I'm sorry, Chase,' said Belle. *'Nothing personal.'*

Yeah. Right. It didn't even *sound* like Belle anymore. And what chilled me most was that I detected a sense of genuine regret. I twisted the handle, punched her buttons, and her lights went out. 'Good-bye,' I said.

'She gone?'

'Yes.'

'What happened to her?' Alex asked. 'Are we okay?'

'It wasn't Belie,' I said. 'Hang on, I'm going to restore gravity.'

'Good,' said Alex. 'If you could make it quick—'

'I'm working as fast as I can.' Artificial gravity is normally controlled by the AI. To reset it, I had to switch over to manual, and punch in more numbers. Our weight flowed back.

Alex sat quietly, looking stunned. 'What's our situation?' he asked, finally.

'Can't be good. We're adrift in a hot area.'

'Hot?'

'There's a lot of radiation out there. Let's get a look.' Despite Belle's claims, the telescopes worked fine. They aren't designed to be operated manually, though. I had to turn each on individually, then aim it. There were six of them, so it took a while. I routed the feed into the displays. One by one, the pictures came on.

The *Belle-Marie* was in the middle of a light show.

Two bright blue lights slashed across the monitors. It was a saber dance, and the sabers were long, twisted beams of light. 'What the hell is it?' asked Alex.

It was the sort of effect an ancient lighthouse might have caused had the lamp been bouncing around inside and spinning wildly.

The lamp itself appeared to be a blue star.

Alex was watching me, reading my face. 'So what is it?'

'Ramses.'

'The pulsar?'

'Yes. Has to be.' I was pressing my earphones, listening to it. I put it on the speaker, and the bridge filled with a sound like waves of ice and sleet rattling against the hull.

'Doesn't sound good,' he said.

'We're headed directly into the lights.'

'What happens when we get there?'

'We'll fry. If we're still alive at that point. Radiation's already going up.'

He didn't take that real well. There was some profanity, which was rare for him. And then he told me in a cool level voice that we needed to do something.

I was in a state of near shock myself. 'I don't believe this,' I said. 'Leave the damned ship under the supervision of nitwits, and this is what happens.' Someone had re-programmed or replaced Belle. Probably the latter.

His eyes were wide, and there was something accusing in that stare. How could you let this happen?

We were getting more warning lights. External radiation levels were increasing. I was checking time in flight, the range from Sacracour to Ramses, the status the quantum engines would have attained before transition. It *was* Ramses. No doubt. A collapsed star. Or maybe the burned-out remains of a supernova. I wasn't really up on my celestial physics. In any case, I knew it was a beast we wanted to stay well away from.

The beams flicked past, moving so quickly they constituted a blur. I froze one of them. 'It's mostly a slug of gamma rays and photons.'

'Can we get clear?'

It was a cosmic meat slicer, and we were headed into it with no power and no way to change course. 'We have no engines,' I said.

'How long?'

'Seven hours. Give or take.'

'What about the jump engines? Can't we jump out of here?'

'They're useless without the mains.' I switched on the hyperlight transmitter. 'Arapol, this is the *Belle-Marie*. Code White. We are adrift near Ramses. Heavy radiation. Request immediate assistance. I say again: Code White.' I added our coordinates, set the message to repeat, and began transmitting.

Help wasn't going to arrive in time. So I began working on the assumption we'd have to save ourselves. To that end, I pulled up everything we had on pulsars in general and Ramses in particular. I'd never really had any cause to concern myself with pulsars. The only bit of information I thought I needed was pretty basic: Stay away from them. 'It has an extremely strong magnetic field,' I told Alex. 'It says here that it bounces around a lot, the magnetic field, sometimes close to light speed. It interacts with the magnetic poles, and that's what generates what you're looking at.'

'The lights?'

'Yep. They're *cones*.' We still had the frozen image on one of the screens. 'There are two of them. Ramses is a neutron star. It spins pretty fast, and the cones rotate with it.'

'Must be *damned* fast. They're a blur.'

'It rotates once in about three-quarters of a second.'

'You mean the star *spins* on its axis at that rate?'

'Yes.'

'How the hell's that possible?'

'It's small, Alex. Like the one that hit Delta Kay. It's only a few kilometers across.'

'And it spins like a banshee.'

'You got it. This is a slow one. Some of them do several hundred revolutions per second.' The two shafts of blue light both originated on the neutron star. Their narrow ends pointed toward the pulsar.

I've discovered since then that, like any superdense star, a pulsar has trouble supporting its own weight. It keeps squeezing down until it achieves some sort of stability. And the more it squeezes, the faster it spins. The point is that as the pulsar gets smaller, its magnetic field becomes more compressed. Stronger. It becomes a dynamo.

'Sons of bitches,' said Alex. 'I hope we can get our hands on the people who did this.'

'Consider yourself lucky the quantum drive isn't too precise. Or they'd have shipped us right into the thing. As it is, at least we got some breathing space.'

We were 60 million klicks from the pulsar. The cones at that range were almost 6 million kilometers in diameter. And they were directly in front of us, dancing all over the sky.

305

Hull temperature was up, but within levels of tolerance. Internal power was okay. Attitude thrusters had fuel left. The AI was dead. We had some computer power available, off-line from the AI.

So how do you change the course of a starship when you can't run the engines?

'Maybe,' suggested Alex, 'we could start heaving furniture out the airlock.'

20

We imagine that we have some control over events. But in fact we are all adrift in currents and eddies that sweep us about, carrying some downstream to sunlit banks, and others onto the rocks.

—Tulisofala,
Mountain Passes, translated by Leisha Tanner

By any reasonable definition of a star, Ramses was dead. Collapsed. Crushed by its own weight. Its nuclear fires were long since burned out. But its magnetic field had intensified. It was a trillion times stronger than Rimway's. Or Earth's. It was throwing out vast torrents of charged particles.

Most of the particles escaped along magnetic field lines. They came off the surface in opposite directions from the north and south magnetic poles. Which meant there were two streams, accounting for the two light cones. They were necessarily narrow at the source, but they got wider as they moved out into space. It was those streams, more or less anchored on a wildly rotating body, that produced the lighthouse effect. But Ramses was a lighthouse spinning so swiftly and so wildly that even the beams of light got confused.

'That's why the cones are twisted at intervals,' I told Alex.

'Ramses spins like a maniac, and the light cones are millions of kilometers long. But the particles can only travel at light speed, so they become spirals.' I'd been punching data into the processing unit and was starting to get results. 'Okay,' I said, 'we're not in orbit. But we're going to go right through the circus.'

The link dinged. Transmission from Arapol. It was a bit like awaiting sentence.

I activated it. A short dumpy man appeared up front. '*Belle-Marie, this is Arapol. Emergency unit Toronto is on the way. Forward situation and location to us for relay to rescue vessel. Radio transmissions are negative your area. Too much interference from Ramses. ETA Toronto nine hours from time of transmission this message. Do not go near the pulsar. I say again, do not approach the pulsar.*'

'Nine hours,' said Alex. 'Call him back. Tell him that's not good enough.'

'Alex,' I said, 'they could get here during the next ten minutes, and they wouldn't be able to find us in time.' With radio transmissions wiped out by the pulsar, it could take *weeks*.

I wasn't feeling very well. 'Me neither,' said Alex. 'You don't think any of that radiation's getting in, do you?'

I'd been watching the numbers. Radiation levels outside were still rising, would continue to rise as long as we kept getting nearer the pulsar. But they weren't yet close to being a problem. 'No,' I said, 'we're fine.' But my head was starting to spin, and my stomach was sliding toward throw-up mode.

'Good.' He looked terrible. 'Back in a minute.' He released himself from his harness and pulled himself out of the chair.

I watched him stagger toward the hatch. 'Be careful.'

He left without answering.

The washroom door closed. A few minutes later, when he came back, he still looked pale. 'I wonder,' he said, 'if they did something to life support, too?'

I ran an environment check. 'I don't see anything,' I said.

'I'm glad to hear it. But something's wrong.'

I saw nothing on the status boards. No evidence of a radiation leak. The ship was holding steady. What was making us sick?

'Alex,' I said, 'I'm going to shut everything down for a minute.' He nodded, and I killed the power. The lights went off. And the fans. And gravity. Backup lamps blinked on. We drifted silently through the night.

And there it was. 'Feel it?' I asked.

'Something,' he said.

It had a rhythm. Like a tide rolling in and out.

'Are we tumbling?'

'No. It's more like a pulse. A heartbeat.'

I wished I knew more about pulsars. We'd done a segment on them at school, but I never expected to go anywhere near one. Nobody *ever* goes near one. My kabba cup was a small metal container with a straw. I removed the cup from its holder and released it.

In the zero-gee environment, it floated away, drifting toward the open hatchway. It disappeared out into the common room. I repeated the experiment with a metal clip. It also went out through the hatch.

'What are you doing?' asked Alex.

'Just a moment.' I tried a handkerchief. Held it out. Let it go. It went nowhere. Just floated there at arm's length. So we had two metal objects that had gone aft, and a handkerchief that simply stayed adrift.

'Which tells us what?' asked Alex.

I brought the systems back up, turned the lights on, but left the gravity off. 'The magnetics are screwed up.' I got grip shoes out for both of us so we could get around. Then I gave myself a crash course on pulsars.

After an hour or so, and several trips to the washroom to throw up, I thought I knew what was happening. The axis of the magnetic field was well off the spin axis of the pulsar. More than thirty degrees. The plane of our vector almost aligned with the spin axis. So the magnetic field, as far as we were concerned, was off center. Ramses was also oscillating, and it was strong. The magnetic forces were rocking the ship.

Alex made an animal sound. 'I'm not following.'

'We're getting eddy currents in the hull. They keep changing our orientation. We have too much movement in too many directions.'

'Well, whatever. Can we do anything about it?'

'No. But the good news is that it's slowing us down.' The hull was warm. 'It's heating up,' I said.

'Praise be!' Alex looked delighted. 'We get a break! Enough that the *Toronto* will be here before we go into the soup?'

'No. Unfortunately not. But it's going to give us' – I tapped a key and studied the result – 'another two hours.'

'I'm sorry, but I don't see how that helps. It's just two extra hours to be sick.' Then he brightened. 'Wait a minute. How about the shuttle? It's got a full tank. Why don't we use it to clear out? Leave the ship?'

I'd already considered it and discarded the idea. 'Its hull is too thin. If we go out in that, we'd be fried in about two minutes.'

'Then how about transferring its fuel? To the mains? Can we do that?'

'Different kind of fuel. And not enough to do any good anyhow.'

'So what do we have left, Chase?' he asked.

'Actually, the shuttle might come in handy. It uses a superconductor system during launch. And we've got some spare wire for it in cargo.'

'How does that help us?'

'Superconductors, at least some of them, don't like external magnetic fields. It's the way glide trains work. You turn it on, and it automatically removes itself from a region of high field strength to low field strength. It's called the Meissner Effect.'

'So we are going to—'

'—Do a little electrical work.'

We had about sixty meters of superconducting wire in storage. We brought it out and cut it in half. We took one segment to cargo, which was located beneath the bridge, to the point farthest forward in the ship. We fastened it to the leading bulkhead with magnetic staples. 'In a spiral,' I told him, adding, 'I think.'

'You're not sure, Chase?'

'Of course I'm not sure. I've never done anything like this before.'

'Okay.'

'If you want to take over—'

'No. I'm sorry. I wasn't criticizing. Listen, get us clear of this, and you get a bonus.'

'Thank you.'

'You can *name* the bonus.'

We took the rest of the wire back into the engine room, at the aft end of the ship, and put it up the same way, on the rearmost bulkhead. 'Now,' I said, 'we need current, the more the better. And a sink.'

He frowned. 'A washbasin?'

'No. A place to put the electricity after it runs through the coils.'

He stood there, looking puzzled.

The gravity control was our best bet. Artificial gravity requires substantial power, and the system has robust cells, which would be sufficient to absorb the dump.

'Why do we need to drain the power?' he asked.

'Because superconductors are a bit different from ordinary circuits. It's easy to get the current going, but to shut it down, we need a place that can drain it off.'

'Okay,' he said. 'I'm glad one of us knows this stuff.'

'Alex,' I said, 'this is all theory to me. I may be missing something. But it has a decent chance to work.'

311

Over his shoulder I could see one of the monitors. The light cones flickered across the screen. They were velvet blue. Lovely. Almost enticing.

The quantum drive uses a slide control device to monitor and regulate the power feed. After we had the coil in place, I removed it, and collected the backup unit from storage. I wired each spiral into one of the slide controls and connected the controls to the AG generator. 'Center position,' I told Alex, 'is neutral. No power. Up, the current runs clockwise; down is counter-clockwise. When it's powered up, it should make the ship a large magnet, with north at the bow and south at the tail. Or vice versa.'

'Or vice versa? You don't know?'

It was as if by explaining it, I gained real control over events. Describe the procedure, and it has to be so. 'We need to align our north to the pulsar's south. And our south to its north. If we can do that, the magnetic field will push us clear.'

'Good. That seems simple enough.'

'Okay. Hang on.' We belted down, and I put the pulsar on the navigation screen. 'First step: Line up.'

I used the alignment thrusters to turn *Belle* around. Get us angled parallel with the north-south axis of the pulsar. Tail up, nose down. When I had it as close as I could get it, I prepared to initiate step two.

'What's step two?' he asked.

'Activate.'

I pushed the sliders up. Current flowed into the system. The ship lurched.

I was thrown sharply against the harness. Then shaken. Up and down, back and forth. Lots of stops and jolts. It was like being on one of those three-dimensional bumper rides in an amusement park, where the bumper car takes you ahead and bangs to a stop and takes you ahead again and bangs to another stop. Except this was serious stuff. We were tossed every which

312

way, jerked back, forth, and sideways, thrown relentlessly against the harnesses. 'No!' I screamed.

Alex was telling me to shut it down. It felt as if *Belle* was coming apart. I switched off the power, and it stopped.

'What happened?' he asked.

'I don't know.'

'Maybe the current needs to go the other way.'

We tried it, with a similar result.

I went back to my data. Eventually I figured out what had happened. 'The magnetic axis at Ramses is thirty degrees off the spin axis,' I told Alex. 'I should have realized that would blow the program.'

'Why?'

'When we turned on the power, the ship aligned with the magnetic field, which it was supposed to do. But because it's thirty degrees off center, the magnetic field kept changing as the pulsar spun. Every three-quarters of a second. That was what banged us around.

'Can we fix it?' Alex asked hopefully. 'Try it again?'

'I have no idea how to compensate.'

'So,' he said, 'what now?'

We were down to about five hours.

On the *Belle-Marie*, the shuttle was launched from the starboard side, and the main airlock was to port. That suggested another possibility.

I reactivated the gravity. I also killed the monitors so we didn't have to watch the two sabers getting brighter and bigger.

The bulkheads were continuing to heat up, and the eddy forces were becoming more pronounced. On the bridge, we developed a drag *forward*. But if we went back to the washroom, which was located at the rear of the living quarters, the effect went in the opposite direction: Metal objects were pulled farther aft.

A buzzer sounded. I shut it off. 'Yellow alert,' I explained. 'Radiation.'

Alex nodded, but said nothing. Occasionally I caught him watching me, waiting for me to come up with something. And I sat there while forces that felt like tides dragged and pushed. I tried to put it out of my mind, to concentrate on what we needed to do. The critical point was that magnetic fields *do* push against one another.

Finally, I thought I had worked out another approach.

'I hope it's better than last time,' Alex said. He must have seen that the comment was irritating because he immediately apologized.

'It's okay,' I said. 'The first thing we need is some wire.'

'We've got plenty of it stapled to the bulkheads. Fore and aft.'

'It'll be too much trouble to get down. We have some on spools in storage. Those will be easier to work with.' I released my harness, got cautiously to my feet, and went out into the common room.

This time Alex didn't ask for an explanation. We went down to cargo and collected four spools of assorted sizes of cable, each sixty meters long. I set one aside. We unrolled the other three and connected the strands to make a single piece. At one end I stripped off a few centimeters of insulation and attached it to one of the handgrips on the hull of the shuttle, metal to metal.

Then I walked it back and taped about ninety meters of it to the back of the shuttle. That left enough to go up to the bridge and still have some slack. The shuttle was going to go out the door, and when it did I wanted to arrange things so the tape would come loose and the wire unravel. Preferably without fouling.

Simple enough.

Alex collected the fourth spool. I took the remaining eighty meters, and we started topside. I was paying the cable out as we went. But I found myself staring at the airlock that separated the launch bay from the rest of the ship. It would have to be closed before I could launch the shuttle. How was I going to get my wire through a sealed airlock?

I stood there wishing I knew more about electrical circuits.

Okay. All I really had to do was get the charge through.

First I needed an anchor in the shuttle bay, something stout enough to pull the wire free of the tape on the back of the shuttle when it launched, and which could withstand a good yank if need be. There were some storage cabinets along the bulkhead, supported by metal mounts. They looked rugged enough to do the job, so I picked one and secured the cable to it, leaving enough to pass through the airlock and reach the bridge.

That wouldn't be possible, of course, because I had to close the hatch. So I led the wire from the cabinet mount over to the airlock, just enough to connect the two, cut off the excess, and taped the piece from the cabinet onto the hatch. Metal to metal, again. We went through the airlock, gently closed the hatch, and taped the remaining piece to it, once again ensuring a metal contact.

The remaining cable was just long enough to reach the bridge. I'd intended to tie it into the AG generator, but we didn't need the same level of power this time. The hypercomm transmitter was sitting there, doing nothing. I connected the line to its power cell. Which meant we had connected a power source with the shuttle. This was the long wire.

We unrolled the final spool. The short wire. I linked it also to the transmitter's power cell, and we walked it out to the main airlock, which opened off the common room. We did much the same thing we'd done with the hatch on the lower deck. I cut the cable and connected it to the inner door. Then I unwound the rest of it from the spool – there was maybe forty meters left – coiled it on the deck inside the airlock, stripped the insulation from the end, and connected it to the inside of the door.

'We need to put the rest of the wire outside,' I said.

Alex looked from the coil to the outer hatch to me. 'We'll need a volunteer,' he said.

'No. Not like that. We'll blow it out.'

'Can we open the outer door without depressurizing the lock?'

315

'Normally, no. But I can override.' We left the lock and closed the hatch. 'Ready to go,' I told him.

'I hope.'

'I'll need you to turn on the juice, Alex.'

'Okay.'

He had to sit down on the deck to get access to the power unit. I showed him what to push. Showed him which lamps would come on when we established the circuit.

'All right,' he said. 'I got it.'

'What we want to do,' I told him, 'is to open the outer door of the main airlock and simultaneously launch the shuttle. The shuttle goes out one side; the air pressure in the lock blows the cable out the other.'

'I'm ready.' We looked at one another for a long moment. 'Just in case,' he said, 'I'm glad you've been part of my life.'

It was the only time I've known him to say something like that. My eyes got damp, and I told him I thought we had a good chance. What I *really* thought, I was trying not to think about. 'Okay,' I said, 'starting depressurization in the shuttle compartment.'

'Chase, do you think it matters whether I turn on the power now? Or should we wait until everything's outside?'

'Probably doesn't matter. But let's play it safe and wait.'

'Okay.'

'Overriding main airlock restraint. Got a green light.'

'Good.'

'I'm going to bleed a little air out of it.'

'If you think. But make sure there's enough left to expel the wire.'

I took the pressure down to about seventy percent, warned Alex that I was about to shut off the gravity again, and did so. It would help ensure that the coil in the airlock got blown clear. When the launch bay showed green – vacuum – I opened the launch doors, activated the telescopes, and eased the shuttle out of the ship. Then I opened the main airlock. Moments later, the port-side monitor showed the cable drifting away.

'Looks good so far,' said Alex.

I'd instructed the shuttle's onboard AI what she was to do. She took the shuttle out slowly while we watched on the monitor. The cable broke clear of the tape and began to pay out.

I gave it a couple of minutes. Then I told Alex to hit the juice.

The outside flux sent charged particles into the shuttle and the cable that was attached to its rear. The shuttle strained toward the pulsar and the cable straightened. The charge came toward the ship along the wire and passed through the open airlock. It circled the cabinet mount and penetrated the hatch on the lower deck. The wire on our side of the hatch picked it up and relayed it to the hypercomm power cell, from which it switched over to the short wire, passed through the main deck hatch, and out the main airlock. A luminous blue arc leaped from the shuttle to the tip of the short wire, connecting them. 'What do you think?' asked Alex.

'Circuit is complete,' I said, trying to keep the sheer joy out of my voice. 'I think we have a magnetic field.'

We got tossed around again, but it wasn't nearly as severe as the previous time.

Within moments, I felt a gentle shove upward and to starboard. 'We're getting a course change, Alex.'

'Yes!' he said. 'You're right. No question.' His face broke into a huge smile. 'You're a genius.'

'Magnetic fields don't like each other,' I said. 'The big one is getting rid of the little one. Had to happen.'

'Of course.'

'I never doubted it would work.'

The push was steady. Up and out. And accelerating. We were riding the wave, baby. Moving at a goofy angle, but who cared as long as it was away from the sabers?

The *Toronto* needed only five days to find us. It didn't matter to us. All we cared about was that we knew they were coming.

It was a party cruise. The ship was filled with the cast and director of the musical *Cobalt Blue,* which had been a huge hit everywhere on Grand Salinas and points west and was currently headed for Rimway. Unfortunately, they did not have fuel available for our thrusters, so we had to go on with them.

The passengers were always looking for reasons to celebrate, and we ranked high. They provided food and alcohol, and we got to see Jenna Carthage, the show's star, performing 'Hearts At Sea.' It's been a lot of years, but 'Hearts At Sea,' which is the second act showstopper, remains a standard. And Alex occasionally refers to it as 'our song.'

I should mention that I caught the eye of Renaldo Cabrieri. Alex didn't care for him, but I liked the guy, and it didn't hurt my self-confidence to have one of the biggest romantic stars in the Confederacy following me around. He was a bit over the top, but he was a charmer nevertheless. He made sure I always had a drink in my hand. He leered at me, purred in my direction, smiled in the most delightful manner, and just generally misbehaved. At one point, Alex told me it was embarrassing. Me, I thought I was entitled.

First, a dictator. Now a certified heartthrob. I wondered what, or who, was next.

21

Most of us deny the existence of ghosts. There is no spectre abroad in the night, we say. No phantom, no presence lingering over the dying fire, no banshee loose in moonlit trees. No spirit eyes peer at us from the dark windows of abandoned houses. But we're wrong. It's all true. And even though we understand that they are the creations of the mind, they are no less real.

—Ferris Grammery, *Famous Ghosts of Dellaconda*

We never found Belle. Presumably, after she was taken from the ship, she was discarded.

The AI that had been inserted in her place turned out to be a standard model, a bit more advanced than Belle. But someone had made a few adjustments. Had prepped it to take us out sightseeing to Ramses. 'Could you have done it?' Alex asked me.

No. I wasn't that good. But I don't pay much attention to the inner workings of AIs. I knew a few people who could make those sorts of changes. 'It's not that hard,' I said.

Fenn heard about what had happened, and an escort was waiting for us when the *Toronto* pulled into Skydeck. They stayed with us until we reached the country house. Fenn arrived moments after we did. 'You can't stay here any longer,' he said. 'We'll have to arrange something elsewhere. These people, whoever they are, seem to be determined.'

It was good enough for me. But Alex said it was okay, no need to make a big deal of it. He wasn't fooling anybody, of course. He was scared, too. But he didn't like showing it, so he continued to tell Fenn not to bother until he thought Fenn was going to back off. Then he caved. For my sake. By early evening, we'd been moved to an inauspicious little two-story town house in Limoges, a medium-sized city two hundred kilometers southwest of Andiquar. There would be security bots constantly in the area, he assured us. We were given fresh identities. 'You'll be safe,' he said. 'They won't be able to find you. But be careful anyway. Assume nothing.'

So we shut down Rainbow temporarily. 'Going on vacation,' we informed our clients. Fenn didn't even want us to do that. Just slip away in the night, he said. But we couldn't walk off and leave everybody hanging. There were projects under way, commitments had been made, and there'd be people who'd contact us and expect a response.

We left the country house and began a careful existence of locked doors and staying away from windows.

At the end of the second week, Autoreach, a salvage company, announced it was ready to go out and get the *Belle-Marie*. Alex stayed home while I went along. When we got to the ship, I installed a fresh AI, an upgrade, in fact, and I fed it a code to ensure that if anyone got to it again I'd know before leaving port.

It felt good to bring the ship back. I arranged extra security for it, and returned to our new home on a blustery winter evening. Alex was sitting quietly in the living room behind his reader and a pile of books. An image of the *Polaris* floated over the sofa. He looked up when I came in and told me he was glad to see me. 'Did you by any chance,' he asked, 'see the *Polaris* while you were on Skydeck? It's here for a few days.'

He meant the *Clermo*, of course. 'No,' I said. 'I wasn't aware it was scheduled in.'

'I don't know how you feel about going back up there,' he said, 'but I think it's time we did the tour.'

'We're going to look at the *Clermo?*'

'We should have done it two months ago.'

'Why?'

'Everson and his people never found what they were looking for.'

'So—?'

'That means it might still be on the ship.'

I called Evergreen, gave them a set of false names different from the ones Fenn had bestowed on us. I was taking no chances. For this trip, we would be Marjorie and Clyde Kimball. I especially liked that because Alex has a thing about names. There are certain ones, he maintains, that you just can't take seriously. *Herman. Chesley. Francis. Frank* is okay. So I knew what he'd think of *Clyde.*

'We're doing a book on the *Polaris* incident,' I explained, 'and we'd like very much to tour the *Clermo.*'

My contact was a quiet, intense young woman, dark hair, dark skin, dark eyes. Professional smile. It put a fair amount of distance between us. *'I'm sorry, ma'am. The* Clermo *isn't fitted out for tours.'* Whatever that meant.

'We're embarking on this project,' I told her, 'under the auspices of Alex Benedict.' That was taking a chance, but it seemed necessary. I waited for a sign of recognition. 'I suspect your employers would want you to agree.' That was a leap, but Alex was pretty well known.

'I'm sorry. Who is he again?'

'Alex Benedict.' When she went blank, I added, 'The Christopher Sim scholar.'

'Oh. That Alex Benedict.' She didn't have a clue. *'Can you hold, please, Ms Kimball? Let me check with my supervisor.'*

The supervisor didn't know either. It took a couple more calls before I finally got through to an executive secretary who said yes, of course, they'd be delighted to have a representative of

Mr Benedict tour the *Clermo*, except that she didn't know when the ship would be available.

We went back and forth for the next couple of days before we finally got an invitation, primarily, I suspect, because I'd become a nuisance.

Evergreen's Skydeck office was located on the 'Z' level, at the bottom of the pile and well out of everyone's way.

The Foundation had purchased the *Polaris* in 1368, three years after Delta Karpis. They renamed it and had been using it since to transport company executives, politicians, prospective customers, and assorted other special guests.

We got our first sight of it from one of the lower-level viewports. It was smaller than I'd expected, but I should have realized that it wouldn't be very big. It was a passenger transport vehicle, with a carrying capacity for the captain plus seven. Not much more than a yacht.

It had a retro look, with a rounded prow, flared tubes, and a wide body. Had it not been for its history, I suspected the *Clermo* would have been retired. But it provided a substantial degree of cachet for Evergreen. It was easy to imagine the Foundation's executives pointing out to their VIP passengers the very workspace Tom Dunninger had used while history was overtaking the ship. Ah, yes, if the bulkheads could only talk.

The retro look added to the charm. But the forest of scanners, sensors, and antennas that had covered the hull in its Survey days was gone. Only a couple of dishes were visible now, rotating slowly, and a few telescopes.

The hull, once gray, was now sea green. The tubes were gold, and there was a white sunburst on the bow. The imprint of the DEPARTMENT OF PLANETARY SURVEY AND ASTRONOMICAL RESEARCH no longer circled the airlock. The *Polaris* seal, the arrowhead and star, had been removed from the forward hull, which now read EVERGREEN, in white letters stylized as leafy branches entangled with vines. The Foundation's tree symbol lay just aft of the main airlock. The only thing that remained from the original designators was the manufacturer's number, barely visible on the tail.

We were met by a middle-aged, thin, officious man wearing a gray company shirt with the tree logo sewn across the breast pocket. He looked up from a monitor as we strolled into the Evergreen offices. 'Ah,' he said, 'Mr and Mrs Kimball?' His name was Emory Bonner. He introduced himself as the assistant manager of Skydeck operations. He'd done his homework and mentioned his admiration for Alex Benedict's efforts in what he referred to as "the Christopher Sim business". 'Magnificent,' he said.

Alex, wearing a false beard and shameless to the last, commented that Benedict was indeed an outstanding investigator, and that it was a privilege to be assisting him in this project.

Bonner said hello to me but never really took his attention from Alex. 'May I ask precisely what your interest is in the *Clermo*, Mr Kimball?'

Alex went off on a long thing about antiquities, and the value of the *Clermo* as an artifact. 'I sometimes wonder,' he concluded, 'whether the executives at Evergreen are aware of the potential market for this ship.'

'Oh, yes,' said Bonner. 'We are quite aware. We've taken very good care of the *Clermo*.'

'Yet,' said Alex, pushing his point, 'you've kept it in operation. That does nothing for its long-term value.'

'We've found it quite useful, Mr Kimball. You'd be surprised the effect it has on our VIP guests.'

'I'm sure. In any case, we'll be writing about a number of artifacts that are currently grossly undervalued. Every one of them, Mr Bonner, will appreciate considerably after publication.' He smiled at the little man. 'If you'd like to make a killing, you might try to buy it from the Foundation. It would make an excellent investment.'

'Yes, I'll talk to them today and make the down payment tomorrow.' Turning serious: 'When do you anticipate publication?'

'In a few months.'

'I wish you all the best with it.' He took a moment to notice me, and asked whether I was also working on the project.

'Yes,' I said.

'Very good.' He'd fulfilled his obligation to basic decency. 'Well, I know you're busy, so maybe we should go take a look.'

He led the way outside. We walked back down the tunnel by which we'd come and stopped before a closed entry tube. He told the door to open, we passed through and strolled down onto the docks. He paused to talk to a technician, giving him instructions that sounded as if they were being delivered to impress us. A few moments later we followed him through another tube and emerged beside the *Clermo*'s airlock.

Beside the *Polaris*.

It looked ordinary enough. I'm not sure what I was expecting, a sense of history, maybe. Or the chill that had come when we'd stood at the crime scene on the Night Angel. Whatever had happened that day at Delta Karpis, had happened right there, on the other side of the hatch. Yet I felt no rush of emotion. I kept thinking that I was really looking, not at the inexplicable, but at an object used in an elaborate illusion.

It was open. Bonner and Alex stood aside, allowing me the honor of entering first.

The lights were on. I went in, into the common room, which was twice the size of *Belle*'s. There were three small tables and eight chairs arranged around the bulkheads. Bonner began immediately jabbering about something. Fuel efficiency or some such thing. The *Polaris* had been luxurious, in the way that Survey thought of the term. But its present condition went well beyond that. The relatively utilitarian furniture that you saw in the simulations had been replaced. The chairs were selbic, which looked and felt like soft black leather. The bulkheads, originally white, were dark-stained. Thick green carpets covered the decks. Plaques featuring Evergreen executives posing with presidents, councillors, and senators adorned the bulkheads. (I suspected the plaques were taken down and replaced regularly, a custom set installed for each voyage, depending on who happened to be on board.)

The square worktable and displays were gone, and the common room now resembled the setting for an after-dinner club. Hatches were open the length of the ship, so we could see into the bridge and, in the opposite direction, the private cabins and workout area. Only the engineering compartment was closed.

There were four cabins on each side. Bonner opened one for our inspection. The appointments were right out of the Hotel Magnifico. Brass fittings, a fold-out bed that looked extraordinarily comfortable, another selbic chair (smaller, because of space limitations, than the ones in the common room, but lavish nonetheless), and a desk, with a comm link hookup.

The workout area would have accommodated two or even three people. You could run or cycle to your heart's content through any kind of VR countryside, or lift weights, or whatever you liked. Maximum use of minimum area. It would have been nice to have something like that on the *Belle-Marie*.

'Evergreen has taken good care of the *Polaris*,' Alex said, as we turned and walked back toward the bridge.

Bonner beamed. 'Yes, we have. The *Clermo* has been maintained at the highest level. We've spared no effort, Mr Kimball. None. I expect we'll see many more years' service from her.'

Good luck to him on that score. The ship had to be pretty much at the end of her life expectancy, with only a year or so left before her operational credentials would expire.

We went up onto the bridge. It's amazing how much difference the brass makes. Although I knew *Belle* was state-of-the-art, the *Clermo* just looked as if it could get you where you wanted to go safer and faster. Its Armstrong engines had, of course, been replaced by quantum technology. It *felt* snug and comfortable. I'd have liked a chance to take her out and tool around a bit.

There couldn't have been much resemblance to the bridge Maddy

English had known. Most of the gear had been updated, and the paneled bulkheads would never have found their way onto a Survey ship. Nevertheless, this was the space she'd occupied. It was the place from which the last transmission had been sent.

'*Departure imminent. Polaris out.*'

She'd been right about that.

'Notice the calibrated grips,' Bonner was saying. 'And the softened hues of the monitors. In addition—' He seemed unaware of why the ship was interesting.

Maddy had been preparing to enter Armstrong space, so the six passengers would have been belted down, probably in the common room, possibly in their quarters. 'If you were the pilot of this ship,' Alex asked me when we had a moment, 'would it make a difference to you?'

'No. Irrelevant. Whatever they like, as long as the restraints are in place.'

'Anything else you'd like to see?' asked Bonner, who was watching me as if he thought I might try to make off with something.

'Yes,' said Alex, 'I wonder if we could take a look belowdecks.'

'Certainly.' He led the way down the gravity tube, and we wandered through the storage area. The lander bay was located immediately below the bridge. Bonner opened the hatch to the smaller vehicle, and we looked in. The lander was a Zebra, top of the line. 'New,' I said.

'Yes. We've replaced it several times. Most recently just last year.'

'Where's the original?' Alex asked. 'From the *Polaris*?'

He smiled. 'It's on display at Sabatini.' Foundation headquarters.

I caught Alex's eyes as we stood beside the lander. Had he seen what he was looking for?

He signaled *no*. Either *no* he hadn't, or *no,* don't say anything.

We strolled out through the airlock. A lone technician was doing something to one of the fuel tanks, and Bonner peeled off to talk to him. When he was out of earshot, Alex asked how difficult it would be for a passenger to seize control of a ship. 'I'm talking about getting the AI to take direction,' he said.

That was simple enough. 'All you'd have to do, Alex, is to get logged on to the AI response list. But the captain would have to do it.'

'But Belle will take direction from me.'

'You own the ship.'

Bonner caught up with us and asked whether we'd found everything we needed.

'Oh, yes,' said Alex. 'It was an exquisite experience.'

'I'm pleased to hear it.'

'One more question, if you don't mind, Emory.' Alex was in his charm mode. 'When Evergreen first acquired the *Clermo*, do you know whether anything left by the original Survey passengers was found on board? Any *personal* items?'

Well, that one floored him, and he didn't mind letting us see it. 'That's sixty years ago, Mr Kimball. Before my time.'

Right. Nothing that had happened before this guy was born could be of any consequence. 'I understand that,' Alex said. 'But artifacts from an historic ship are valuable.'

'I was under the impression,' he said, 'that Survey scoured the ship when it originally came back.'

'Nevertheless, they might have overlooked something. If they did, it would be worthwhile to know about it, and I suspect somebody at Evergreen would have been smart enough to hang on to it.'

'I assume you're right, Mr Kimball. But I just have no way of knowing.'

'Who *would* know?'

He led the way into an exit tube. 'Somebody at the Sabatini office might be able to help.'

'Thanks,' Alex said. 'One final thing.' He showed him a picture of Teri Barber. 'Have you ever seen this woman?'

He squinted at it and arranged to look unimpressed. 'No,' he said. 'I'm afraid I don't know her. Should I?'

* * *

We caught the ground-side transport and transferred to a flight to Sabatini. Alex sat staring out at the clouds. We'd been in the air only a half hour when the pilot warned us of turbulence ahead. Within minutes we sailed into heavy weather and started to sway. Alex made a comment about the storm, how it looked pretty dark out there. I said yes it did and asked whether he still thought Walker was involved.

'No question about it.'

'How could that be? We know they couldn't have taken Maddy and the passengers aboard the *Peronovski*. Are you suggesting Alvarez lied?'

'No. Alvarez appeared before the Trendel Commission. He tested out, so we know he kept nothing back. But they never checked Walker. No reason to.'

'But they couldn't smuggle seven people onto Alvarez's ship and maintain them without his knowing.'

'That's the way it looks.'

'It's impossible.' I took a deep breath as raindrops began to splatter against the windows. 'Not only couldn't it be done without the captain's knowledge, it couldn't be done at all. We've been over this. There's no way the *Peronovski* could have supported nine people.'

He took a deep breath, sighed, but said nothing.

'There might be another possibility,' I said.

'Go ahead.'

'We've been assuming the conspirators were a majority. Pretty much everybody except Dunninger.'

'Yes.'

'We've also been assuming there was a kidnapping. But I can tell you how things could have happened.'

'Go ahead.'

'Somebody, one or two, take over the ship. They have six days before the *Peronovski* will arrive. So they go elsewhere in the system.'

'I'm with you so far.'

'It's not a kidnapping, Alex. They *kill* everybody. Get rid of the bodies. Then go to wherever the *Peronovski* found them. With Walker's help they get aboard without being seen by Alvarez. And all Alvarez finds is an empty ship.'

'Good,' Alex said. 'That seems to account for everything.'

I felt pretty good. 'Thank you,' I said.

He was smiling, too. 'Why?' he asked.

'You mean, what was the motive?'

'Yes.'

'The same thing we've been talking about. To prevent Dunninger from completing his work.'

'You think any of these people were capable of murder?'

'I don't know.'

'I like your solution,' said Alex, 'but I just don't believe it happened that way. It's too bloody-handed. And I can't imagine Boland or White or any of them consenting to commit murder. For any reason.'

'What about Maddy? She was fairly ruthless.'

'Maddy had no motive.'

'Maybe she was bought.'

'To murder six people? And to disappear herself? I don't think so.' He took a deep breath. 'But you agree that there could have been an extra passenger or two on board the *Peronovski* without the captain's being aware of it?'

Yes. They could have used the belowdecks compartments. Walker would have had to get extra supplies on board. Extra water. But if he had done that, it could have been managed. The captain has no reason to go prowling around in storage. 'I don't see why not,' I said.

Alex closed his eyes and appeared to go to sleep. We left the storm behind, and the sun reappeared. Two hours later we crossed the Korali Mountains and began our approach to Sabatini. A cloud of vehicles floated through the sky.

Evergreen's headquarters was located among rolling hills, on the southern gulf. I'd called ahead and established that, yes, they did have a display room that held exhibits and artifacts from their two-century-long history, that it included the *Polaris* shuttle and a few other items that had been found on the ship, and yes, they would provide a tour.

Our guide was Cory Chalaba, a middle-aged, steely-eyed woman who felt strongly about endangered reefs in the Minoan Sea, overflowing population on half a dozen Confederate worlds, and the recklessness, as she put it, with which people introduced secondary biosystems onto living planets. We sat drinking coffee and munching donuts for about twenty minutes in her office, talking about Evergreen's role in what she referred to as the human adventure. 'Because that's what it is. There's no plan, there are no stated objectives, no thought for the future. All anyone cares about is profit. And power. And that means development.'

'What about Survey?' I asked. 'They must make an effective partner for Evergreen. At least you're not in it alone.'

'Survey's worst of all.' She was heating up. 'They want to find out how a given biosystem develops, how it got to be what it is. And then record its characteristics. Once they've done that, they don't give a damn what happens to it.' It was easy to imagine her in the protest line outside Dunninger's lab at Epstein.

The Foundation's display was both more and less than I'd expected. It consisted primarily of clothing worn by Evergreen collaborators during historic events, instruments used by them, notebooks, pictures, VR records. There were rocks from Grimaldo, where a small band of Evergreen's people had died trying to protect that world's giant lizards from hunters who had flocked to it with a vast array of high-tech cannons. Several of the species, according to an accompanying placard, were now extinct. They had the shoulder patch from Sharoun Kapata's blouse, dating from the Mineral Wars on Dellaconda. Replicas of boats and ships were mounted along the walls, along with their histories. *Transported the Ann Kornichov team to the Gables, 1325.* And, *Rammed and sunk by net-draggers in the skies of Peleus, 1407.*

The *Polaris* shuttle was there, occupying an alcove. It still looked serviceable. The public wasn't permitted inside, but we could get up close enough to see everything. Carrying capacity was four. The harness arrangement was different from anything you'd see in a modern vehicle. Heavier, and more intrusive. Cabin design felt old-fashioned, but you'd expect that. Standard set of controls. Standard guidance system. A basic thruster package that could have come right off *Belle*'s shuttle. Two storage cabinets behind the backseat, filled with spare parts. And a cargo compartment in the rear, accessible through a separate hatch. The shuttle retained the *Polaris* and Survey markings.

The rest of the *Polaris* display was inconsequential, and was stored in two glass cases.

One held a shirt. 'Urquhart's,' Chalaba said. She consulted a notebook. 'It was found in the foldaway bed.'

'The Survey people must have missed it,' said Alex.

'Apparently.'

There were also a pen, a remote, a book, and a makeup kit. 'The makeup kit, of course, belonged to one of the women. We're not sure which. The pen, we don't know. It was found in its holder on the bridge.'

'You've done the archeologically correct thing,' Alex said. 'Recording the locations of the finds.'

'As if it matters. But yes, our people did a decent job.' She went back to her notes. 'The remote is an electronic key of some sort. It was found in the cargo locker of the lander. We don't know who that belonged to, either.'

'An electronic key?' Alex peered down at it. It was about the size of a candy bar, with five buttons, one red, four blue, and a display. Each button was marked with a symbol:

$$\uparrow \downarrow \circlearrowright \circlearrowleft \boxdot$$

'What's it operate?' asked Alex.

Back to the notes. 'It doesn't say. I doubt anybody knows.'

It was hard to imagine why anyone would need a key on the

Polaris. Aboard a ship, everything operates off the AI. Or by simple voice command. Or by pushing a button.

'What do you think?' Alex asked me. 'Would they need it maybe for the lander?'

'I can't imagine why,' I said. 'No, there'd be no point.'

A remote. In an age when most devices were voice-activated, there's not much use for it. Kids use them for games. They operate flying models. They open hotel room doors. They can be used to adjust water temperature in pools.

What else?

Alex shook his head. 'Anybody have any idea what the symbols mean?'

'The bottom one looks like a negative,' said Chalaba. 'Maybe somebody just brought it from home,' she said. 'Forgot they had it.'

It looked very much like a standard hotel key. Five buttons: *up* and *down* for the elevators, *lock* and *unlock* for the apartment, and a transaction button. That would be the red one. The rectangle represented a press pad.

The book was *Wilderness of Stars,* by Emanuel Placido. It had been a big hit with the environmental people in the last century. 'It belonged to White,' Chalaba said. 'We have a virtual copy available if you'd like to see it.'

Alex caught my eyes. *Maybe she wrote something in it. Maybe it's what they've been looking for.* 'Cory,' he said, 'since we're in here, I assume the exhibit area is open to the general public.'

She nodded. 'Yes. But we don't advertise it, so I doubt many people know it's here.'

He showed her the picture of Barber.

'No,' she said. 'I've never seen her.'

He gave it to her, along with his code. 'It will get you to our office,' he said. 'We'd be grateful if you'd keep an eye open. If she shows up, please give us a call.'

She looked at us suspiciously.

'It's all right,' he said. 'If you're reluctant to call *us,* let the Andiquar police know. You'll want to talk to Inspector Redfield.'

'All right. You mind telling me what it's about?'

'One other thing,' he said, bypassing the question. 'I'd like very much to buy a copy of the key.'

'Oh, I'm sorry, Mr Kimball, but that's really not feasible.'

'It's important,' he said. 'And I'd be grateful.' He produced his link, typed in a figure, and showed it to her. 'Would this cover it?'

Her eyebrows went up. 'Yes,' she said, drawing the word out. 'If it means that much, I suppose we can manage it.'

'Thank you,' said Alex. 'Please be sure it's a working duplicate.'

'What are you going to do with it?'

'I think it's what Barber and Kiernan were looking for.'

'Really. Why?'

'Because it's the one object that has no possible use on the *Polaris*.'

'I'm not sure I follow.'

'Ask yourself what it was doing in the shuttle's cargo compartment.' He looked around to be sure we were alone. 'Chase, I know how it was done.'

We were walking across a white stone bridge that separated the Foundation grounds from the landing pad. He stopped and gripped the white handrail and leaned out over a brook as if he were really interested in seeing whether it contained fish. He could be infuriating sometimes. I waited for the explanation, which did not come. 'How?' I said at last.

'You suggested the ship went elsewhere in the system.'

'Yes.'

'Why not *outside* the system? They had six days before the *Peronovski* would arrive.'

'It's possible. Sure.'

'Everybody assumed the ship went adrift right after the last message. But that's not what happened. It jumped out of the system. Took the passengers somewhere. To a drop-off point. Then they unloaded everyone. The place, wherever it was, had living accommodations. That's where the key came from.'

'There's no place like that near Delta Kay.'

'You sure? We're talking three days available for travel, one way. How far was that in 1365?'

'Sixty light-years.'

'That's a pretty big area. Even out there.' He dropped a pebble into the water. 'The key, in effect, is a hotel key. Whoever had it unloaded his passengers, got a good night's sleep, and in the morning he started back in the *Polaris* to Delta Kay.'

'—Where the ship was found by the *Peronovski*—'

'Yes.'

'And, with Walker's help, he was able to slip aboard and hide below. Until they returned to port.'

'Very good, Chase.'

'You really think that's what happened?'

'Except one thing.'

'What's that?'

'Change the pronoun. *She* slipped aboard.'

'Maddy?'

'I don't think there's any question. She's the one in the ideal position to pull it off, provided she had help from other passengers. And she was a pilot. The conspirators had arranged in advance to make another ship available for her at Indigo. When she got back, she collected it and went out to recover them.'

'I'll be damned.'

'All the objects that were looked at by our burglars belonged to Maddy. Nobody else.'

'But Alvarez should have seen her when he searched the *Polaris*.'

'She hid in the shuttle cargo compartment. That's when she lost the key.'

'They had no reason to open the cargo compartment.'

'Right. And when the search was over, Alvarez and Walker went back to the *Peronovski*. That night, Alvarez goes to sleep—'

'—And Walker brings her aboard.'

334

'He stashed her in one of the compartments belowdecks. *Voilà*, the alien wind has swept them all away.'

'Incredible,' I said. 'That simple.'

Alex shrugged modestly.

'They did all this just to head off Dunninger's research?'

'They saw it as life and death for millions of people. And they were all idealists.'

'Fanatics.'

'One man's idealist is another's lunatic.'

'But why is anyone worried about it now? Is someone still in power from those years?'

His eyes were troubled. 'No. I've checked. Everyone who could have been involved, either at Survey, or in the political world, is dead or retired.'

'Then who's behind the attacks on us?'

'I have an idea, but let's put that aside for now.'

'Okay. So where'd the *Polaris* take them?'

'That's what we have to find out.'

We stayed in Sabatini and returned to Limoges the next day by train. Alex liked trains, and he also thought it might be smart to change our travel plans. Just in case.

We rode a taxi to the station and arrived just as the Tragonia Flyer was pulling in. We got into our compartment, and Alex lapsed into silence. The train made a second stop in Sabatini, then began its long trek across the Koralis.

We were still in mountain country when the service bot brought lunch. And wine. Alex gazed moodily through the window at the passing landscape.

I thought about Maddy while I ate. I liked her, identified with her, and I hated to think she'd been part of a conspiracy to put Dunninger out of action.

'First thing we need to do,' I told Alex, 'is to go back and look at the shipping schedules again. We'd assumed that any black ship would have to go all the way out to Delta Kay. But this changes things. We need to check, to see whether anyone was in a position to get close enough to manage a rendezvous.'

'I've already looked,' he said. 'It was one of the first things I did.'

'So you're telling me nobody would have been able to do that either?'

'That's correct. Nobody was unaccounted for. Nobody, other than the *Peronovski,* was anywhere near the target space. And not for weeks afterward. Which means Maddy didn't immediately go back to pick them up. But that's just smart planning.'

He finished his meal and pushed it aside.

'You know,' I said, 'I think I prefer the alien juggernaut theory.'

'Yeah. I feel that way, too.'

'I have a question.'

'Go ahead.'

'What was the last-minute emergency that kept Taliaferro off the flight?'

'Chase, I don't think Taliaferro ever intended to go. I think everybody on board that ship was part of the conspiracy to shut down Dunninger. Taliaferro got volunteers, people who were willing to give up their everyday lives to stop something they thought would be a major calamity. But there was a limited number he dared ask. Not enough to fill the ship. Taliaferro couldn't go himself, because they needed him to direct things from Survey. They were going to need money, for example, and eventually a base. So Taliaferro set up Morton College. But there were a lot of people who wanted to make the *Polaris* flight, so they had to be able to claim it was filled.'

We passed through a small town, lots of lights, someone on a runabout. Otherwise, the streets were empty.

22

Do not underestimate the woman. Provoke her, anger her, infuriate her, and in her hands every object, every knife, every pot, every pebble, can become lethal.

—Jeremy Riggs,
Last Man Out

The train ride required a bit more than fourteen hours. We slept most of the way and got into Limoges an hour or two before midnight. Once off the train, we hurried through the terminal like a couple of fugitives, watching everybody and wondering when someone would throw a bomb. But we got back to the town house without incident.

Neither of us was ready to call it a night. Alex poured two glasses of Vintage 17, made a sandwich, and sat down in an armchair in a manner that suggested big things were about to happen.

I've forgotten the AI's name at the town house, but he directed it to provide a display with Delta Karpis at the center. 'Make a sphere around it, with a sixty-light-year radius.' Sixty light-years, of course, was the maximum range the *Polaris* could have traveled in the three days it had available. 'How many habitable worlds are there?'

'*One moment, please.*'

Alex was in excellent spirits. He looked across at me and grinned. 'We've got them,' he said. His sandwich showed up, and he picked it up without looking at it, took a bite, chewed and swallowed, and washed it down with his wine.

I was feeling less jovial. Alex says I worry too much. 'I hate to point this out,' I told him, 'but I think we've done enough. Why don't we walk away from this? Give everything to Fenn and let him deal with it? Before more bad things happen?'

He shook his head. It's a hard life when one is surrounded by such imbecility. 'Chase,' he said, 'don't you think I'd love to? But they're going to keep coming after us. And there's no way we can stop that until we stop *them*. Fenn's not going to run out to Delta Kay and look around.' His voice softened. 'Anyhow, don't you want to be there when we confront these people?'

'Probably not,' I said.

'*Three*,' said the AI. '*There are three habitable worlds.*'

'Three? Is that all?'

'*It's a sterile area. Most of the stars in the region are young.*'

'Delta Karpis wasn't young.'

'*Delta Karpis was an exception. And there is also an outstation.*'

'Where?'

'*Meriwether. It's actually a bit farther than the parameters you set. It's sixty-seven light-years out.*'

'Where is it? Show me.'

A swirl of stars appeared in the middle of the room. A prominent yellow one began blinking. '*Delta Kay,*' said the AI. An arrow appeared above a side table, pointing toward the back porch. '*That way to Indigo.*' Then we got another blinker, this one red, over a love seat. '*The Meriwether outstation.*'

Alex looked pleased. Only four possibilities. 'Chase,' he said, 'we've caught a break.' And, to the AI: 'Tell me about them.'

'*The worlds first. Terranova has a small settlement.*' Its image formed in the middle of the room. '*It's the home of the Mangles.*'

'What's a Mangle?' I asked.

'They're a back-to-nature group who like isolation. They ascribe, more or less, to the philosophy of Rikard Mangle, who thought that people should get their hands dirty, build their own homes, and grow their own food. To do less, he maintained, is to fall short of knowing what it truly means to be human. Or something like that. Aside from an occasional hermit, they've been the sole inhabitants on Terranova for two centuries. They claim to be the most remote human outpost.'

'Are they?' I asked.

'Depends where you put the center of the Confederacy, ma'am.'

'And they're still functioning?' said Alex.

'Oh, yes. They're still there. But they don't have much contact with the outside world. A little trading. And every once in a while somebody escapes.'

'That's a gag, right?' I said.

'Not at all. Their children don't always want to stay. Some, when they can, clear out.'

'The brighter ones.'

'I'm not equipped to make that judgment.'

Alex wore a wry smile. 'These Mangles,' he said, 'would they be likely to let an outside group move in?'

'Judging by their history, as well as their code of regulations, I'd say not. Unless you adopted their political philosophy.'

Well, I thought, that part of it doesn't matter. A planet's a big place. The *Polaris* had a lander. The Mangles sound fairly primitive, so the lander could have gotten to the surface unseen easily enough. 'How many Mangles are there?'

'Fewer than sixty thousand, Chase. Terranova is the only Confederate world that shows a consistent decrease in population.'

'Okay,' said Alex. 'Tell us about the other two.'

'Markop III. And Serendipity. Neither has been settled. Gravity approximates one point four at Markop. It's uncomfortable under the best of circumstances. Serendipity's air is thin, and the surface is hot to intolerable. Any human settlements would have to be placed near the poles.'

'But the air is breathable.'

'Oh, yes. It's not a place you'd want to go if you like comfort. But you could certainly put a group of people there and, assuming you provided food and shelter, you could have every hope they'd survive.'

'What about the outstation? Meriwether?'

'It services a bare handful of missions each year. It's probably the oldest of the operational stations. Completely automated.'

'Could I use it without leaving a record?'

'I don't know. That information is not available.'

That was my area of expertise. 'The answer's no, Alex. The station AI logs everything. Any attempt to juggle the log, to gundeck it in any way, is considered a criminal offense. And it gets reported.'

'No way it could be done?'

'I don't think so. At the first sign of tampering, the AI would send out an alarm.'

'Okay. I think we'll want to have a look at it.'

'Could we wait until morning?'

He laughed. 'Yes, I suspect we can do that.'

It was supposed to be a joke. 'You do mean we're leaving *tomorrow?*' I'd been hoping for two or three days off.

'Yes,' he said. 'I think it's prudent we end this thing as quickly as we can. We'll be targets until we do.' Did I want more wine? I declined, and he refilled his glass. 'Now, can we trust *Belle*'s new AI?'

'Yes,' I said. 'We have a security system that will alert us if anyone so much as looks twice at the ship.' Nevertheless, I took an early transport up to Skydeck and spent the morning going over her, just to be on the safe side. I'd had enough surprises.

The Meriwether platform is located in solar orbit around Meriwether A, which is the largest component of a triple star system. The other two suns, however, are so dim and so far away, they're not distinguishable from distant stars. The station is, of course, an excavated asteroid. As we approached, lights came on, and a cheerful radio voice welcomed us.

With the advent of the quantum drive, the outstations had all become essentially obsolete. A few were kept in operation to assist ultralong missions; but there weren't many, and they were being maintained at a limited level. 'Belle says Meriwether doesn't get more than a half dozen missions a year,' I told Alex.

'That can't be enough to pay the upkeep,' he said. 'I suspect they'll be closing the place within a few years.'

I put visuals on-screen. 'It's been here a long time.'

'How old *is* it?'

'Seventeen hundred years. It goes back to Commonwealth days.' I was running data across the monitor. 'Says here it was originally a naval base.'

There'd been a period early in the history of the Commonwealth in which warfare had flared sporadically among the various worlds. It had been an era of shifting alliances, of occasionally intense conflict, and of an ongoing struggle for supremacy.

The station continued transmitting. '. . . *to have you in the area. Please state your requirements.*' The voice was male. Careful diction. Vague projection of superiority. Aristocratic.

I submitted a list of needed supplies. Fuel. Water. We had plenty of food.

'*Very good,*' said the station. '*Follow the lights. You'll be coming in through Bay Four.*'

'Thank you,' I said.

'*We're pleased to help. Is there anything else?*'

Guide lamps came on around the curve of the rock. A portal was opening. Then more lights.

I invited Alex to respond. He nodded. 'Yes,' he said. 'I wonder if we could get some information about the history of the station.'

'*Of course. We have a fully automated gift shop with several applicable volumes and VRs.*'

'Excellent,' Alex said. 'By the way, this is Chase Kolpath, and my name is Alex Benedict.'

'*I am pleased to meet you both.*'

'May I ask your name?'

'*George.*'

We docked. The portal closed, the bay pressurized, lights came on, doors opened, and robots began attaching fuel and water lines to the ship. We climbed out. I could see several other bays, all empty. It looked as if we were the only ones currently at the station. Ahead, deck lights came on and showed the way to an exit ramp.

We turned into a brightly lighted carpeted sitting room. An avatar was waiting. He looked authoritative, official, competent. 'Hello, Mr Benedict,' he said cheerfully. '*Ms Kolpath. It's good to see you. I am Captain Pinchot.*' He was tall and trim, white-haired, with craggy features and a congenial smile. He wore a white uniform with an arm patch, epaulets, decorations, and a sash. The patch depicted a torch and a motto in unfamiliar characters. He smiled politely and steered us toward a group of three armchairs, centered around a dark-stained table. He waited until we were seated, then joined us. '*We don't get much company here anymore.*'

His feet didn't quite touch the deck. The station AI needed adjustment.

Panels opened in the table, and we were looking at two glasses of red wine and a bowl of assorted cheeses and fresh fruit. '*Please, help yourselves.*'

'Thank you.' I picked up a slice of melon. It looked just off the farm, tasted that way as well, and I wondered how they managed it.

'*Your ship will be ready in one hour, ten minutes,*' he said. '*To get to the gift shop, simply go out the door, turn right, and follow the corridor. It's about a three-minute walk. Do you require any other assistance?*'

'No, thank you, Captain,' I said, trying the wine.

'*I regret I can't join you.*' The avatar graciously let me see that I'd gained an admirer.

Alex crossed one leg over the other. 'May I ask how old you are, Captain?'

Pinchot was sitting ramrod straight. *'The station has been here sixteen-hundred forty-one standard years.'*

'No. I mean *you*, Captain. How long have you been the operating intelligence here?'

The avatar tapped his index finger against his lips, apparently deep in thought. *'I was installed in 1321 on your calendar.'* A little more than a century ago. *'I was an upgrade.'*

'Are you familiar with the *Polaris* incident? With the loss of that ship?'

'You mean with the loss of the travelers aboard her?'

'Yes. I see that you are.'

'I'm familiar with the details.'

'Captain, we're trying to determine what might have happened.'

'Excellent. I hope you succeed. It was, certainly, a puzzling incident.' He gazed around the room. *'One of the search vessels stopped here shortly after the event. I'm not sure what they expected to find.'*

Apparently, someone else had been thinking the way Alex had.

'You know who the seven victims were?' Alex asked. 'The ones who vanished?'

'I know their names. And I knew one personally.'

'Really,' I said. 'Which one?'

'Nancy White.'

'You're suggesting she visited here?'

'Yes. Twice.'

'Physically?'

'Oh, yes. She sat right there where the young lady is.'

'I see,' said Alex. 'Did you by any chance see her again *after* the incident?'

'After the incident? Oh, my, no.'

'Did you have any visitors at all during the time period, say, three weeks on either side of the event?'

'We had one ship during that span. Did you wish specifics?'

343

'Yes, please.'

We listened while Captain Pinchot gave us chapter and verse. The vessel had been returning from the Veiled Lady and docked seventeen days before the *Polaris* incident. *'En route to Toxicon.'*

Alex looked thoughtful. 'When was Nancy White here?'

'In 1344. And again in 1362.'

'Twice.'

'Yes. She told me the first time that she would come back to see me again.'

'She must have been quite young. The first time.'

'She was about nineteen. Scarcely more than a child.' Something mournful had entered his aspect.

'Tell us about it,' said Alex.

'She and her father were passengers aboard the Milan, *which was returning from a survey mission. The father was an astrophysicist.'*

Alex nodded.

'He specialized in neutron star formation, although the mission was a routine survey effort.'

'Just see what's out there.'

'Yes. There were six of them on board, not including the captain. Like the Polaris. They'd been out five months and had stretched their supplies until they were exhausted.'

'So they stopped here before going on to Indigo,' I said.

'Indigo was closed down at the time, Ms Kolpath. Undergoing maintenance. This was all there was.'

'What did you talk about?' I asked. 'You and Nancy?'

'Nothing of consequence. She was excited because she had never been off Rimway before, and her first flight had taken her so far.'

'And she came back to see you years later. Why do you think she did that?'

'Actually we maintained contact during the intervening years, and in fact right up until the time she boarded the Polaris.'

'Really? She sent messages from Rimway?'

'Oh, yes. Not often. But occasionally. We stayed in touch.' The avatar looked from Alex to me. He seemed lonely.

'May I ask what you talked about?'

'What she was doing with her life. Projects she was involved in. There were practical advantages for her. When her career as a popularizer of science began to take off, I served as a symbol for some of her presentations.'

'A symbol?'

'Yes. Sometimes she used me to represent an advanced life-form. Sometimes a competitor. Sometimes an indispensable friend. I served quite well. Would you care to watch one of the shows?'

'Yes,' I said. 'If you could make a copy available.'

'We have several selections in the gift shop,' he said. 'Priced quite reasonably.'

It occurred to me that one of the books, Quantum Time, was dedicated to a Meriwether Pinchot. 'That's you, isn't it?'

'Yes.' There was no missing the note of pride in his voice.

'Captain,' Alex said, 'the Polaris passed close to this station during the final flight. She must have thought of you.'

The avatar nodded. 'Yes. In fact, I had two messages from her.'

'I don't suppose either of them shed light on what happened?'

'Unfortunately not. The last time I heard from her was shortly after the event they went to observe. After the neutron star hit Delta Kay. She described it to me. Told me it was "compelling." That's the word she used. Compelling. I would have thought witnessing the destruction of a sun called for a stronger reaction, but she was never much on hyperbole.' He looked momentarily wistful. 'That was a good many hours before Madeleine English sent that last message.'

'What else did she have to say?'

'Nothing out of the ordinary. On the way out she'd told me how anxious she was to see the collision. To see the neutron star actually destroy Delta Karpis. She said she wished I could be there with her.'

Alex looked at me. He was finished. 'Captain,' I said, 'thank you.'

'*It is my pleasure. I don't often get to sit down with guests. People come so seldom, and they don't have time to talk. Fill the tanks, recharge the generators, thank you and good-bye.*'

'Well, Captain,' I said. 'I want you to know I'm pleased to have met you, and to have had a chance to spend a little time with you.'

'*Thank you, Ms Kolpath.*' He beamed. Even the uniform got brighter.

It was good to be out of the *Belle-Marie* for a bit, and we decided to spend the night. There was a suite of rooms in an area the AI referred to as the Gallery. He showed us to them, chattering the whole way. '*I have a wide choice of entertainment, if you like. Drama, athletic events, wild parties. Whatever you prefer. Or, we can simply sit and talk.*'

'Thanks, Captain,' I said.

'The shows might be interesting,' said Alex.

'*You may design whatever guests you wish. We also have an inventory of historic figures, if you'd like to participate in some stimulating conversations.*'

Tea with Julius Caesar.

'*The keys for your rooms are at the doors. Please be sure you return them before you leave.*'

The keys were remotes. Alex reached into a pocket, produced the one we'd found at Evergreen, and compared them. They didn't look much alike.

I collected mine, aimed it, and pressed the *open* function. The door folded to one side, revealing a living room. Alex showed the duplicate to the avatar. 'Captain,' he said, 'sixty years ago, would this key have worked on this station?'

The captain examined it and shook his head. '*No,*' he said. '*Setting and design are quite different.*'

I stuck my head into my apartment. Lush curtains, polished

furniture, chocolate on the coffee table. A large bed piled high with pillows. Private washroom and tub. Not bad.

'*If you elect to stay five days or more,*' said the avatar, '*the fifth night is free.*'

'It's tempting,' said Alex, not meaning it. The weight of centuries and the sense of decline pressed on the place. Furthermore, Meriwether felt *remote*. On *Belle,* we could be a couple hundred light-years from anybody else, but you didn't notice it. In the outstation, though, you knew precisely where you were. The nearest person was one hell of a long way off, and you were conscious of every kilometer. Alex saw me grinning. 'What?' he said.

'I could use a good party.'

Markop III was hardly worth a visit. But we went anyhow, because Alex insisted on being thorough.

It was an attractive world, lots of blue water, fleecy white clouds, herds of big shaggy creatures that made great targets if you were into hunting. The weather through the temperate zones was almost balmy.

If it was inviting, however, it was also potentially lethal. Unlike the vast majority of living worlds, its viruses and disease germs loved *Homo sapiens.* So you couldn't drop a group of people onto the surface and expect to retrieve them unless you took a lot of precautions. That fact certainly ruled out tourist spots, and with them, hotels.

There was no talkative AI this time to tell us whether anything out of the ordinary had happened. Markop III had more land space than Rimway, 180 million square kilometers, much of it concealed by forest and jungle.

There had been a settlement at one time. That was ancient history, in the extreme. Four thousand years ago. The records are sketchy on details, but the Bendi Imperium established a colony there, and it lasted about a century before the plagues began to get ahead of the medical people. They eventually gave up.

We weren't really equipped to do a major planetary scan. But we went into low orbit and took a long look. We spotted some ruins. A couple of long-dead cities, so thoroughly buried in jungle that no part of them was visible to the naked eye. In remote areas that might once have been farms, we saw walls and foundations.

We spent three days in orbit. There was nothing that looked like a viable shelter.

23

There'll always be a Rimway.

—Heinz Boltmann,
during an address to the Retired Officers' Association,
in the early days of the Confederacy, when survival
seemed problematic

Terranova, the new Earth, was well named. It orbited a nondescript orange star, it had a twenty-one-degree axial tilt, its gravity
was a fraction of a percent below standard; it had an oversized
airless moon, and there were a pair of continents that, seen from
orbit, resembled Africa and the Americas.

The most remarkable aspect of the planet was that terrestrial
life-forms integrated easily with the biosystem. Tomatoes grew
nicely. Cats chased the local equivalent of squirrels, and the
temperate zones proved to be healthful places for human beings.

But the critical piece of information for us was that the Mangles
had a system of satellites in place, and it had been up and running
over a century. Nobody came or went without their knowledge,
and it didn't take long to find out there had been no activity
during the target time period. The *Polaris* had not gone there.

The only noteworthy event during our visit to Terranova

occurred when a piece of rock got too close and had to be taken out by the Hazard Control System. The HCS consists of a black box mounted on the hull that detects and identifies incoming objects and coordinates the response, which is delivered by one or more of four particle-beam projectors.

The rock at Terranova was strictly a one-beam operation. It was only the second time in my career that we actually used the device.

Serendipity was the fourth world in the Gaspar system, and our last candidate. It was effectively a collage of desert broken by occasional patches of jungle near the poles. A few small seas were scattered across the surface, isolated from each other. The equatorial belt was boiling hot and bone-dry, its vegetation consisting mostly of purple scrub. Even the local wildlife avoided the area.

Gaspar was a yellow-white class-F star. According to the data banks, the three inner worlds were all pretty thoroughly cooked. The sun was in an expansion cycle, getting hotter every year, and would soon burn off whatever life still clung to Gaspar IV. Serendipity. *Soon* seemed to be one of those cosmic terms, which really meant several hundred thousand years.

The life-forms were big, primitive, hungry. Not dinosaurs, exactly. Not lizards at all. They were mostly oversized, warm-blooded, slow-moving behemoths. Their considerable bulk was favored by the low gravity, which was about three-quarters of a gee.

The world was called Serendipity because everything had gone wrong on the discovery flight. The ship had been the *Kismet,* a private vessel operated by fortune hunters functioning several decades before the Confederacy established guidelines for exploration. Like requiring a license before external life-forms could be introduced into a biosystem.

A field team member was killed by one of the behemoths. Walked on, according to the most popular version of the story. Another had stepped in a hole and broken his leg. A marriage had disintegrated into a near-violent squabble. And the captain suffered a fatal heart attack the day after they arrived. In the midst of all that, the *Kismet's* Armstrong engines died, so they had to be rescued.

From orbit, we looked down at a surface that was dust brown and wrinkled, dried out, cracked, broken. Lots of places were emitting steam. Serendipity had the usual big moon that seems to be a requirement for large, land-based animals, and its skies were almost cloudless. It had a breathable atmosphere, and there were no pathogens known to be dangerous to humans. If you wanted to hide someone for a few weeks or months, this would be the perfect place. Except where would a hotel key fit in?

'I was hoping we'd get lucky,' said Alex.

'Doesn't look like it. This place is primitive. Does anybody live here at all?'

He grinned. 'Would you?'

'Not really.'

'We're here,' he said. 'Might as well do the search. I'd guess we're looking for a cluster of modules. Some sort of temporary shelter. Anything artificial.' He was visibly discouraged.

I told Belle to run a planetwide scan.

We passed over a miniscule sea and back over desert. The place was so desolate and forlorn that it had a kind of eerie beauty. When we crossed the terminator and slipped into the night, the ground occasionally glowed with ethereal fire.

But there was nothing, no place, certainly no hotel, where anyone could have stashed visitors.

After two days, Belle reported the scan complete. *'Negative results,'* she said. *'I do not see anything artificial on the surface.'*

Alex grunted and closed his eyes. 'No surprise.'

'Time to go home,' I said.

He took the key out of his pocket and stared at it. *Up. Down. Lock. Unlock. Transfer funds.* 'Barber was willing to kill to keep its existence secret,' he said.

Why?

I looked down at the surface and thought how nothing would ever happen there. The oversized critters would continue to chase one another down while the climate kept getting hotter. By the time survival became impossible even for these hardy life-forms, the human race would probably be gone, evolved into something else. It got me thinking about time, how it seems to move faster as you get older, how it runs at different rates in gravity fields or under acceleration. How we assume that the kind of world we live in is the status quo, the end point of history. There'll always be a Rimway.

'You know,' I said, 'we may have made an assumption about the key.'

An eyebrow went up. 'Which is what?'

'That it came from around 1365.'

'Of course it did,' he said. 'It was lying in the back of the shuttle.'

'That doesn't mean it belongs to that era.' I took the key from him and stared at it. 'People have been barging around in the Veiled Lady for thousands of years.'

'We've ruled out planetary surfaces and outstations,' Alex said. 'And we've ruled out a rendezvous with another ship. What's left?'

Not much. 'Somebody else's outstation?' I suggested.

He considered it. 'Maybe. Maybe we're looking for an artifact. Something left over that's not in the record.'

'It's possible,' I said. 'But it can't be too old. If you're going to use it to shelter people, even for a just a few days, it has to be capable of functioning.'

'By which you mean it has to be able to hold a charge.'

'Yes. That's part of it.'

'How old?' he asked.

When did I become the professional on outstations? 'I'm not an engineer, Alex. But I'd guess maybe two thousand years at the outside. Maybe not that long. Maybe not nearly that long.'

We were moving back into daylight again, watching the sun climb above the arc of the planet. 'Two thousand years,' he said. 'That sounds like the Kang.'

'It could be.' They'd been active in this region for a period of about twelve hundred years, beginning during the ninth millennium. After that they'd gone dormant. Only in the last century had the Kang begun showing some of their old vitality. 'Belle,' I said, 'has anyone other than ourselves and the Kang Republic been prominent in the exploration of the region that includes Delta Karpis? Out, say, to seventy light-years?'

'The Alterians maintained a substantial presence, as did the Ioni.'

'I'm talking about recent times. Within the last three millennia.' I realized what I'd said and must have grinned.

'That's good,' Alex said. 'We're thinking big.'

'It appears,' Belle said, *'that no one else has invested in the subject area. Other than the Commonwealth, of course. The forerunner of the Confederacy.'*

Alex poked a finger at the AI. 'Belle,' he said, 'what kind of character did the Kang use to represent their currency? During their period of ascendancy?'

'There were many. Which currency, and during what era?'

'Show us all of them.'

The screen filled with symbols. Letters from various alphabets, ideographs, geometric figures. He looked at them, shook his head, and asked whether there were more. There were.

It was in the second batch. The fifth symbol from the key. The rectangle. The press pad. 'That looks like it,' he said.

It was impossible to be certain, but it did seem to be the same character. And I thought, Finally! 'Belle, please provide the position for any remnant outstation from the Kang era located within the subject area.'

'Scanning, Chase.'

Alex closed his eyes.

'We lack data,' said Belle. *'The locations of the Kang*

outstations were lost during the Pandemic revolutions. The stations themselves were long abandoned by the time the polity collapsed, and apparently no one cared enough to save the details. The locations of six are known, none of which is in the area of interest. But there were substantially more.'

'But we don't know where they were located.'

'*That is correct.*'

Serendipity is only twelve light-years from the place where the dwarf plowed into Delta Kay. Had Delta Kay still been a living star, it would have been at almost a right angle to the plane of the local solar system, bright and yellow in Serendipity's northern skies.

'Might as well go home,' said Alex.

Belle stepped onto the bridge, blond and beautiful and wearing a workout suit. Her shirt said ANDIQUAR UNIVERSITY. This one, whose programing was virtually identical to the original's, enjoyed making personal appearances. She shook her head, signaling that she wished she could help.

It was out there somewhere, a forgotten station where the *Polaris* passengers had found refuge. But where? A sphere with a diameter of 120 light-years makes a pretty big search area. 'Not so fast,' I said. 'How did Maddy know it was there? If there is such a place, how'd they happen to find out about it?'

'I have no idea,' said Alex.

And I remembered Nancy White at the outstation, the fact of its existence borne away by the ages. '*Given enough time,*' she'd said, '*it's what happens to us all.*'

'I beg your pardon?'

'Nancy White. She was especially interested in things that get abandoned. Worlds, cities, philosophies. *Outstations.*'

'She knew of one in this area?'

'I don't know. She does a show that includes a tour of one of them. Chai Ping, or Pong, or something like that.' I looked at Belle.

'*Checking,*' Belle said. She leaned back against a bulkhead and let her gaze drop to the deck.

Alex wandered over to the viewport and looked down into the darkness. 'I can't imagine,' he said, 'that we ever thought they might have come here.'

'Had to look, Alex. It was the only way to be sure.'

Belle lifted her eyes. '*I've reviewed the show in question. White locates Chai Pong at a point eleven hundred light-years from Delta Karpis.*' Well out of range.

Alex grumbled something I couldn't make out. The air felt thick and heavy. 'Maybe she found more than one.'

'It's possible,' I said.

'If so, it might be in her work somewhere. In her commentaries, her essays, her notebooks. Maybe even in another of the shows.'

'*Starting a comprehensive review,*' said Belle. '*This will take a few minutes.*'

'Meantime,' said Alex, 'there's no point hanging around here.'

'Let's sit tight,' I said, 'until we know which way we'll be going.'

Belle brightened and raised a fist in triumph. '*It's in her* Daybook,' she said. '*In a collection of ideas for essays and programs.*'

'What does it say?' asked Alex.

'*Are you familiar with Roman Hopkin?*'

'No.'

'*He's a longtime friend of White's. An historian who seems to have spent most of his time doing research for her. Anyhow, he discovered Chai Pong. In 1357.*'

The *Daybook* appeared on-screen:

3/11/1364

Hopkin has found another. How many lost pieces of the Kang are out there? This one, he says, is near Baku Kon, in the dusty embrace, as he put it, of one of the gas giants in the system. (He always tends to over-state things.) He says it's going down soon. Into the atmosphere. He thinks it'll happen sometime during the next few centuries. It's apparently been abandoned for two thousand years. He says it looks as if they cleared out in a hurry, and left everything. Ideal site for reclamation. It's a microcosm of the Kang culture of the period. He's going back in a month, and he promised I can go along.

I read it several times.

'*Nancy White,*' continued Belle, '*is the only one of the* Polaris *passengers to do extensive off-world travel. She has, as you know, a reputation for a cosmic perspective. She is celebrated primarily because—*'

'Skip it, Belle. A Kang platform would have been a major discovery. Why didn't we hear of it before?'

'*Hopkin was dead three months later.*'

'Another murder?' I asked.

'*It doesn't seem so. He died trying to rescue a woman who was attempting to commit suicide from a skyway. She climbed over the railing. He tried to stop her, but she apparently put up a fight and took him with her.*'

'And Nancy White kept the second Kang discovery quiet,' I said.

'Belle,' said Alex, 'where's Baku Kon?'

A star map flashed onto one of the screens. Here was Delta Karpis. And *there*, at a range of forty-five light-years, a light blinked on and grew bright. 'It would have been easy for them,' Alex said.

Belle caught his eye. '*Alex,*' she said, '*I have a transmission for you. From Jacob.*'

'From Jacob? Okay. Let's see it.'

She put it on-screen:

Alex, I've received a message from one Cory Chalaba, who's with the Evergreen Foundation. I take it you know her. She says the woman in the picture came by to look at the exhibit. She didn't want to comment further except to ask me to relay the message and to get back to her. I assume you know what it means.

Teri Barber.

Alex nodded. 'She wants to know whether Barber might try to steal the artifact.'

'What are you going to tell her?' I asked.

'It should be safe enough. It's been in that case for sixty years. Barber will realize that stealing it would only call attention to it. No, that's not where the danger lies.'

'You're talking about Baku Kon?'

'Yes, indeed. She'll assume that we know. That we've figured it out.'

'And she'll be waiting for us when we get there.'

He pushed back in his chair and folded his hands. 'Wouldn't you?'

Baku Kon was a class-B blue-white star, surface temperature twenty-eight thousand degrees Kelvin. The catalog indicated it was relatively young, only 200 million years old. Like Sol, it had nine planets. And, as if it had been designed by a mathematician, the gas giants were the inner- and outermost, and the third, fourth, and fifth.

The inner giant was in a marked elliptical orbit that would literally carry it through the sun's atmosphere. The Kang weren't going to put a station there.

Generally, when you were deciding the location of an outstation, you would want to be close enough to the sun to be able to take advantage of the free energy it supplies, but you don't want to have to put up a ton of shielding to protect yourself from radiation.

'The third one,' I told Alex.

Finding an outstation after it's been shut down is not an afternoon at the beach. If it's not lit up, if it's not putting out a signal, you've no easy way to distinguish it from the thousands of other rocks that are usually orbiting a big world. So we had to start an elimination process. Pull in close to a candidate, look for antennas, dishes, collectors, whatever, cross it off the list, and move on to the next. You could be at it for a while. And we were. Days and nights began to run together.

Life on board settled into a routine. Alex spent a lot of time reading White's work, hoping to find something that Belle might have missed. 'She tells stories here,' he said, 'like being with her father on Rimway when she was a girl, and both moons lined up during a total solar eclipse. It happens at sporadic times, sometimes not for thousands of years. But this was 1338, and it was going to happen again just fourteen years later. They talked about where each of them would be when it did, and she said she wanted to be with him, made him promise. But he died two years early, and she describes watching the event alone, or at least watching it without him.' He nodded and took a sip from a coffee cup.

'Hard to believe,' I said, 'someone like that could be part of this.'

'It would take somebody like that,' he said.

We moved slowly through the field of orbiting rocks. They ranged in size from pebbles to moons twice the size of the big moon at home. The planets were recently formed, still in the process of clearing gas and assorted debris out of the neighborhood. Roman Hopkin had not been exaggerating when he described a dusty embrace. Belle did the examinations, of course, while we looked out the windows. She was far more efficient than we would have been, checking out whole clusters of the things simultaneously. Had it been necessary for Alex and me to do it, we'd still be there.

It took just over a week.

Belle woke me in the middle of the night to say she had a hit. *Ninety-nine percent probability,* she added. It was a big, misshapen asteroid, craggy, broken, its surface covered with ridges and craters. Communication, sensing, and collection equipment bristled from its higher ground. It had at least six attitude thrusters. We could even see where a section had been cut away to provide easier ingress to docking bays.

'Any sign of another ship?' I asked her.

'*Negative, Chase.*' She didn't add, didn't need to, that this area would be easy to hide in.

'Okay, Belle. I want you to position the ship one kilometer from the outstation. Match course and speed with it.'

'*Complying.*'

Outstations are designed so that arriving ships find the docks wide open. You just glide in, tie up, exit through a boarding tube, and you're inside. That's all there is to it. The way we did at Meriwether.

But here we were looking at an asteroid that just hung there in the night. No doors had opened on our approach, no transmission informed us of the virtues of the Wong-Ti Restaurant, no lights came on.

It appeared to be in tidal lock, always showing the same face to the big planet. The surface was a tangle of jagged rock and craters. I could see hatches scattered here and there. Most were designed to provide access to fields of sensors, antennas, telescopes, and/or collectors. That's what you'd expect, of course. They were service hatches. I found what looked like a main access near the docking area. It would take us right into the concourse.

We'd need extra air tanks. And a laser. In case the airlocks weren't working.

If Barber were there, she'd probably already been alerted that we'd arrived. So there was no reasonable chance of sneaking up on her at four in the morning. I decided to let Alex sleep, but I didn't go back to my own cabin. If something happened, I wanted to be on the bridge.

When Alex appeared a few hours later, his first question was whether I'd seen any sign of Barber. No, I said, everything's quiet.

'Good,' he said. 'Maybe we'll be okay.'

I showed him the hatch I thought we should use.

He frowned. 'No.'

'Why not? It's ideal.'

He indicated a service hatch buried among ridges in a remote antenna field. '*That* one,' he said.

'Alex, that's a long way from the docks. If we go in there, it's going to be a major hike into the operating spaces.'

'That's exactly right.'

'So why are we using it?'

'Because if Barber's here, she'll think the same way you do. She'll expect us to use the hatch by the docks.'

He had a point. 'Okay,' I said. 'But that's rough country. I'm not excited about taking the ship in close to those ridges.'

'We'd have to jump, wouldn't we?'

'Yes, we would.' Maybe twenty meters or so.

Unaccountably, he seemed to think that was good. 'We'll use the lander,' he said. 'Or at least, *I* will.'

'What do you mean? We're both going over, right?'

He delivered that familiar mischievous grin.

24

The power of illusion derives primarily from the fact that people are inclined to see what they expect to see. If an event is open to more than a single interpretation, be assured the audience will draw its conclusion ready-made from its collective pocket. This is the simple truth at the heart of stage magic. And also of politics, religion, and ordinary human intercourse.

—The Great Mannheim

EXTRACT *BELLE-MARIE*/LANDER DAY 32 OF MISSION; 0717 HOURS

LANDER: On my way, Chase.

BELLE: Flight time will be four and a half minutes, Alex.

LANDER: That checks with onboard data.

BELLE: Be careful when you get out. Just step across to the airlock. You have the generator, right?

LANDER: Yes, Chase, I have the generator. And the laser.

BELLE: When you get inside, we're going to lose radio contact.

LANDER: I know.

BELLE: That means you exercise extreme caution.

LANDER: Chase, we've been over this. I'll be careful.

BELLE: Don't forget you get back to the lander ninety minutes after arrival. If I don't see you within that time, I'm coming over.

LANDER: Have no fear, my pretty. I'll come out and wave to you.

BELLE: I don't like this arrangement, Alex.

LANDER: Just keep cool. Everything's fine. Did you give the AI her directions?

BELLE: Yes. Nobody's going to get on board. If anyone tries, we'll accelerate, and whoever's out there will get tossed.

LANDER: Very good. I don't think there's anything to worry about, but . . .

BELLE: . . . Better safe than sorry. *(Pause.)* Target hatch is to starboard.

LANDER: Pity we can't open the access doors. Just take *Belle* right in.

BELLE: This place has had no power for centuries, Alex.

LANDER: Okay. Coming up on it now.

BELLE: Don't forget the tether.

LANDER: It's not really a big deal. All I have to do is lean out the airlock and the hatch is right there.

BELLE: Do me a favor and let's do this the way we said we would.

LANDER: You'll make somebody a good aunt one day.

BELLE: I already am somebody's aunt.

LANDER: I'm not surprised.

BELLE: Alex, after you're on the ground, Belle will pull the lander back a bit.

LANDER: Okay. I've arrived.

BELLE: Contact.

LANDER: That's what I said, Chase. Beginning depressurization.

BELLE: I read you. Keep in mind there'll be no artificial gravity on the rock.

LANDER: I know.

BELLE: And no maintenance for a long time. Watch what you grab hold of.

LANDER: I always watch what I grab hold of.

BELLE: Let's try to stay serious, Alex. This thing has collectors, and it's just barely possible it still has power somewhere. Stranger things have happened.

LANDER: I hear you.

BELLE: Anything metal is dangerous.

LANDER: Stop worrying, Beautiful. You're talking as if I've never done anything like this before.

BELLE: It's a dreary-looking place.

LANDER: Hatch is open. I'm tethered and on my way.

BELLE: You've got everything?

LANDER: Would you please stop?

BELLE: It's the price you pay for leaving me behind.

LANDER: I'm out of the lander. It's a jump of about fifty centimeters.

BELLE: Okay.

LANDER: I think I can make it.

BELLE: I hope so.

LANDER: On the ground. Releasing tether.

BELLE: Standing by to retract tether.

LANDER: Approaching the entry hatch.

BELLE: I can see you.

LANDER: *(Pause.)* Chase, I've got the manual release.

BELLE: Gently . . . It probably won't work after all this time.

LANDER: Wait one . . . No, I'm in business . . . It's open. I'm in.

BELLE: Very good, Alex.

LANDER: I'm inside the airlock. Trying the inner hatch.

BELLE: There may still be air pressure on the other side.

LANDER: Apparently not. It's opening up.

BELLE: Keep in mind, you have a two-hour air supply. And I want to see you back at the airlock in ninety minutes. Okay?

LANDER: I'm through. I'm in a tunnel, Chase.

BELLE: Acknowledge my last.

LANDER: What did you say?

BELLE: Back in ninety minutes.

LANDER: No problem.

BELLE: Say it. I will be back within ninety minutes.

LANDER: I will be back within ninety minutes.

BELLE: What can you see?

LANDER: Nothing but rock.

BELLE: It figures. It's a service hatch. Regular traffic would have been in and out through the docking areas.

LANDER: The tunnel goes about twenty meters and then it curves. Can't see what's beyond.

BELLE: Moving the lander.

LANDER: Okay. I'll see you in an hour and a half.

BELLE: Alex, you're starting to fade.

25

O Solitude! where are the charms
That sages have seen in thy face?

—William Cowper

EXTRACT FROM ALEX BENEDICT'S JOURNALS

I was, of course, in zero gravity, wearing grip shoes, but still half-adrift. I've never learned to walk properly with them. Experts say that a novice will be tempted to try to fly. In my case, at least, they're wrong. I tend to be cautious. I don't like being weightless, I get ill easily, and I always feel disoriented when it's not entirely clear which way is down.

I came through the airlock wondering whether I'd find Teri Barber waiting for me with a bomb. But that was imagination run wild, and I knew it. Nevertheless, I breathed a sigh of relief when the inner hatch opened up, and I was looking down a long, empty corridor.

I had a generator with me, so that, if the need arose, I could introduce some power into the place. I also had a black marker, to ensure I didn't get lost, and a scrambler. I've never used one of the things, but I knew if Barber turned up, I'd have no trouble blasting away.

The corridor was cut through rock. I turned on my wrist lamp and put it at its lowest setting, so it wasn't much more than a soft glow. I kidded myself that I was less of a target that way. And I plunged ahead. Straight down the passageway for about twenty meters, then around a curve. Looking back on it now, I think continuing around that bend, convinced there was a psycho waiting for me somewhere in the place, was the gutsiest thing I've ever done.

The walls were uniformly gray, flinty, reflective. Strips that had once provided lighting ran along the overhead and the tunnel floor.

The tunnel curved and dipped and rose, so that you could seldom see more than twenty or thirty meters at a time. Ideal for an ambush. Don't ask me why there were so many convolutions. It seemed to me that if you're driving a passageway through rock, you go straight. But what do I know?

It would have been nice to be able to hear. But, of course, someone could drop a ton of bricks in that vacuum, and you'd never know. I trailed one palm against the walls, on the theory that any movement in the tunnel might create a vibration that I could detect. But that was wishful thinking, and I knew it.

I kept going. Past three or four doors that didn't look promising so I didn't try to open them. Past a couple of intersections, where, since the connecting tunnel seemed no more interesting than the one I was in, I stayed straight. Through two more hatches, both, I'm happy to report, open.

Eventually the tunnel forked. I marked it and went right.

I was beginning to relax a bit until I came around a curve, saw a light, and almost jumped out of the pressure suit. But it turned out to be a reflection. Off a sheet of metal. It turned out to be a door that had broken loose, probably from a cabinet.

Another hatch lay ahead. That one was closed, and it didn't respond when I tried to open it. Usually if that happens, it's because there's air pressure on the other side. In this case, it felt as if the problem was simply a matter of age. I wrestled with it for a minute then finally cut my way through with the laser.

The corridor continued on the other side. I passed a series of storage areas, filled with cabinets, cases, and crates. These were loaded with spare parts, bedding supplies, cable, hardware, electronic gear. When they left, the Kang had apparently not bothered to clear the station. It made me wonder whether the last ones out had realized nobody would be coming back.

Some stuff was afloat. Benches, chairs, fastenings, rock-hard fabrics, accompanied by a fine mist of particles and gunk that might have been anything, the remnants of towels or clothing or filters or food. Everything had drifted against one wall, which must have marked the far side of the station's orbit.

I'd been in the passageway about three-quarters of an hour when I went through a final hatch and the stone walls ended. They were replaced by something that had been board or paneling at one time. It was rough, dry, hard, and all the color had drained from it. The floor was carpeted, but my grip shoes tore small pieces out of it. I approached a set of double doors, one of which was open. I passed through and was gratified to see that I'd arrived in the station proper. Doors, rather than hatches, began to appear. They were on both sides of the corridor. None was easy to open, but I forced my way past several of them. One room housed a workout area, with a treadmill, some bars, and a few other pieces of exercise gear. Another contained an empty pool, its diving board still in place.

Two more rooms were filled with lockers and benches. Each had showers.

I came to a staircase and drifted up to the next level, which opened out into a lobby. There was a long, curving counter on one side and a series of shops opposite. The shops were all empty shelves and tables. A wrench and a mallet were climbing one wall. They forget the tools and take the personal stuff. I've seen it before, and it's as if people are being deliberately vindictive. Any of those shopkeepers could have achieved immortality by the simple expedient of leaving his name and his stock.

Several passageways opened off the area. There were more shops and more doors. I wandered into an apartment. A worktable was anchored to the deck. Two chairs floated against a wall. And a cushion. Everything was stiff and dry.

There were also shards of glass adrift. And an electronic instrument. A music player of some sort, I guessed.

I went next door, where it was different. The furniture was bolted to the floor. Fabrics were old, but not ancient. The room wasn't exactly the Golambére, but it was livable. Had, in fact, been lived in within the recent past. A (relatively) modern chest of drawers stood in a corner. The only objects adrift were a coffee cup, a pen, and a doily.

I walked over to the bureau and inspected it. There were four drawers, all empty. I cut it loose from its anchors and looked on the back. A plate said MANUFACTURED BY CROSBY WORLDWIDE. In Standard characters.

I opened my channel to Chase. 'I don't guess you can hear me, love,' I said, 'but I think we found it. This is where they stayed.'

I felt pretty good at that moment. End of the trail, at last.

Chase, of course, didn't respond.

And now for the icing on the cake: All that remained was to hook up the generator, feed some power into the circuits, and watch my key work one of the locks.

'You needn't go any farther, Benedict.' The voice came out of my receiver, but I saw movement to my left in the doorway. 'I really hoped you wouldn't push so hard.' Another lamp blinked on. It blinded me, but I could see someone behind it. A woman.

She was holding a military pistol, one of those things that blows large holes in walls. I'd gotten so caught up in the search that I'd put my scrambler into a pocket. Not that it would have made much difference against the cannon she was carrying.

'Turn off the lamp,' she said quietly. 'That's good. Now turn around slowly and don't do anything that might surprise me. You understand what I'm saying?' She stood in the doorway, in a white pressure suit with a Confederacy patch on one shoulder, her face hidden by the helmet and the light. The weapon was in her left hand.

'Yes,' I said. 'I understand.'

'Put your hands straight out where I can see them.'

I complied. 'How long have you been waiting here, Teri?'

'Long enough.'

I couldn't get a good look at her. 'Or should I say Agnes?'

I could hear her breathing over the radio link. 'You have it all figured out, do you?'

'No. I don't. I don't understand how Maddy English could resort to murder. You killed Taliaferro, didn't you?'

She didn't answer.

'He was going to talk to Chase. Warn her about you. Am I right?'

'Yes.'

'Was he going to tell her who he really was? Was he going to blow the whistle on the whole operation?'

'He said no. He promised he wouldn't do that. But I couldn't trust him.'

'Too much to lose.'

'Yes. Everything to lose.' She edged into the room. 'But there's no way you can understand what I'm talking about.'

'Try me.'

'You know, Alex, I feel as if I've come to know you pretty well.'

'You're a mystery to me, Maddy.'

'I guess.' She sounded wistful. 'Listen, I had no wish to kill anyone.'

'I know that. It's why you warned Survey when you planted the bombs.'

'Yes. That's right. I tried to do the right thing. I wouldn't have killed anybody if I could have avoided it. Especially not Jess. But too much was at stake.'

'What was at stake, Maddy?'

'You know what I am now.'

'Yes. Forever twenty-five. Must be nice.'

'It changes your perspective about a lot of things.' She said nothing for a long moment. Then: 'Don't misunderstand me, Alex. I won't hesitate—'

'Of course not. Still, it must have hurt when you pushed Tom Dunninger off the cliff at Wallaba Point.'

'It wasn't Tom Dunninger. It was Ed. Or maybe it wasn't. I'm not sure anymore who it was.'

'What happened?'

'I didn't push him.'

'What happened, Maddy?'

'I loved Ed. I would never have harmed him. Never.'

'You loved him? You betrayed him.'

'You're talking about Dunninger again. They were different people. At Walpurgis, when he was Eddie Crisp, I loved him. And before that, in Huntington, and before that, on Memory Isle. Appropriate spot, that was. Memory Isle.'

'What happened to him?' I was thinking about Wallaba Point, but she answered a different question.

'He wouldn't give in. After they brought him here off the Polaris, to this place, he still wouldn't give in.'

'Wouldn't agree to stop his work.'

'It was too late by then anyway. He'd already done the final test. Taken the nanobots aboard.'

'You mean injected into his own system?'

'Yes. Of course. What else would I be talking about?' She used the weapon to wave me into the middle of the room. 'They were here for almost four months. During that time they could see that he was getting progressively younger. When I got here, with the Babcock, to pick them up, I couldn't believe what I saw.'

'He was a young man.'

'I wouldn't go quite that far. But I'd never have recognized him.'

'So Boland did a reconstruction job on him.'

'Yes. Chek wiped his memories. Gave him a new personality. Eventually created a fresh identity and got him a job. We used to take turns watching him. To make sure he was okay.'

'But you had to move him periodically. Right? Because he didn't age.'

'Yes. He didn't understand that. He had false memories, implanted by Boland. But every eight years we had to do it again. Take his memories. Make him someone different.'

'It must have been hard on him.'

The light wavered. 'We were killing him. Over and over. That's what it is, when they do a wipe. Somebody else takes over your body. You're gone.'

'So you—'

'He used to get flashbacks. He'd remember pieces of his former life. Sometimes as Tom Dunninger. Sometimes as one of the others. By the time we were at Walpurgis, he was in his fourth incarnation. Flashbacks were coming more often, and I was trying to persuade Boland to take him in at Morton, put him with others who didn't age and give him a permanent identity. But Dunninger kept reappearing. More and more often as time went by. Boland said no. He said a permanent identity would eventually restore him altogether.'

'There was no satisfactory solution,' I said.

'No.'

'So you decided to push him off the summit at Wallaba Point.'

'No. I told you I didn't do that. I would never have done it. I loved him.

'We used to go up there on summer evenings. We enjoyed the place. It made everything else seem unreal. Ed was good. And funny. And sometimes sad on occasions when he didn't seem to know why. But he loved me. They were getting ready to move him again. Change his identity. People in Walpurgis were beginning to notice. Every time they did that, we had to start over.

'Whenever Boland was done with him, he never remembered

who I was. It was killing me, too. So I decided I was going to explain everything to him that night. Roll the dice. Persuade him to join us. Tell him the truth. And while I was doing it, up there on the brink – God, how could I have been so stupid? – Dunninger came back. Just like that, it was Dunninger looking at me out of Ed's eyes, knowing who I was, knowing who he was. And he hated me. Oh God, he hated me.

'But he seemed to have forgotten where we were. He snarled at me and pushed me down. Then he turned to walk away and he tripped over something, a rock, a root, something.' Her voice caught. 'He lost his balance.' Her voice shook and trailed off, and she stood a long time without moving. 'I watched him flailing on the edge, watched him fall. And I never moved to help him.'

'I'm sorry, Maddy.'

'Yeah. I'm sorry, too. We're all sorry.'

I wondered whether tears were running down her cheeks. It sounded like it. Tears in a pressure suit are a major problem.

'Once,' she said, 'at Huntington, he met somebody else. And married her.'

I watched her lower the pistol a few degrees, and I thought maybe it was over. That she'd seen what she had become, but when I took a step toward her, it came back up. I thought about trying to charge her, get to her while she was distracted, but the barrel never wavered.

I asked what had happened to the other wife.

'Jasmine. Who the hell would name their kid Jasmine?' She was breathing heavily. 'He didn't like her anyhow. The marriage didn't work.'

'What happened?'

'Chek came one night, and we just spirited him away. Jasmine never knew what happened. One day her husband was there, the next he was gone.'

The muzzle looked very large. Keep her talking, I thought. 'Why was he getting flashbacks? I thought personality change was permanent.'

372

'It's not supposed to happen. But Boland says, you put some-body under stress, and sometimes it does.'

'Tell me about Shawn Walker.'

'Walker was a son of a bitch.'

'What did he do? Threaten to tell what he knew?'

'He didn't really understand what it was about, didn't realize it was for him as well as for everybody else. All he saw was that he had a chance to make a killing. He knew we'd pay to keep him quiet. So he kept pushing. Pushed until we'd had enough.'

'Did Taliaferro help with that?'

'No.' All I could see was the pressure suit and the helmet. Her face was completely in shadow. 'He didn't have the stomach for it. Jess wanted him dead, just as I did, but he didn't like the idea of having to do it.'

'So you took care of it.'

'Listen. I don't need any moral lectures from you. You buy and sell the past. Make your money. You don't care whether everything goes into private collections, whether people hoard it so they can sell it off down the line. All you care about is turning a profit. I did what had to be done. And I can tell you I'd have preferred to see you walk away from all this. But you just didn't know when to let go.'

I could feel the scrambler lying against my thigh. But it was down in a cargo pocket. It might as well have been in the Belle-Marie. 'As soon as the Sentinel and the Rensilaer started back,' I said, 'you sent your last message.'

'Yes.'

'And then you brought the Polaris here.'

'Of course. We left in the late afternoon, ship's time, and we were here early next morning. I even spent a couple of nights here before going back.'

'Why'd you do it, Maddy?'

'Why'd I do what?'

'The whole Polaris thing. You were giving up who you were.

Going into hiding for a lifetime. Was it that they promised to make you young again?'

She kept the lamp pointed at my eyes. 'I think it's time to end this. It's getting up to an hour and a half since you came down here, and your buddy will be getting antsy. I want to be out at the airlock when she shows up. To say hello.'

'You were listening—'

'Of course I was.'

'So you're going to have to kill two more people.'

'As soon as she sticks her face in the hatch. I'll make it quick. Like you. She won't even know I'm there.' Her finger tightened on the trigger. 'Good-bye, Alex,' she said. 'Nothing personal.'

26

Reach out, Herman. Touch the stars. But not with your mind. Anyone can do that. Touch them with your hand.

—Silas Chom,
speaking to Herman Armstrong, in *The Big Downtown*, a drama celebrating the invention of the Armstrong Drive

'Chase, where are you?'

'She can't hear you down here, Alex.'

It must have been a nervous moment for him, but I had her in my sights and could have taken her out at any time. She was standing in the doorway, half-in, half-out, paying no attention anywhere except to Alex. Completely fooled by a scripted conversation. The plan, of course, was to let her talk as long as she wanted. But obviously not to let her shoot anybody.

I suspected she would not give up meekly, and she had the pistol. If I told her to put it down, she could keep it trained on him, and we'd have a standoff. So I decided to go the safe route. Shoot first, talk to her later.

I aimed and fired. Scramblers, of course, are not lethal. There are some people who say that's their drawback. Maddy gasped, and her lights went out. The pistol drifted away from her, and she just hung there, locked to the deck by her grip shoes.

Alex took a deep breath. 'Chase,' he said, 'where've you been?'

'Been right here,' I said. 'The whole time.' I pushed past the woman into the room. She swayed.

'I was afraid maybe you got lost.'

I took her pistol and put it in my belt. Then I slipped the scrambler into a pocket. 'I was behind you the whole way, Big Guy.'

'I'm glad.'

I put my lamp up close to her helmet. 'Is it really Maddy? How can it be?' I was looking at Teri Barber.

'Yeah, it is.'

'Incredible. I hope I look that good at a hundred.'

'She's not quite that old.'

We stood quietly, trying to absorb the reality of the moment. 'How did you know?'

'I didn't, for certain. But I couldn't think of any scenario that would account for three women, Barber, Shanley, and Maddy, who looked so much alike. And the fact that Kiernan looked like Taliaferro, and Eddie Crisp resembled a young Dunninger. Even parents and their kids don't look that much alike.'

'They could have been clones.'

'Not this bunch. Maddy, maybe. The others? There was no record of any clones. And anyhow, they were population-control types. Opposed on principle to cloning except in special cases.' He shook his head. 'I couldn't imagine any reason for them to do that.'

'So you decided Dunninger had already achieved his breakthrough—'

'—And that it did more than extend life. It restored damage caused by the ageing process. Yes.'

'So they're all alive? Except Dunninger?'

'And Taliaferro. Yes, I think so.'

'And they're at Morton College,' I said.

376

'Very good, Chase. I don't know whether they actually spend time there or not. But I don't think there's any question that's their base.'

'Margolis? Is he one of them? He didn't look like anybody.'

'I don't think so. I think he's just hired help.'

I was shining my light around the room. Taking my first good look at the place we'd been searching for. 'Taliaferro,' I said. 'What happened to him? I mean, why'd he disappear?'

'He benefited from Dunninger's discovery, like the rest of them. Except a couple of years passed before they administered it to him. I assume Mendoza was handling that.'

'Why would they wait?'

'Probably because they wanted to keep Taliaferro in charge at Survey. Once he became like them, his ageing process would go into reverse. He'd start getting younger every day.'

It was hard to swallow. 'Alex,' I said, 'I always understood age reversal was impossible.'

'That's what the experts say. Obviously, Dunninger, and maybe Mendoza, figured out a way.'

I tied the generator into one of the circuits and adjusted the voltage. Alex hit the switch, and the lights came on. He took the key out of his pocket and handed it to me. 'Do the honors,' he said.

We went into the corridor, picked a closed door at random, aimed the remote, and pressed the ○ button. Nothing happened, and we moved to the next door. 'It's here somewhere,' said Alex.

It was at the far end of the hall. I will never forget watching a guide light activate while the door tried to swing inward, but it wouldn't because it was wedged tight so Alex gave it a kick. That broke it open and a table lamp came on. Maddy's apartment. 'Congratulations,' I said.

'Yes.' He was wearing a large smile. 'We do seem to have done it, don't we?'

'And the rest of them stayed in these other units,' I said.

Alex nodded. 'I wonder what the mood was like.'

I could hear Maddy breathing over her open channel. 'So what's next?' I asked.

'We take Maddy back and figure out what we're going to do with her. And then we'll have a conversation with Everson.'

'You think he'll agree to that?'

'Oh, yes,' Alex said. 'In fact, I'll be surprised if he's not in touch as soon as he hears we're back.'

'Do we need to do anything else here?'

'No. I think we should be heading out.'

I looked down the corridor. Some of the lights were on, lending an appearance that was less romantic than it had been, and more dilapidated. I wondered what it had been like in its glory days, when the place was alive and the Kang were on the premises. What would a functioning AI from that era be worth? Which called to mind Alex's idea about tracking ancient radio signals.

Ah, well. Let's stay with the business at hand.

I could no longer hear Maddy breathing. She'd turned off the link. I slipped away from Alex and retreated down the corridor to the room in which we'd left her.

She was gone.

I let Alex know and checked the lobby. There was no sign of her.

'You've got her pistol?' asked Alex.

'Yes.'

'Then it doesn't matter.'

The scrambler should have put her down for thirty minutes or so. We'd been gone less than ten. 'Maybe her body is more resistant than normal,' he said.

Oh, damn. I should have realized. 'It's the pressure suit. It would have shielded her.'

Alex made an irritated noise deep in his throat. 'Well, we got what we came for. Let's head out.'

'And quickly,' I said.

He picked up on my sense of urgency, asked no questions, and we hustled out of the lobby and back down the passageway. It was about three kilometers out to the airlock. That was not good news. I assumed that since we hadn't seen Maddy's ship, she'd been able to get the docking area working, and that was where she was moored. Docking areas are always close to the living spaces. She would get to her ship long before we could reach ours. It didn't help that Alex wasn't the quickest creature on two feet.

'I'm going ahead,' I told him. 'We need to secure *Belle*.' I charged through the tunnel, wishing I'd kept in better shape.

Noncombat vessels aren't armed, in the normal sense of the word. But they do carry the HCS, with its particle beam deflectors. The system is activated automatically when a rock approaches on a threatening vector, as had happened to us at Terranova. But it had parameters, preventing it from firing at an approaching vessel. There was, however, nothing to stop Maddy from rewriting the parameters. She'd have to do that physically, have to poke the change in. That was a safety feature, to avoid inadvertent firing at the wrong target. But she'd only need a couple of minutes. Once she'd done that, she could blast *Belle* and leave us stranded.

It's hard to run in a pressure suit. In zero gee. In a tunnel. Every time the tunnel turned, I hoped maybe I'd see her ahead, but I knew that wasn't likely. And sure enough the passageway stayed dark and empty. Finally, gasping for breath, I was tumbling through the airlock, and there was the lander, about fifty meters overhead, above a field of elevated power collectors. I opened a channel to Belle.

'Hello, Chase,' she said.

'Belle, are you okay?'

'*I'm fine, thank you. How are* you *doing?*'

'Never mind that. Do you see any other ship?'

'*Yes. There's one approaching from the port quarter.*'

I looked and saw a cluster of lights above the horizon. Growing brighter. I'd been wrong. She hadn't docked, but had succeeded in keeping her ship hidden among the orbiting debris. Now it was coming to pick her up.

The AI in the lander had been named *Gabe,* after Alex's uncle. 'Gabe,' I said, 'I need the lander. Bring it in close.'

The station hatch was in a narrow gully, but the primary hazard to the spacecraft was the field of antennas surrounding it. Gabe eased the lander down among them.

'Could you hustle it up a bit, please?'

'The terrain in which you are located—'

'—I know that, Gabe. But we don't have time at the moment for safety first.'

He made a noise that sounded like disapproval but brought the lander in quickly. I got in, and we made for the oncoming ship.

The gas giant floated on the opposite side of the sky. It was sludge brown, with no features whatever except a disturbance of some sort in the northern hemisphere. Probably a storm. I could see several inner moons, all crescents.

The planet and its satellites cast an eerie glow across the chopped surface of the asteroid. I saw Maddy, standing atop a ridge, watching her ship approach. I could make out Bollinger thrusters, and a boxy bridge. It was a Chesapeake, probably a 190. A yacht, really, a dual hull, reduced-mass luxury runabout designed exclusively to travel among ports. It wasn't intended for use elsewhere. Which was why Maddy had to bring it in close to board: It had no lander. Her back was turned to me, and she was utterly exposed. Whatever she might have been sixty years ago, she was homicidal now. I'd left the lander's hatch open, and I thought seriously about using her own pistol to take her out. To finish it. The scrambler wouldn't be adequate at this range, and if I tried to move in close enough to use it, she'd spot me. And the truth was I didn't know whether she had a second weapon available. I didn't want to take any more risks. Or maybe I just wanted to kill her and be done with it. I don't know.

In any case I got as far as leaning out the hatch and drawing a bead on her. But I couldn't bring myself to do it. I remembered lecturing Alex years before during the Sim business when he had a helpless Mute ship in his sights and was about to pull the trigger on them.

So I let her be. Instead, I arced around and came in over the Chesapeake. The area where Maddy was waiting was well off to one side of a collector array. It was relatively flat, and there was room for the Chesapeake to descend.

Its thrusters were firing, moving it in closer to Maddy, lining it up, and slowing it almost to a stop. The ship's hatch began to open.

At that moment she spotted me. But I wasn't interested in her just then. I was looking for the HCS, specifically the controller, the black box, without which the particle beams were useless. I spotted it as the ship snuggled in beside her. It was red and white, located on the hull just forward of the bridge.

Alex's voice broke over the link: *'Chase, where are you?'*

'Back in a minute,' I said. 'Keep in mind she's listening.'

He spoke again, but this time not to me: *'Maddy, give it up. Come back with us. You need help.'*

The Chesapeake drew abreast of Maddy, and she scrambled inside. But that was okay. I was within can't-miss range. I leaned out the hatch, aimed at the black box, and pulled the trigger. 'Bang,' I said.

It was an easy shot. The weapon bucked, there was a satisfying flare, and the black box disappeared in a belch of smoke.

The Chesapeake lifted into the night.

I was wondering about the extent of the damage as I put about and started back to pick up Alex. *'I saw what happened,'* he said. Then he was talking to the Chesapeake: *'Maddy, are you okay? Do you need help?'*

Thoughtful, considering that she'd tried to bushwhack us.

She didn't answer. 'She might just want to get clear,' I told him.

Then I got two voices at once: Gabe and Alex both yelled at me to look out.

The Chesapeake was diving on me, trying to ram me. I guessed that settled any questions about Maddy's state of mind. I swerved to starboard.

Even though the lander is far slower, it's much more maneuverable than a ship, even a small one like the Chesapeake. She made a second pass before I got back to the airlock where Alex waited, but she never had a good shot at me. I took it down among the antennas, and she backed off.

Alex looked dismayed as he climbed in. 'So what do we do now?' he asked.

'She's not going to let us ride the lander out to *Belle*,' I said.

'So okay. We bring the ship here. In tight.'

I opened a channel to Belle and got a surge of static. Switched off and tried again. 'She's jamming us,' I said.

'Can she do that?'

'She's doing it.'

We could see her, a group of five lights now, just off the rim of the gas giant. Waiting.

'If she tries to ram us, isn't she risking serious damage herself?'

'Not if she does it right. It wouldn't take a whole lot to punch a hole in the lander.' I glanced around the cabin. It looked suddenly fragile.

I turned the engine off.

Alex had removed his helmet. Now he reached for it and seemed to be considering putting it back on. 'I have an idea,' he said. 'The windows are polarized, so she won't be able to see into the cabin. She won't know what's in here. We've got a whole station at our disposal. How about we make a bomb, put it on board the lander, and let her ram *that*?'

'That's a good idea. Great idea.'

'Do you know how to make a bomb, Chase?'

'No. I haven't a clue. You?'

'Not really.'

He went back on the circuit, hoping to talk with her. I guess he thought he might be able to cut a deal of some sort. But all

382

channels were blocked. 'We'll just have to make a run for it,' he said. 'She wasn't able to get you a few minutes ago so maybe we'll be all right.'

'I was close to the ground. Not an easy target. Trying to get up to *Belle* is a different game altogether. It's strictly desperation.' The temptation to say the hell with it and make a sudden move was strong. But it would get us killed. *Belle,* like the Chesapeake, was only a set of lights. In her case, there were six. She was directly overhead.

'Does Belle actually have instructions to take off if Maddy were to try to board?'

'Oh, yes. I wasn't leaving that to chance.'

'Good.' For a long minute he was quiet. His eyes drifted to the air tanks. Between the air supply in the lander and the spare tanks, we were good for a few more hours. 'Damn it,' he said. 'Let's try it. Maybe we'll catch her in the washroom.'

'No. We won't make it that way.'

'You have a better idea?'

'Yes,' I said. 'I think I do. I like your bomb idea.'

'But we don't know how to make one. For that matter, there might not even be materials on the platform.'

'There's another possibility.'

'What?'

'First thing we have to do is get the spare air tanks out. We're going to need them.'

'And then—?'

'We arrange things so that Maddy runs into a brick.'

We put our helmets back on, got out of the lander, and climbed down into the station airlock.

We shut off our radios so we couldn't be overheard. Alex touched his helmet against mine to speak to me. 'She can see us,' he said.

'Doesn't make any difference. She'll know we have to try for the ship. Sooner or later.'

383

The laser that Alex had brought was a household unit, a little handheld device for a guy working at home, rather than the industrial strength I would have liked to have. But it was functional, and if it was a trifle short on power, it should nevertheless be adequate.

The airlock hatches and bulkheads looked like steel. Probably made from iron mined on the asteroid itself. They would have been ideal for our purpose, but the metal was resistant to the laser. We could have cut through the hinges and freed the two hatches, but they were too big to get into the lander.

We'd have to load up with ordinary rock.

Alex signaled: You cut, and I'll haul.

I shook my head no. We needed to keep an eye on Maddy, so she didn't slip down and seize the lander while we were preoccupied. I indicated I'd do the first round of work, and he should go back and keep watch.

The work was easy. Just cut a large slab of rock, then haul it out to the airlock. Even that part of things, in zero gee, was simple enough. After a half hour or so, we switched.

I moved the lander directly over the airlock to block Maddy's view of what we were doing. I measured the dimensions of the lander's hatch. It was smaller than I'd remembered, about three-quarters my height. Width was shoulder to wrist.

I ripped off one of the seat covers and moved the backs of the seats down. That would make it easier to load the cabin. The windows protected against outside glare, so Maddy wouldn't be able to see who, or what, was in the cockpit.

I picked up one of the pieces of rock that I'd stowed just the other side of the airlock, put the seat cover over it as an extra precaution, floated it out to the lander, and loaded it into the cabin. Alex was bringing up more chunks, but I could see the doubtful expression on his face. He was wondering whether it would really work, because all the rock didn't weigh anything. That was true. The weight was gone, but it retained its mass. It would resist getting shoved in a new direction.

I started getting warning beeps from my suit's life-support system. Time to switch to fresh air tanks. We had another two sets for each of us, four more hours apiece. And it occurred to me that we would have to be done and back inside *Belle* by then, since we were not going to have the lander at the end of the operation. At least not if everything went according to plan.

We loaded the rock. The warning lamp on the laser began to blink, but we kept working until it gave out. The last piece was too big to fit into a cabin already filled, so we put it in the cargo hold. Acceleration was going to be pretty slow, but Maddy wouldn't have a lot of time to think about it.

When we were ready to launch, Alex made a show of opening the hatch and getting in. But we kept the lander airlock turned away from Maddy's telescopes, so she had no way of knowing what was actually happening. To her it must have seemed we were just going to roll the dice.

Alex slipped back out of the spacecraft, kept down as best he could, and went back into the tunnel. Then it was my turn. I stood at the lander's hatch, my head sticking up so Maddy could see me. I ducked as I normally do and climbed aboard. Then it got complicated. I closed the hatch, pressurized the cabin, and, when I could take off my helmet to speak, I instructed Gabe to start the engine after I got back out.

'*Best approach comes if I leave in six minutes,*' he said.

'Okay. Do it.' It occurred to me that I should take out some insurance, so I gave Gabe a final instruction. Then I put my helmet back on and started depressurization. I also turned off the lander's lights in what was supposed to look like part of an effort to sneak past Maddy's watchful eye.

My conscience, which I usually try to keep under control, reminded me I was abandoning Gabe. I know AIs are not sentient, but sometimes it's hard to believe that. I whispered a goodbye that he couldn't hear.

When I was able to open up, I slipped out, closed the door, and joined Alex in the tunnel.

A minute or two later, the lander lifted away.

Alex touched his helmet to mine. 'Good luck,' he said, keeping his voice low as if even there, inside the rock, with the radio links turned off, Maddy might hear us.

The jamming stopped. She'd spotted the lander and figured she had us now. I half expected her to say something, some final expression of regret, or maybe a taunt. But there was nothing.

Our pressure suits were white, so they didn't provide much camouflage. Nevertheless, we had to know what was happening, so I edged out close to the airlock hatch and took a look. The lander was ascending slowly, trying to accelerate with its load of slabs. I hoped that Maddy was too emotionally played out to notice that it was struggling. But it was moving away from the surface, ascending to an uncertain rendezvous with the *Belle-Marie*.

For a long minute I couldn't find the Chesapeake. But then it passed across one of the moons. I was able to follow it, nothing more than a cluster of lights, moving through the night, curving in, descending, gliding across the barren moonscape.

It was coming.

Alex tugged at my leg. What was happening? We still couldn't talk, especially at that moment. I tried to signal with my hands that she was on her way. Taking the bait.

The Chesapeake came close enough that I could see her clearly, burnt orange in the ghastly light. The twin hulls looked like missiles riding slowly beneath the stars. Her attitude thrusters fired once, twice, lining her up, then she made a final adjustment and began to accelerate.

Here we go, I thought.

But no. She was slowing down again.

Alex's helmet touched mine. He was up beside me now. 'She's thinking it over,' he said.

If she took too long, if the lander actually reached *Belle*, we were dead.

He was baring his teeth. 'Look at her!' The Chesapeake was still tracking the lander, still closing, but still slowing down. 'Maybe she's figured it out.'

'She's wondering whether she can do it without sustaining major damage herself.' I opened my channel to the lander and spoke one word, trying to disguise my voice as something else. *Anything* else. 'Blip,' I said. Then I shut it down again.

Gabe, using my voice, said, *'We're right here, you dumb bitch. If you have the guts.'*

For several seconds the tableau remained virtually unchanged. The lander struggled to gain altitude. And then the Chesapeake fired its main engine and lurched ahead.

Maddy knew that if she hit the lander too hard, there was a possibility of an explosion. Nevertheless she continued to accelerate, raced across a range of about six hundred meters, and blasted into the smaller vehicle, knocking it sideways. But the Chesapeake literally bounced off. The lander's engines erupted in a fireball.

The Chesapeake went spinning toward the east.

We scrambled out onto the surface. Alex had hold of one of my arms, a death grip. 'What do you think?' he asked.

'Don't know.'

The starship gradually faded into the night.

We waited.

A star appeared where it had been. It expanded, burned brightly for a minute or so, faded, and vanished.

27

We are all transients. None of us is any more than a visitor
who has dropped by for coffee and a few minutes' conversation. Then it's out the door and don't let the damp in.

—Margo Chen,
The Toxicon Chronicles

I don't know how Tab Everson arranged to be informed about us,
but we were still fourteen hours out of Rimway when Belle reported
we had a transmission from him. (We'd arrived back home well
off target and had been inbound by then almost three days.)

I took a longer look at him this time. Black beard, gray eyes,
the mien of a young and gifted scholar. We were still too far out
for a meaningful face-to-face, so all we had was a recording.
'*Alex,*' he said, '*I'm glad you got back safely. It's important that
we talk. I'll be waiting at Skydeck. Please take no action until
we've had a chance to discuss things. I beg you.*'

That wasn't the kind of language a young man uses. 'He knows
the cat's out of the bag,' said Alex.

'You want me to contact Fenn? Have him arrange an escort
for us?'

He'd been reading. It was a novel, and I wondered how long

it had been since I'd seen him read anything other than *Polaris*-related stuff. 'No,' he said. 'I don't think we need worry about our safety.'

'Why do you think that?'

'For one thing, he doesn't know what kind of information we've already given Fenn.'

I was trying to figure out who he was. Since Maddy had turned up looking twenty-five, I assumed Everson was also one of the *Polaris* passengers. But which? I tried to imagine what Everson would look like after another thirty or forty years. If he were aging normally. But none of the other passengers looked remotely like Tab Everson. Boland had been more handsome; Urquhart bigger with more presence; Mendoza was shorter and more intense.

And that left only—

'That's right,' Alex said. 'That's exactly who he is.' He scribbled some notes onto a pad, studied them, changed his mind and struck something out, and finally looked satisfied. 'Belle,' he said. 'Reply for Everson.'

'*Ready.*'

'Mr Everson, we'll be weary on arrival and in no condition to carry on a discussion. I'll be happy to talk with you. But not at Skydeck. I'd like you, and the others, to come by my office tomorrow, nine o'clock sharp. I don't need to tell you that if you're unresponsive, I'll have to consider my options.'

Despite my qualms, we abandoned our false identities and the town house and went directly to Andiquar. Alex was reassuring, but I thought we were putting ourselves at risk. He invited me to stay over at the country house, and I agreed and took one of the guest rooms.

We had a leisurely breakfast in the morning. By eight o'clock, Alex had drifted into the back somewhere, and I was in the office, utterly unable to concentrate on anything. At nine, a skimmer appeared overhead, hovered for a few moments, and descended onto the pad.

Four people got out. Everson, two other men, and a woman.

Ordinarily I'd have gone to the door and met them at the front of the house, but in this case I wasn't sure they wouldn't shoot the first person they saw. I notified Alex.

He was at the door talking to them when I arrived. All looked as if they were in their twenties. Everson was talking about 'difficulties encountered throughout the entire process, absolutely unavoidable.' He wished things might have gone otherwise. Alex smiled coldly and turned to me. 'Chase,' he said, 'I'd like to introduce Professor Martin Klassner.'

I'd known it was coming, of course, but still, seeing the reality was something of a shock. Old and dying in 1365, his brain damaged by Bentwood's, this was the man they'd suspected might not survive the flight. He stood before me like a young lion, watching me curiously. He was taller than he'd seemed on the *Polaris*.

I'd spent most of the last few weeks building resentment against the people who'd been trying to kill us. And most of the last few days, since seeing Maddy, trying to digest the reality of age reversal. And here they were. The legendary passengers of the lost flight.

Nancy White was tall and elegant. Distant now, not at all like the figure who'd charmed everyone with her science chats. Her hair, which had been brown at the time of the *Polaris,* was blond. She was dressed casually, trying hard to look relaxed and confident.

And Councillor Urquhart. Once one of the seven most powerful people on the planet. This version had red hair and was so young it was barely possible to see the great man concealed within the trim youth. I couldn't believe it was actually him. He looked barely twenty. But the amiable expression belonged to the older man, the Defender of the Afflicted. He'd lost most of the bearing he'd possessed during his political years. Can't really give the impression of wisdom and *gravitas* when you look just out of school.

And Chek Boland. He could have been a leading man. His hair

had gone from black to blond, but there was no mistaking the classic features and the dark eyes.

Mendoza was missing.

I pulled my attention back to Klassner. 'Good morning, Professor,' I said, without offering my hand.

He took a deep breath. 'I think I understand how you feel. I'm sorry.'

It *was* they. No question. In the prime of their lives, apparently. Young and strong, as people are before gravity sets in.

Alex steered them into the living room, where we'd have more space. Please make yourselves comfortable. I'd left the door to the office open purposely. We'd moved the display case so that Maddy's jacket was visible. Not prominently displayed, but set in a way that visitors could not miss it. Klassner saw it, nodded as if some great truth had just been revealed, and took a seat by the window. He checked his wrist, probably assuring himself that we weren't running a recording system. It struck me that, in this most extraordinary of meetings, we nevertheless retained the usual social niceties. Could we get anyone something to drink? Did you have any problem finding us? You don't look entirely comfortable; would you care for a cushion? (That last was directed at Klassner, who chuckled and allowed as how, yes, he was not entirely at ease, but the furniture had nothing to do with it.)

They passed on the refreshments. Everyone got more or less comfortable, and there was some clearing of throats and a couple of comments about what a nice place the country house was.

'I expected one more,' said Alex.

'Before we get to that,' said Klassner, 'I wanted to ask about Maddy.'

Their eyes met. 'She's dead,' Alex said.

'She attacked you at the Akila?'

'The Kang outstation? Yes, she did.'

'I'm sorry.' He swallowed. 'We're sorry she did that. We're sorry she's been lost. We'd have prevented it if we could. The attack.'

'Why didn't you?'

'I spoke with her when she came to me. She told me you'd found the key. I thought we were still safe. That you wouldn't put it all together.' He smiled. Wearily. Regretfully. 'I underestimated you.'

It was hard to get used to. This *kid*, with the demeanor, not merely of a mature adult, but of an *accomplished* one.

'Why didn't you stop her?'

'How would you suggest I might have done that? She was a free agent.'

'You also stood by while she killed Taliaferro.'

That brought guilty glances from everyone. 'We didn't expect her to do that,' said Urquhart. 'She was more desperate than we realized.'

'And you knew she was trying to kill *us*. She made three attempts. While you people did nothing.'

'No.' Klassner's face clouded. The others shook their heads. 'We didn't know. She didn't tell us what she was doing. We had no way. She and Jess, we thought, were simply trying to find the lost key. Jess was our contact at that time. He thought there was really no problem, that she might have left the key at the outstation, that even if it was found, no one would understand the significance anyhow. Not after all this time. But Maddy was worried, so he tried to help her.'

Well, I'll confess I was a bit intimidated in the presence of a former councillor. But I wasn't just going to sit there like an old shoe. 'Come on,' I said, 'she killed Shawn Walker, too. What's the big surprise?'

'Yes,' said White. 'We knew that. After the fact. We wouldn't have condoned it.'

'Good. I'm glad to hear you think that was maybe a bit extreme. But I assume you weren't too unhappy when it happened.'

'That's hardly fair.' White turned large, intelligent eyes on me. 'There's more to this than you realize, Chase.'

'We're not talking *fair*,' I said. 'We're talking about what actually happened.' Alex caught me with a glance, and I read the message: Let him handle it.

'What did you do,' he asked, 'when you found out what she'd done to Walker?'

'I treated her,' said Boland.

'Not a mind wipe.'

'No. I didn't think it was necessary.'

'The treatment didn't work,' I said.

'Maddy was under a lot of pressure,' he continued. 'But I thought she'd be okay.'

'And you couldn't very well turn her over to the authorities.'

Klassner let his eyes slide shut. 'No. We would have preferred to do that, but there was no way.'

'And eventually she killed Taliaferro.'

'That was a tragedy,' said Boland. 'We didn't think she was dangerous. Even afterward, we didn't – *I* didn't, I'll speak for myself here. Even after Jess died. I didn't believe she'd killed him. She had no reason to.'

'He was going to warn us,' said Alex.

'Yes. But he hadn't shared with us the information that she'd gone psychotic again. So we had no way of knowing what was happening. She told us Jess fell off the roof at the Archives because he was hurrying and was distracted.'

'People have a habit of falling from things,' I said, 'when Maddy's in the neighborhood.'

White's eyes flashed. 'I don't believe she killed Tom. That *was* an accident. She loved him. She'd have done anything for him.'

'We didn't know,' said Klassner, 'that she'd gone after you. At the outstation. We were concerned she'd been emotionally affected by Jess's death. When we went looking for her and couldn't find her, we got worried. Then we found out that *Mathilda* was gone.'

'Who's Mathilda?' asked Alex.

'Our ship. I assume you've seen it. It's a Chesapeake.'

'It *was*,' I said, showing more satisfaction than was seemly, I guess.

Urquhart was staring out at the woods. 'I told you,' he said to

Klassner, 'it would be a mistake to come here.' He looked across at me. 'We never condoned what Maddy did. We tried to stop her. We did everything we could. Why is that so hard to understand?'

'No,' I said. 'You never condoned it. But you knew. You knew, and you were secretly pleased to get Walker out of the way, without getting blood on your own hands. You probably knew Taliaferro was in danger. And if you didn't know she was trying to kill us, you should have. You're contemptible. All of you.'

Urquhart's jaw quivered. Klassner was nodding, yes, guilty as charged. White was looking at me, shaking her head, no, it's wasn't like that at all.

'Professor,' Alex asked, 'where is Mendoza?'

Klassner was seated on the sofa, beside White. 'Dead,' he said. 'He's been dead a long time.'

'How'd he die?'

'Not the way you think,' he said accusingly. 'He died of heart failure. About nine years ago.'

'Heart failure? Didn't the process work on him?'

'He never wanted it. Refused it.' He took a deep breath.

'Why?'

'He felt he'd betrayed Tom. He didn't want to profit by it. Didn't want to live with the knowledge of what he'd done.'

'The rest of you seem to have adjusted pretty well.'

Urquhart looked as if his patience was exhausted. 'We don't claim to be saints.'

'Are there any others?' Alex asked. 'Other than yourselves? Anyone else who knows about this? Any more immortals?' He let the word hang in air.

'No,' said Klassner. 'No one else knows the truth.'

'And no one else has received the treatment?'

'No. Warren was the only one who understood how to do it. And he swore, after us, no one else.'

'Is the process on record somewhere? Do you know how it's done?'

'No. He destroyed everything.'

Something on wings banged into a window and fluttered away. For a long time after that, no one spoke.

'I suppose I should congratulate you,' Alex said, finally.

The room remained quiet.

'Why?' I asked.

'They buried Dunninger's work. Prevented its being used.'

'They took it for themselves.'

'No,' Boland said. His voice was simultaneously subdued and impassioned. 'That was never our intention.'

'It happened.'

White held a hand up, fingers spread in defense. 'It was too tempting,' she said. 'To be young again. Forever. Who could resist that?'

'That's the whole point, isn't it?' said Alex. 'Nobody can say no. Other than, apparently, Mendoza.'

I was getting annoyed. 'You sound as if you think they did something admirable.'

Alex took his time answering. 'I'm not sure they didn't.'

'Oh, come on, Alex. They kidnapped Dunninger. They're responsible, at least indirectly, for two murders.' I turned and looked at them. Klassner's eyes never left me. Boland stared out the window, wishing he was somewhere else. White's gaze had turned inward. Urquhart glowered, daring anyone to challenge him. 'You've done all right for yourselves,' I continued, getting into a rhythm. 'You grabbed the treatment that you denied everyone else. I'd say you haven't done badly.'

'Had we not intervened,' said Boland, 'the population of Rimway would have doubled over the past sixty years. Earth would have over twenty billion people by now.'

White got in: 'Except that it wouldn't. Earth doesn't have the kind of resources to support a population anywhere close to that. So a lot of those people, millions of them, would have died. Of starvation. Or in wars over natural resources. Or disease. Governments would have collapsed. Most of the survivors would be living in misery.'

'You don't *know* that,' I said.

'Sure we do,' continued White, relentless. 'The numbers tell the story. Food production, clean water, even living space. Energy. Medical care. It's just not there for twenty-plus billion people. The same as it wouldn't be for us if we had twice the population. Take the trouble to inform yourself, Chase.'

'Damn you,' I said, 'you're taking millions of lives into your hands. What gave you the right to make that sort of decision?'

'Nobody else was in a position to,' said Klassner. 'Either we took it into our own hands, or it went by default in Dunninger's direction.'

'You couldn't dissuade him?' said Alex.

Klassner's eyes closed. 'No. "They'll find a way." That was his mantra. "Give them the gift, and they'll find a way."'

'There are other worlds,' I said. 'Help was there if someone was willing to ask.'

Urquhart snorted. 'It would have been the same everywhere,' he said, in a rich baritone. 'The tidal wave would fill all ports. It would have introduced such suffering and catastrophe as the human race has never seen.'

Upstairs, as if right on schedule with all the talk about doom, a clock struck. Nine-thirty.

I heard shouts outside. Kids playing. 'Where did the money come from?' asked Alex. 'It took considerable resources to pull this off.'

Urquhart replied: 'The Council has a number of discretionary funds. They can be accessed if the need is sufficiently great.'

'So some of the councillors knew about this.'

'That doesn't necessarily follow. But yes, it was known on the Council. Although not by everyone.'

'They thought you were doing the right thing.'

'Mr Benedict, they were *horrified* by the possibility that this would get out.'

'And they didn't ask to share the secret?'

'They didn't know Dunninger had gotten as far as he had. And they certainly weren't aware that the project would also produce a rejuvenation capability. We didn't disabuse them.'

'What kind of life span are you looking at?' I asked. 'Is it indefinite?'

'No,' said Boland. 'We have parts, stem cells, nerve cells, with which the nanobots have limited capability.'

'Barring accidents,' said Klassner, 'Warren thought we'd live about nine hundred years.'

'Our lives,' said White, 'are not what they might appear to you. We had to abandon everything we cared about, including our families. Today, we can make no long-term commitments with anyone. We can establish no permanent relationship, take no mate, have no child. Do you understand what I'm saying?'

Klassner folded his hands and pressed his lips against them, like a man in prayer. He confronted Alex. 'Look, none of this matters at the moment. If you go to the authorities with this story, you'll succeed in punishing us. But it will be the story of the age. And all the researchers will need is a blood sample from any of us, and they'll be able to work out the secret. So the question now is, what do you and your associate plan to do?'

What, indeed?

It had been growing dark outside. Gathering clouds. Four lamps began to glow, one at either end of the sofa, one in a corner of the room, one on a table beside Urquhart.

Klassner cleared his throat. Young or not, this was a man accustomed to having people pay attention when he spoke. 'We were gratified that you did not immediately blow the whistle. That tells us you understand the consequences of a rash decision.'

'It would do nothing for your reputation either, Professor.'

'My reputation does not matter. We risked everything to make this work.'

I sat staring at Maddy's jacket. I thought about how sweet life was, how good young men and jelly donuts and ocean sunsets and night music and all-night parties are. What would happen to the way we live if the secret got out?

Throughout the conversation I'd been trying to think of a compromise, a way to seize permanent youth and simultaneously persuade people to stop having children.

It wouldn't happen.

'You don't have to worry,' Alex said. 'We'll keep your secret.'

You could hear everyone exhale. And I have to confess that at that moment I had no idea what the right course of action might be. But I was annoyed, at Alex, at Klassner, at all of them. They were starting to get up. Smiles were breaking out. 'One second,' I said, and when I had their attention: 'Alex doesn't speak for me.'

28

Like as the waves make towards the pebbled shore, So do our minutes hasten to their end.

—William Shakespeare

I'd been sitting there wondering how Dunninger's gift had changed them. Perspective. Empathy. A sense of proportion. What's it like not to have to worry about getting old? To see other people as creatures of a day?

It had begun to snow. Big wet flakes. No wind was blowing, and they were coming straight down. I wished for a blizzard big enough to bury the problem.

All eyes were on me, and Klassner, his voice calm and reasonable, apologized that I had been overlooked. 'Surely, Chase, you can see the wisdom of letting this go no further.'

It was hard to believe I was speaking to Martin Klassner, the cosmological giant of the previous century, reinvigorated, somehow returned to life and sitting in our living room. Not only because the event seemed biologically unlikely, but also because it was hard to believe such a man could have known about Maddy and not found a way to heal her. Or at least render her harmless.

'I'm not sure I do,' I said. 'You of all people, *Martin*, know what it is to be old. To watch the years pile up, and feel the first pains in joints and ligaments. To watch the outside world grow dim. You have it in your power to step in, to prevent people from being betrayed by their own bodies. And you've done nothing. For sixty years, you've not lifted a finger.'

He started to speak, but I cut him off. 'I know the arguments. I know what overpopulation means. If I didn't realize it earlier, I certainly came to understand it these last few weeks. So we have an ethical dilemma.

'You've withheld Tom Dunninger's gift. No, don't say anything for a moment. You and your friends would be in a far stronger position to bring up ethics had you not grabbed the opportunity for yourselves.'

'That's no reason,' rumbled Urquhart, 'to compromise every-thing we've accomplished. Simply because we couldn't resist the temptation. Our failure makes the point.'

'You're right. The issues are too serious for that. Alex has said he'll keep your secret. But I won't. I see no compelling reason to protect you.'

'Then,' said Klassner, 'you doom everybody.'

'You have a tendency to overstate things, Martin. You're in a position to stop the ageing process. Or not. Either way, as you would have it, people will die. In large numbers.

'But if we make the treatment available, *maybe* we'll learn to live with it. We survived the ice ages. And the Black Plague. And God knows how many wars. And thousands of years of political stupidity. We even picked a fight with the only other intelligent species we found. If we survived all that, we can survive this.'

'You don't know that's so,' said White. 'This is different.'

'It's *always* different. You know what's wrong with you? The four of you? You give up too easily. You decide there's a problem, and you think we have to arrange things so we don't have to deal with it.' I looked over at Alex, whose face revealed nothing. 'I say we put the Dunninger formula on the table where everybody can see it. And then we talk about it. Like adults.'

'No,' said White. Her eyes radiated a hunted look. 'You really don't understand.'

'No, I don't. I can't understand your giving in without a fight. I don't want to live the rest of my life watching people die, knowing I had the means to save them.'

Lines showed up around Boland's eyes and mouth. He literally looked in pain.

'I'll go this far for you: We'll be in touch with you within the next few days. We'll arrange to have one of you donate a blood sample. We'll get it analyzed and let the chips fall. I'll say nothing about where I got it. And I'll say nothing about you or the *Polaris*. You can keep your reputations intact, and you can go on living happily for the next thousand years or so.

'Although I should tell you that if you're as virtuous as you like to think, as I'd like to believe, you'll reveal yourselves, admit to what you've done, and argue your case in the public forum.'

It wasn't what they were expecting. Alex frowned and shrugged. I hope you know what you're doing.

Well, it was, as they say, the old conversation stopper. One by one they got to their feet. Klassner hoped that after I had a chance to think things over, I'd reconsider. White took my hand, pressed it, and bit her lip. She was close to tears.

Urquhart asked me not to do anything irrevocable until I'd had a chance to sleep on it. 'When it starts,' Boland said, 'when governments become oppressive about containing the birth rate, when we run out of places to live, when the first famines hit, it's going to be *your* fault.'

They filed out, each of them sending silent signals to Alex, pleading with him, or directing him, to use his influence to get me to make sense. I watched them walk through the intensifying snow down to the pad and climb on board their skimmer. They didn't look back. The doors swung shut, and the aircraft lifted into the sky and disappeared quickly into the storm.

Alex asked me if I was okay.

Actually, I wasn't. I'd just made what might have been the biggest decision in human history, and I most definitely was not okay.

'Nevertheless,' he said, 'it was the right thing to do. We've no need of secret cabals.'

'You voted with them,' I said.

We were standing out on the deck, watching the snow splat against the windows. He put his palm against the glass, feeling the cold. 'I know,' he said. 'It was the easiest way out. The least painful. But you're right. This needs to be in the open.' He kissed me. 'I suspect, though, that we're going to find it's a mixed gift.'

'Because we'll get too many people.'

'That, too.' He lowered himself into one of the chairs and put his feet up. 'We might discover that when life goes on indefinitely, it's not quite—' He struggled for the word. '—Quite as fulfilling. As valuable.'

Well, I thought that was nonsense, and I said so.

He laughed. 'You're a sweetheart, Chase.'

'Yeah. I know.'

'How about we go out and get something to eat?'

The storm was intensifying. We could no longer see the line of trees at the edge of the property. 'Are you serious?' I said. 'You want to go out in *this*?'

'Why not?'

'No,' I said. 'Let's eat here. It's safer.'

We had just finished when Jacob interrupted. *'There is a news report that may be of interest,'* he said. *'Something exploded out over the ocean a few minutes ago. They don't know what it is yet.'*

God help me, I knew right away. So did Alex. 'How far out, Jacob?' he asked.

'Fifty kilometers. Over the trench.' A deep part of the ocean. *'The way they're describing it, it must have been a pretty big blast.'*

Damn.

'They're saying no survivors.'

Epilog

True to the end.

Whatever they used as an explosive device, it was pretty thorough. All the authorities ever found was a charred piece of one of the antigrav pods.

The interest in the *Polaris* generated by the anniversary events and the attack at Survey had subsided. Everything went back to normal.

We passed messages to several microbiologists that we had reason to believe that Dunninger had been on the right track. They assured us they'd look into it.

Morton College is still in operation. The Lockhart Foundation, which specializes in education for genius-level types, has taken it over.

I've always thought of that morning as if two separate conversations took place, one between Alex and the men, the other between Nancy White and me.

She looked young and vibrant and, in some ways, more than human. Or *different* from human. Maybe knowing you won't grow old, at least for a very long time, does that for you, adds a certain sense of who and what you are, that you've stepped outside the ordinary run of mankind, and indeed of the natural

405

world. Maybe at that point you become almost a neutral observer, sympathetic to humanity in the way that one might be sympathetic to a lost kitten, but nevertheless possessing the sure and certain knowledge that you are *different* in kind, and not simply in degree.

When the people you meet in daily life become *temporary, transient,* their significance must necessarily lessen. Jiggle the equipment in Shawn Walker's skimmer so that he goes into orbit, and what is lost? Only a few decades. In the short term, he was dead anyhow. Is that how it is?

I've thought of it often, sitting on the big porch at the end of the day, before setting out for home. Nancy White was trying to tell me something that morning, something more than simply that she'd had to jettison everyone and *everything* she knew and start life over. I think she was trying to underscore what Alex said later, that the treatment would have been, at best, a mixed gift. That she had become something else.

Metahuman. The next stage. Whatever. Maybe it was the original Nancy White, locked up somewhere inside, trying to connect with me.

You know about the cemetery at the edge of the woods. You can't get a good look at it unless you go up to the fourth floor. But there has never been a day, since the visit from Klassner and the others, that I haven't thought about it. When I come in each morning, dropping down past the trees, my eyes are drawn to it, to its pale white markers, and its stone figures. Last stop. Terminal City. I'm a little more conscious of it than I used to be.

It reminds me every day of Klassner's rejoinder when I told them I wasn't going to sit on everything for them. *Then you doom everybody.* Over the top, I'd thought. People never really talk like that. And I'd assumed he meant Alex and me as well as the four of them, and the entire human race. But I don't think that was it at all. We were in the office, and he was talking about the device they'd planted in the skimmer, that they planned to use if the meeting didn't go well.

It hadn't gone well.

'But I think we've answered one question,' said Alex.

'And what's that?'

'Maddy *was* an aberration. The mere fact of having your life prolonged doesn't cause you to become something other than human.'

'—Because the more sensible thing for them to do would have been to blow *us* up—'

'Absolutely. Instead they found an elegant solution to their problem.'

'*Elegant?* You call committing suicide elegant?'

He was grinning. Big, wide, ear-to-ear. 'Are you sure they died?'

'Alex,' I said, 'that *had* to be their skimmer. They never got back to Morton, and nobody else is missing.'

He nodded at Maddy's jacket. 'Chase, don't forget – these are the same people who disappeared out of the *Polaris*.'

A Talent for War

Everyone knows the legend of Christopher Sim. An interstellar hero with a rare talent for war, he changed mankind's history forever when he forged a rag-tag group of misfits into the weapon that broke the alien Ashiyyur.

But now, in a forgotten file, Alex Benedict has found a startling piece of information. If it is true, then Christopher Sim was a fraud.

If he is to see it through, Alex Benedict will have to follow the dark track of a legend, into the heart of an alien galaxy, where he will confront a truth far stranger than anything he could have imagined. . . .

Praise for Jack McDevitt:

'The logical heir to Isaac Asimov and Arthur C. Clarke'
Stephen King

'Another highly intelligent, absorbing portrayal of the far future from a leading creator of such tales'
Booklist

'Combines hard science fiction with mystery and adventure in a wild tour of the distant future. Stellar plotting, engaging characters, and a mastery of storytelling'
Library Journal (starred review)

978 1 4722 0307 6

headline